THE SHAAR PRESS

THE JUDAICA IMPRINT
FOR THOUGHTFUL PEOPLE

FATAL
JUDGMENT

A NOVEL OF SUSPENSE BY
YISROEL MAYER MERKIN

Published by **SHAAR PRESS**

This is a work of fiction. Names, characters, places, and incidents are either the product of the
author's imagination or are used fictitiously. Any resemblance to actual persons, living or dead,
or locales is entirely coincidental.

Distributed by MESORAH PUBLICATIONS, LTD.
4401 Second Avenue / Brooklyn, N.Y 11232 / (718) 921-9000

Distributed in Israel by SIFRIATI / A. GITLER
6 Hayarkon Street / Bnei Brak 51127

Distributed in Europe by LEHMANNS
Unit E, Viking Business Park, Rolling Mill Road / Jarrow, Tyne and Wear, NE32 3DP/ England

Distributed in Australia and New Zealand by GOLDS WORLD OF JUDAICA
3-13 William Street / Balaclava, Melbourne 3183 / Victoria Australia

Distributed in South Africa by KOLLEL BOOKSHOP
Northfield Centre / 17 Northfield Avenue / Glenhazel 2192, Johannesburg, South Africa

ISBN 10: 1-42261-383-6 / ISBN 13: 978-1-42261-383-2

Custom bound by Sefercraft, Inc. / 4401 Second Avenue / Brooklyn N.Y. 11232

Prologue

SHE COULD NOT RECALL HOW LONG IT HAD BEEN: DAYS, maybe even weeks. All she knew was the darkness that filled her small, dank, and chilly cell. Yet though she trembled uncontrollably in the cold and the blackness, she never lost her resolve. She was going to defy her captors, no matter the cost.

The defiance began with ignoring their orders. If they told her to eat, she would sleep. If they ordered her to stand, she would sit. Although she knew that her captors could kill her, she also felt that they needed her alive. Though she had no idea what they wanted, if she were still alive, she reasoned, they must want something from her, and she wasn't going to give it to them.

Unable to move around her cell, the prisoner replayed memories of happier times, when she and her husband would walk in the park with their young children. Her boys, ages seven and five, were rambunctious and mischievous youngsters who loved to have fun and laugh. She pictured going to the lake and feeding the ducks with her boys and recalled the lavish picnic she had prepared for her family; she remembered the gusto and happiness with which they ate. But with these memories came the frightening realization — she might never see her children or her husband again.

The cell door opened, interrupting her thoughts. A hooded figure entered. The unexpected glare of the bulb from the hallway hurt her eyes and she instinctively covered them with her hands. The man began to speak, and she realized that she recognized his voice. She'd heard it on the night that the nightmare began.

"My men tell me that you seem to have trouble following orders," he said, his tone icy. "If you think that just because I have chosen to keep you alive that means that I will not hurt you, you are gravely mistaken."

The prisoner didn't respond. Although she was frightened, she didn't want to give her tormentor the satisfaction of seeing her fear. She believed that she could handle anything, and she knew that she would need to.

"This will be the last time that I will be visiting you," the man declared. "From today you will listen to my men and you will do as they say. Because if not, I will bring upon you a pain that you have never experienced or imagined, and after I am finished, you will beg me to end your pathetic existence."

The hooded man motioned for the guards to open the door. As he neared the entrance, he faced the prisoner. "To show that I am serious, I leave you this as a reminder of how much you truly stand to lose," he said, dropping a picture on the floor as he left the room.

For a short moment the door was left open. A beam of light shone into the room before it was shut with a sickening clang. It was enough time for the prisoner to see the photograph.

The wails and the screams bounced off the walls. She banged on her cell door, pleading for her guards to come and allow her to make amends for whatever she had done. After a few minutes of sobbing and pleading, she collapsed to the floor trembling, her raw hands clutching the picture, bringing it close to her heart.

■ ■ ■

Eitan Adiran sat by his computer. It was three in the morning and all was quiet. With all the turmoil that was raging in Eitan's mind, he could have used a little clamor to drown out the intense fears that were flooding his brain.

How could he have been so careless? He was a pro, at the top of his field, head of the leading computer security firm in all of Israel. Datcom Secure even numbered the Knesset among its clients. That was how he'd acquired the information in question — and that was how he'd made his colossal error.

On the cutting edge of high-tech security, Eitan had always been careful in every business deal that he brokered. But he hadn't done his due diligence this once, and now he was realizing the magnitude of his mistake.

When Eitan had been contacted for the information, he had thought the person was a member of the paparazzi looking for an exclusive to fill the pages of his tabloid. The money was great, and, Eitan reasoned, what harm would it do if the information leaked out?

That was until Eitan found out who wanted the information and why he wanted it.

Now Eitan debated his options. He couldn't just go the police and admit his mistake without putting his career, and maybe even his family, at risk. But he couldn't keep quiet either. The one thing that he was certain of was that he needed to make a decision quickly.

In the pre-dawn silence, Eitan could have sworn that he heard footsteps in the corridor outside his office.

"Who's there?" he called out.

When he heard nothing more, Eitan rose from his desk. He was probably just imagining things. It was late and he needed to get home to sleep. The decision could wait until tomorrow.

He turned off his computer, slipped his phone into his pants pocket and headed for the door. Before he reached it, he felt the cold weight of metal come crashing down on his skull. Eitan fell to the ground and cried out in pain.

"Did that hurt, Eitan?" an icy voice asked.

The man slammed his foot into Eitan's nose. The sickening sound of breaking bone was obscured by a scream of pain.

"I guess that one did hurt," the man laughed. "Do you know who I am?"

"Please don't kill me," Eitan whispered.

"That isn't what I asked," the man roared as he slammed the butt of his gun into Eitan's gut. "Now let us try that again. Do you know who I am?"

"No," Eitan gasped, tears streaming down his face.

"Let me introduce myself. My name is Rasheed Salaam and I will be the last person that you will ever see."

"Please don't kill me. I'll give you whatever you want."

"You already have given me whatever I want. You have done well. But sadly, you are now useless to me."

"No!" Eitan cried

"May Allah have mercy on your soul," Rasheed cried as he pointed his gun at Eitan's chest and fired.

Rasheed pocketed his weapon and walked toward the exit. Eitan's eyes fluttered as he felt the blood pouring out of him. Through a haze of pain and nausea he felt a stirring of determination: his death would not be in vain. With his last bit of strength, Eitan pulled his phone out of his pocket and feebly pressed a few buttons. He only hoped that his message would be received in time.

■ ■ ■

It was an unseasonably cool September morning. The morning fog was just clearing off the lake. The hunter positioned himself in the brush, out of the sight of his prey.

Gripping his Winchester rifle, the hunter eyed the young doe as it came into view. Though his idea of hunting didn't usually involve animals, the hunter knew that he needed to practice his marksmanship, and this young deer would have to do. As he watched his prey, delicately bending down to eat a blade of grass, the hunter sighed. It wasn't that long ago that he was hunting not for sport, but for something he believed in. For justice. Now the hunter was tracking a deer and not an enemy.

Still, holding a weapon again for the first time in almost three years symbolized that his years of waiting were finally over.

As Khalid al-Jinn steadied his finger on the trigger, he thought back to the day when his new life had begun.

Khalid checked to make sure that everything was in order. His specialty Heckler & Koch PSG1 rifle was disassembled and ready for transfer. Though he would have enjoyed using his bare hands on his victims, he knew that if he wanted to stay out of prison, he would have to stick with his sniper rifle instead. He had already managed to kill three soldiers, and that was only the beginning. As he looked at the picture of his next victim, Khalid knew that when he was successful in his mission, he would become the most wanted man in Israel, and that was exactly what he wanted.

As Khalid closed his backpack, he heard footsteps outside his apartment. He listened closely by the door and waited. Once he was certain that the intruder was just outside, Khalid whipped open the door, catching his visitor by surprise. Khalid gripped the man's throat and dragged him into the apartment. Throwing all of his weight onto his visitor he slammed him into the ground, all the while keeping his grip on the man's throat. The man tried to speak, but couldn't get any words out as Khalid's grip intensified.

The man struggled to breathe. Khalid's eyes shone with glee at the sight of his victim's suffering. The intruder used his free hand to whip his pistol out of his pocket, pointing the weapon squarely at Khalid.

Khalid released his grip and rolled off the man. The visitor struggled to catch his breath. After a few moments, he regained his composure.

"Are you crazy?" he yelled in Arabic.

"You are of the Faithful?" Khalid responded, shocked.

"Of course I am. Did you think that I was an Israeli?"

"I thought that they were coming to arrest me."

"Why? Because of the three murders that you have already committed?"

Khalid's eyes widened. "How do you know about them?"

"Or maybe they were coming to arrest you for the attempted murder of General Oren?"

"How do you know all this?" Khalid asked in disbelief.

"The question you should be asking isn't how I know every-thing," the man corrected him. "You should be asking yourself, if a total stranger knows this much, then what do the Israelis know?"

"They don't know anything," Khalid replied. "If they did, then why haven't they arrested me yet?"

"Lack of evidence," the man answered. "You have been good, but not perfect. They know that all the soldiers were killed with the same gun, but judging by the bulge in your bag over there, they haven't been able to find the weapon. They know about your plan to assas-sinate the general in Afula. They know about the apartment across from the plaza where the general will be eating. They are setting a trap for you. Once you enter that apartment, you will have the entire Israeli army converging on you to take you to prison."

Khalid did not want to believe what this stranger was saying. He had thought that he had outsmarted the Israelis, but it turned out that they were onto him and were lying in wait. The thought that they had actually outwitted him and were playing him for a fool infuriated Khalid.

"AHHH," he screamed as he smashed his fist into the wall. He barely realized that blood was streaming from his fingers; in his rage he didn't care.

Seeing the look in Khalid's eyes, his visitor raised his gun for protection. He knew all about Khalid's uncontrollable fury, and he was taking no chances.

"Maybe you are really an Israeli and you are trying to fool me," Khalid spat out.

"My name is Rasheed Salaam and if I were an Israeli, I wouldn't be giving you this," the man responded as he threw a manila enve-lope to Khalid. Khalid caught the envelope and dumped its contents onto the table. A passport and several bundles of cash fell out.

"What is this?"

"This is your redemption."

"I don't understand."

"I just handed you a passport with all the proper visas and docu-mentation, and over twenty thousand dollars in cash. You can fly to America immediately. The money should be enough to get you started."

"Started where?"

"America," Rasheed stated.

"Why would I want to be in America if my life is here in Jenin?"

"You have nothing in Jenin," Rasheed countered. "Right now there are three Israeli agents waiting for you to leave your apartment. As soon as you leave, they plan to enter your apartment and plant bugs everywhere. Then they are going to take whatever information they gather and use it against you in court. You are a wanted man, Khalid. Your only chance to survive is to leave with me tonight."

"But what about my war?" Khalid growled. "I want those Zionist pigs to pay for all the pain that they have brought to our people."

"I fight the same war that you do, my brother. I am working on a plan to hurt the Israelis in a way that they will never recover from. But in order for me to accomplish my goal, I need your help. Together we can show the world the power of our jihad and bring about a revolution that Allah would be proud of."

Khalid eyed Rasheed with concern. He was not a trusting man by nature, and to follow Rasheed halfway across the world would require a lot of trust. Rasheed, sensing Khalid's skepticism, spoke.

"If you don't believe me, look outside." Rasheed handed him a small pair of Swarovski binoculars.

Khalid went to the dusty window, taking care not to be seen.

"What am I looking for?"

"The third vehicle on the left. Do you see what is painted on the door?"

"It's a plumbing company."

"Look at the sunglasses on the driver. When did you see a plumber in Jenin with such expensive designer glasses? Details, Khalid, that is the difference between genius and failure."

Khalid adjusted the lenses. The figure in the van grew clearer. He paled.

"If they are watching me, how are you going to get me out of here?"

"I have a loyal soldier waiting around the back who believes in our cause. If you agree to my conditions, he will come into this apartment, take your clothing and your backpack, and lead the Israelis toward the apartment in Afula. Once we are certain that the Israelis are gone, together we will fly to America."

"What conditions are you talking about?"

"You will need to take this every day," Rasheed informed him, tossing a plastic bottle at Khalid. "It is called fluvoxamine."

"What is that?"

Rasheed grinned. "You know very well what it is. I know all about your anger. These pills will help."

"I won't take them," Khalid declared. "They cause my hands to shake and won't let me do what I do best."

"You will take those pills or you will not be getting on a plane with me."

"Why would you want me to take the pills? Don't you want me to be able to perform in our jihad?"

"Of course I do," Rasheed replied. "And there will come a day when I will tell you to stop taking them and let our enemies feel the terror of your wrath. However, for what I want to accomplish, we need patience and discipline. That requires you to stay out of trouble until our opportunity arises. The only way that I can be sure that you will stay out of trouble is if you can hold your anger in check. And the only way you can do that is to take these pills."

"So what will I do with myself in America?"

"You will keep a low profile and wait for my call. I don't know how long it will take. It may take a few months or even a few years. I need you to be patient and to stay out of sight until the time comes."

Khalid looked at Rasheed and debated his options. For most of his life, he had done things on his own and had never taken orders from anybody. What Rasheed wanted him to do was not going to be easy. But as he looked back out the window and saw the Israeli agents sitting in the van, he realized that he didn't have much of a choice.

"Fine," Khalid agreed. "I will do exactly as you ask."

Khalid steadied his hands and brought his finger to the trigger.

The unsuspecting animal nibbled the grass without a care in the world. Khalid, holding the rifle in his hand, felt a rush of power that he hadn't felt in years. He controlled the fate of his prey, as he used to control the fate of those Zionist soldiers. The past was coming back and the feeling was euphoric.

Khalid pulled the trigger. The shot shattered the innocent silence that had enveloped the peaceful forest. The birds flew away in fright, but the young deer wasn't as lucky. Khalid rose from his hiding place and approached his victim. As he saw the animal struggling in front of him, a blast of anger consumed him. It was a feeling he hadn't felt since that day in Jenin, and he relished the sensation of the rage as it flowed through his veins.

Khalid drew a metal rod from his pocket and began to pummel the defenseless animal. As the screams of the deer continued, the beatings intensified. Khalid's joy grew with every blow. The wails of the dying animal were drowned out by Khalid's corresponding howls of glee.

Within minutes the deer's cries and Khalid's roaring came to a halt. But the real damage had been done. The beast within Khalid had been unleashed.

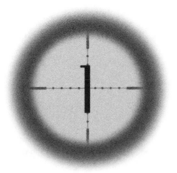

"TATTY, I CAN'T FIND MY SHOES," SARA CRIED OUT.

"Are you sure that they aren't in your room?" Shea asked.

"I told you that I looked there already and I can't find them."

Shea headed toward his daughter's room and found her jumping on her bed without her shoes on. Looking down, he spotted her black Mary Janes peeking out from under the dust ruffle.

"Sara," her father called out, "I thought that you told me that you looked for your shoes."

"But I did," responded his daughter, panting as she bounced up and down.

"So why did I find them right under your bed?"

"I don't want to wear those shoes," Sara protested. "I want to wear my pink ones."

"But sweetie," Shea responded from between clenched teeth, "I thought we decided that since the pink ones are too small on you, you weren't going to wear them anymore."

"But Tatty, Elky wears pink shoes, and I want to wear mine."

"I know that you want to wear them, sweetheart, except they are too small on you and they will hurt your feet."

"I don't care if they are too small!"

Shea couldn't believe what was happening. He had helped broker deals worth hundreds of millions of dollars and negotiated plea bargains with district attorneys, and yet he couldn't convince his daughter not to wear a pair of pink shoes. As he turned to face her, he saw that she had stopped jumping and that tears were forming in her eyes. Shea knew that this wasn't a good sign. He needed to bring in the cavalry.

"Shira," he called out to his wife.

"Yes?"

"I think we have a situation that could use some mommy intervention."

"I'm sorry, but I am kinda busy right now."

"Well, your daughter wants to wear the pink shoes and I can't convince her not to."

"That is a problem, but your son wants to wear his elephant pajamas to school and I think that is a bigger issue. You're on your own, counselor."

Shea looked at his watch and then looked at his daughter. The tears were only beginning to flow. Shea had some leeway, but not much. His daughter Sara was a cute, sweet, and charming little girl. With her dimples and ponytails, she was a joy to behold. But that was when she wasn't crying. As cute and enjoyable as she was when her eyes were dry, she was equally as terrifying when crying. Although her episodes would start with only a whimper, they would grow in intensity to a point where her tantrums could rival the roar of Mount St. Helens erupting.

Because of his heavy work schedule, Shea was not nearly as adept in handling his daughter as his wife was. But now he was on his own and he needed to stop the impending explosion. After examining his options, he chose the only thing that he knew would definitely avoid a tantrum.

"Sarala," he began, "I know that you really want to wear those pink shoes. I will make you a deal. Are you listening to me?"

Sara nodded meekly, waiting to hear what her father was going to offer.

"If you don't wear the pink shoes, I will take you to the Candy House on Erev Shabbos to get your own special nosh."

"Can I get my own giant jaw smasher?"

Shea debated before answering. Those jaw smashers were twice the size of his daughter's mouth. He could just imagine the dentist's delight when he would count his young patient's cavities.

Shea looked at his watch. He was running late.

"Yes," Shea said reluctantly, "you can get your own giant jaw smasher. But make sure you don't tell your brother, okay?"

"I won't tell anybody," Sara said with a big smile on her face.

"Won't tell anybody what?" asked Shira Berman, as she entered the room

"Good news, Mommy," Shea said quickly. "Sara just decided to wear her school shoes and not the pink ones."

"And how, might I ask, did she come to such a decision? Did you offer her anything?"

"What are you referring to?" Shea asked coyly.

"I am referring to the fact that every time your daughter cries, you offer to buy her something. What was it this time, a taffy rope?"

"No," answered Sara, "it was a giant jaw smasher."

"Hey," Shea said, "that was supposed to be our secret."

"You offered her a giant jaw smasher to not cry?" Shira asked incredulously.

"I refuse to answer that question on the grounds that I will incriminate myself," Shea answered.

"That stuff only works in the court of law, not in the court of Berman," Shira responded.

"Look, I would love to continue this conversation, but I have a real court date and I am running late. We can continue this when I get home."

With that, Shea said goodbye to his wife and kissed his kids. He looked at his watch once more. If he didn't move fast, he was going to be in a lot of trouble.

Jumping into his car, he turned on the radio and sped out of his driveway. Living right near the Garden State Parkway definitely had its advantages. One of them was the fact that Shea could leave his house at 7:30 in the morning and not encounter any local traffic. That allowed him to coast on eighty all the way to New York. Only once he was on the Turnpike would he be subject to the usual heavy city-bound traffic. Tuning the radio, he found out that there were no accidents on the Parkway. Even with the morning's near disaster, he wasn't going to be late to court.

Shea breathed a sigh of relief and shifted his focus to the task at hand, defending Merzeir Pharmaceuticals.

Attorney Shea Berman was a junior associate for the law firm of Crane, Gardner, and Scott, one of the prominent legal firms in the United States. It had offices in eighteen cities in ten states. The New York office was the firm's largest, with nearly one hundred attorneys and over two hundred associates. Within the litigation department there were only two junior associates, and Shea was one of them.

Shea was finishing his first year as a junior associate in the firm. With all the long hours he had put in, Shea felt that he made a strong impression on the managing partners. Due to the downturn in the economy, many of his law school friends had been laid off. Shea had heard nothing about layoffs in his office, and he hoped that it would stay that way. But he knew that there were no guarantees in life and that a lawyer was only as good as his last case.

Shea's last case of the year was certainly his biggest.

This past year he had spent most of his time working with several senior partners in the firm. The Merzeir lawsuit was the first case where Shea had first chair, and he was seeking to make the most of his opportunity. With the case winding down, Shea knew that if he was going to make a splash he had to do it quickly. Today was the last day of trial and he needed to make sure that he didn't blow it.

Merzeir was a large pharmaceutical company that was being sued by an Arab-American woman named Fatima Assad. The company had been running drug trials for a new drug called Zenonox. The drug promised a revolutionary way to treat lung cancer. Although most lung cancers are caused by smoking, there had been research indicating that some cancers were caused by a genetic flaw on chromosome six. People with this flaw were found to be highly susceptible to cancer, while those with a mutated form of the p53 gene had been found to be unable to prevent the growth of cancerous cells. Zenonox was a ground-breaking drug that treated the faulty genes and enabled the body to fight back. The drug trial was restricted to people who had not smoked during the past three years, and that was why the company had rejected Fatima as a candidate.

Fatima Assad was a thirty-year-old woman who had suffered from lung cancer since her teens. Although she had originally blamed her cancer on her heavy smoking, Fatima now believed that her cancer had nothing to do with her two-packs-a-day habit. She contended that she hadn't smoked in over three years and yet after she had been cancer- free for over five years, the disease had returned. Fatima believed that her renewed bout with lung cancer was a result of the faulty gene. She had hoped that the drug would cure her once and for all. The company, however, disagreed with her; they believed that her excessive smoking as a teenager had ruined her lungs forever. When they informed her that she'd been rejected for the trials she decided to sue, claiming that the company could have rejected her only if she had smoked within the last three years, and they had no proof that she had. The problem for Shea was that she was right. According to the rules of the drug trial, only recent smoking could cause a person to be rejected. Unless Shea could prove that she had smoked recently, the company would be found liable and Fatima was suing for thirty million dollars. Shea knew that it was a long shot that the jury would award her all that money, but with the way she looked, bald and emaciated from all the radiation and chemotherapy, it wasn't a risk he was willing to take.

The plaintiff's attorneys had built their case by recalling other misconduct by the company during various drug trials. They had tried to establish a pattern of discrimination by the company against foreigners, specifically, in Fatima's case, against Arabs. They had shown that in two previous drug trials conducted by

Merzeir, suit was brought against the company by Arab women for not allowing them to participate in the trials. Although Shea had countered their argument successfully by showing that the women in question were found to be ineligible due to their age and diet habits, it seemed that the damage had already been done and the jury had begun to sympathize with Fatima.

Fatima's attorney, sensing the jury's sympathy, had decided to call Fatima to the stand. In Shea's mind, the move was brilliant. Either way they were going to make Shea and Merzeir look like the bad guys. Just the sight of her, a thirty-year-old woman dying, needing to be pushed in a wheelchair to the stand and breathing oxygen through a cannula, would cause the jury to cry. If Shea dared object to any of her testimony, he would be seen as the enemy.

Shea's primary goal was to prove that through her own actions Fatima had been ineligible under the terms of the trial. No matter what she said on the stand, if Shea could prove that Fatima had smoked within the last three years, Merzeir wouldn't be found liable.

Pulling up at the courthouse, Shea parked his car. As he entered the building, he saw numerous guards searching the visitors and requiring them to walk through the metal detectors. Though he had never heard of a suicide bomber disguised as a lawyer, he had heard of many disgruntled clients who would have liked nothing better than to get back at the lawyer or the district attorney who'd failed them.

He placed his briefcase on the conveyor belt and allowed the guards to search him. Once they were convinced that Shea wasn't packing any weapons, they allowed him to proceed to the courtroom. As he entered, he could feel the tension surge through him. By nature Shea wasn't a nervous person, but the gravity of today's decision wasn't lost on him. Merzeir was one of his firm's biggest clients, and he wanted to do everything in his power to keep it that way.

Another reason for his dry mouth and pounding heart was that his senior managing partner, Allan Shore, was going to be in court. All the junior associates were assigned a senior managing partner to lead them and guide them through their first year. Although Shea had assisted Allan on other cases, Allan had never observed him work on his own. Shea knew that his future in the firm likely depended on Allan's opinion of him.

Allan greeted Shea as he made his way to the defendant's table.

"So, have you thrown up yet?" Allan asked jokingly.

"Do I really look that nervous?" Shea wondered.

"Nah, you just look like the weight of the world is about to fall right on top of your shoulders."

"What should I do? Should I go out and have a drink to calm me down?"

"That may have been a good idea before you walked into court. Now you are on your own. But don't sweat it. You are a good lawyer and I am sure that you will win this case."

"And what happens if I don't?" Shea asked, only half kidding.

"Well then, you can always check the unemployment section in the paper," Allan said with a smile as he went to sit with the other spectators in the gallery.

Shea returned Allan's smile with one of his own, but he wasn't convinced that Allan had been joking.

As he approached the table he saw Dennis Merzeir waiting for him. Dennis rose to speak to his attorney.

"How is it looking?" Dennis asked

"A lot will depend on today," Shea explained. "Without Fatima's testimony, they have no case. They are hoping that the jury will feel for her and award the settlement just because she has suffered so much."

"So how can we prevent her from testifying?"

"We can't, but that doesn't mean that we will lose the case. If I attack her on the stand, the jury will think that I am some kind of a beast. So we are going to let her talk and repeat her story no matter how hard it is for us to hear and no matter how many jurors' eyes begin to tear. After she is finished her story, then we will prove that she did not meet the criteria of the trials. But we need to let her speak."

"Are you sure that will work?"

"The judge will not allow the jury to award her anything if she in fact broke the rules, no matter how bad he feels for her. As long we stick to the plan, we should be fine."

"So what do you want me to do?" Dennis asked

"I need you to remain calm and stone faced. I know that you are going to be frustrated while Fatima tells her story and blames your company. But if the jury begins to sympathize with her, they will only resent you more if you show anger at her."

Dennis Merzeir nodded in agreement and took a seat at the table. Shea joined him and they waited for the judge to arrive. A few minutes later, Judge Arthur Abernathy arrived in court. Abernathy was a Democrat and normally his liberal views would have been a concern for Shea, but the judge had been very fair to the defense so far. Shea hoped that wouldn't change.

He looked over to the other side and saw Fatima Assad conversing with her attorney, William Drillings, aka Slick Willy. Drillings was infamous for his ridiculous lawsuits against the city and for his high-profile clients. He had defended one of New York's most notorious gangsters, Eduardo Bastetti, before Bastetti checked himself into witness protection and was never seen again. When Shea had heard that Drillings was taking Fatima's case, he wasn't surprised. Merzeir was a newsmaker and Drillings would do anything to get his name in print.

After finishing his talk with Fatima, Drillings approached Shea.

"Are you sure you don't want to settle this case?" Drillings asked teasingly. "Once my client takes the stand, you are going to wish you had taken our deal. When the jury hears her story, there won't be a dry eye in the building and I am going to be a very rich man."

"Now, William," Shea responded, "I never thought it was about the money. I always thought that you were only doing this for the good of your clients."

"Say what you want, Berman, but as soon as I turn around the deal is off and you take your chances with the jury."

"Well then, you better turn around," Shea responded, "because you aren't going to get a dime from my client."

The judge, sensing the tension between the two lawyers, asked if they were ready to proceed. Drillings answered affirmatively and called Fatima as his final witness. The jury gasped as they saw the young woman struggle to walk to the witness box. All the color had drained from her face and she looked like a walking skeleton. Drillings helped her to the stand, peering at the jury to make sure they saw what he was doing. After helping her be seated, Drillings cleared his throat and Fatima was sworn in.

"Would you please state your name for the record," Drillings requested.

"Fatima Assad."

"Now Miss Assad, how old are you?"

"I am thirty years old," Fatima answered.

"Well, you surely don't look thirty to me," Drillings stated.

"That is because I am sick."

"What is the nature of your illness?"

David leaned over to Shea and whispered in his ear.

"Are you really going to let him do this? I mean everybody knows that she has cancer. Can't you object or something?"

"I told you already," Shea answered quietly while maintaining eye contact with the jury, "we have to let her tell her story. I need you to trust me."

Dennis pulled back and nodded slowly. Reluctantly.

"I have lung cancer," Fatima asserted.

"Now this isn't the first time you have contracted lung cancer, is it?"

"No, I also had it when I was a teenager. I underwent surgery and chemotherapy and the cancer went into remission. But eight years later it returned."

"So have you gone for additional surgery or chemotherapy?"

"No," Fatima answered.

"Why not?"

"When I first contracted cancer, the doctors believed it was because I had smoked when I was younger and also because I was surrounded by secondhand smoke in my house. I assumed that they were correct in their diagnosis and proceeded to take their treatment. However, my cancer returned, even though I stopped smoking."

"This must have been quite a shock to you. How did the doctors react?"

"They said that since I had contracted cancer before, I was at a greater risk to get it again."

"But you didn't agree with their diagnosis?"

"No," Fatima answered strongly. "It didn't make sense to me that I could get cancer again, without smoking."

"So what did you believe was the cause of the cancer?"

"Well, I began to read up on different causes of cancer. Of course, I saw the reports about smoking and various toxins. But then I read a report about a possible genetic flaw that could cause cancer and that made the most sense to me. I believed that I had gotten the cancer because I had a genetic flaw on chromosome six that was causing the cancer. I even paid for a test out of pocket, that cost me thousands of dollars, to prove my theory."

"What were the results of the test?"

"They proved that my theory was right. It showed that I had the genetic flaw, and therefore it was probably that that was the cause of my cancer."

"So what did you do next?"

"I started to look for ways to treat my condition. Although it was rare, I learned that there were a lot of possible treatments for my condition. But with all of them, the risks were very high and the success rates were very low. I started to lose hope. And that is when I heard about Zenonox."

"How did you hear about it?"

"I read an ad in the paper about a clinical trial for a new drug that was going to treat my condition. I immediately picked up the phone and called for more information."

"What happened next?"

"I went down to their offices for an interview. They asked me a lot of personal questions which, although I felt they were a bit intrusive, I didn't mind answering."

"Why did you feel compelled to answer their questions?" Drillings asked.

"I was willing to tell them anything if it would help me get the help I needed."

"So were you accepted into the trial?"

"No," Fatima answered bitterly.

"Why not?"

"One of the requirements of the trials was that any subject could not have smoked within the last three years. The company accused me of having smoked and therefore disqualified me from the trial."

"How would they have known that you smoked?"

Shea rose from his chair. Even though he had told Dennis that he wanted to give Fatima a chance to say her story, he didn't want the jury to think that he had fallen asleep either.

"Objection!" Shea exclaimed.

"On what grounds?" questioned Judge Abernathy.

"It calls for speculation. Ms. Assad has no idea how my client would have known she smoked. Those reasons were never disclosed."

"Sustained," the judge responded. "Mr. Drillings, please rephrase the question."

"I am sorry," Drillings said halfheartedly. "Ms. Assad, in your best judgment, do you have any idea why the defense would have accused you of smoking?"

"I think it had to do with a photo that I had posted online. "

"You are referring to exhibit G, are you not?"

"Yes," Fatima answered, pointing to a photo that had been enlarged on a screen next to her. The photo showed a picture of a healthier, younger-looking Fatima Assad, smoking a cigarette. It wasn't a very professional picture. Fatima was flanked by two men, whom she'd identified as her two brothers. There was also an arm draped around one of the brothers, a muscular arm with a large burn mark near the elbow, belonging to someone who'd been cut off in the photo.

"This picture clearly shows you smoking, does it not?"

"Yes, but that photo was taken over five years ago. I haven't touched a cigarette since."

"Can you prove that the photograph was taken over five years ago?" Drillings asked.

"No, but they can't prove that it wasn't," Fatima countered.

"So you told them you hadn't smoked for five years," Drilling repeated, shooting a glance at the jury box. "Ms. Assad, why do you think that the defendant disqualified you from the trials? Do you think it was because they didn't believe you?"

"No, I think they did believe me, but it didn't matter to them."

Shea leaned toward Dennis and whispered in his ear.

"I know what she is going to say right now and I need you to be calm."

"What are you talking about?"

"She is going to accuse you of some things that aren't true and we are going to use it against her. But right now you have to stay calm and not react."

Dennis nodded and sat back in the uncomfortable chair.

"Why do you think that it didn't matter to them?" Drillings asked, bending toward his client.

Fatima pointed to her headscarf. "Isn't it obvious? They wouldn't help me because I am an Arab. As soon as I walked into the interview all they saw was the headscarf, not the woman who is dying from a terrible disease."

Drillings walked toward the jury. This would make it seem as if Fatima would be addressing the jury directly and Shea would not be able to object.

"I am so scared," Fatima continued. "I have no idea if I will even be alive next month. I don't want to die. I want to live and start a family of my own. But they took that chance away from me. Only because I am an Arab! You have the power to make sure that they never do this again to anybody else. Please help me and don't let them get away with this."

Dennis rose halfway to his feet, and Shea gently pulled him back down.

"How can she say those things?" Dennis muttered. "My

company has never denied anybody anything based on their race or religion. What she just said up there was a hundred percent false. How can you let her get away with that?"

"I knew exactly what she was going to say and I told you that we were going to use it against her."

"Well, you better know what you are doing, because right now it looks like the jury bought her story hook, line, and sinker."

"Don't worry," Shea said reassuringly as he rose from his chair to question Fatima. Everything was going according to plan. Now Shea just had to make sure that his plan would work.

"GOOD MORNING, MS. ASSAD," SHEA BEGAN. "PLEASE accept my wishes and the wishes of my client for you to have a speedy recovery from your illness."

"Thank you," Fatima answered weakly.

"Ms. Assad, were you aware of the criteria of the trials before you applied?"

"Yes."

"How were you made aware?"

"Well, the representative that I contacted on the phone emailed me the requirements needed to be a candidate for the trials."

"Did you read them?"

"Yes," Fatima replied. "As soon as I received the email, I printed out a copy and read it to make sure that I qualified."

"Did the paper you receive look like this?" Shea asked holding a piece of paper and bringing it toward Fatima

"Yes."

"Can you please read for the jury the highlighted portion of the paper in front of you?"

"Objection," Drillings called out. "This isn't a library and my client is extremely weak. Answering all these questions is taxing enough. I see no reason why she should have to read something for the jury."

"I am sorry, Your Honor, but if Mr. Drillings called his client as a witness, he must have deemed her capable of answering questions. I am merely attempting to lay the foundation for my case."

"Overruled," the judge announced. "The witness may read the portion for the jury."

"Requirement number seven, any potential candidate must have not smoked within the last three years," Fatima read.

"Were you aware of this requirement?" Shea asked.

"Of course I was aware, but I told the interviewer that I hadn't smoked in five years and therefore I should have qualified."

"But if it were to be proven that you did smoke, wouldn't you agree that the company had the right to disqualify you from the trials?"

"Objection!" Drillings shot out. "This calls for speculation. My client is not an employee of the drug company and isn't privy to their rules and regulations."

"I am just trying to establish that Ms. Assad understood the rules of the trials and was aware that smoking was a cause for dismissal," Shea defended himself.

"I agree with the defense, Mr. Drillings," the judge declared. "Your witness is claiming that she was disqualified because of her religion. The defense is attempting to establish that she knew the rules before applying. I see nothing wrong with that."

"Yes," Fatima answered nervously. "I knew that if I had in fact smoked within the last three years, then I would be disqualified. But the fact remains that your client had no proof that I had smoked and had no right to reject me."

Shea turned and walked toward the defense table, ignoring Fatima's last comment. He was about to blow the case apart, and he wanted to take his time and enjoy it.

Shea withdrew a photograph from his bag and held it face down against his chest. Walking toward the bailiff, Shea shot Allan a glance and smiled. He then proceeded to give the picture

to the bailiff to enter it into evidence as exhibit S. Drillings immediately raised his voice.

"Objection!" Drillings exclaimed.

"But I haven't even said anything," Shea countered.

"I am referring to that photo that you just entered into evidence. It was not included in discovery."

"Actually, it was."

"What are you talking about?" Drillings asked.

"The picture that I just handed in has already been entered into
evidence."

"Your Honor, will you help me out here," Drillings said.

"Mr. Berman, I must admit that I am also a bit confused," the
judge agreed. "I don't remember seeing this picture in the original
items placed in discovery."

Shea waited for a few moments before he answered the judge.
He hadn't expected anybody to recognize the picture that the bailiff had now placed on the screen. Unless one would look closely
it was almost impossible to recognize, but that is what Shea had
done and that was how he was going to save his client millions
of dollars.

During the pretrial meetings, Shea had been very upfront with
Merzeir. He had told them that the facts were not in their favor.
The likelihood was, according to Shea, that the jury would side
with the plaintiff. It was a classic David versus Goliath and everybody knew how that story had ended. The only way Shea felt that
the company could win was if they could prove that Fatima had
in fact not been eligible since she did not meet the criteria of the
trials. But when he pressed Dennis Merzeir on whether or not the
company had proof that Fatima had smoked, he had answered
that his only proof was the photo that Fatima had posted online,
which was at best inconclusive. They had no way of determining
when it had been taken and therefore couldn't prove that she had
smoked within the past three years.

Shea had studied that picture for hours trying to see if there
were any clues that would help him strengthen his client's case.
Then one night, at about three in the morning, the answer came to

him, and he thanked Hashem that he had never really grown up.

Shea had always been an avid sports fan. He could name the starting lineups for every team in every professional sport. Even though his love for any sport was great, his love for football was even greater, especially when it came to his beloved New York Pilots. Shea had been a Pilots fan ever since he learned how to read. Although they hadn't won the Super Bowl in nearly forty years, Shea still followed them. He would study all their players and their stats. When he was young he would watch every game they played. If they lost (a common occurrence), Shea would be so enraged that his parents knew to avoid him for the rest of the afternoon. It would take him till Wednesday to calm down, and he only did so because another game was approaching and there would be a chance for redemption. His mother would often say that if he expended a quarter of the energy into learning *Gemara* that he did in sports, he would become a Rosh Yeshivah. Her only solace was the hope that Shea would outgrow his obsession and that his priorities would change as he got older.

Well, he did get older, and his priorities did change, but he definitely did not outgrow his obsession. His love for the Pilots was still strong, and Shea followed them with a great passion. But it was because of this passion that Shea was able to notice something in the picture that everyone else had missed.

In the photograph where Fatima was smoking with friends, Shea noticed that the television was on in the background. Not only was it on, but he could have sworn that he was looking at a football game. When Shea realized this, he downloaded the photo and brought it to a friend of his who was a wizard with computers. He enlarged the photo, so that the scene on the TV came into focus. Once Shea saw what had been playing on the TV, he knew that he would be able to prove that Fatima had in fact broken the rules of the trials.

Now he was about to share that revelation with the rest of the courtroom.

"Your Honor," Shea said, "I would ask you to recall exhibit G, which was introduced into evidence by the plaintiff."

"I do recall that picture showing the plaintiff smoking with a couple of others."

"Well, in that picture the TV was on in the background. The picture that I have just introduced into evidence is a blown-up version of what was on the screen."

"Objection!" Drillings stated. "The defense has no proof that this picture was in fact on the TV screen."

"I am sorry, but Mr. Drillings is mistaken," Shea corrected. "I have a sworn affidavit from one Andrew Carsten, who is the CEO at Access Technologies, that exhibit S was in fact a blowup of the TV screen featured in exhibit G."

Shea brought the affidavit to the judge and handed it to him. The judge read the affidavit and turned to Drillings.

"Mr. Drillings, it does seem that the photo is credible and I am going to allow it. Please continue, Mr. Berman."

Shea suppressed a smile before he continued. Drillings looked anxious, as well he should, thought Shea. He had no idea what was coming. And when he would finally find out, it was going to be too late to recover.

"Ms. Assad, do you know what that is a picture of?" Shea asked, pointing toward the picture.

"I think it is a football game," Fatima answered.

"You are correct. Are you a football fan, Ms. Assad?"

"No, not really. I mean, my brothers are fans, but I have never really cared much for the game. "

"Well, I am a major football fan and I happen to follow the New York Pilots. Are you familiar with that team?"

"I have heard of them. My brothers are big fans."

"Looking at the screen, do you recognize either of the teams playing in the game?"

"It seems that one of the teams is the Pilots," Fatima answered. "But I don't recognize the other team."

"Well, let me help you with that one," Shea offered. "The team that they were playing was the Miami Sharks. Can you please identify for the jury what the score on the screen was?"

"It says that the Pilots were leading the Sharks seven to five."

"Can you please tell us what quarter it was and how much time was left?"

"It says that the game was in the third quarter and there was three minutes and thirty seconds remaining."

"Objection," Drillings said weakly. "What does a football game have to do with this case?"

Shea knew that the objection raised by Drillings was in total desperation. Drillings knew exactly what the football game had to do with the case and it frightened him greatly.

"I was just getting to that, Your Honor," Shea interjected. "Ms. Assad, did you know that the Pilots have played the Miami Sharks over fifty times in their history. But only once has the score been seven to five with exactly three minutes and thirty seconds left in the third quarter."

"I was unaware," Fatima answered nervously.

"Did you happen to know the date of the only game between the Pilots and the Sharks where the Pilots led seven to five with exactly three minutes and thirty seconds left in the third quarter?"

"No," Fatima whispered.

"Well, you see I happen to know the exact date because I remember exactly where I was when that game took place. But your attorney Mr. Drillings would never allow me to base my information on my own personal recollections. So I rather refer to the Elias Sports Bureau which has the game taking place on November seventeenth, two thousand and eleven. Do you know what this means, Ms. Assad?"

Fatima didn't answer the question, but she didn't need to.

"That means," Shea continued, "that the picture of you smoking with your friends did not take place as you originally claimed, over five years ago. In fact, it took place less than two years ago. Which according to my calculations means that you in fact did break the rules of the trials and therefore my client, Merzeir Pharmaceuticals, was correct when they disqualified you and therefore aren't liable for anything."

Fatima was stunned and the courtroom was in an uproar. Her family and friends in the gallery were shouting, and the judge was banging his gavel trying to restore order in his courtroom. Shea looked over at Drillings, who seemed shell-shocked. As Shea walked over to his table, Dennis Merzeir rose from his seat to shake Shea's hand. While Shea embraced Merzeir, he saw Allan Shore exiting the courtroom with a big smile on his face.

■ ■ ■

Shira Berman walked around her house, not knowing what to do first. Even though she was presently out of a job, that didn't mean she was bored. Besides caring for three healthy, growing children, Shira also had assumed the role of contractor for her home.

When Shira and Shea decided to buy a home in Lakewood, New Jersey, they were excited and apprehensive at the same time. Although Shea had learned in *kollel* in Lakewood, neither of them had any family there. A native of California, Shira was anxious about buying a home so far from her family. She had never deluded herself into thinking that she would move back west. She knew that Shea's friends and family were on the East Coast and that was probably where they would end up. However, once they started looking for houses to buy, the reality started to settle in. There was one thing that made Shira able to forget that she was several thousand miles away from her family, and that was the community that she and Shea had chosen to move to.

PineMist was on the outskirts of Lakewood. It was filled with detached houses on large properties. Growing up in Los Angeles, Shira didn't have a large backyard and that was something that she always wanted for her children. Even when they first moved to Lakewood, Shira and Shea's townhouse was in a crowded development. Although it was perfect for a new couple starting out, Shira knew that development life wasn't for her. She wanted her kids to be able to play and run outdoors, and the houses in the community of PineMist provided that. But it wasn't only the large properties that drew the Bermans to PineMist. Most of the families living there were at the same stage of life as the Bermans:

couples in their early thirties with three to five children. It also didn't hurt that three of Shea's closest friends lived in the community. But for Shira, it was all about the house. From the outside it didn't look like much, but the potential was there and that is why Shira fell in love with it.

The house was a small, three-bedroom colonial with an attached two-car garage and an unfinished basement. It sat on an acre of land with a gorgeous in-ground pool. As soon as they signed on the house, Shira began making plans for the construction. She had seen that the garages could be converted and additional bedrooms could be built on top. She didn't see a three-bedroom house. She saw a seven-bedroom house with a large playroom and dining room. However, all these plans required money and that is why she thanked Hashem for Shea's job.

When Shea and Shira had been going out, he had explained to her that he didn't know what he wanted to do with his life. He wasn't sure if he wanted to go into *chinuch,* or possibly business. Shea's father was a real estate developer and philanthropist who traveled the globe to help Jews and Torah institutions. There was hardly an institution in the Jewish world that hadn't received some assistance from the renowned Dovid Berman. Shira had assumed that Shea would follow in his father's footsteps. But after a few years of marriage, Shea informed her that he wanted to go into law. Shira was concerned. She understood that law school would be very time-consuming and that was nothing compared to the number of hours that Shea was going to be spending at the office once he finally found a job. Even though she had some doubts, she never shared them with Shea. If he wanted to be a lawyer, she was going to support him in his ambitions. It didn't hurt that Shea's starting salary was over six digits. So as she mused over the various designs for the house, she understood that although Shea wasn't home that often, he was supporting the family and enabling her to realize her dreams.

As Shira looked over the plans, she gave a faint sigh. She couldn't complain. Her husband had a job; in today's market, that meant a lot. But to tell the truth she didn't want to be her own contractor. Even though she had great ideas, she still felt over-whelmed by the responsibility, and she thought it would be best if they hired a professional.

That had been the original plan. However, right after they started to think about the construction, Shea had told her that they needed to start cutting back on their expenses. He had explained to her that his student loans were due, and they had to be paid immediately. Even though the thought of becoming her own con-tractor was less than appealing, she realized that there was no other option and she took on the task. In the back of her mind she sensed that Shea wasn't being one hundred percent honest with her, but she shrugged off the doubts. After all, didn't she trust her husband to be completely up-front with her? Instead, she threw herself into her new profession.

As she sifted through the cards showing various paint colors, she found it hard to keep her focus. Her mind was on Shea's latest case. Shea had explained the basics, without going into too much detail. He had told her that he wasn't allowed to disclose every-thing because it would have violated attorney-client privilege. But there was one thing that he had said that had brought out tiny worry lines near her eyes: Shea had told her that he needed to win the case if he wanted to keep his job. That is what was troubling her, and what was pushing the latest designer paint shades out of her mind.

Shira knew about the current state of the economy and Shea had told her many stories of friends of his from law school who couldn't find jobs. Shea's firm was one of the most successful in the United States, and it wasn't easy to hold a job there. It seemed that firm paid very well and they expected major returns on their investments. Shira had never seen Shea so concerned about a case before, and it worried her.

It was ironic that while she was worrying about Shea's case, she was choosing colors for the new bedrooms. Because accord-ing to Shea, if he lost the case, there weren't going to be any new bedrooms.

Looking for a way to calm her nerves, Shira took out a *Tehillim*.

In seminary, her teachers had taught her that in times of distress and confusion, one could always open up a *Tehillim* and *daven* for help and comfort. Even though she had been out of seminary for many years, she still turned to her *Tehillim* whenever she was troubled.

She had just finished a few *perakim* when she received a text on her phone. It was from Shea. She knew he was sending her the results of the trial. With trembling hands she picked up the phone. As she read his text, a huge smile lit up her face.

■ ■ ■

Shea left the parking lot and headed to his office. Before entering the massive structure, he stopped and stared upward. Standing on the corner of West 12th and Broadway, the building that housed his firm was an enormous structure. Shea's firm occupied the top ten floors. The rent was very expensive, to say the least. But as Shea realized, it was an expense that his firm could definitely afford.

Riding in the elevator, he felt a strong sense of unreality come over him, almost as if he were dreaming. *Is this really happening?* he wondered. Crane, Gardner, and Scott was known as a Harvard firm. All the managing partners were Harvard alumni. Out of the more than two hundred associates, over ninety percent had graduated Harvard. And of those ninety percent, eighty-five percent had made Harvard Law Review. When Shea had originally applied for the job, his friends told him that he was wasting his time. Even though he had graduated from Fordham Law magna cum laude, he wasn't from Harvard and the chances that he would get the job were slim, almost nonexistent. But Shea had never backed down from any challenge, and he didn't back down then. Now those friends were unemployed and Shea was on his way to celebrate his first win with the rest of his fellow associates.

As he exited the elevator, he looked around. It always seemed that the firm was running on wheels, but in reality it was tightly oiled machine. The senior partners' offices were on the top floor, while the junior partners shared the other floors with the associates. Because the firm handled so much business, there weren't separate floors for each department. All the lawyers were expected to be able to deal with all different types of law and therefore there was no need for specialized divisions.

Before arriving at any of the junior partner's offices, one had to walk through a series of cubicles known as associate row. There, all the associates would tackle whatever task the partners demanded.

Shea headed straight for the row, and he was greeted by an overwhelming round of applause. All the associates rose from their cubicles in unison and congratulated him. Even though there was a serious sense of competition between the associates, there was also a strong feeling of loyalty and camaraderie. After Shea accepted the congratulations of his fellow associates, he headed for his desk. As he turned into his own cubicle, he was met by one last firm handshake. It belonged to Kyle Ross, Shea's main competition.

Kyle was one of those associates who had graduated from Harvard, and he let everybody know it. He was a cocky and tenacious lawyer who seemed to be headed straight for partner. Like Shea, he also reported directly to Allan Shore. Though they never spoke about it, Shea and Kyle knew that Allan was only going to retain one associate and each hoped that he would be the one.

"Great job out there," Kyle applauded.

"Thanks," Shea responded.

"I mean, that photo idea was amazing. Not that I wouldn't have thought of it. But hey, it's pretty good for a Fordham guy."

"I am going to ignore that last comment and assume that you are trying to congratulate me," Shea said with a pinched smile.

"That's good, because it's the closest thing to a compliment that you will ever get from me," Kyle answered.

Shea sat at his desk to type his case report. The firm had a policy that no matter what the outcome of a case, the lawyer in charge submitted a report about the proceedings to the supervising senior partner, who would return it with his comments. Although it was a bit tedious and time consuming, Shea liked the idea and appreciated the feedback. He knew that the only way to become great was to learn from the best.

Before he was able to start typing, he heard Kyle calling his name.

"Hey, Shea," Kyle said, "you coming out with us later for celebratory shots?"

Shea paused before answering. The firm had an age-old tradition that the associates would go out together after work and toast the various attorneys who had won that day. For obvious reasons, Shea had explained to his fellow associates that although he would have loved to spend the quality time with them, he had other obligations to attend to. But tonight would be different. Tonight they would be celebrating Shea's achievements, and he didn't want to insult anybody.

"I would love to," Shea responded, "but you know Allan. He is going to have some case for me to get working on bright and early in the morning."

"Wait," Kyle interrupted. "You don't know the firm policy?"

"What policy?"

"The firm has a rule," Kyle explained, "that after every trial that an attorney wins, he is given the following day off. They want the attorney to enjoy his victory and recharge his batteries."

"So you are telling me that I don't need to come in tomorrow?" Shea asked, shocked and delighted.

"Not only do you not need to come in, but you don't even have to turn on your phone."

"Wow."

"So I guess that means that you *can* come out with us tonight?" Kyle asked

"Well um ...," Shea stammered.

"It's all right. I know you can't come out with us. You being married and religious and all that. Don't forget that I am Jewish, too," Kyle said.

"I didn't forget," Shea responded. "By the way, you still have to come to us for a *Shabbos* meal."

"I haven't forgotten. Tell your wife to make more of that

delicious *challah* that you brought in last week, and I will be over there in no time."

"Will do," Shea stated.

"I'll make sure to drink some shots for you tonight, okay?"

"I knew I could always count on you, Kyle," Shea answered.

BEFORE SHEA COULD GO BACK TO HIS REPORT, HIS PHONE rang. His face lit up when he saw the caller ID.

"Shea, you are the man!" a voice exclaimed.

"How do you figure, Danny?" Shea asked.

"You just made me a ton of money."

"By doing what?"

"Well, when the market opened, Merzeir was down ten percent because of the lawsuit. But I knew that they had the world's best attorney on their side. So I bought one thousand shares. Later in the day, you win the case and the stock jumps twenty percent. I love you, man."

Danny Abramson not only happened to be one the smartest traders on Wall Street, but he was also Shea's oldest and best friend. They had been inseparable ever since kindergarten.

It had started when they were five. Shea's parents had just moved from Long Island and it was Shea's first day with his new classmates at Yeshivas Tiferes Yitzchak. Worried that as the new boy in the classroom he might have a hard time making friends. Shea's parents bought him the newest Superman action figure. They had hoped that Shea's classmates would want to see his new toy and therefore would want to be his friend. The problem for Shea was that he wasn't the only person who had brought a Superman action figure to school that day. Moshe Robinson, who was the principal's son, also had brought his Superman to school. Now, Moshe had reasoned that there couldn't be two Supermen in the class. So he decided that Shea's Superman was going to be the bad guy. The whole class proceeded to spend their recess period chasing after Shea and trying to destroy his action figure.

The mayhem came to an end when a short and pudgy kid stood up to Moshe and told him to leave Shea and his Superman alone. That boy was Danny, and ever since then, Shea and Danny had been inseparable.

"Are you sure what you did was legal?" Shea asked "This isn't some kind of insider trading, is it?"

"Are you kidding me? Of course it's legal. Look, just because all of Wall Street thought that you were not capable of winning this case, doesn't mean that I had to agree with them."

"I am sure that *some* people thought that I could win the case," Shea argued.

"No way. Well, there may have been one blind guy. But he thought you were Alan Dershowitz, so I guess that doesn't count."

"You sure know how to make a guy feel great, don't you?"

"I just call it the way that I see it. But anyway, how are you celebrating the big victory?"

"By working," Shea responded.

"Why?"

"I need to write a report for my boss. It could take me all night to complete. Danny boy, go and spend your millions. We'll continue this conversation later. If I don't finish writing this report, I will never get out of here."

"No problem," Danny responded. "I guess that means that we won't be learning tonight?"

"I don't think so."

"You finish the report and don't worry about me. I still need to review the *parashah* from last week. We'll pick it up again tomorrow night."

"Thanks, Danny and have a great night."

Shea returned to his typing, a small smile playing on his lips. Danny's luck in the market was the icing on the cake. Life was going great. He had a wonderful job and a gorgeous family. He was living in a terrific community with friends who really cared about him. Life couldn't get any better.

If only he had been able to hold onto those thoughts for a little while longer. Because with what was about to transpire over the next couple of days, Shea's life was about to implode right before his eyes.

■ ■ ■

The crowd was mesmerized by the speaker. His powerful voice echoed both through the hall and within the hearts of all those who had come to listen. His towering frame only added to the power that he exuded. For most of the listeners, the rabbi's words would provide inspiration that would, they hoped, last at least until their next encounter with the challenges of modern-day life. But for Shea, listening to Rabbi Felder, his rebbi provided much more than a fleeting moment of inspiration. His rebbi's words guided him every moment of every day. Shea rarely did anything without consulting his rebbi first. Today, Shea badly needed his guidance.

Even though he had heard his rebbi's speeches many times, he always felt the words uplifting his soul; giving him the feeling that spiritually he had the potential to accomplish anything and everything if he really wanted to.

He knew that if there was anybody who had the answers, it would be his rebbi. And tonight, he needed some answers.

"So that is the message that we are trying to understand," Rabbi Felder stressed to the crowd. "No matter what the challenges that we may face, we are given the strength to overcome them. The *refuah* is always given before the *makah*. The real challenge isn't the test itself. The real obstacle is understanding and finding the courage that we all possess in order to overcome our own insecurities, and triumph over the *yetzer hara* that whispers to us that we can never succeed. May we all merit to find our inner strengths as we wait for the coming of *Mashiach* in our days."

"Amen," mumbled the crowd.

"Let's *daven* Maariv now," Rabbi Felder said cheerfully as he prepared to lead the service.

After *davening*, the congregants rose from their chairs and formed a line to approach Rabbi Felder. He received each member individually and inquired about his well-being, this one's health, that one's new baby. Once the crowd had dispersed, he looked up and saw his favorite student waiting patiently.

"Come now, Shea, and please do me a favor," Rabbi Felder requested.

"Anything," Shea answered.

"Be honest with me. You have heard this speech at least fifty times. Does it sound the same every time? "

"Honestly?"

"Please," Rabbi Felder implored him. "My congregants are nice, but they would never tell me the truth. But you, a *talmid*, I am sure that you could be honest with me."

"Well, as long as we are being honest, I think I could have given the speech word for word. Even with all the same hand motions and stops."

"You were always able to do a great impersonation of me," Rabbi Felder reminded him.

"But that doesn't mean I don't get something out of your words, even if I know them by heart," Shea hastened to add, hoping he hadn't hurt his rebbi's feelings. Rabbi Felder hardly heard him. He was chuckling softly to himself, remembering Shea's antics in years gone by.

"You think I didn't know about that time when you called the yeshivah office saying that you were me and that school was cancelled because of snow? You might have gotten away with it had it not been seventy degrees outside and sunny."

"You knew about that?"

"Shea, I knew about everything. Just because I didn't speak to you about it, doesn't mean I didn't know what was going on."

"How did you realize it was me?" Shea wondered.

"Whenever something was going wrong in your life, you always had this puzzled look on your face. So the next day in yeshivah, when I went over to you, the look on your face told me everything I needed to know. It looked kind of like the look that you have on your face right now."

"I am sorry, rebbi," Shea apologized, "but what I am supposed to do?"

"First things first. Did you win your case?"

"Sure did," Shea grinned. "The opposing counsel never saw it coming. I must admit, it felt really good."

"Does that mean that you definitely have a job next year?"

"I have no idea. I mean, Kyle Ross is a really good lawyer, and a Harvard grad, and I don't know how I am going to be able to beat him no matter how well I do."

"Look, you can only worry about your own success. You can't worry about what other people are doing."

"But how can I not? The debt is growing by the day and I am really feeling squeezed. I can't imagine what I would do if I lost this job."

"Shira still doesn't know?"

"No, and I am doing my best to make sure that she never finds out. But she is getting suspicious."

"How do you know that?"

"She isn't stupid," Shea answered. "She knows that I handle the finances and she rarely asks questions. But ever since we bought the house, I get the feeling she knows something is wrong."

"Why?"

"I told her that she could take care of all the renovations in the house. She gets to pick out the paint colors, the tiles, and the kitchen appliances. The problem arises when she picks out a tile or a freezer that is too expensive for our budget."

"Doesn't she understand that things may cost a little too much for you to spend?"

"But she does the math," Shea countered. "She knows how much I'm making and she doesn't understand why we can't spend for certain things."

"What do you tell her when she asks you?"

"I tell her that we need the money to pay off student loans."

"Does she believe you?"

"I guess," Shea replied. "But I keep wondering if I'm right."

"Right about what?"

"About not telling my wife the truth. It's killing me having to lie to her. I mean, before this whole episode, I never told her an untruth, not even once. She would often remark to me how much she cherished our openness. Now every time I look at her I'm reminded of the lie that I have created."

"Let's look at your choices. Can you really tell her the truth?"

Shea thought about what Rabbi Felder was asking. He wanted so badly to be able to tell him yes. He wanted to be able to tell his rebbi that Shira could handle anything and would accept Shea no matter what he had done. But when he thought about it, he knew that Shira was human and even Shira had her limits.

His silence said it all.

"I know that you can't see it now," Rabbi Felder said gently, "but there will be a time when you will be able to tell your wife the truth. Now is too early. Give it some time and then you can tell her. I know this isn't easy, Shea," Rabbi Felder consoled him. "Soon it will be all over and then you and Shira can go back to living your lives like you had before."

"I know," Shea responded, grinning despite his uneasiness. "If Hashem gave me a *makah*, then he gave me the *refuah* to overcome it."

"Maybe next time, I will have you give the *shiur* instead," Rabbi Felder said with a smile. He glanced at his watch. "It's getting late."

"Would Rebbi like a ride home?"

"A ride?" Rabbi Felder asked. "Who needs a ride? I need to walk. The doctor says that it is good for my cholesterol. You young people and your cars. You forget that you were born with two long limbs called legs and they are meant to be used."

"Okay, so I will walk you home," Shea said.

"And ruin your *shalom bayis*? Your wife is waiting for you. I don't think so. I can get home fine by myself. You go home to your wife as quickly as possible."

"Are you sure?"

"Of course I am sure," Rabbi Felder answered. "Now get out of here and call me tomorrow."

"I will and thank you again, Rebbi."

"There isn't anything that I wouldn't do for you, Shea. You know that, right?"

"I know and we will speak tomorrow. Good night, Rebbi."

"Good night, Shea."

Shea got into his car and started the ignition. He saw his rebbi walking and waved to him. He debated turning off the engine and walking Rabbi Felder home, but he decided against it. His rebbi had been adamant and he knew it was useless to argue with Rabbi Felder.

As he turned onto Coney Island Avenue, he realized how much better he felt since he had spoken to his rebbi. He made a mental note to call him the next day to thank him.

But as Shea was going to find out, that was one phone call he would never make.

■ ■ ■

Though it had been hours since he'd returned from the forest, Khalid still felt the delicious rage surging within him. He forced himself to think of Rasheed. Khalid knew what he needed to do: get back to his apartment without a problem. But Khalid was hungry. Starving. The blood, the cries of the wounded animal had given him a huge appetite.

He smiled. His favorite Middle Eastern takeout place was only a few blocks from home. As soon as he got his shwarma, he would run straight home and stay there.

It almost worked.

Khalid got to the takeout counter. While the old lady ahead of him took her time with her order, Khalid was able to control his frustration, and he waited quietly for his food to arrive. As soon as his order was ready, Khalid left the store and headed home.

Had he not looked ahead of him and just walked with his head down, maybe things would have ended up very differently. But as he neared the intersection, Khalid's eyes, trained to take in every detail, scanned the area. That is when he saw him. He had seen the old man on many occasions, and though he had often felt the familiar stirring of anger and violence at the sight of the rabbi, the medicine that Rasheed forced him to take had helped him to dominate his desires. But Khalid hadn't taken his medicine for three days, and he could still smell the blood of the dying deer.

Knowing what was at stake, Khalid tried to fight his compulsion. But then the man passing him smiled. Memories of suffering flooded Khalid's brain. He would punish the old man and make good on the oath of vengeance that he had sworn. Although a quiet voice deep within him warned that there would be consequences to his actions, Khalid took out the metal rod he had used on the deer.

■ ■ ■

Rolling out of bed at eight o'clock definitely had its advantages. Because Shea had the day off, Shira had gotten the kids off to school and enabled Shea to go to a later *minyan*. For a guy who usually woke up at 5:30 in the morning, the extra rest definitely felt good. After *davening* was finished, Shea looked at his watch. It was 9:30 and he had no idea what to do next. He had told Shira that he would meet her for breakfast at 10:30. That gave him an hour. Shea looked for a *sefer* that he could learn while he waited for his wife. As he pulled a *Mishnah Berurah* off the shelf, he turned on his company cellphone to check for messages from the office.

What was going on? Danny had sent him more than ten text messages since 6:30 in the morning, all begging Shea to call him.

Danny answered the phone after the first ring.

"Where have you been?" Danny yelled. "I've been trying to get in touch with you the whole morning."

"My phone was off," Shea answered.

"So you haven't heard?"

"Heard what?" Shea asked, obviously confused.

"Look, I'm just finishing up a meeting. I can't go into everything now. Check out Frumnews.com, okay. You'll find out everything you need to know. Once you have checked out the site, call me back. I should be available in five minutes."

The phone went silent.

Shea clicked the browser on his phone and pulled up Frumnews.com. He didn't even have to scroll down the page to see the story that Danny was referring to.

In his shock, he dropped the phone.

Struggling to regain his composure, he bent down, picked up the phone, and speed-dialed Danny.

"Is this for real?" Shea asked, his voice trembling.

"I don't think that the website would be mistaken about something like this."

"But when did this happen?"

"As far as I know, it was late last night. I mean that is what the website is reporting."

"Is it as bad as they are making it seem?"

"I don't know what to tell you," Danny answered. "I don't know more than you do. I don't even know where they are keeping him. According to the papers, they are keeping his location a secret. "

"Why would they do that?" Shea wondered.

"I really can't give you the answers. The only one who can is Yechiel, and I think you should give him a call."

Yes. Action. Something to do. Something to help him steady his nerves.

"I'll call him right away."

"Hey," Danny added, "if you find out anything, give me a call, please."

"Will do."

How could this have happened, he wondered. *Why would anybody do something so cruel?*

As Shea waited for Yechiel to answer, he reviewed the story he'd just read.

It seemed, according to reports, that at 11:30 last night, on his way home after giving his nightly *shiur*, Rav Gedaliah Felder was brutally attacked, seemingly by a lone assailant. The incident occurred on Coney Island Avenue, between Avenues R and S. The extent of the damage was horrifying. Although the exact details could not be confirmed, initial reports stated that Rabbi Felder had suffered six broken ribs, a broken nose, and a severe concussion. But because his location had been kept a secret, nobody had an update on his condition.

Finally, Yechiel Felder answered his phone.

"Yechiel," Shea began, "what happened?"

"Shea, it's not good," Yechiel answered gravely. "I have no idea what the media is reporting, but I can tell you that it is much worse."

"I am so sorry, Yechiel. Do you have any idea what happened?"

"Not really. My father finishes giving his *shiur* at about 10:45. The yeshivah then *davens* Maariv and he usually walks home at about 11:15. It is about a ten-minute walk to our house and you know my father, no matter the weather, he always walked. But at about 11:45, he still hadn't come home, so my mother called his cell phone. It rang and rang and then went into voicemail. My mother got concerned, and she called *Hatzalah*. She asked them to canvass the area where he usually walks, and they found him lying on the sidewalk unconscious."

"Where did they take him?" Shea inquired.

"I don't know if I can tell you."

"Why not?"

"Look, Shea, my father was brutally attacked. His face is so swollen from all the bruising that I can barely recognize him. The doctors told me that both of his femurs were fractured and he suffered a collapsed lung. He is still unconscious."

"I feel terrible for you, but why aren't you telling people where he is?"

"If he was attacked like this, we don't want the perpetrator coming to finish off the job."

"You think that he is coming after your father in a hospital?"

"Shea, I know it sounds farfetched, but you didn't see the damage that this madman inflicted. This wasn't just a robbery gone bad. There was real hatred behind this crime. We are really afraid for my father's life."

Shea was in shock. His rebbi was the kindest, most generous man he knew. He didn't think that anybody could bear ill will toward Rabbi Felder, let alone attack him viciously. None of this made any sense.

"Do the authorities have any suspects?"

"If they do, they haven't told us. Right now there is a police officer outside my father's room guarding the door. Nobody is allowed within fifty feet of the door unless one of us recognizes the person."

"I'll make a few calls," Shea offered. "I have a friend who works with the district attorney. If there are any suspects, he would know about it."

"Thanks, Shea."

"I need to see him, Yechiel. What hospital are you guys in?"

"I don't know what to say, Shea," Yechiel answered.

"Look, this isn't just some person, and I am not just some student. You know how much your father means to me, and I would never do anything to hurt him. So please, just tell me where you are."

Yechiel thought a moment before answering. Shea was his father's closest student. If anybody deserved to be at the hospital, it was Shea.

"We're at Lutheran Medical Center, on the fourth floor. Make sure you call me before you come, or else the cops won't let you get near the door."

"I'm on my way. And Yechiel, remember, if there is one person who can overcome anything, it's your father."

"I know, Shea, and thanks for the kind words. I'll see you soon."

Shea ended the call and ran to his car. As his mind struggled to grasp what had just transpired, he took out his phone and dialed his wife.

"Hello," she answered cheerfully.

"Where are you?" Shea asked.

"I am on my way to Bagel World. You told me to meet you there by 10:30."

"Well, plans have changed."

"What's wrong?" Shira asked, concern in her voice.

"It's Rabbi Felder," Shea replied. "It seems that he was involved in some kind of attack last night. I spoke to Yechiel and I am going to the hospital right now."

"*Hashem yerachem*," Shira exclaimed. "Is he okay?"

"I'm not sure. According to Yechiel, he still hasn't regained consciousness. I'll call you later, whenever I know anything."

"Shea," Shira added. "My *Tehillim* group is meeting today. Text me Rabbi Felder's name, and we can say *Tehillim* for him."

"Great idea. I'll get it from Yechiel."

Shea hung up and ran through the contacts on his phone. He remembered what he had told Yechiel, and he searched for a specific number. Once he found the number, he hit send on his phone and waited for the person to answer.

"Shea Berman, is that really you?"

"How are you Moshe?" Shea asked

"I am doing fine, B"H," Moshe responded. "What about you? How is it working for the dark side?"

"Come on, Moshe," Shea answered, "not all attorneys are evil."

"You are right," Moshe agreed. "But the all good ones work with me for the DA's office. The ones who work with you, those guys are scary people."

Shea laughed at Moshe's comment. It so happened that Moshe Cohen was the lone *frum* attorney working for the Brooklyn District Attorney. They had met while they were at Fordham. Moshe had originally started out in Stanford, but decided to transfer to Fordham so he could learn in a yeshivah at night. Though Moshe's parents weren't religious, they loved the idea of their son going to school near home, even if he was spending time in a yeshivah. Shea had befriended Moshe during his second year of law school, and they had kept in touch ever since.

"Just because we have beaten you the last five times doesn't mean that you have to be bitter," Shea teased.

"Ouch," Moshe said. "But seriously Shea, what's up?"

"You heard what happened to Rabbi Felder?" Shea asked.

"Of course. That's all anybody is talking about here. This one is bad, Shea. Whoever did it better have a good lawyer. The DA has already given the speech about this one. He is going hard after this guy, without any mercy. He knows that if they let this one get away, it's going to end up being a media nightmare."

"Why?" Shea wondered. "I mean, Yechiel explained the brutality of the attack, but why would this be different from the dozens that your office deals with daily?"

"It looks like this one is racial," Moshe answered.

"What do you mean?"

"I really can't say."

"Moshe," Shea pressed, "I told Yechiel that I would try to get answers. He told me that the police at the hospital aren't saying anything until his father wakes up. The poor guy is suffering. Please just tell me something that I can take back to him."

Moshe thought before answering. He could imagine the fear and grief that Yechiel and his family were going through. He wanted to help them in any way possible. But he also knew the volatility of the situation and he didn't want anything to blow out of control.

"Tell Yechiel that the police will probably have a suspect in custody within the next hour," Moshe finally said.

"Do you have a name?"

"You know I can't tell you that, Shea. But right now I really need to run. Once they get the suspect into custody, all mayhem will break loose. I can't tell you much about the suspect, but you can tell Yechiel that he is a Palestinian," Moshe added, as he hung up the phone.

As he drove toward the Garden State Parkway Shea mulled over what Moshe had just told him. If it was true that Rabbi Felder's assailant was a Palestinian, then Moshe was right. The media was going to have a field day. There would be protests and demonstrations demanding justice. The Jewish assemblymen would hold press conferences reassuring the public that justice would be done. The DA would state that justice would be served and that the streets of New York would be safe again. Elections were approaching, and the politicos would be jumping on the bandwagon; there were lots of Jewish voters out there.

Amid all the chaos, Shea realized, one very important fact would be forgotten. There was a very special man at the center of this calamity, and that man was currently struggling to stay alive.

As Shea got onto the New Jersey Turnpike, memories of his rebbi flooded his thoughts. The fact that he may have been the last person to see Rabbi Felder before he was attacked was not lost on Shea. He tried to imagine the elderly man lying on a hard Brooklyn sidewalk, unconscious, bloody, but the only thing that he could think about were the warm memories. He saw Rabbi Felder's affectionate smile, which would radiate love while he was explaining *pshat* in a difficult *sugya*. Shea recalled the powerful speeches that he would deliver, demanding that the boys live up to their potential. There was one story that Shea was able to remember better than anything else. It was the story that defined the relationship between him and Rabbi Felder. It was also the story that changed Shea's life forever.

■ ■ ■

Shea Berman didn't really have an interest in learning. Everyone agreed that he was very smart, but he never had the patience to sit and learn. He was passionately interested in sports, particularly playing basketball, and that is where he devoted most of his energy and interest. Even though Shea's yeshivah did not have a basketball team, Shea participated in an intercity league where Jewish boys would be split into teams and play each other. Tall and athletic, Shea was a natural and was one of the top players in the league. Shea loved playing so much that his studies took a backseat, which was fine with him but not with the yeshivah. His menahel, Rabbi Forst, had called him into his office and told him that unless he stopped playing basketball he would be expelled from the yeshivah. Shea was fuming. It did not help matters that his parents agreed with the administration and would not permit Shea to play. It was around Purim time and Shea decided that he would show his parents and the yeshivah.

In the weeks preceding Purim, yeshivah students around the globe spend their time trying to conjure up ideas on how to pull off the perfect Purim prank. Whether it is ringing the fire bell in the middle of class, or putting crazy glue on the teacher's markers, students look for the best way to create the most mayhem, all in the name of "Purim shtick." Shea saw the upcoming Purim holiday as the ideal cover to vent his disappointment at Rabbi Forst and the yeshivah.

One afternoon, Shea had stopped on his way home from school to purchase mice from a local pet shop. He brought them to school in his backpack and waited for the perfect opportunity. To Shea's glee, the school was having an assembly that day and all the students, from ages six to seventeen, would be in the auditorium. In the middle of the assembly Shea opened his bag and pandemonium immediately followed. Boys were running in every direction trying to avoid the tiny creatures and it was a miracle that nobody ended up getting hurt. The janitors spent an entire week trying to capture all the mice.

When Rabbi Forst found out that Shea had orchestrated the chaos, he was fuming. Shea for his part, wasn't the least bit contrite. He was angry with the school and he was showing them how he felt.

Rabbi Forst was livid and wanted to expel Shea immediately. Rabbi Felder, who was Shea's rebbi, asked Rabbi Forst if he could speak with Shea before a final decision was made. Rabbi Forst relented and Rabbi Felder called Shea into his office.

Entering the office Shea was calm and composed. If the yeshivah wanted to kick him out, he was fine with that. At least he might be able to go to a school where they had a basketball team. He waited for Rabbi Felder to yell and scream, but there was no fiery tirade.

Rabbi Felder motioned for Shea to sit down. Shea glanced at his rebbi, waiting to see the burning anger in his eyes. Instead he saw *genuine sadness. Before Shea had a chance to speak, Rabbi Felder took his hand and grasped it. Over and over, Rabbi Felder uttered the words, "Shealeh, Shealeh, what is going to become of my Shealeh …." Tears streamed from his eyes. He didn't speak directly to Shea; he didn't have to. The sight of his rebbi's genuine pain and disappointment was all Shea needed to see.*

With Rabbi Felder's intervention the yeshivah allowed Shea to stay. They didn't regret it: from that day on, Shea became a diligent student who grew into a true ben Torah.

As he entered the fourth floor of Lutheran Hospital, Shea wasn't sure that he could handle seeing his rebbi under such horrific circumstances.

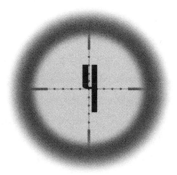

DETECTIVE JOEY NELSON STOOD IN THE STAIRWELL AND grimly eyed the suspect's apartment. Though he wasn't the most imposing figure, Nelson cast fear into many criminals. With his fiery personality and wiry frame, criminals understood that this cop meant business.

Nelson liked to be one hundred percent sure before he made an arrest. Something about this case didn't seem quite right. For one thing, the apartment house was a fairly upscale residence for a recent immigrant. And it was convenient that the police had received an anonymous tip as to the whereabouts of the suspect. Maybe a little too convenient?

These doubts were mitigated by the fact that the suspect's home was only a two-minute walk from the scene of the crime. More important, according to surveillance reports the suspect matched an eyewitness' description of the man who had attacked the rabbi.

As Nelson approached the door, he pushed all doubts out of his mind, and raised his voice.

"Khalid al-Jinn," Nelson shouted, banging on the door. "Police, open up."

When there was no response, he checked the warrant in his hand. He didn't need to wait for al-Jinn to politely open the door. He motioned for his partner to break it down. His partner gave a swift kick directly under the doorknob. Nelson rushed over the threshold, his hand firmly on his pistol.

Whatever he'd expected, it wasn't this. Al-Jinn was crouched on a rug on the floor, seemingly unaware of the officer's presence, praying. Nelson froze, not sure how to proceed. But as al-Jinn raised his head and locked eyes with Nelson, the policeman sprang into action. He ordered al-Jinn to stand up. Al-Jinn, ignoring Nelson, continued mumbling Arabic words under his breath.

"Khalid al-Jinn," Nelson began as he slapped the handcuffs on al-Jinn, "you are under arrest for the attempted murder of Gedaliah Felder. You have the right to remain silent."

For the first time, the Arab looked directly at the policeman. "Do you know what the Koran says about the Jewish swine and their Christian friends?"

"Honestly, I couldn't care less," Nelson answered gruffly, checking the cuffs.

"It says 'May Allah kill them because they turned away.' Do you think that I am afraid of you?"

"You should be."

"I fear no man. I fear only Allah, and he would be proud of what has been done. That Zionist pig deserved what he got and all of you will soon get what you deserve."

"Tom!" Nelson yelled to his partner. "Get Mr. al-Jinn out of my sight before I do something that I know I'll regret."

His partner shoved al-Jinn and led him outside. Nelson took out the crime scene tape and closed off the area leading into the apartment. After he booked this arrogant thug, he would return to the apartment to collect any evidence needed to prosecute him. And oh, how he would enjoy seeing him thrown into jail for a long, long time.

Nelson radioed into the precinct for backup to make sure that the apartment wasn't touched until he got back. After he received confirmation from dispatch that the backup was on the way, he headed to his car. There he found his partner guarding the car with al-Jinn secured inside.

"Is this guy for real?" Tom asked.

"What else did he say?"

"I don't know. Just a lot of praise Allah this and death to Zionists that. I mean, this guy seems like a certified wacko."

"Well, then it shouldn't be hard to prove that he did this. But hey, we did our job and now it is up to the DA to put this guy away for a very long time," Nelson responded.

■ ■ ■

"Shea," Yechiel called from down the hall, "come over here."

Shea nodded to the officer guarding the doorway and walked quickly toward Yechiel. He embraced his friend with a heart-felt hug. As Yechiel pulled away, Shea could see that his friend's brown eyes were red from crying. His thinning hair was a mess and he looked like he hadn't slept in weeks.

Noticing Shea's gaze, Yechiel commented, "I know I look like a wreck. My father would not have been pleased. He was always very insistent that we looked our best. He would have said that if we are truly the children of the King, then we must adorn our-selves like princes."

"Stop referring to your father in the past," Shea corrected him gently. "He is going to survive this, I know it."

"Look, I know that my father is a strong person, but you haven't seen what was done to him."

Shea turned to Yechiel. There were tears in his eyes.

"I spoke to him after his *shiur*, Yechiel. I offered him a ride, and he refused. I should have insisted."

"This isn't your fault, Shea."

"I just can't stop thinking about what might have happened if I had walked with him."

"Go in, look at him. It is so bad, Shea. Nobody could have stopped this madman, not even you. Most likely you would just have wound up in the hospital with him."

Shea nodded slowly. He realized that he couldn't have done anything to prevent what happened to his rebbi. But that didn't make him feel any better.

"Did you hear anything about my father's attacker?" Yechiel asked.

"My contact told me that the suspect was going to be arrested within the hour."

"*Baruch Hashem*," Yechiel exclaimed.

"But there is more," Shea continued. "Did the police give you any clue about possible suspects?"

"Like I told you before, they weren't talking much. They said that they had some questions for my father, when he wakes up, and they didn't want to tell me anything until he answered them."

"One more thing," Shea said. "Besides me, who else knows that your father is here?"

"Other than the family, nobody else. Why are you asking these questions, Shea? What do you know that you aren't telling me?"

"Right now you need to make sure that your father's location is a secret."

"Why? If the cops have the suspect in custody, why should we be afraid?"

"I am not worried about the suspect coming to hurt your father. I am more concerned that you and your family are given the proper space and privacy that you need."

Yechiel stared at him, perplexed. "Why would anybody, other than our close friends, really care about my father being attacked?"

"The suspect that the police are arresting is a Palestinian," Shea answered gravely. "According to my source, once the media finds out about this, they will be swarming everywhere. You won't be able to go home, to yeshivah, or even to shul without a camera in your face. "

Yechiel took a step back. He had known that his father's attack was brutal, but he had had no clue that it was racially motivated.

"Do you know that name of the suspect?" Yechiel asked.

"My source wouldn't tell me anything. But once they arrest him and his name is revealed to the media, all mayhem will break loose. We need to keep you and your family as far from the circus as possible."

As they entered Rabbi Felder's room, they saw Yechiel's mother, Rebbetzin Felder, sitting and saying *Tehillim*. The tears rolled down her face as she said each word with conviction and concentration.

"Do me a favor," Yechiel whispered. "Don't tell my mother any of this. She is already broken from the whole ordeal. I think if she hears about this guy being an Arab, it will just bring her more pain."

"Not a word."

Mrs. Felder lifted her gaze up from the *Tehillim* and turned reddened eyes toward Shea.

"Hello Rebbetzin," he said, a little uncomfortable in face of her obvious grief. "I am not sure if you remember me."

"Of course I remember you, Shea," Mrs. Felder said quietly. "My husband would spend many nights talking about how proud he was of you. When he danced at your *chasunah*, he told me that he felt the same way that he did by Yechiel's. But now, I just don't know what is going to be."

Rebbetzin Felder began to cry and Yechiel went over to comfort her. He then motioned to Shea. With great apprehension, Shea walked slowly toward the motionless figure lying, ever so still, in the hospital bed.

■ ■ ■

Nelson pulled the toothpick, or whatever remained of it, from his mouth. Though he didn't like to admit it, his wife was right. Chewing on toothpicks was definitely a disgusting habit. She once told him that if he wanted to get his suspects to talk, all Nelson needed to do was show them the mutilated toothpick and they would confess for sure. Nelson wasn't sure about that, but as he eyed his latest suspect through the glass, he knew that he was going to get a confession no matter what he had to do to get it. And it would take more than a chewed-up toothpick.

Joey Nelson wasn't a racist by nature. His parents had raised him to be a caring individual who was accepting of all types of people. That was the reason he originally joined the police force. He wanted to make a difference and to create better lives for his neighbors and friends. But that all changed six months ago, with the death of his partner Raymond Coleman.

Raymond had worked with Nelson for over ten years. Ray was a heavy fellow, while Nelson was on the slim side. People used to refer to them as the "Odd Couple," and to Nelson that was fine. The odd couple had the most successful arrest record in the entire city and both Nelson and Coleman had received numerous awards for their bravery and heroism.

All this came to an abrupt end, when one day Raymond Coleman showed up in the wrong place at the wrong time.

Ray always took the subway to work and he was on the platform when he heard a cry for help. He saw an Arabic man wearing a kaffiyeh, lying on the ground writhing in pain. Ray ran over to the fallen man to see what he could do to help. When he bent down and asked him what he needed, the man answered that he needed Ray to die, and he pulled out a gun and shot the officer at point blank range. Before anybody had a chance to react, the terrorist screamed out, Allahu Akbar, and shot himself as well.

Nelson was the one who told Raymond's wife and kids that their father would never come home again. After leaving his partner's house, Nelson broke down and wept. From that day, he was a changed man.

As he opened the door to the room to face al-Jinn, he could only see Ray's big hearty smile. The anger began to take control. Khalid al-Jinn sat on an uncomfortable wooden chair with his eyes closed. He seemed to have been mumbling something, but Nelson couldn't make out the words. After waiting a few moments, Nelson took his files and slammed them full force onto the table right in front of the suspect. Khalid didn't flinch, which only infuriated Nelson even more.

"Hey," Nelson yelled, "do you hear me talking to you?"

Al-Jinn was silent. Nelson slammed his fist on the table. Al-Jinn finally opened his eyes and turned to the officer.

"*Hal beemkanimosa'adatuk?*" al-Jinn replied

"What did you just call me?" Nelson asked

"*Hal beemkanimosa'adatuk?*" al-Jinn repeated

"Do you think this is a joke? You can call me anything that you want, but I am the one holding all the cards."

"I did not call you anything," al-Jinn responded in perfect English. "I just asked you what is it that you want from me."

"Sorry to rain on your parade, Ali Baba, but I don't want anything from you," Nelson responded confidently. "You see, what we have here is something that we in the police force like to call a slam dunk."

Nelson waited for a reply from al-Jinn, but he received none. *This guy is crazy*, Nelson thought to himself. *How could he just sit there all smug and confident? I need him to realize how great the stakes really are.*

He then moved to the other side of the room before continuing. When he attended the police academy, the cadets were taught to continually move around when interrogating a suspect. His instructors told them that the suspect must be kept off balance. As Nelson paced the room, he could see the fear building in al-Jinn's eyes.

"Usually," Nelson continued, "it takes hours to get a suspect to confess. It would hasten the process and save me the hassle of collecting evidence and building a case. But see here, you little jihadist, I don't need your confession. Your case is already wrapped up. Not only do I have the weapon and not only do I have motive, but I even have a witness who saw your dirty evil self attacking a defenseless rabbi. She says that she saw your face perfectly as you struck the rabbi repeatedly with that metal rod. But I haven't even told you the best part. She also heard you yelling some crazy Arabic words which I am sure, with the help of some court appointed translator, we will be able to figure out what they mean. Once the prosecutor sees all the evidence, he isn't going to charge you with aggravated assault. Oh no, he is going to charge you with a hate crime. And do you know what the penalty for a hate crime is in the beautiful state of New York? It is life in prison without parole. So you can whisper your prayers to Allah or Mohammed or whatever else it is that you psychopaths pray to. Because where you are going, you are going to need all the help you can get."

Al-Jinn didn't flinch. Most suspects, when they heard the mention of life without parole, would usually react. Al-Jinn said nothing. Nelson was impressed, but not really surprised. He had dealt with a few extremists in the past, and none of them showed any emotion when they were initially interrogated. They would usually break down after being left alone with their thoughts, which is exactly what Nelson planned to do with al-Jinn.

"I am going to let you think about what I just said," Nelson informed him. "But just remember that I don't care if you confess or not. So when I come back in here, if you wanna deal, you better offer me something good."

Nelson thought that he had finally broken al-Jinn as the suspect peered down toward his hands. But then al-Jinn raised his eyes toward Nelson and clapped his hands.

"*Mabrouk, mabrouk,*" al-Jinn mocked. "They should give you an award for such a performance."

"How dare you ridicule me?" Nelson said, seething.

"I am sure that your tough-guy speech has won you many cases in your time. But you see, mister detective, I don't care for your theatrics. Like I told you before, I fear no man and no court other than the court of Allah. And in his eyes I know that I am pure and innocent. So you can spray your venomous lies all over this room, but Allah knows the truth."

With a roar Nelson lunged for al-Jinn's neck. The door to the interrogation room flew open and an armed officer restrained Nelson and marched him out of the room. Nelson's superior, Lieutenant Simpson, was waiting in the hallway.

"How could you have done that to me?" Nelson spit out. "I was so close to breaking him."

"No, Nelson," Simpson corrected him, "you were so close to getting yourself thrown into jail for police brutality. If this case is as airtight as you say it is, the last thing we want is this guy getting sympathy from a jury for police misconduct."

"Everything I told him in there was true. The evidence is right here in this folder," Nelson answered, handing the folder to Simpson.

"Don't give me the information," Simpson ordered. "Make sure that he," Simpson said, pointing to a young man standing nearby, "has all the evidence he needs."

The young man wearing a yarmulke stopped in front of Nelson and stuck out his hand. Nelson recovered his composure. He returned the handshake warmly and spoke.

"Mark Cohen, I haven't seen you around here lately. Where have you been?"

"I've been working on a RICO case against Stefano Dimassi," Moshe answered.

"I thought they found his body washed up on some shore in Italy," Nelson said.

"I am not going after him. I am really going after his partner, Louis Scallini. But once I can prove my case against Stefano's estate, then going after Louis will be much easier."

"Well, good luck with that. The more of them behind bars, the better it will be for all of us."

"Thank you," Moshe replied. "But let's get back to the business at hand. Tell me more about Mr. al-Jinn."

"Just take a look at him," Nelson said, his anger rising once again. "You will learn all you need to know just by observing him."

Moshe peered through the one-way glass into the interrogation room. He saw the suspect sitting in his chair calmly muttering words, which Moshe assumed were prayers, to himself.

Moshe also saw Nelson growing more and more infuriated.

"Detective Nelson, let me begin by telling you how sorry I am for what happened to your partner."

"What does that have to do with this?"

"I see you are visibly upset with the suspect," Moshe answered.

"Of course I am upset. This guy attacked a defenseless old man and deserves to be punished for it."

"That is true, but you are making this personal and the defendant knows it. How many Muslim extremists have you dealt with in your career?"

"Honestly, not too many," Nelson replied. "Why do you ask?"

"When I became an attorney in the DA's office, I took a course given by Rami Aretz. Have you ever heard of him?"

"The name doesn't ring a bell."

"He used to be one of the heads of Shin Bet, the Israeli counter-terrorism unit. He was giving a course on dealing with Muslim extremists. The Israelis have the most extensive history in dealing with terrorists, and the course was designed to give an insight into the psychological makeup of the terrorist."

"So why did you take the course?" Nelson questioned. "You are with the DA's office, not the FBI."

"I felt it was important. The spread of Muslim radicalism is everywhere. Every day there are plots being hatched to murder and injure people in this city. I felt if I was going to prosecute these animals, I needed to be able to understand them first. And do you know what the first thing they taught me was?"

"What?"

"Never let the terrorist feel that he is in control. Aretz told us that the typical terrorist will want to get a rise out of you. He will spew his radical views and expect you to react. The trick to controlling him is to not let him control you."

Nelson nodded slowly. As he peered through the glass, he saw exactly what al-Jinn had tried to do. What he had succeeded in doing.

"Don't be hard on yourself," Mark comforted him. "They all talk a great game. But when they get thrown behind bars, that is when the reality hits home. All the hate that they have been indoctrinated with falls to the wayside. When the cameras are off and nobody is listening, it's just them and their demons and they end up falling apart."

"Agreed." Nelson grunted. "But I want this guy to suffer for what he has done. If I have to wait for him to get behind bars, that means that we need to nail this guy. Are you sure that you can put this guy behind bars for the rest of his life?"

"If everything in this folder can hold up in court," Moshe answered, sifting through the evidence folder, "then we will have no problem putting this guy away for good."

"But what about the other side?" Nelson asked. "Many times I have given your office an airtight case, only to have some big-shot defense attorney get the perp off on some technicality. The evidence is good, but how good are you?"

"I am really good," Moshe answered confidently. "But even if I wasn't, I have taken a look at al-Jinn's financials. He immigrated to the States a few years ago, and he does menial jobs. He has no cash in the bank and no equity to speak of. All he is getting is a court-appointed attorney, and the last thing that a court-appointed attorney wants is to go to trial."

Moshe eyed al-Jinn as the suspect turned toward the one-way window. Even though the Muslim couldn't see Moshe, it seemed as if their eyes locked, and it sent shivers down Moshe's spine.

"Don't worry, Detective Nelson. Mr. al-Jinn will pay for his sins. I guarantee it."

■ ■ ■

Shea approached the hospital bed with great trepidation. Although Rabbi Felder was well over six feet tall, he looked miniscule, dwarfed by the equipment surrounding him. Steeling himself to look at his rebbi's face, Shea felt a wave of horror begin to overwhelm him. The tremendous swelling had made his rebbi all but unrecognizable. Both of Rabbi Felder's arms were covered in bandages and both his legs were in casts. Shea could not begin to imagine the degree of pain that he was in. He had told Yechiel that if anybody could pull through this, it was Rabbi Felder. But now looking at him, even Shea had his doubts.

Shea neared the bed and grasped his rebbi's hand. The flood

of emotion was overpowering. He began to recall all the times that his rebbi had embraced him. Whether it was when Shea had asked a good question on the *gemara*, or when he was simply giving Shea a warm and hearty *shalom aleichem*, his rebbi's grasp was always firm and true. But now, as he held his rebbi's hand, Shea could no longer feel the vitality that his rebbi had exuded, and it frightened Shea terribly.

A shrill ringtone broke through Shea's thoughts. He glanced at his cell phone and knew that he had to answer it.

"Hello, Donna," Shea said to Allan Shore's secretary.

"Are you okay?" she asked. "You don't sound too good."

"Yeah, I'm fine, don't worry about it."

Donna left it alone.

"Where are you?" Donna asked.

"In Brooklyn."

"Well, you need to get down to the office right away."

Shea was concerned. Kyle had told him that he had the day off, so why did Donna need him at the office? Had Kyle lied to him?

"I thought that I had the day off," Shea said.

"You did, but Allan needs to see you right away."

"Did he say why?"

"Not really, but knowing Allan, if he wants to see you then it must be important. So how long will it take you to get here?"

Shea looked at his watch. "Twenty minutes or so."

"Make it fifteen," Donna advised, "Allan is running on a tight schedule today."

"Will do," Shea replied. "See you soon."

Shea hung up the phone and turned toward his rebbi. He didn't want to leave him, but if Allan Shore needed him, there was no choice.

As he left the room, he struggled to think of what Allan could possibly want that couldn't wait until tomorrow.

"DID YOU GET IN TOUCH WITH SHEA YET?" ALLAN Shore asked his secretary.

"Just spoke with him a few minutes ago. He told me that he is on his way."

"Good. Make sure that you let Bennet and Williams know that I am going to be a few minutes late."

"I already did," Donna responded.

"What would I do without you?"

"You would be helpless," Donna grinned.

"I can't argue with that one. Tell Shea to come right in when he gets here, and please hold all my calls."

Allan clicked off the intercom and abruptly turned his ergonomic executive chair to face his office window. As he gazed outside, he was struck by the beauty of the New York skyline on a crystal-clear day. The view from his penthouse office was truly remarkable. It also reminded him how far he had gone in the firm and how much he expected from Shea.

Allan had been with the firm for twelve years. In that time he had become their highest-billing attorney. With all the billables that he had put in, plus the record number of corporate deals that he had put together, Allan had become a senior partner sooner than anybody else in the firm's history. His reputation was sterling. According to company legend, he had never lost in court. It was partially because of his spectacular success that the firm had grown so rapidly within the last decade. But it was also because of his success that he expected his junior associates to be flawless, and that is why he liked Shea.

In this "Harvard firm" almost every attorney on staff had graduated Harvard Law. The firm was one of Harvard's biggest donors, forking over three million dollars a year to the school. Each of the managing partners had made Harvard Law Review. In a world of blue bloods, Crane, Gardner, and Scott was the bluest. So the big question in the firm was how Shea Berman of Fordham had landed a job there, and that was a secret that Allan wasn't sharing.

He remembered it quite clearly. Jessica Scott, one of the founding partners, had told Allan that he should hire an associate he could train and retain. Despite all his other successes, Allan had not managed to hold on to the associates assigned him. It seemed that after a little while either Allan would get tired of coaching, or the prospective associate would quit due to Allan's high demands and hectic schedule. Jessica had told Allan that he needed to hire and train an associate by the end of the year, or else there would be severe repercussions. The firm needed new associates and if Allan wasn't willing to train them, Jessica was going to find someone who would. Allan had told her not to worry and began his search immediately.

Finding Kyle Ross wasn't hard. Out of the two hundred graduates from Harvard, Kyle was the most qualified. He had made the Dean's list on numerous occasions and was chosen valedictorian of his class. When looking at Kyle, Allan had seen a vision of his younger self, and he felt confident that Kyle was going to be a great attorney. To no one's surprise, Allan offered Kyle the position and Kyle accepted immediately.

Jessica, knowing how competition increases productivity, then announced that she wanted two associates to compete for the permanent position. Allan needed to find another lawyer who would give Kyle a run for his money. He decided to look for something different. He wanted the second associate to be the total opposite of Kyle. Whereas Kyle was tenacious and cutthroat, Allan wanted his counterpart to be thorough and thoughtful. He wanted to see which style of lawyer would be the perfect fit for the firm.

The search wasn't easy. It seemed that most first-year lawyers coming from schools other than Harvard were frightened away by the firm's reputation and didn't bother applying for a position. Those who did apply spent all their time trying to convince Allan that they were just like any Harvard lawyer. Allan was about to give up his search, when a young, clean-shaven Orthodox Jew walked into the room and blew Allan away.

"What is your name?" Allan asked.

"Shea Berman," Shea answered confidently.

"Well, it seems that you are wasting your time, Shea," Allan responded while glancing through his resume. "I am sure that you know that my firm only hires the best lawyers. The best lawyers are from Harvard. According to your resume, you didn't go to Harvard. I mean, you didn't even go to Stanford. So please tell me why you bothered to waste my precious time this morning."

"You really don't get it, do you?" Shea said.

"What are you talking about?" Allan inquired, taken off-guard.

"You sit up there in your fancy leather chair, surrounded by your antique mahogany furniture, thinking that you know it all."

"That is because I do," Allan interrupted "But let me just stop you there. If you think that you can give me one those 'you gotta give the underdog a chance,' type of speeches, then you are wasting your time. Maybe in another firm, one that doesn't make the amount of money that mine does, maybe that speech would work. And maybe the senior partners, who aren't busy making money, have some time to coach the underdog and show him the ropes. But you see, kid, you aren't in the minor leagues. As soon as you waltzed yourself into my office, you entered the big leagues, where the players don't care about your heartwarming story. They just care about one thing and that is the bottom line. So I am sorry if I don't have time for your speech, but that is the way we play ball in the majors."

"If you would have let me finish," Shea answered abruptly, "I would have told you that I agree with you. I don't want this job because I want someone's charity. I want this job because I feel that I am the best man for it."

"That would be great, if it were true," Allan corrected, "but according to your resume, you simply don't have the credentials that the other candidates have."

"But I have something that no one else has," Shea responded.

"And what might that be?"

"Look, I have done my research. You have been interviewing for this position for the last three months. If you wanted somebody from Harvard, you would have hired that person already."

"Maybe I haven't found the right person yet," Allan countered.

"But you have interviewed almost ninety percent of the graduates from last year's class. If you haven't found the one you are looking for, you probably aren't going to find it in Harvard."

Allan nodded. He had to admit that Shea had a point. Score one for Berman to have figured it out.

"Let's say that you are right," Allan said. "Let us say for argument's sake that I am not interested in a typical blue-blooded lawyer. Why would I hire you? It can't be just because you didn't go to Harvard. There are thousands of lawyers who would fit that description."

"But I possess something that most lawyers don't. I possess a background in a type of law that even you are unfamiliar with."

"And what type of law would that be?" Allan asked, intrigued.

"Talmudic law."

"And how does your expertise in Talmudic law have anything to do with our current judicial system? As far as I know, no judge on the bench will refer to any precedent found in Talmudic law as a basis for court rulings."

"I agree with you. But my expertise in Talmudic law has given me two skills that are vital to being a great lawyer. The first is my attention to detail. When one studies Talmudic law, he is trained to pay attention to every single detail. No word in the Talmud is extraneous and I was taught to focus on every word in order to

extrapolate its meaning and essence. This skill would be vital as it would allow me to properly understand different documents and witness' testimonies, and to expose any inaccuracies."

Allan found himself smiling. This kid is good, he thought. More importantly, he was the exact opposite of Kyle Ross, which was what Allan was looking for. But he wasn't still one hundred percent convinced.

"What other skill did Talmudic law provide you?" Allan asked.

"Please don't take this the wrong way, but I have done a lot of investigating into your firm and I found an alarming statistic."

"What was that?"

"Out of all the suits that your firm brought against various companies last year, do you know how many involved single plaintiffs?"

"I am not sure."

"How about only three percent?" Shea answered. "That means that your firm only defended forty individual-plaintiff suits last year. Why would that be?"

"Maybe it is because we don't staff a bunch of ambulance chasers and don't have time for every frivolous lawsuit that comes our way."

"That might be true, except that I contacted some of the potential plaintiffs and asked them about their cases."

"And what did they tell you?" Allan wondered.

"These were not your typical, 'ouch I burnt myself on hot coffee so now I want to sue the restaurant,' type of cases. Most of those that I spoke to were victims of major malpractice. One person I spoke to needed five surgeries just to undo the damage that was inflicted by her first doctor. Another was misdiagnosed and had undergone radiation therapy for five months for a cancer that he never had. These weren't the only cases. Almost everybody I spoke to had a similar story behind his suit."

Allan was fascinated. As a senior partner, he rarely dealt with individual cases. Those were handled by the junior associates. Allan spent most of his time on corporate deals or class action lawsuits. But if these cases were really legit, why didn't his junior associates have more of them to handle?

"So why did these plaintiffs decide to use a different firm?"

"When one learns Talmud, not only do you learn the various laws, but you also learn character traits. You learn how to properly deal with people and how to conduct yourself in the workplace. According to most of the plaintiffs, they didn't feel that this firm truly appreciated the pain that they had gone through. They felt that most of the lawyers just saw them as a dollar sign, and didn't treat them with the respect and dignity that they deserved."

Shea paused and looked Allan straight in the eye. "If you choose to hire me, there will never be a client who walks out of my office feeling slighted in any way. I will do my best to empathize with the pain that my client has endured and that will allow me to pursue the justice that my client so rightly deserves."

Allan hired Shea right on the spot.

Up until now, Shea had made good on his promises. He was a wonderful lawyer who had an amazing attention for detail. Very few lawyers, even Allan himself, would have been able to catch Fatima's lie as Shea had done. Shea's empathy was legendary and many potential clients requested him because of it. Shea never had a problem identifying with the client and truly fighting for the client's rights. But that was until now.

As Allan waited for Shea's arrival, he debated how he was going to tell Shea about his next case.

Shea was perspiring heavily as he raced toward Allan's office. *What could he possibly want from me*, he wondered. As he sprinted out of the elevator and ran toward Donna's desk Shea knew he was going to get the answer, whether he liked it or not.

"He's been expecting you," Donna said matter-of-factly.

"Did he say what he wanted?" Shea asked.

"Nope," Donna answered, not moving her gaze from her computer. "All he said was that I was to cancel all his meetings until he finished meeting with you. And he isn't alone, by the way. The big boss lady is inside with him. So whatever he wants from you, it has gotta be big."

Shea thanked Donna and approached Allan's office. He

knocked and was told to come in. As he entered, he was happy Donna had warned him. There was a woman there about whom Shea had heard many stories, but had never met personally.

"Shea," Allan announced, "thank you for coming in today. And after that amazing job with Merzeir Pharmaceuticals, you definitely deserved a day off."

"Thank you for your kind words," Shea said quietly.

"I don't make kind statements," Allan corrected him, "only true ones. Isn't that right, Jessica?" Allan asked, turning toward a woman sitting on a sofa in a corner of the room. "Shea, meet Jessica Scott."

Shea nodded a greeting. Until now, he had never been introduced to the mythical Jessica Scott. All his cases were overseen by Allan, and until this last case, none had involved major clients. Jessica worked a very busy schedule and had very little time for pleasantries. If she was at this meeting, that meant something big was going down and Shea had no idea what it was.

"I heard that you did a fabulous job on the Merzeir case," Jessica commented. "I just got off the phone with Dennis Merzeir. He was so impressed with your skills that he requested that you be his primary counsel for the next year. I wish I had been there to see it. According to Allan, you really stole the show."

"What can I say?" Shea answered, embarrassed. "I guess I had a great teacher."

"That would be nice, if it were only true," Jessica responded. "Allan may be a lot of things, but a wonderful teacher he is not. From what your colleagues say, Shea, your humility is well known. But a good attorney knows when he has knocked one out of the park, and you hit a grand slam."

"Thank you."

"Allan," Jessica stated, "I think this calls for a celebration, don't you?"

"I'm always ready for a good drink," Allan said, stepping to his liquor cabinet. "So tell me what will it be, bourbon or scotch? I just bought a great bottle of Macallen 25."

Shea looked at Allan by the liquor cabinet. Normally, Shea

wasn't one to turn down a drink, especially a good bottle of scotch. At a *kiddush* Shea was always willing to make a *l'chaim*. But after just leaving his rebbi's bedside, he just didn't feel like drinking.

"I am sorry, Allan, but I am not really in the mood for a drink right now."

Allan looked disappointed but he put down the bottle and returned his attention to Jessica. She looked toward Shea and smiled.

"A win is a win, no matter how you celebrate it. I would love to shake your hand, but as Allan has explained to me, that would go against your religious beliefs and I really respect that. So thank you for all your hard work and I hope we can have these meetings again in the future. You keep up this type of success and you will be making partner in no time."

"Thank you so much for this opportunity," Shea responded.

Allan escorted Jessica to the door. As she turned to leave she bent her head toward Allan's ear and whispered into it.

"Just make sure that you get this done, Allan."

"I will try, but I can't force him to do anything."

"Just make him understand that if he wants to continue working here, then he needs to play ball."

"Will do," Allan assured her as she walked briskly out of the office.

Allan returned to his desk and took a seat. Shea could see that he was nervous, but he had no idea why.

Shea broke the silence that was beginning to feel awkward. "Jessica seems like a really nice person."

"She is, when she gets what she wants. And normally she gets what she wants."

"So what does she want from me?"

"Who says that she wants anything from you?" Allan asked coyly.

"Something is obviously going on. If you wanted to congratulate me, you could have sent me a card. You didn't need to clear your schedule for the entire morning. So just level with me, what is going on?"

"Don't get me wrong," Allan began, "what Jessica said before was true. What you were able to pull off during the Merzeir trial was truly amazing. I don't think even I would have been able to catch that picture on the TV screen."

"Really?" Shea asked in wonderment. Allan had never admitted that he couldn't do something. This was definitely a first.

"Okay, maybe I would have been able to catch it," Allan admitted. "But another attorney definitely would have missed that one. You see, that is why I hired you. You have an amazing eye for detail."

"But?" Shea asked.

"But what?"

"You wouldn't be telling me all this stuff, unless there was a catch. So tell me already. What is it? What did I do wrong?"

"You actually didn't do anything wrong. It seems that you did your job too well."

"I am sorry, but I don't follow," Shea responded, confused.

"I am sure that you have heard that the firm is opening a branch in Paris next month," Allan stated.

"Of course," Shea said. "That's all that anybody is talking about around here. A lot of the associates are afraid that they are going to be assigned to Paris."

"Well don't worry, you aren't going anywhere."

"That's a relief," Shea said "My wife would not enjoy living in Paris. But if I am not moving to Paris, what am I doing here?"

"I am sure that you are aware of what is going on in Europe these days," Allan continued.

"Regarding what?"

Allan looked uncomfortable. Whatever he knew, he definitely didn't want to tell Shea. Shea waited for him to continue.

"The Muslim presence in Europe generally, and specifically in France, is growing. As a matter of fact, the UN estimates that by 2040, 55 percent of Europe's population will be Muslim."

Shea felt a stab of uneasiness. He didn't know where this was going, but he didn't like the direction it was taking.

"When the firm chooses to open up a branch in Paris, we can't be seen as an anti-Muslim firm. If we are, we won't stand a chance of attaching any clients."

"That makes sense. But what does this have to do with me?"

Allan rose from his desk and went around toward Shea. He looked his junior associate straight in the eye before continuing.

"Your case, even though it helped us here a lot, did some serious damage overseas."

"What are you talking about?" Shea asked in disbelief.

"Our European investors believe that by winning the Merzeir case, people will assume that our firm is anti-Muslim."

"Why, because Fatima is a Muslim?"

"Look, I am not saying that it makes any sense, I am just telling you what the reality is. We live in a viral society. Once one guy believes something, he spreads his views over the net, and people accept it as truth. So right now, a month before we are scheduled to open our doors, we are being vilified in Europe's social media as an anti-Muslim firm."

Shea couldn't believe what he was hearing. He hadn't done anything wrong. Never once had he made any anti-Muslim remarks toward Fatima. Even though she staked her case solely on race, Shea fought on the merits of the truth, and the truth had prevailed. So why was his firm suffering?

"So what does Jessica want from me?" Shea asked. "Does she want me to issue an apology to the Muslim Rights Organization? "

"What should you apologize for?" Allan said. "You did nothing wrong. If anything, you were respectful and courteous during the proceedings. That is more than I could say for the plaintiff, Ms. Assad."

"But it doesn't matter how I conducted myself. If the world thinks that we are anti-Muslim, then we need to change that image. So if I need to apologize, then that is what I am going to do."

"You are right," Allan admitted, "we do need to change our image. But it isn't going to happen through an apology. A good lawyer never apologizes when he wins, only when he loses. However, an opportunity has come up. A new case just came across my desk and Jessica feels that if the firm fights this case valiantly, it will show our potential Muslim clients that we can be trusted."

"What case are you talking about?" Shea asked.

"It's a pro bono that just opened up this morning. It seems that once this case gets out, there will be a real media firestorm and we will be in the center of it. That is exactly what we need if we want to change our global image."

"What happened?"

"Well," Allan answered, "the details are still a little sketchy, but here is what we know. Our client is a twenty-two-year-old Palestinian man named Khalid al-Jinn."

The name meant nothing to Shea.

"It seems that Mr. al-Jinn was arrested earlier this morning. He is being held at the 61st precinct in Brooklyn. He is charged with attempted murder and possibly a hate crime."

The 61st precinct wasn't far from where his rebbi had been attacked. It couldn't be a coincidence. Shea felt his hands shaking as he asked his next question.

"Allan, was this guy arrested for attacking a rabbi?"

"How did you know?" Allan answered in surprise.

"The rabbi who was attacked is my rabbi. I have known him since high school. I saw him last night, thirty minutes before he was attacked. The reason that I was late getting here was because I was at his bedside. That is why I couldn't drink anything. I am too torn up about the whole episode."

Shea looked up and saw Allan averting his gaze. The reason behind this meeting suddenly became clear to Shea. No doubt Allan had somehow found out that Shea was close with Rabbi Felder, and he was probably worried that Shea was going to have a problem if the firm represented his rabbi's attacker. That was also why Jessica had been in the office, Shea realized. They needed to make sure that he wouldn't cause a conflict of interest.

Shea needed to show Allan that no matter how upset he was, he wouldn't get in the way of somebody from the firm defending al-Jinn.

"I am sure that you think that I will bear some grudge against the firm if we represent my rabbi's attacker," Shea said firmly. "Allan, I'm a pro. No matter who is responsible for defending this man, I will show that person the same respect and courtesy that I have always shown. It will not create any disruption in the workplace."

"That is good to hear, Shea," Allan responded "I'm glad to hear that you are a team player. Jessica had her doubts, but I always knew that you had your eye on the big picture."

"So who is going to be lead counsel?" Shea asked. "Is Kyle going to handle it or are you going to give it to over to someone with expertise in criminal law?"

Allan shook his head grimly before answering. He thought that Shea had understood the true purpose of the meeting, but he realized that he was mistaken. It didn't matter, though. This decision had come down straight from the top and Allan was only following orders. But that didn't make this task any easier.

Allan took a deep breath and answered Shea's question.

DETECTIVE NELSON SAT AT HIS DESK AND FINISHED HIS paperwork. Even though he hadn't appreciated the way that Mark Cohen spoke to him, he had to admit that the lawyer had a point. The last thing Nelson wanted was to have al-Jinn walk because of Nelson's temper.

He also wanted to make sure that the police report was in order and that is why he checked it over for the umpteenth time. Once Nelson was finally satisfied, he sighed. He never used to have to write the reports. That had been his late partner's job. Coleman had always complained that Nelson's poor grammar and terrible penmanship made his reports impossible to read. Nelson had never told his partner that he intentionally wrote sloppily to get out of writing the reports. Nelson used to think that the real police work was done on the beat and not behind the desk. But now, with a rookie cop at his side, Nelson knew that the paperwork was his responsibility, and he wanted to make sure that there were no mistakes.

As he was about to file the al-Jinn reports, he saw Assistant DA Cohen stride down the hallway.

"Where is the prisoner?" Moshe asked.

"Why?" Nelson replied curtly.

"We need to move him now."

"What's the rush? Let him cool his heels for a while. A night in the slammer might do him some good. It might help him remember what happened and get us a confession."

"Normally, I would agree with you. But we need to act now. Is everything in order? Is the prisoner ready for transfer?" Moshe asked, motioning for Nelson to show him where al-Jinn was being held.

Nelson caught up to Moshe as he hurried toward the holding cell. As Moshe motioned for the guard to step aside, Nelson stuck out his arm and blocked Moshe's path.

"Whoa, counselor," Nelson exclaimed. "I think it is time that you explained to me what is going on. A few hours ago, the plan was to let this guy sit on ice. Now you are running around like we gotta hide this thug before al-Qaida comes in and busts him out. So can you please enlighten me?"

"Remember how I told you that according to al-Jinn's financials, he couldn't afford a real attorney?" Moshe asked.

"Yeah," Nelson recalled. "You said something about this guy getting a court-appointed attorney and us striking some kind of a deal."

"Well, I was wrong. It turns out that this terrorist just got himself representation from one of the best defense firms in the city."

"Which one?" Nelson wondered.

"Crane, Gardner, and Scott," Moshe answered.

Nelson was surprised. Crane, Gardner, and Scott was one of the most successful firms in America.

"But I thought you said that this guy couldn't afford an attorney. How does this guy go from not affording one to getting the most expensive lawyer in the city?"

"It seems that even evil law firms have a heart," Moshe said, his voice dripping sarcasm. "Supposedly, they are taking this case pro bono. Although between me and you, these big firms never do anything for free. They have got to have an angle; I am just not yet sure what it is."

"But here is what I don't get," Nelson continued. "How did those guys even hear about our case? Al-Jinn hasn't said a word to anybody since you left. All he has been doing is reading from the Koran and praying on the floor. Who told them that this guy even needed a lawyer?"

"Well, it wasn't from my office," Moshe said. "Someone must have slipped to the media from your end."

Nelson was upset. He didn't appreciate Moshe pointing a finger at his fellow police officers. "I take offense, counselor. You can't come in here and make those kind of accusations. My fellow officers are good people and they deserve to be treated better."

Moshe looked straight at the door in front of him. In truth, he had no idea who had told the firm that al-Jinn needed a lawyer. The leak could have come from his office the same way it could have come from Nelson's department. He was just frustrated. But he also realized that he needed Nelson on his side and didn't want to create any issues between them. "You are right," Moshe admitted, "and I am sorry. I guess this whole thing just took me by surprise. I never expected things to move so fast and right now I am trying to make sure that we don't lose control of the situation."

"If you need things to slow down, why are we moving al-Jinn?" Nelson asked. "Why not leave him here until his lawyer gets here?"

"Are you a football fan, Nelson?"

"Are you kidding me? I am a major Pilots fan. My family has had season tickets for the past twenty years."

"You know the term, 'the best defense is a good offense'?" That is exactly what I want to do. Al-Jinn's attorney undoubtedly is concocting strategies as we speak. I don't want to give him time to file motions and try to suppress as much evidence as he can. I want to apply the pressure right away."

"Sounds like a good strategy, but how do you expect to implement it?"

"Very simply," Moshe answered. "Right now al-Jinn hasn't met with anyone. The last thing we want is to have al-Jinn confer with his attorney before the arraignment and discuss strategy. If we can get him arraigned immediately, then the defense won't have time to meet with al-Jinn. In order to beat Crane, Gardner, and Scott, we have always got to be two steps ahead of them."

"But what judge will grant you an arraignment so quickly, especially if the defendant hasn't had time to consult with his legal counsel?"

"I took care of that already," Moshe answered confidently. "I just got off the phone with Judge Daniels at the criminal court. I told him that we have a possible hate crime that could attract a lot of media attention. I asked him if we could have the defendant arraigned immediately."

"And he said yes, without asking any questions?" Nelson asked in surprise.

"Well, it just so happens that Judge Daniels is up for reelection. When I told him about the possibility of a media circus, he jumped at the opportunity. He wants to judge this case as much as anybody. He wants the publicity that trial would bring. If he arraigns the defendant, he can set the trial date and put it on his docket. It also doesn't hurt that Judge Daniels has strong ties to the Jewish community."

Nelson was impressed. He had heard through the grapevine that Mark Cohen was the heir apparent to the current District Attorney. Even though Nelson had worked with Moshe in the past, he had never seen Moshe display the political savvy that is needed to be a star on the Brooklyn DA's staff. But after what Moshe had just pulled off, Nelson could see what all the buzz was about.

"We've got to move," Moshe said. "The arraignment is scheduled to begin in one hour and we don't want to be late and have the judge push it off."

Nelson nodded in agreement and followed Moshe into the room to retrieve their prisoner.

■ ■ ■

Mohamed Farouk sat in his late model Toyota, his unblinking

eyes focused on the front door of the building. Even though he could have thought of better ways to spend a Thursday morning, Rasheed's instructions had been very specific and Rasheed was not the type of person one wanted to disappoint. Still, Mohamed reflected, he had taken on this mission with a heavy heart, and he only hoped that he was doing his best.

To pass the time, he tried listening to music on the radio, but there was nothing that captured his interest. All the songs sounded the same, he thought. He then tuned in to a talk station, but that too he found confusing. It seemed that he had stumbled onto a sports radio station where the host and the caller were yelling at each other regarding the starting quarterback for the New York Pilots. Mohamed chuckled. He understood the passion of fans. In his home country he could remember many days spent at the local stadium cheering on his favorite soccer team. But he still could not understand why the Americans referred to their game as football. The only football he knew was the game played with feet and not with hands.

Having grown tired of the tirade, he changed stations once again and found himself listening to the news station. After being bored by the latest lotto numbers and weather report, his interest was piqued when he heard the day's top story.

"Breaking news from the Middle East," the newscaster declared. *"According to unsourced reports, Israeli Prime Minister Yitzchak Schechter will be making a surprise visit to the United States at the end of the month. While it had been widely speculated about for over a week, the Prime Minister's office has finally confirmed Schechter's visit. Schechter has been an outspoken critic of the Palestinian Authority and has threatened to halt all talks between Israel and the Palestinians. President John Brady has requested a special meeting with Schechter in Washington to discuss various options prior to severing ties."*

Mohamed turned off the radio and focused again on the building. When he saw three people exiting, he used his phone to call his employer.

"Sabah el kheer," the voice answered.

"Good morning to you as well," Mohamed responded.

"*Kaifahaloka?*"

"I am doing well and thanks for asking."

"If you are doing well, why are you calling me?" Rasheed asked with a tinge of annoyance.

"They are moving the prisoner right now," Mohamed stated.

"To where?"

"I am not sure. If I had to guess, they are probably taking him to downtown Brooklyn to the criminal court."

"But why so soon?"

"I am not sure," Mohamed answered. "I do recognize one of the men with the prisoner as the assistant district attorney."

"They are going to arraign him now?"

"It seems that way."

"Did the prisoner get a lawyer?"

"I don't know," Mohamed. "I have been watching the door of the police station ever since the prisoner was arrested. Though I cannot say for certain, I have not seen any lawyers entering the building within the last two hours."

There was an uncomfortable moment of silence. Mohamed realized that this was not a good sign. Rasheed was not an easygoing man and he liked things to go his way. The prisoner being moved this quickly was definitely unexpected.

"I have no idea what they are up to, but I need you to keep an eye on our prisoner. We have to make sure that everything goes according to plan. We cannot afford to have anything go wrong. Is that understood?"

"Loud and clear," Mohamed responded.

"You will call me as soon as you find out who will be defending the prisoner."

"Definitely."

"*Ma'asalama,*" Rasheed wished him coldly.

"*Ma'asalama,*" Mohamed responded.

As Mohamed turned his car into traffic and headed toward the Prospect Expressway, he looked into his rearview mirror and caught a glimpse of himself. He was only twenty-seven, but a life of hardship and suffering had taken its toll, and the gray hairs that streaked his beard attested to it.

He hadn't been completely honest with his boss. It wasn't a mystery to him who the prisoner's counsel would be, but he could never let his boss find out. As he turned onto Ocean Parkway he knew that he was playing a very dangerous game. He only hoped that he wouldn't be caught.

■ ■ ■

"You can't be serious," Shea exclaimed.

"What do you mean?" Allan asked evasively.

"What do I mean? How about the fact that the man that you want me to represent brutally attacked my rabbi?"

"You mean allegedly, don't you?"

Shea ignored Allan's comment and turned back to the issue at hand. "It doesn't matter whether he did it or not. All I know is that I can't defend him. Rabbi Felder is like a father to me; how can I possibly defend the person who is accused of attacking him?"

"But he *isn't* your father, is he?" Allan asked.

"What does have that to do with anything?"

"As long as he isn't your father, you will have no problem with a conflict of interest. As you know, conflict of interest only deals with direct relatives, not close acquaintances. So as far as I am concerned, you should be able to do your job."

"But why me? Why is it my job? There are many better and more qualified attorneys in this firm. There are so many lawyers who would sell their souls to defend this case. So why are you putting it on the one guy who can't do it?"

Allan was annoyed and he was about to let Shea know it. "You think that I am punishing you by giving you this case? You are not a child, Shea, and you better start realizing that right now. I gave you this case because, more than anybody else in this firm, you need it."

"Why?" Shea asked.

"Because if you don't take it, you will be out of a job by the end of the summer," Allan answered matter-of-factly.

"What are you talking about? I have been doing a great job at this firm. Jessica just said so herself."

"Jessica only knows what I tell her, and right now she thinks that you are doing great. But what do you think is going to happen at the end of the month when the partners review the numbers? Don't kid yourself. The truth is going to come out."

"What truth are you referring to?"

"Your billables, Shea," Allan answered bluntly. "Remember, when I hired you, I told you that you were competing against Kyle for the permanent position. In this profession, the bottom line is all that matters and Kyle has brought in more revenue than you have."

"You know I have always done my best for the firm."

"I know," Allan agreed, "and that is why I am asking you to think about your family right now. You have got to keep your eye on the big picture and not get caught up in the details. I like you Shea. You are a good lawyer and a better man and that is why I really want you to be able to stay at this firm. But I can't create numbers that aren't there."

Shea didn't want to believe what Allan was saying. He had tried so hard to be a great lawyer. He knew that he didn't bring in the amount of money that Kyle had. But he had always hoped that Allan would be able to look past the numbers and see the progress that Shea was making.

"Do you remember the day that you hired me?" Shea asked.

"Of course I do."

"Do you remember the promise I made when I told you that no client would ever leave my office feeling slighted or degraded?"

"You were the only applicant I ever interviewed who actually cared about the feelings of the client."

"Haven't I made good on my promise?" Shea pleaded. "Haven't I done everything that you have asked me to do?"

"You have been a great lawyer and you will be an even better lawyer," Allan responded. "But that doesn't change the facts. Right now with the way that the economy has been going, the partners only care about one thing and that is money. It is all about what you do and not who you are."

"So I don't get it," Shea responded. "Why are you pressuring me to take this case? You already told me that it is pro bono. That means the firm isn't going to be making anything. How is this going to help me keep my job?"

"Very simple," Allan answered. "It is all about loyalty. Right now our European investors doubt our ability to support and accommodate Muslim clients. But we can show them where our true loyalty lies. You see, if I can show the partners that you were willing not only to defend a Palestinian, but you were willing to defend the man who allegedly attacked your rabbi, the investors and our partners will love you."

"Yeah, but I will hate me."

Allan regarded Shea with a mixture of pity and sadness. He wasn't happy putting him in this position, but he also knew that without this case, Shea didn't stand a chance.

"Do you have any idea what this is going to do me? I mean, do you realize that my friends will probably never talk to me again?"

"Do your friends provide your paycheck every month?"

"No."

"Then who cares what they think."

Shea turned his gaze to meet his superior's. Allan took Shea's hand in his own and grasped it.

"Look, I know this isn't easy, but I also know how much you need this job."

"What are you talking about?" Shea asked.

"How about the ten grand that leaves your account every month on the fifteenth?"

"How do you know about that money?"

"Because," Allan explained, "I know everything about my associates. You think that I would not need to know that my junior associate has a gambling problem and needs to pay up his bookie every month?"

Shea glared at him, his cheeks burning. "It isn't like that. I don't have a gambling problem and frankly what I choose to do with my money is my business and not yours."

"You are probably right," Allan agreed, backing off. "I believe you. To be honest, if I had to pick one guy in the firm to have a gambling problem, it wouldn't be you. You are too strait-laced and proper. Kyle, on the other hand, now he is a wild card. But either way, if you are laying out that kind of money every month, you really need this job."

Shea looked at the carpet. How did Allan know about the money — and who else in the firm knew? It didn't matter because Allan was right. Shea needed the money and he couldn't lose this job.

"I don't mean to say that it is going to be easy," Allan said softly. "You are probably going to have to deal with issues and problems that you have never dealt with before in your life. But never forget the bottom line: you need this case. Without it, you will be on the unemployment line with the rest of your law school buddies."

Shea hung his head in disbelief. *How could things have gone downhill so quickly?* he wondered. Twenty-four hours earlier, his life was going great. But now his rebbi was in a coma and he, Shea Berman, was being pressured to defend the man responsible for putting him there. Was it even possible? How could he defend such a barbarian? The thought of sitting next to that monster in a courtroom made Shea sick. At the same time, Shea knew that there was one reason why he would need to defend Rabbi Felder's attacker. It was the thing that was keeping him up at nights and invading his daytime thoughts.

He needed to make a decision, maybe the most important decision of his life, and it couldn't be made in Allan's office.

"This is how we are going to proceed," Shea declared, his voice carefully controlled. "Right now I have no idea if I am going to take the case or not. I know that you may think that I would be a fool for bypassing this opportunity, but I would rather be a fool than be somebody that I can't look at in the mirror. I can't make this decision without speaking to somebody first and that person is currently unavailable. I will handle the arraignment, and if need be,

I will pass the rest of the case off to another member of this firm."

"Fine," Allan responded. "I wouldn't want you doing something that you weren't completely comfortable with. If you take the case, you shouldn't worry, because you will have all the firm's resources available to you. You aren't alone on this one. This is going to be a full team effort."

Shea drew in a deep breath and forced himself to get into the mode of a top legal professional.

"Okay, let's start. Do we know anything about our client?"

"Nothing," Allan answered.

"What do you mean nothing? Hasn't anybody spoken to him?"

"Not as far as I know."

"But if nobody has spoken to him, how did he hire us as his counsel?"

"He didn't hire us. We got an anonymous call from some guy claiming to be a friend of al-Jinn's. He said that al-Jinn had just been taken into custody by the police and needed legal representation."

"Hold on," Shea said, shocked. "You mean that I am about to defend a guy who not only put my mentor into a hospital, but who doesn't even know that I am going to be his lawyer?"

"Makes it exciting, doesn't it?" Allan smiled.

"But if this guy didn't ask for counsel, how do we know he didn't admit everything to the cops already?"

"Honestly, we really don't know anything. We are walking into this blind. So here is what you are going to do. You will drive down to the 61st precinct and meet with your new client. "

"Allan, you have a phone call," Donna's voice informed him.

"I thought I told you to hold all my calls," Allan reminded her.

"That you did, but I figured that you would want to take this one."

"Who is it?"

"Denise Feller from Judge Daniel's office."

Allan was concerned. Why would Denise be calling the office and asking to speak to him? Well, there was only one way to find out.

"Put her through," Allan ordered.

Allan lifted the receiver and began his conversation. Shea was lost in his own thoughts, but he perked up as he heard Allan yelling into the phone.

"They can't do that," Allan screamed. "When is this going down?"

Allan waited for a response that Shea couldn't hear. After receiving his response, he spoke again into the phone. "Thank you, Denise, I really owe you one."

"What was that all about?" Shea asked.

"You need to get out of here quickly," Allan said.

"What's going on?"

"It seems that the prosecution is already trying to get ahead of us in this case. They have moved al-Jinn to the criminal courthouse in downtown Brooklyn for his arraignment."

"Arraignment?" Shea asked. "But I haven't had a chance to meet with my client yet. And what about a grand jury?"

The grand jury investigation was the stage in the legal process right before indictment. If the prosecutor feels that he has enough evidence to charge a defendant with a crime, a jury is convened and the preliminary evidence is offered. If the jury feels that there is enough evidence to warrant a trial, the defendant is indicted and put on trial.

"Denise says that al-Jinn has waived his rights to a grand jury. Says he wants to face his 'enemies' without delay."

Normally a defendant would have no reason to waive the grand jury and proceed directly to trial. Warning bells were going off in Shea's head. Al-Jinn was either crazy or incredibly naïve.

"What am I supposed to do now?"

"Look, all you need to do is issue a plea and set bail," Allan explained. "Remember that this is an election year for Daniels, so he probably will not want to alienate the Jewish vote. That means that you aren't going to have a friend on the bench. We can discuss the issue of recusal, but not now. Just get over there and make sure you enter a plea."

"What exactly am I pleading?" Shea demanded. "We have no

idea what happened and we don't know if this guy is guilty or not. We don't even know if he is sane enough to stand trial."

"Just enter a not-guilty plea and try to get the trial pushed off as long as possible. That way you will have as much time as you need to prepare your case."

Shea was hesitating and Allan could see it. He took Shea by the arm and led him to the door.

"Remember, you aren't alone on this case. You will have the full resources of the firm standing behind you. Just get yourself down there now. Daniels does not like it when the attorneys are late."

Shea got into his car and headed for the FDR drive. His mind was swirling with questions, but he needed to focus on the task at hand. No matter how much he wanted to change things he was stuck with this case, and if he wanted to keep his job, he needed to give his best performance. On his way to the criminal courthouse, he focused on various strategies that he was going to implement. He knew that he couldn't worry about the fallout, because that would just cloud his thinking and prevent him from doing his job. But as they say, ignorance is bliss. Because no matter how bad Shea thought things could get, he had no idea of what was really in store for him.

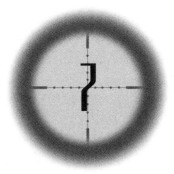

DRIVING TO THE COURTHOUSE, SHEA STOPPED AT A RED light. He slowly, reluctantly keyed a number in on the cell phone hooked to the dashboard. He knew he shouldn't be trying this case. *What kind of a person would defend his rebbi's attacker?* Shea wondered. But he also knew that he couldn't say, no, at least not until his other issue was resolved. So as he impatiently listened to the phone ringing on the other end, Shea prayed that he wouldn't be forced to make an impossible decision.

When he was growing up, Shea was extremely close to his father, Dovid Berman. Shea had often thought of his father as his best friend. They learned together, went to ball games together, went on trips together, just the two of them. The only son, with three younger sisters, Shea was the apple of his father's eye. Shea confided everything to his father, and that only brought them closer. But everything had changed the day that Shea's father visited him in his office less than a year ago.

His father, normally impeccably dressed, looked shattered and torn. His eyes were bloodshot and his normally close-cropped beard needed trimming. As he sat in a chair across from Shea's desk,

Dovid Berman looked as if the weight of the world had come crashing down on his shoulders. Shea, not sure what his father wanted, waited for him to begin.

"You have a really nice office here, Shea," his father stated, looking around. "I really like what you have done to the place."

"Abba," Shea smiled, "you are sitting in a four-by-four cubicle. There is very little that is nice about it. But you aren't here to give me decorating tips, so please tell me what is going on. You look terrible."

Suddenly, incredibly, Shea's father began to weep. In his whole life, Shea had never seen his father crying. As the tears streamed down Dovid Berman's face, Shea felt paralyzed, too shocked to respond.

"I can't believe this happened," Dovid Berman whispered, tears still streaming down his face. "How could I have let it go so far? I put all of you at risk."

Shea found his voice. "Abba, what are you talking about?"

"Do you know that I haven't slept in three days?"

"Does Mommy know about this?" Shea asked.

"Your mother thinks that I went to a meeting in Miami. But all I have been doing is pacing the floor in my office trying to figure out how to get out this mess."

"What mess are you talking about?"

Dovid Berman didn't answer and he just stared blankly at the bare walls of his son's office. Shea's father was usually a rock of unwavering strength. But that rock was crumbling right before Shea's eyes.

"I never meant for any of this to happen," Dovid Berman said hoarsely. "When I started, I figured that I would be able to handle myself, but it just got the better of me. And now, I have no idea how I am going to get out."

Shea forced himself to speak slowly and patiently. "Abba, tell me what happened. I am not a child anymore and you don't have to protect me. If there is something terrible going on, I want to know what it is. Maybe I can help you."

"Sons shouldn't have to help their fathers. It is my place to help you, not the other way around."

Shea went to his father's chair and looked into his eyes. Those eyes would radiate strength and confidence when Shea would pour his heart out to him. But now they looked shallow and weak, and more than anything Shea wanted to help restore their clear sparkle.

"It all began last summer," Dovid Berman began. "When your sister Devorah started dating Chaim. We were so thrilled with the shidduch. Chaim was a great guy and Devorah wasn't getting any younger. When the shadchan proposed the match, we immediately said yes without thinking twice. However, as the weeks went by and all systems said go, we realized that we had a situation on our hands. When we were originally approached with the shidduch, we were told that Chaim's parents had no money at all and the entire financial burden would be placed upon our shoulders. At the time that didn't matter to me, but when it looked like they were going to be engaged, I realized that I needed to come up with a lot of money very quickly."

"Chaim's side didn't pay for anything?" Shea asked, surprised.

"Not a thing," Mr.Berman answered. "Chaim is one of fifteen children. His parents couldn't even afford to buy him a new suit for the wedding. I was going to have to foot the entire bill."

"But I don't understand!" Shea exclaimed. "We have never had a problem with money. Your construction business has always been successful."

"Shea, there is no business anymore."

"What do you mean?"

"I mean, the business is finished. The recession has crippled me. I had to stop three projects in the middle, because we had no tenants to fill the apartments. You know that new development, Shady Woods, that I was building right down the block from where you live?"

"Sure I remember it. I had a bunch of friends that really wanted to buy houses there."

"Well, nobody came forward. I lost over two million dollars on the project. I had to sell off all my assets just to stay out of bankruptcy. I have nothing left, Shea. Nothing!"

"Does Mommy know about this?"

"No way," his father responded. "I couldn't bear facing her if she knew that we had no money. So I make believe that we are doing fine and she doesn't ask any questions."

"How are you paying for food and clothing?"

"I took out another mortgage on the house. I was hoping that the money that I took out would hold me over till things got better. But things have only gotten worse."

Shea couldn't believe what his father was telling him. Growing up, the Bermans were quite comfortable. Shea always wore the latest style and had the newest toys. His parent's house, though not a mansion, was always tastefully decorated in up-to-date decor. But what Shea remembered most about his father's success was the long line of tzedakah collectors who would surround his dining-room table. His father would give away a handsome chunk of his wealth each year. He was known as one of the most generous philanthropists in all of Brooklyn.

And now, it seemed, he was the one in need of charity.

"Why didn't you come to me?"

"I could never ask my own son for money. You were just settling into your new job and you had a family of your own. I wasn't going to make my problems, your problems."

"So how did you come up with the money for the wedding?"

Dovid Berman looked at Shea and then looked away. He knew that his son had viewed him as a role model and that was all about to change.

"There was still one project that I had going. A couple of investors had bought a property in Sheepshead Bay and they wanted to turn it into a strip mall. When I had made a bid on the project, my company was still viable and they knew about my sterling reputation, so I won the bid. I saw it as min haShamayim, and hoped that this project would allow me to get back on my feet.

"As the construction progressed, I was even saving my clients a lot of money by finding cheaper supplies and inexpensive workers. So when I saw the amount of money we were saving, I also saw a way for me to get the extra money that I would need for the wedding."

Shea felt his breath coming faster. He thought he had heard his father correctly, but he didn't want to believe it.

The words came out before he could even think about what he was saying. "You stole the money from your investors?" he asked incredulously.

"I didn't steal it, I merely borrowed it," Dovid Berman wearily defended himself.

"What does that mean?"

"I knew that the business was losing money and I needed to diversify my assets. I wanted to have some money invested in other ventures. At the time of your sister's engagement, I had already put in motion a series of investments that were supposed to provide the necessary funds to not only pay for the wedding but to get myself out of financial turmoil. But the problem was that I didn't have the cash on hand. All of it was tied up in the business. So I borrowed the money from my investors and fully intended to pay it back when the investments came through."

"So where is the money now?"

"It's gone," Dovid Berman cried out. "All of the money that I invested was stolen. It turned out that the person I invested with was a con artist. He ran a convoluted scheme and stole over thirty million dollars from me and other investors."

"Did the cops catch him?"

"Sure they caught him, but not the money. It seems that he stashed all the money in some offshore account. And even if they are able to somehow get part of the money back, I will never see any of it. My loss was pretty small in comparison to the losses of other people."

"Does anybody know that you took the money from the investors?"

"No," Dovid Berman answered. "Not yet, but that will change."

"Why?"

"Because the project failed. The strip mall never materialized and the investors were forced to sell the property at a loss. Now in a few months, the sale is going to go through and they are going to open the books to see how much money they really lost. What is going to happen to me when they see an additional shortfall of over ninety thousand dollars?"

Shea looked at his father with pity and surprise. He knew that his father hadn't meant to do anything wrong, but rules were rules and his father had broken them. He'd stolen from the investors — there was no other way to describe what he'd done — and now he had no way of repaying them.

But something else needed clarifying.

"You said you took ninety thousand dollars?" Shea asked.

His father nodded wordlessly.

"Why did you need so much money? How much did the wedding cost?"

"About forty thousand."

"So why did you need an additional fifty thousand dollars?"

His father looked even more uncomfortable. "If you can remember what was going on around the time of the wedding, I am sure that you can figure out where the rest of the money went."

Shea tried to recall what was going on at that time. When the answer finally came to him, he let out a gasp.

"The fifty thousand dollars you gave us for the house?"

"Yes."

"Are you telling me that the money that you gave us for the house wasn't yours?"

"I am so sorry, Shea."

"Abba, why?" Shea cried. "Why did you need to do that? Why couldn't you have just told me that you didn't have the money? I never would have asked you for it if I had thought that you would need to steal to get it."

"But I wanted to give you the money," his father responded. "I was proud of everything that you had accomplished. You were successful and you were bringing up a wonderful family that was giving your mother and me so much nachas and joy. What kind of a father would I have been if I couldn't help you make the most important purchase of your life? I had never failed you before and I wasn't going to fail you now. And I told you," he added quietly, "I never thought I wouldn't be able to repay it."

Shea walked over to his father. Although he was ashamed of what his father had done, he knew that his father had only done it because of his love for his children. His father had been weak, not greedy or evil.

"So what do we do now?" Shea asked.

"I guess I am going to need a lawyer," Dovid Berman said. "Know any good ones?" he added, with a faint smile.

"That's not the way," Shea said emphatically. "How many more months until the investors will realize that the money is missing?"

"These things take time," Dovid Berman answered. "The sale has to be finalized and the audit has to run its course. I would estimate I have about nine months."

"Here is what we are going to do," Shea told his father briskly. "I am going to deposit ten thousand dollars a month for the next nine months from my account to yours. By the time the sale of the property is finalized and the audit completed, all the money will have been put back and nobody will know that anything had ever happened."

Dovid Berman shook his head and looked away. "I can't have my son pay back my debts."

It was brutal, but Shea knew he had to say it. "And I can't have my father facing a jail term."

"But how are you going to be able to survive?"

"Don't worry about me. The firm pays well and for the next few months, I will just have to live a little tighter. Look, Abba, this isn't your choice, it's mine. You have been taking care of us for a very long time; now it's time that somebody took care of you."

Dovid Berman looked at his son with a mixture of sadness and pride. Tears welled up in his eyes. "I didn't come here to ask you to bail me out. I just needed to tell somebody what was going on. This entire episode has been weighing on me like a ton of bricks. But thank you, Shea. You are a great son, and I am so lucky to be your father. But this isn't a gift. I will pay you back every penny. I don't care how long it takes."

"Don't worry about it, Abba. Everything is going to be fine," Shea declared, with more confidence than he felt.

Now, as he listened to his father's phone ringing on the speaker, Shea knew that everything would not be fine. On one hand, if he quit his job there was no way he could keep his promise to his father. But the more he thought about it, the more he realized that he couldn't go through with it. There was no way that he was going to be able to defend his rebbi's attacker. He only hoped that his father would understand.

"Abba," Shea called out as his father answered the phone.

"Hi, Shea, how have you been doing?"

"Not great," Shea responded. "I am sure that you heard what happened to Rabbi Felder."

"Of course, I heard. That is all everybody is talking about. Do you know how he is doing?"

"Not good, Abba," Shea answered glumly. "I just saw him today, and it looks really bad."

"How did you see him?" Dovid Berman asked. "I thought that they were keeping his location a secret?"

"I called Yechiel and he told me where he was being treated."

"Wow, that must have been really hard for you. How are you holding up?"

"Not well," Shea answered. "I am telling you, Abba, you can't even recognize him because the swelling is so bad. I am really a wreck right now."

"I am so sorry. Is there anything I can do to help?"

Shea thought about his father's question before answering. What his father had in mind was probably a listening ear or maybe a nice dinner cooked for the Felder family. But what Shea needed was a lot more complicated.

"There is something that you can do for me," Shea answered.

"Name it."

"My firm was hired to represent Rabbi Felder's attacker."

"That is horrible," Dovid Berman exclaimed. "A monster like that doesn't deserve any representation, certainly not from a top-notch firm like yours. How could your firm agree to do such a thing?"

"It gets worse."

"What do you mean?"

"My firm assigned me the case. I am first chair on this one."

Shea succinctly explained the situation: the firm's opening in France, the necessity to prove that they were not anti-Muslim.

"But that is crazy," Dovid Berman exclaimed. "How can they expect you to do such a horrendous thing? Why can't you just tell them no?"

"I want to, but Allan told me that there will be repercussions if I do."

"What did he mean by repercussions?"

"He meant that I would be fired if I didn't take the case," Shea said plainly.

"They can't do that. You are a great lawyer."

"Thanks for the vote of confidence, but they can do whatever they want. It is their firm. And besides, I haven't been able to bring in enough money for the firm. So Allan laid it out for me nice and simple. If I want to keep my job, then I need to take the case."

"So what are you going to do?" Dovid Berman asked.

"I don't want to take the case. I want to be able to tell Allan that I quit."

"Does he know that you are thinking about quitting?"

"Sure he does," Shea answered. "He knows how difficult the decision is for me and he understands very well why I would want to leave. However, he also knows something else."

"What is that?"

"He knows about the money that I give you every month."

"How does he know about it?" Dovid Berman asked nervously.

"Apparently, he has sources. He knows all the financial activity of all his employees. But don't worry," Shea reassured his father, "he has no idea why I take out the money. All he knows is that on the fifteenth of every month, for the past four months, I've been transferring ten thousand dollars out of my account. He has no idea where the money goes."

"So what are you going to do?" Dovid Berman asked his son.

"I don't know. With the money I would get from unemployment

and my savings, my family should be okay until I land something else."

"But you wouldn't be able to pay off the rest of the money," Dovid Berman interjected.

"That's right," Shea agreed.

Shea's father was silent and Shea waited for him to respond. Shea didn't see that his father had much choice. He had done his father a favor for the last few months, but now he needed his father to come through for him.

That's why, when his father finally spoke, Shea couldn't believe what he had to say.

■ ■ ■

Mohamed sat in the corner of the courtroom. He tried to blend in, but with his choice of clothing, that was impossible. It didn't really matter. Let people think what they wanted. To some, he would be viewed as an interested civilian. Others might see him a sympathizer of the defendant or a civil rights activist. As long as nobody knew his true reason for being there, the man was safe.

He stared at the defendant. He saw him in handcuffs, his eyes in another world and his mind on a different planet. Only Mohamed knew what the defendant was truly thinking. It would surprise most people, but to this man, who knew the defendant well, it would come as no surprise. Making sure that the defendant could not see him, he looked more closely at the defendant; he could have sworn that he saw a tear in his eye. That did surprise him, and Mohamed knew that it wasn't a good sign.

■ ■ ■

"I am sorry, Shea," Mr. Berman responded.

"What do you mean, you're sorry?"

"I can't help you."

"I'm not sure that I understand."

"Shea, if you are asking me whether or not I can pay the rest of the money without your help, the answer is no. I need you to pay off the rest of the debt."

"But Abba, I already gave you forty thousand dollars. Are you telling me that you have no way of getting the rest of the money?"

"Yes," Dovid Berman responded. "I'm telling you exactly that. I can't just go to someone and ask them for fifty grand. Especially, if I have no idea how I am going to repay it."

"But you have plenty of friends and former business associates. Won't they lend you the money?"

"Of course they would," Dovid Berman answered. "But they would want reasons and assurances. They would want to know why I need the money and how I intend to pay it back. Those are questions that I can't answer."

Shea couldn't believe what his father was telling him.

"So what do you want me to do?" he asked in desperation.

"What do you mean?"

"I mean that I don't want to take this case. I have no problem going over to my boss and telling him that I would rather quit than have to defend my rebbi's attacker."

"But Shea, you can't," Dovid Berman countered. "If you quit and stop the payments, in a few months investors will open the books and realize that the money is gone. As soon as they figure where the money went, they won't hesitate to call the cops. Forget about me. Besides the pain and embarrassment it will cause your mother, think about your sisters. You still have two sisters who need to get married. Do you think either of them will get *shidduchim* if I am sent to prison? Nobody will want to marry them. You need to think about your family!"

Shea was quiet and Dovid Berman waited on the line for him respond. In truth it was killing him to have put Shea in this terrible position. But what choice did he have?

Shea's eyes burned with anger. Didn't his father realize how much Shea had done for him already? Didn't he know how painful it was going to be for Shea to have to defend that monster? Why couldn't he have just done the right thing and allowed Shea to quit and not force him to make an impossible decision?

In his fury, hardly thinking about his words, he spoke. "Did you realize how selfish you were when you did this?"

Dovid Berman was taken aback. Shea had never spoken to him like that.

"You talk about family and responsibility, but where was your responsibility to your family? You put everybody in danger when you stole from the business and now I am left to clean up the mess."

"I am sorry, Shea," Dovid Berman whispered.

"Do you realize that for the past four months I have had to lie straight to my wife's face because of you?"

"What do you mean?"

"Shira asks me every day why we can't spend money on the house. She knows that I make a good salary and she can't figure out why we have to live so tightly. So I look her in the eye and lie to her."

"But why couldn't you just tell her the truth?"

"Because I have been trying to protect you," Shea answered. "I don't want her thinking any less of you."

"You don't need to protect me."

"Really? So then why are you forcing me to take this case?"

Dovid Berman was silent. He couldn't blame Shea for his anger. Everything that Shea had said, Dovid Berman had already said to himself a million times. But he also knew that he couldn't think of any other option.

"I am so sorry, Shea."

"*Sorry* isn't very useful," Shea answered coldly. "But I don't have the time for this. I have a client waiting for me in court," he added, as he ended the call in disgust.

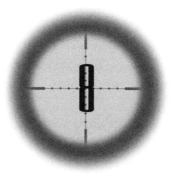

J UDGE ANDREW DANIELS LOOKED OVER HIS COURTROOM like a general surveying his troops before battle. He expected civil behavior from all parties and never allowed anyone to speak out of turn. He believed that the law was sacred, and he demanded the respect that it so greatly deserved. But as Daniels eyed the notes on his next case, he feared that his precious and fragile decorum would be disrupted. He was determined to make sure that would never happen.

"Bailiff, please call the next case," Daniels requested.

"Case number one eight six seven four nine, State versus Khalid al-Jinn. Charges are attempted murder in the first degree, assault with intent to kill in the first degree, and a hate crime."

"Thank you, bailiff," Daniels said. "Who is trying this case for the state?"

"Assistant district attorney, Mark Cohen," Moshe answered.

"Mr. Cohen, to your knowledge, has the defendant retained counsel?"

"We do believe that the defendant has retained counsel; however it seems that his lawyer is late to these proceedings. I am greatly sorry, Your Honor. I know how much Your Honor loathes tardiness."

"Your concerns are appreciated, counselor. Well, if the defendant's attorney is not present, I guess we will proceed without him."

"Wait," came a voice from the rear. Shea raced toward the front of the courtroom and stood next to al-Jinn.

"Shea Berman, from Crane, Gardner, and Scott, here on behalf of the defendant."

"Mr. Berman, where do you think you are?"

Shea was startled by the question. He had just run up a flight of stairs and was struggling to gather his thoughts. He had no idea what the judge was referring to, but he was about to find out.

"I believe I am in a courtroom," Shea answered nervously.

"That is good to hear," the judge responded, "because from the tone of your voice yelling 'Wait,' I would have thought that you were trying to catch the bus."

"I am sorry, Your Honor," Shea answered sheepishly.

"There are rules of conduct, Mr. Berman, and I don't want you to forget them. And speaking of rules, I am very particular about punctuality. You are late, Mr. Berman. Attorneys who are late in my courtroom usually find themselves in contempt."

"I am sorry, Your Honor, but I was informed of the arraignment hearing less than an hour ago."

"Why would that be? The district attorney had told me that all parties involved wanted a fast arraignment."

"Well, I am sure that the district attorney wanted a fast arraignment, but he never told me or my firm about it."

"Is this true, Mr. Cohen?" Judge Daniels asked harshly.

"Well," Moshe said slowly, stalling for time, "at the time I scheduled the arraignment, I wasn't sure who would be the lead counsel for the defense. I therefore proceeded without informing them."

"That is untrue," Shea countered. "You knew that my firm was going to represent Mr. al-Jinn. You just wanted to get the arraignment scheduled before I had an opportunity to meet with my client."

"Are you accusing me of doing something underhanded to try

to get an advantage? That is a tactic usually employed by firms like yours."

"Gentlemen," Daniels raised his voice while rapping with his gavel, "that's enough! While I appreciate a good verbal sparring match as much as anyone, there is a time and a place for everything. Save your verbal attacks for the trial. Now, all I want to hear is a plea by the defendant and then we will discuss bail. Can we proceed?"

"Yes, Your Honor," both attorneys answered.

"Mr. al-Jinn," the judge addressed the defendant. "Your attorney believes that you are ready to issue a plea. How do you plead to the charges?"

While Moshe and Shea were having their verbal spat, al-Jinn seemed to be off in his own world, ignoring the whole episode. He had not even acknowledged Shea's presence. However, once the judge addressed him, rage burned in his eyes and he rose to speak.

"You think that I care about the Zionist pig defending me? Do you know what Koran says about the Jews? It says that Allah will curse them because they do not believe in him. To have this filthy pig stand near me," al-Jinn said pointing at Shea, "makes me sick."

Shea turned to face al-Jinn, a look of shock on his face. While he knew that defending al-Jinn wasn't going to be easy, he never thought that his own client would turn against him. Especially before they even had time to meet.

The judge, appreciating Shea's situation, reprimanded al-Jinn.

"Mr. al-Jinn, I have no idea where you think you are, but let me inform you. You are standing in my courtroom and in my courtroom, you will treat everybody with the dignity and respect that they deserve."

"And why should I listen to you?" al-Jinn challenged. "Do you think that I fear you or your sham of a court? You are no better than the Jew. You enable him and allow him to steal from the resources of the world while he enslaves all my brothers and sisters. The Koran says that you and the rest of this cursed country are non-believers, you are the vilest creatures on earth, and you shall burn in Hell for eternity."

Moshe and Shea exchanged shocked glances. Nobody ever spoke to Judge Daniels that way, especially in his own courtroom.

Daniels composed himself before responding. Shea saw a fury in his eyes that he had never seen before. "Mr. al-Jinn, the great thing about our wonderful country, the country that you happen to despise, is that everybody has the ability to say whatever they want and whatever they feel. That power is given to us by the First Amendment. However, I must also inform you of another law that exists in our wonderful country. That law allows me, as a judge, to run my courtroom the way I see fit. If I feel that a participant's conduct, whether the defense attorney, the prosecutor, or even the defendant himself, will result in disrupting the proceedings I can order that participant to be escorted from my courtroom and I can even hold that person in contempt. So before you erupt into one of your hate barrages again, I must warn you that if you do I will ask the bailiff to remove you from my courtroom."

Al-Jinn began to laugh. "What do I care about your rules and laws? Do you think that I am afraid of jail? I am not even afraid to die. Allah has guaranteed me a place in Paradise for my belief in him. This is what I think about your threats." Al-Jinn drew a deep breath and spat across the room, straight at the judge.

Daniels rose majestically from his seat and commanded, "Bailiff, remove the prisoner at once and put him in the holding cell. I don't want to see his face around here today."

The bailiff shoved Shea aside, grabbed al-Jinn, and led him toward the courtroom door. Shea watched as his new client was ushered from the room. Judge Daniels used his gavel to attempt to regain order in the courtroom. Once he was confident that order had been restored, he turned to Shea.

"Well, Mr. Berman, I assume you will enter a plea for your client."

"I am sorry for what just transpired, Your Honor. I had no idea that my client would behave in such a matter."

"Let it go, because right now I have ten additional cases that need to be arraigned. Let us proceed."

"Thank you, Your Honor," Shea said. "My client will be pleading not guilty, Your Honor."

"A plea of not-guilty has been entered. We will need to schedule a date for the trial."

"The state requests that the trial date be set as soon as possible," Moshe stated. "Because of the political nature of the crime, we feel that the longer we prolong the trial, the more tainted the jury pool will be."

"I tend to agree," Daniels admitted.

"Your Honor," Shea interrupted. "As you can tell, my client will need psychological evaluation before we even begin the trial. These types of tests, along with the necessary discovery proceedings, can take a long time. An expedited trial date may not allow me to prepare a proper defense."

"While I appreciate your dilemma, counselor, I have to agree with the prosecution. Right now we are sitting on a ticking time bomb that will explode if we delay the trial. The racial and political implications of this crime reach far beyond my courtroom. I do not want this case being tried in the court of public opinion. But the longer we wait for a trial, the more probable that it will be."

"But what about my defense?"

"From what I have heard about your firm, you have the resources to proceed with a trial tomorrow, let alone in two weeks."

The last comment was meant as a shot against Shea's firm, but Shea didn't react. He wondered if there was any bad blood between Daniels and the firm; perhaps that would be grounds for recusal.

In any case, the judge's reason for a speedy trial did give Shea the basis for something that he wanted and needed very badly.

"Your Honor," Shea said, "if we are afraid that this case will be tried in the media, I ask that as of this moment, Your Honor issue a gag order. That way, all the participating attorneys will not be able to influence the potential jury pool and we will not have this trial become a media circus."

Moshe looked dismayed. Shea knew that Daniels was up for reelection and he also knew that Moshe Cohen wanted as much political pressure and heat put on this case as possible. A gag order would hurt them both; that was Shea's intention. If the judge refused the gag order, then Shea would request a later trial date and give himself more time to prepare. Either way, Shea would get something that he wanted and Moshe Cohen knew it.

"Your Honor," Moshe attempted a reply, "the public has a right to know what is going on during these proceedings."

"Not if it will prevent proper justice from being served," Shea countered.

"I am sorry, Mr. Cohen, but I have to agree with the defense. If we are going to expedite the trial date, then it is only right that we issue a gag order on this case."

Shea had to suppress a smile. Even though the situation with al-Jinn was out of control, at least Shea could prevent Moshe from inciting the local media. All the Jewish publications would do their best to undermine any possible defense Shea could create. By keeping the media out of the trial, Shea hoped that he could control some aspect of this case.

"Before we end this arraignment, there is the issue of bail that needs to be decided," the judge reminded them.

"The prosecution requests that the defendant be remanded until and throughout the trial."

"On what basis?" Shea challenged him. "My client has no prior history of any violence and is not a known flight risk."

"Your client," Moshe corrected him, "has emigrated from the Palestinian city of Jenin, where his entire family resides. He would have no problem disappearing and heading back to Jenin. He has relationships with various organizations throughout Brooklyn that have been known to harbor and aid terrorists. I am quite confident that if he is issued bail, we will never see him again."

Shea didn't answer Moshe's claim because he had no idea what to answer. He didn't know about al-Jinn's relationships. He didn't even know that al-Jinn had grown up in Jenin. Shea wondered how the state had managed to dig up so much information on his client while he knew nothing.

"I must agree with the prosecution," the judge stated. "Bail has been denied and the defendant will be remanded to the custody of the Rikers Island Correctional Facility. We will reconvene in two weeks for pretrial motions. I will advise the prosecution to turn over all its evidence for discovery."

Daniels banged his gavel. The arraignment was over.

As the attorneys walked out of the courtroom, Moshe gave Shea a look of disgust. "So how much did it cost them?" he muttered.

"What are you talking about?" Shea asked.

"When you sold your soul to your firm," Moshe answered. "I was just wondering how much it cost them. I mean, to defend the attacker of one's rebbi must be a pretty expensive proposition. So I was just wondering, how much does one's soul go for these days?"

Shea stalked silently away. What scared him was that he had nothing to respond. What Moshe was saying was true. He had sold his soul, and he had never felt worse in his life.

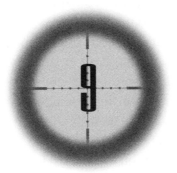

SETTLING INTO THE DRIVER'S SEAT, SHEA HEADED FOR THE Prospect Expressway. He turned on the radio, hoping that they would be discussing something that didn't have to do with his case. But for once the urgent and vocal debate on who the Pilots were going to pursue during free agency didn't interest Shea. He couldn't get the image of his rebbi lying in the hospital bed out his mind. How he hated himself for defending the man who put him there!

Had Shea not been so preoccupied, he might have realized that a dark sedan kept appearing in his rear-view mirror. But as he wove expertly from lane to lane, his thoughts in turmoil, Shea didn't notice a thing.

The sound of his cell broke through his dismal thoughts. He looked at the caller ID and answered the phone.

"Hey," Shea said.

Shira Berman had a quick ear. "Why do you sound so beat?"

"It has been a really long day."

"I'm sorry. When do you think you'll be home? We have PTA tonight for Yehuda."

"Oh," Shea said, "I almost forgot. If there are no traffic hold-ups, I'll be home in about an hour and a half."

"Should I have supper waiting for you when you get home?"

"No, I don't think I will have time to eat. Besides, after what happened today, I really don't have much of an appetite."

"Are you sure that you are up to going to PTA?" Shira asked in concern. "I can really go by myself."

Shea thought about it. Even though Yehuda, Shea's oldest, was a wonderful boy and was doing amazingly well in school, Shea believed that it was important for every parent to go to PTA. It was not only a chance for the teachers to meet the parents and share with them praises of their children, but it also showed the teachers that the parents appreciated all the effort that they were putting in on behalf of their children. However, on this night Shea just wanted to go home and go to sleep, and he strongly considered his wife's offer. But after a few moments of deliberation, he realized that PTA might be the perfect diversion that he needed. It would also allow him to concentrate on what was really important in his life, and that was his family.

"Thanks for the offer, but I really want to go to PTA with you," Shea responded.

"Okay, I'll be waiting at home for you and we will go together. I'll call Tirtza Jacobs and see if she can babysit."

Shea heard their other line ring. "Gotta go, Shea, there's a call coming through. I'll see you soon."

■ ■ ■

With the kids fed and bathed and the babysitter given her instructions, Shea and Shira headed out. As they drove to the yeshivah, Shea was grateful that his wife was sitting quietly. Usually Shira was full of news of her day: the wallpaper samples she'd pored over, the bathroom tiles she'd finally picked, the kids' antics. Tonight, though, she seemed lost in thought, and that was fine with Shea. There was so much he had to think about, he needed a little space. He wanted to tell Shira everything, but now wasn't the time.

As they pulled up to the school, Shea saw that the lot was full and he parked on a side street.

Yeshivas Kol Nearim was one of many elementary schools in Lakewood. Even though it had been in existence for over twenty years, only recently had it grown in popularity. For the school's first fifteen years, there had been only one class per grade. However in the past five years there had been sufficient registration to create three parallel classes in each grade. Shea had a wonderful relationship with its successful and charismatic principal, Rabbi Eliezer Israel, and Shea's son was thrilled with the school.

As he looked around the building, Shea let out a sigh. The school was beginning a major expansion campaign, and Shea could understand why. To accommodate the growing numbers of students the classrooms had been divided. They were now small and dark and the tiles on the floor were cracking. Colorful posters and bulletin boards couldn't hide the water stains on the ceiling and the walls' chipped paint. The school was falling apart right before Shea's eyes. To make things worse, even the playgrounds were shrinking. The boys used an empty lot for their recess play, but a builder had bought the property adjoining the school and was planning to construct ten duplex apartments. By the end of the school year, the kids would have nowhere to play.

Shea knew that there was only one answer. The yeshivah needed a new building, and that was why the dean of the school, Rabbi Yerachmiel Hirsh, approached Shea as soon as he walked through the door.

"Reb Shea, Mrs. Berman, how are you?" Rabbi Hirsh greeted them.

"Just fine, Rabbi Hirsh," Shea answered.

"Only just fine? From what Rabbi Israel tells me, your son is doing extremely well in *shiur*. If I am not mistaken, he just finished *shakleh vetariah* on the first four *blatt* of *Eilu Metzius*. With a child like that, you can't just be doing fine. You have to be doing amazing!"

For the first time that day, Shea gave a sincere smile. "I guess you are right," he responded, realizing that Rabbi Hirsh had a point. "Life is great. *Baruch Hashem*."

"That is what I want to hear. Please do me a favor and thank your father for me."

"Why?"

"Well, not only I am thankful for the donation that he gave last year, but he also introduced me to a couple of his friends who gave generously. Your father is really something special."

If only you knew the truth, Shea thought. *What would Rabbi Hirsh think of my father then?* But he kept silent.

Shira waved to another mother, and, with a polite nod to Rabbi Hirsh, walked off to speak to her. Shea turned toward his son's classroom.

"I see that you are impatient to go and get your *nachas*, so I will only bother you for another minute," Rabbi Hirsh said. "You know, of course, that our expansion campaign is in the planning stages."

"Yes, and not a minute too soon."

"Reb Shea," Rabbi Hirsh said, his voice compelling and persuasive, "there is nobody that I would feel more comfortable in having chair our expansion campaign than you. Not only are you a wonderful and involved parent, but you are a pillar of the Lakewood community. You are successful in what you do, but you are still a true *ben Torah*. Who better to be the face of the new building for Yeshivas Kol Nearim?"

Shea didn't know what to say. Even though he would have loved to help out his son's school, he wasn't usually home till very late. The last thing that his wife would want would be for him to leave to some school meeting minutes after he got home.

"Sure he'll accept it," sounded a booming voice coming from behind him.

"I don't get a choice in the matter?" Shea asked, spinning around to face his friend Danny.

"Like you have one? Do you see the condition of this building? We need a new building, Shea, and as a successful New York City attorney, you will know how to get us one."

"What about you, Danny? Isn't Danny Abramson the famous investor whose clients are worth hundreds of millions of dollars?

I am sure that you would love the opportunity to approach your clients and ask them to help support a worthy cause by building your son a school."

"Well, I am not sure," Danny said, for once losing his trademark confidence.

"You know Reb Daniel, Shea has a point," Rabbi Hirsh smiled. "There is plenty of room for two people to run our building campaign."

Danny looked at Shea and grinned. What he was going to say was going to surprise Shea. In reality, it even surprised Danny.

"Fine," he stated. "I will help chair the building campaign as long as Shea is at my side. There is no better cause than my son's education. I think that together, we can really convince the parent body to get involved and raise the money."

"That sounds great," Rabbi Hirsh said, in the voice of a man who has gotten even more than he'd hoped for. "Looking at the lines forming by your children's classrooms, I figure that you both should get going. But don't worry, we will be in touch. How about we reconvene in two weeks to discuss the future of Yeshivas Kol Nearim?"

Shea and Danny nodded in agreement and walked together toward their children's classrooms. "I cannot believe that you volunteered me for the job," Shea accused his friend.

"You volunteered me," Danny countered.

"That was only after you told Rabbi Hirsh that I would be the perfect man for the job."

"Well, I happen to think that you would."

"Are you for real? Don't you remember the last time that I tried to raise money? It was during second grade for the Moshe Chai Tzedakah drive."

Danny chuckled as the memory came back to him.

Danny and Shea's Rebbi, Rabbi Donowitz, had encouraged the boys to raise money for Moshe Chai, an organization that raised tzedakah funds for poor families in Israel. Rabbi Donowitz told his students that any boy who raised over one hundred dollars would qualify for a special bowling-and-pizza trip. All the boys in class ran home that night and began collecting. All the boys, except for Shea. He was too nervous to approach total strangers for money. He went his room and cried all night because he wasn't going to be able to go on the trip. His parents, feeling sorry for him, donated the one hundred dollars to the organization and Shea was able to participate. He never told anybody except Danny what had really happened.

"Yeah, that was pretty funny," Danny recalled, laughing.

"It was not," Shea shot back.

"Sure it was. I remember everybody bringing in all their small bills and coins in their special envelopes. But all you brought was one crisp one hundred-dollar bill. When Asher Frank asked you what happened, you told him that you exchanged all the money in the bank because the change was too heavy for you."

"I am happy that you are having a great laugh at my expense. But the truth is that I could never go over to a complete stranger and ask him to give money to the school."

"Who says that you have to ask? I'll do the talking and you just sit there."

"And what good would that do?"

"You don't get it, Shea," Danny exclaimed. "No matter how much you want to deny it, people really respect you. You are an honest guy that people just gravitate to. Your just being there while I say my spiel will give the school the credibility that we need."

"Okay, Danny, if that's the way you want it, I'm aboard."

"Great, but we have plenty of time to discuss this. Right now, my wife is going to kill me if I don't join her to talk to the English teacher."

"Why?"

"Do you have any idea what my little Shimon did last week? He covered the board markers with crazy glue and the teacher couldn't get them off her hand. This was after he put salt in her water bottle. I don't think my wife wants to hear all the *nachas* stories alone."

"Well, you go enjoy yourself."

Shea joined Shira outside Yehuda's classroom. As he waited in line he replayed Danny's words in his mind and sighed. No matter what people thought about him before, Shea knew that was about to change. Because once everyone found out who Shea's new client was, no one was going to want to go anywhere near him.

■ ■ ■

Once again Mohamed was waiting in the car. While he waited for his subject to reappear, he replayed the conversation with his employer that he'd had moments after the arraignment had ended.

"We might have a problem," Mohamed had stated.

"What would that be?" Rasheed asked.

"The arraignment has just ended. Our friend was taken away in handcuffs."

"Isn't that what we wanted?"

"Not quite," Mohamed responded. "He was taken away before the arraignment finished."

The word came out like a pistol shot. "Why?"

"The judge found our friend in contempt. He was saying some unfavorable things about Jews and America, and the judge sent him out of the courtroom."

There was a laugh, and a voice that did not sound amused. "So this is America's famous freedom of speech?"

"It seems that the right of freedom of speech does not exist in this judge's courtroom. And another thing," Mohamed continued, "He's got himself a hotshot lawyer to defend him."

Another pistol shot. "Who?"

"His name is Shea Berman from Crane, Gardner, and Scott."

"I thought that our friend was going to be defended by a public defender," the voice said quietly. "The plan was for this case never to get to trial. How did our friend end up with a high-priced attorney?"

Mohamed didn't want to tell his employer the truth. He knew what would happen if he did. And it wasn't pretty.

"What does it matter how he got the attorney? All that matters now is that our friend has competent legal counsel and this case will be going to trial."

"This wasn't part of the plan," Rasheed said angrily. "What do we know about this Shea Berman?"

Again Mohamed chose not to tell the truth, the very dangerous truth.

"He is an Orthodox Jew who is a junior associate for the firm. As far as I know, he isn't very experienced in criminal matters."

"I don't like this at all," Rasheed declared. "Here is what you are going to do. You are going to follow this Mr. Berman and watch his every move. I don't want you to take your eyes off him. If he does anything out of the ordinary, you will tell me immediately. We cannot afford any more surprises."

And so here was Mohamed, sitting and watching this Jewish school.

Suddenly he saw Shea and his wife leaving the building. As he started the engine he felt a rare pang of sympathy for the young man he was following. Because whatever this lawyer thought he knew about this case, he had no clue to what was really going on.

■ ■ ■

The babysitter had done her job well. When they returned home, the children were all sleeping peacefully, and the house was quiet.

After she'd checked on the kids Shira came into the kitchen. She found her husband sitting at the table with a despondent look on his face. In his hand, he held a small shot glass filled with single malt scotch. Shea, who never drank alcohol during the week.

"Shea, we've got to talk."

"Yes, we do. But you'd better sit down for this," her husband said glumly.

Shira opened her mouth as if to speak, then seemed to think better of it. She silently took a chair on the other side of the table. Her fingers slowly traced a random pattern on the tablecloth.

Shea cleared his throat. "After I visited Rabbi Felder, I went back to the office."

Shira looked up, surprised. "I thought it was your day off?"

"It was supposed to be, but Allan called me into a very important meeting. Jessica Scott was there."

"Jessica? I thought she never deals with the junior associates."

"Originally, I thought it had to do with the Merzeir case. But I found out later that she had a totally different agenda."

"Which was …?"

"The firm wants me to take on a new case. The managing partners feel that this new case is vital to the firm's ability to expand in Europe."

"What is the case?"

Shea debated before answering. The last thing that he wanted to do was disappoint his wife, which he knew he was going to do.

"I was asked to defend a young Palestinian man accused of attempted murder. The man's name is Khalid al-Jinn."

"Isn't that the guy who …"

"Yes. He's the Arab who attacked Rabbi Felder."

Shira's eyes opened wide. "Are you telling me that your firm has asked you to represent the man who attacked your rebbi?"

"That is exactly what I am telling you."

"And you're going to do it?"

"Yes."

Shira's voice came out in a harsh whisper. "But why?"

"Because I need this case. You know that it is only going to be one of us, either me or Kyle, who will survive after this year. Well, Allan ran the numbers and I came up short."

"What does that mean?"

"I don't have the billables that Kyle has. He has put in many more hours than I have and has brought in a lot more money."

"But you have a family and you are religious. Doesn't your firm realize that?"

"The firm doesn't take that into consideration. That's why Allan asked me to take this case. The equity partners care about one thing and that is the money. If Kyle has brought in more money, then he gets the job. But if I can show the firm that I am loyal and do a good job trying this case, Allan thinks that the partners will either choose me or maybe even choose to keep two associates."

"But don't you see that the reason they want you to take the case is because you shouldn't. The only reason that taking this case shows that you are loyal is because nobody in their right mind would take it."

"But what choice do I have?"

"Ever thought of saying no?" his wife said sarcastically.

"And if I did, where would that leave us? Do you know how many of my friends are out of work? The economy is horrible for lawyers right now."

"We would be able to figure out something."

"How? You don't have a job and you haven't worked in years. We put all of our savings into this house."

"Which you haven't let me spend any money on," Shira countered.

"I told you that was because of my student loans," Shea reminded her. "Can you imagine what would happen if I lost my job and we needed to pay off all those loans and the house?"

Shira didn't respond. In mounting desperation, Shea watched a tear roll down his wife's cheek; his wife, who was always joyous, always full of *simchas ha'chaim*.

"I don't want to take this case. I may never forgive myself for doing it. But if we lose our home and are forced to the streets, I also won't be able to forgive myself."

Shira brushed away a tear from her cheek. When she spoke next, her voice was colder than Shea had ever heard it.

"But you can forgive yourself for lying to me?"

Shea paled. "Lying?"

"I called the law school," Shira said quietly.

Shea fought for time. "Why would you do a thing like that?"

"I know that you said we can't spend a lot of money on the

house because you needed to pay back your loans. But we still need lights in the playroom. So I called down a couple of electricians to give me an estimate."

"What does that have to do with my law school?"

"Well, one electrician wanted more money, but he also said that he would install ceiling fans in the bedrooms for that price. So I didn't know whom to choose. "

"Why didn't you call me?" Shea asked. "We agreed that before we sign on to do any work, you would discuss it with me."

"I tried to call you all afternoon, but I couldn't get through. So I figured, let me call the law school myself and find out exactly what you owe, and then I could decide which electrician we could afford. I left a message, and they called back while I was speaking to you in the car."

Shea braced his head on his clammy hand. If Shira had spoken to the law school office that meant she knew the truth.

As he lifted his head to meet her gaze, he saw fire burning in her eyes.

"Shea, how could you?"

Not knowing what else to say, Shea played dumb. "How could I what?"

"Don't be coy with me. The office told me that there was no balance. When I informed them that it had to be a mistake, they told me that not only was it not a mistake, but you had never owed any money. You were given a full academic scholarship. "

Shea looked at his wife, her face pale and set, and he sighed. He wanted so much to tell her truth, but how could he embarrass his father?

"Look," Shea began, "I need you to trust me."

"Why should I? How can I believe anything that you say?"

"That isn't fair," Shea defended himself. "I know that you're angry right now, but you can't deny the fact that I have been honest and truthful with you throughout our entire marriage."

Shira laughed harshly. "Don't you realize how ridiculous that sounds? You expect me to believe that you have been honest with me? The only thing that I know for sure is that ever since we bought this house, you've been lying to me. How do I know that you haven't been lying to me since the beginning of our marriage?"

Shea looked crestfallen. He hadn't realized that Shira would react so strongly, but he couldn't blame her either. He needed her to trust him, but from the look in her eyes, he knew that wasn't going to happen.

"You want me to trust you, then answer one question. Where is the money?"

"What money?"

"All the money that we have been saving every month and that you were supposedly putting away to pay your school tuition. Where has that money gone? If you want me to trust you, then you are going to have to be honest with me."

Shea looked at his wife in desperation. He wanted to unburden himself to her. He wanted to share with her the pain and the anguish that he had felt over the past few months because of what his father had done. Then he thought about his father. He thought about the embarrassment that Shea would be causing him by disclosing what he had done. And he realized something else. Shea's father was viewed by everyone as an infallible human being who commanded universal respect. As he saw the hurt in his wife's eyes, Shea feared that his wife wouldn't even believe him. She probably would think that Shea had done something terrible and was blaming his father for his own mistakes.

He wanted to tell Shira the truth, but he didn't think that she was ready to hear it.

Shea looked at his wife with compassion and anguish. He only hoped that one day she would understand. But today wasn't going to be the day.

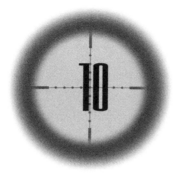

"**E**XCUSE ME SIR, BUT I THINK WE'RE JUST ABOUT finished," Ariel Moore said.

"Are you sure?"

"Positive," Ariel affirmed.

"Fine, then make sure that the car is waiting for me. I'll be out in a moment."

"No problem."

Prime Minister Yitzchak Schechter rubbed his eyes as he looked toward the street outside his office. It had been a trying couple of days, and he knew that it was going to get worse. The press was all over his comments and his party was feeling the heat. The liberals were threatening to bring down the government and there wasn't a lot that Schechter could do to prevent it. *But still,* he wondered, *would everybody have reacted this way had my father made those same comments?* He knew the answer, and that is what was troubling him.

Being the youngest prime minister in the history of the State of Israel wasn't an easy job. There were people who doubted Schechter's mental toughness and ability to properly run the country. What made it harder was the fact that his father, Yehonatan

Schechter, was not only a war hero, but also his predecessor, and Yitzchak was always being measured against his father's successes.

Yehonatan Schechter, one of Israel's youngest generals, was considered the military genius behind Israel's stunning Six-Day War victory. During the Yom Kippur War he had carried out operations behind enemy lines. But even after all those victories, Yehonatan was not finished; upon his retirement from the army he formed his own party, ran for prime minister, and won handily. He would have still been prime minister today had he not suffered a heart attack and died suddenly. Schecter's party, *Am Kulam*, not wanting to lose control, nominated his son Yitzchak to take his place in the special elections. Riding on his late father's popularity, Yitzchak defeated his opponents easily and settled in as prime minister at the age of thirty-nine.

While his experienced and wealthy backers thought that he would be a puppet who would dance to their every command, Yitzchak had proven in a short time that he was hardly a patsy and would not take orders from anybody. Although that attitude went a long way toward establishing his own credibility, he also alienated members of his own party, and now he was facing some tough decisions.

"Ariel," Schechter called out to his aide before he left the room.

"Yes sir."

"Can you be honest with me?"

"Of course, aren't I always?"

"Well sometimes you are and other times you are afraid that I might fire you."

"I do like my job, sir," Moore grinned.

"So please answer me. What did I say that was so wrong? If my father had said what I said, that we were halting talks with the Palestinians because of their failure to stop the missiles, everybody would have cheered his bravery and confidence. So why am I being vilified by the media and my own party?"

"Because you aren't your father."

"What is that supposed to mean?"

"Your father was a hero," Moore explained, "who took this

country from the brink of destruction and helped it rise to promi-
nence. He rescued his homeland from the clutches of her enemies
and saw to it that her safety would never be in jeopardy again. So
when your father would make a statement, people would listen
and obey. You are only his son and until you can establish your
own reputation and legacy, you will never be afforded the same
respect that he was."

"But all I care about is my homeland's safety. Those kassam
rockets fall on our cities every day and the Palestinian government refuses to do anything to stop them. I am forcing their hand.
If they want concessions from the Israeli government, they are
going to have to do something first."

"Nobody is saying that you aren't right," Moore reasoned.
"However, it doesn't help that you ignored a plea from our closest ally when you made your statement."

"But President Brady was out of line," Schechter said. "He
never should have told King Abdullah of Saudi Arabia that a
Palestinian state was inevitable, no matter what was going on in
Israel's border cities."

"You know how it is," Moore responded. "The Americans need
the oil so they will tell the Saudis whatever they want to hear. But
you can never question America's support for us."

"How can I not? When the president of the United States tells
the world that he supports a Palestinian state even if it means
we're going to have to put up with their missile attacks, how can
I not question his loyalties?"

"First of all, he didn't tell the world," Moore corrected him.
"He only told King Abdullah behind closed doors when the
microphones were supposed to be off. Secondly, he wasn't saying anything that you don't already know. We all know that the
Palestinians are going to get their own state. The only questions
are when and where their capital will be. On those two issues,
President Brady did not make any inflammatory remarks. "

Schechter closed his eyes and tried to think. Had he really made
a colossal error? He had thought that he was right when he made
those harsh statements, but now he wasn't sure. He had wanted

to show the Israeli people that they had a fearless leader who would stand up to anybody to protect them. But it seemed that all he had really shown was that he was still young and unable to control his emotions.

"How do we fix this situation?" Schechter asked solemnly.

"Don't worry," Moore reassured him. "We have the summit at the end of the month. You can repair all the damage by reassuring the president and the world that you are committed to peace. Until then, allow your staff to use back channels to inform our friends in the media of your true intentions. Don't be so hard on yourself. Everybody makes mistakes; we just need to be able to learn from them."

"Thank you, Ariel. You are a true friend."

"It is my pleasure, sir. However, there is one more thing that we need to discuss and that is your itinerary for the trip."

"What is the concern?" Schechter asked.

"Mostly nothing," Moore answered. "Everything looks good and all of your scheduled visits can be arranged. However, there is the matter of you visiting your mother that I wanted to discuss."

"There is nothing to discuss. We have gone over this a million times and my answer is still the same."

"But sir, according to your travel requests, you wish to travel alone to visit her."

"That is correct; she is after all my mother and I feel it wouldn't be respectful if I visited her with the entire Shin Bet at my side."

"If you do not allow us to accompany you, I cannot guarantee your safety."

"I am sure that you will think of something."

"But sir, you cannot be serious. There are at least a million people in this world who would like to kill you. How can you be so careless with your security?"

"I am not being careless; I am expecting Shin Bet to do its job. I am not saying that I don't want my security detail sweeping the area to make sure that everything is safe. I am just saying that I don't want anybody close by during this visit. Is that understood?"

"Perfectly," Moore answered reluctantly.

"If there is nothing else, please make sure that my car will be waiting outside for me."

Moore left the prime minister and headed outside. He motioned for the guard to summon the driver and waited. Because he couldn't force the prime minister to inform the Americans of his travel plans, Ariel knew that the prime minister was taking a major risk. And he was not happy about it at all.

■ ■ ■

The woman awoke from another restless night and tried to stretch her muscles. She'd fallen on her back when they'd thrown her into this dark, evil room, and it still ached. She was strong enough to disregard the throbbing, but there was another pain gnawing at her that she couldn't ignore. It wasn't the pain that disturbed her, but what the pain meant. She had experienced that feeling only two times before: when she had been expecting her children. If she was feeling the pain again, she knew what that signified, and it terrified her.

But as she stood up, she scolded herself. She had always been taught that a child was a blessing, no matter what the situation. If she was, in fact, expecting a child, she needed to find a way out of her prison. She would not allow her child to be born under such horrible conditions.

As thoughts of escape entered her mind, she shivered. She would never forget the horror of seeing the photo her captor had thrown at her; a picture of her young two sons. Her beloved, sweet children were vulnerable and the implication of his remarks was terrifyingly clear: continue to disobey and they will die.

As she paced her small cell, the irony brought tears flowing down her cheeks. She needed to escape to save her baby, but if she escaped her other children would die.

A sudden rush of light interrupted her dismal thoughts. Shielding her eyes, she was unable to see the man who entered her cell. As soon as she heard his voice, though, a shiver of terror ran down her bruised spine.

"I see that you are starting to understand the seriousness of your situation," Rasheed said. "My men tell me that you have begun eating again. That is good."

He spoke in a pleasant, everyday voice, like a stranger commenting on the weather. Somehow it made him all the more frightening.

The bile started to rise as she listened to him talk. She had no idea why she had been taken captive. Her captors had never told her and she never dared to ask. They obviously had a plan and a reason for keeping her as a prisoner, but why?

Finally, she could not keep silent any more. "Why do you want me here?" the woman cried. "What have I done to you? I don't have any money and my husband is only a teacher. We won't be able to pay you. What have I done?"

"Who says that you have done anything?" Rasheed asked. "In times of war, even innocent civilians must do their part. Though you may not understand how, you are playing a pivotal role in the destruction of our adversaries."

"What war are you talking about? I don't want to be part of any war. I just want to see my husband and children again."

"And you will, my dear sister," Rasheed assured her in that same calm, terrifying voice. "Just continue to do your part and obey my instructions, and everything will be okay. You have my word. However, if you attempt to escape at all, you will never see your family again. You have my word on that as well."

The woman trembled. She knew that what he'd said was true. Her captor meant business and she was confident that he would kill her if she tried to escape. What she didn't believe was that he would let her live, even if she did as she was told. As she struggled to see his face through the blinding light, another man entered the room. He, too, was a dark figure, though it seemed to her that he had a beard.

"It is time to go, sir."

"Thank you," Rasheed said as he turned once more to his prisoner. "Remember, do as you are told and no one will be hurt."

He walked out, leaving the other man behind. When he was

sure that he was alone with the prisoner, he spoke. "Do as he says," he said, his voice a plea. "It will soon be over and you will again see your children." Before the woman could respond, he'd left the room, and darkness fell once again.

As she replayed his words, something struck a chord within her. While she had not been able to see his face, that voice was familiar. She definitely recognized it, but she couldn't remember from where. Tired, frightened, and nauseous, it was hard for her to focus, but she forced herself to sit and think and, after a few moments, the answer came to her. It brought her no comfort: as she realized whose voice it was, the ramifications were far more terrifying than anything she had ever expected. She ran toward the door of her cell and cried out his name in the darkness.

"Mohamed! Mohamed!"

There was no answer. None at all.

■ ■ ■

Shea arrived at his office early on Monday morning, and for once he was actually glad to be there. Shira had ignored Shea throughout the weekend. They ate the Shabbos meals together, speaking to the children but not to each other; all his attempts to talk were coldly rebuffed. While Shea had never seen Shira act that way, he couldn't blame her. He had lied to her, and worse, she had no idea why. There had been so many times when Shea had looked into her sunken eyes and wanted to tell her the truth, but he couldn't bring himself to do it.

As he entered his office, he knew that he had a lot of work to do. He was scheduled to make pretrial motions at twelve o'clock and he wasn't even close to ready.

Someone was waiting for him in his cubicle, and Shea wasn't happy to see him.

"Hey, Mr. Berman, why haven't you called me back?"

"Lenny," Shea addressed him, "I told you that I don't have the time right now to deal with your case."

"But you see that's just what I'm talkin' about. All those other lawyers think they're too good for ol' Lenny. But not you, Mr. Berman. You treat Lenny like Lenny should be treated. You treat Lenny like a human bein'."

Shea sighed as he looked at his client. Lenny Jones was one of the largest men Shea had ever encountered, and he was also one of the nicest. Lenny made up for his lack of education with his heart and compassion. No matter how tough things got for Lenny, he was always smiling.

Shea had met Lenny almost one month earlier. Lenny was the proud father of two boys and had always provided them with shelter and food. But recently Lenny's brother had been sent to prison on drug charges. Rather than have his nieces and nephews become part of the foster care system, Lenny offered his brother's five kids a home. While that was a very generous act, Lenny hadn't taken into account the additional financial burden he had put on his family. He had been working at the same electronics store for over twenty years, but now the money wasn't enough. He needed a second job and he responded to a want ad placed by the Halal Market on Chamber Street.

It seemed that the food market needed someone to stock the shelves at night. Lenny would be able to keep his job at the electronics store and be at the market in plenty of time to start working. The job was exactly what Lenny had been looking for and for the first few weeks all went well, until the day that his new boss called Lenny into his office. He said that things weren't working out and that he needed to let Lenny go. When Lenny asked for an explanation, he was told that the business was going in a different direction. Lenny had noticed all the stares directed his way by the patrons of the market and he knew what was really going on. They weren't comfortable with a black man working in the market, and that was why the manager had decided to fire Lenny.

Lenny wouldn't go down without a fight. He took his story to a neighborhood advocacy group and they wanted to sue the Halal Market for discrimination. The group had offered to pay for all of Lenny's legal expenses. That is how Shea had ended up meeting

Lenny, but with everything that was going on, Shea didn't have the time to deal with him.

"Look Lenny," Shea replied. "I want to help you, but right now I am swamped. I can't do more than I have already done. I informed the defendant that we intend to sue, and I am waiting for their response. As soon as I receive the paperwork, we can proceed with the lawsuit."

"Okay," Lenny smiled, the relief evident in his grin. "I trust you, Mr. Berman, and if you say that everythin' is gonna be fine, then I know it's gonna be fine. You just let me know if you need anythin'."

Lenny clapped Shea on the shoulder and proceeded down the hallway. In truth, had Shea been more on top of the situation, he could have forced the Halal Market's attorney to send over the paperwork and begun the negotiations toward a settlement. But Shea didn't have the time and Lenny would have to wait. Right now, Shea had more pressing matters to deal with.

As soon as he had turned on his laptop, he heard a familiar voice blaring over his intercom.

"Shea, you there?" Donna asked.

"Right here."

"Allan wants to see you right away."

Shea knew what Allan wanted, but he wasn't eager to give it to him. Still, Allan wasn't a person one kept waiting. With a sigh Shea closed his laptop and made his way toward Allan's office.

Allan was speaking heatedly on his phone and motioned Shea into the office.

"This is urgent. Just make sure that it gets done today," Allan barked as he hung up the phone.

"Anything I can do to help?" Shea asked.

"Don't worry," Allan reassured him. "It's nothing we can't handle. Your main concern right now should be your new client. I heard what happened on Thursday. For the record, I never had a client thrown out of court before. But it seems like you recovered like a pro."

"Thanks, but I have no idea what I am going to do next. Did

you see how this guy reacted during the arraignment? He is capable of anything."

"By the way," Allan interrupted, abruptly changing the subject. "That was a great move, asking for a gag order. Daniels must have hated it."

"I am sure that he did, but there was nothing he could do about it. Not after he gave in on the quick trial date."

"Well, just remember, you don't want to alienate your judge. You need to pick your battles wisely."

"I know and that is why I am really going to be careful with my pretrial motions. I am going to try to argue solely based on the prosecutor's case."

"What is the DA's plan?"

"It seems that they are going to call three witnesses: the arresting officer, the crime scene technician, and the supposed eyewitness."

"Are you prepared for the witnesses?"

"Yeah. It doesn't seem like there will be a lot of problems discrediting the officer and the forensic technician. However, I need more information on the eyewitness, and I was hoping that you could send Brad down to help me."

"That was something I wanted to talk to you about. I know you were probably banking on Brad being able to dig up some information on your witness. However, something has come up and Brad is needed elsewhere."

This was upsetting news. "I thought that the firm found this case to be so important."

"The case is important. If it wasn't I wouldn't have asked you to take it on."

"So then why can't I have Brad's services?"

"Remember, the al-Jinn case is a pro bono and right now the firm needs as many money-making cases as possible. Just this morning, the firm was offered a major proposition."

"What happened?"

"Well, it actually concerns Merzeir Pharmaceuticals and your previous case," Allan replied.

"I thought the case was finished."

"It was. However, we found out today something very interesting. Didn't you ever wonder how Fatima Assad was able to afford Slick Willy Drillings?"

"I assumed that Willy gave his services on commission."

"Shea, you are naïve if you think that Willy would ever do something that he isn't guaranteed money for. He was paid upfront and he was paid handsomely."

"Who paid him? Fatima didn't have any money."

"Well, that question bothered David Merzeir a lot and he decided to do some investigating. Turns out that Slick Willy's tab was covered by Aragon Pharmaceuticals, Merzeir's top competition. "

"Wow!" Shea exclaimed.

"Yep, so since the case got thrown out of court, Merzeir wants to sue Aragon for libel and slander. They are listing the suit at five hundred million dollars."

So that explained it. Even in his defeat, Slick Willy hadn't looked concerned or worried. Shea had found that odd, but he figured it was because Willy had many other clients who could supplement the amount of money that he lost. But now everything made sense. Willy had already been paid, so he didn't really care about losing.

Something more important was bothering Shea.

"If the firm is planning on suing Aragon on behalf of Merzeir, why am I not taking over the suit? Jessica told me that Merzeir wanted to retain me as their head counsel. Plus, nobody knows the Assad case better than I do."

"I know that, and Merzeir actually requested you. But we told them that you were busy and didn't have the time take on their case."

With an effort, Shea reined in his fury. When he spoke, his voice was cold and controlled.

"I can't believe that you did this."

"Did what?" Allan asked

"The only reason I am stuck with this al-Jinn case is because Kyle has brought more money into the firm than I have. But if I would win this new suit, I would be way ahead of Kyle. We're talking a fifty million-dollar fee here! Why are you sticking me with a case that you know I don't want to try and I don't want to be anywhere near? Why can't you just let me try this new case?"

"Because you are the only one that I trust to defend al-Jinn properly. I don't believe that Kyle could do half the job that you could."

"But what about what I want? I stand to lose so much if I defend al-Jinn. Why can't I show the partners that I am worth their while by netting them an additional fifty million dollars?"

"You don't get it," Allan argued. "This suit is going to be on trial for months and in appeals for years. You don't have that much time. You need to show the partners now how valuable you are to them. Shea, you need to trust me. I am not punishing you by giving you the al-Jinn case. I am trying to save your job."

Shea didn't know what to answer. Allan had never steered him wrong, but Shea felt that something else was going on, something big. Something dirty.

"Look, you've got to get to court; you better get moving," Allan said, clapping his hand on Shea's shoulder. "Don't worry; I am going to be in your corner. You shouldn't feel that you are alone on this one."

Shea rose from his chair and slowly walked out. Allan was wrong: Shea had never felt more alone in his life.

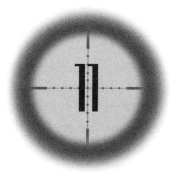

SHEA ARRIVED IN JUDGE DANIEL'S CHAMBERS FIFTEEN minutes before twelve. He'd thought that would give him enough time to prepare his arguments prior to delivering them in front of the judge. When he arrived, he saw that Moshe Cohen was already there speaking with Daniels. Shea rushed into Daniels's office and shut the door.

"I am sorry," Shea apologized. "But I thought our hearing didn't start till twelve."

"It doesn't," Daniels answered with an agreeable smile. "Mr. Cohen and I were discussing a totally separate matter, not one that pertains to your case. But if you are ready to proceed, then so am I."

Shea bit his tongue before responding. While he didn't like the fact that Daniels and Moshe were schmoozing it up before pre-trial motions, Shea also remembered what Allan had said. No, he didn't want to alienate Daniels. So Shea composed himself, and then began to speak.

"The defense does have a few motions that it would like to present."

"Please proceed," Daniels requested.

"The defense moves to suppress the metal rod."

"What?" exclaimed Moshe. "This is insanity. The rod is the weapon that was used by his client."

"Allegedly," Shea corrected.

"If that is what helps you sleep at night," Moshe retorted. "Irrespective of what the defense claims, the officers at the scene had a right to remove the rod from the defendant's apartment."

"They had no right to search his apartment," Shea challenged him. "They only had the right to search Mr. al-Jinn and his immediate surroundings. The club was not found on my client."

"Yes, but it was found on the coffee table, in plain sight. The arresting officers would not have needed a search and seizure warrant."

"He does have a point, counselor," Daniels said to Shea. "As long as the club was in plain sight, the officers did have a right to seize it."

"But I am arguing that the officers had no right to be in the apartment in the first place."

"What are you talking about?" Moshe interjected.

"I am moving to suppress the rationale of the search warrant for lack of probable cause."

"I am not sure I understand, counselor," Daniels said.

"According to the reports, the police received an anonymous tip that my client had attacked Rabbi Felder. However, according to the officer's notes, he made no other inquiries. The only thing he did was to approach a local judge, get an arrest warrant, and arrest my client. Everything was only based on anonymous tip. No other legal basis was provided."

"Your Honor," Moshe interjected, "the defendant lived only two blocks from the scene of the crime. The anonymous tip described the defendant perfectly. The officer felt that he had enough information to be able to arrest the defendant."

"But that was only because my client was a Muslim and the officer knew that. If my client had been a white Catholic, he never would have been a suspect."

"If your client were a white Catholic, he probably never would have committed this crime."

"That is enough," Daniels exclaimed. "You can save your sparring for the courtroom. I have heard all that I need to hear and I am ready to rule."

Shea kept his focus on Daniels, but pondered Moshe's behavior. He had never seen Moshe act like this before, but it didn't surprise him. Even though Moshe wasn't a *talmid* of Rabbi Felder, the vicious attack had clearly touched him, and he wanted to make sure that the assailant was punished. Truthfully, Moshe was just saying everything that Shea believed. Shea should have been the one prosecuting his rebbi's attacker. Instead, Shea was on the other side — and he needed to fight for his client.

"Even though the defense may have a point regarding probable cause, the fact was that the police did have a legal warrant and did not do anything improper in the arrest of the defendant and the seizure of the weapon. Now Mr. Berman, if you wish to bring this point up at trial, I will allow some leeway, but for now the weapon is in."

Shea sighed audibly, casting a furtive glance at Moshe. He never really thought that he would win that motion. The warrant was legit and even if the police hadn't done their due diligence, they were within their rights to arrest al-Jinn and remove the weapon. Shea thought that it was a little too convenient that the weapon had been left out on the coffee table, but that wasn't a point to bring up at a pretrial hearing. Right now, the prosecution had won the first battle and Moshe would be feeling pretty confident. Exactly the way Shea wanted him to feel, because the main reason for Shea filing his first motion was in order to catch the prosecution off guard when he filed his second one.

"The defense requests that my client's religion not be allowed into evidence. We feel that due to the volatile climate surrounding this crime, if the jury were to find out that my client is in fact a devout Muslim, it would be severely prejudicial and prevent my client from receiving a fair trial."

"That is ludicrous!" Moshe exclaimed.

"Excuse me," the judge broke in. "Mr. Berman, you know perfectly well that the DA plans to charge your client with a hate crime."

"For which he has no basis," Shea interjected.

"We have an eyewitness that will testify to the fact," Moshe said quickly.

"That eyewitness's testimony has not been verified nor has it been subject to cross examination," Shea countered.

"What exactly is the argument of the prosecution?" Daniels inquired, turning to Moshe.

"The state wishes to prove that Mr. al-Jinn is a Muslim extremist who singled out a defenseless elderly rabbi to further his own jihadist agenda."

"Do you have any evidence to support that theory?"

"We have an eyewitness who will testify that she heard Mr. al-Jinn yelling inflammatory and racist remarks while attacking the rabbi. Our argument is based on the premise that Mr. al-Jinn is a Muslim. If we are unable to introduce this piece of evidence, our entire case is undermined."

"Your Honor," Shea said firmly, "you cannot deny that my client's religion, in this instance, will be extremely prejudicial."

"Mr. Berman," Daniels addressed him, "does your client deny the fact that he is a Muslim?"

"I am not sure," Shea had to admit.

"What does that mean?"

"As you were able to see during the arraignment hearing, my client doesn't really care to have me as his attorney. I have not been able to even speak with him. He refuses to see me."

"So how do we know that your client wouldn't happily admit to being a Muslim and therefore your motion would be superfluous?"

"But until we do, how can we add another element to this case that will turn the jury against my client? You have already banned him once from the courtroom."

"Which was his own doing," Daniels reminded him sharply.

"I understand that," Shea agreed. "However, my client does deserve a proper defense."

"Which I am sure you can give him," Daniels interjected. "Mr. Berman, I see no reason to grant your second motion. Your client's religion is only prejudicial if the prosecution can prove that he in fact committed a hate crime. There are plenty of Muslims walking these very streets who would never think of attacking anybody, let alone a rabbi. If you do your job well, counselor, then there will be no reason for the jury to be prejudiced against your client because of his religion."

Moshe smiled at Shea, but Shea ignored him. Moshe was feeling good, but Shea was about to ruin his day.

"If the DA is going to attempt to prove that my client committed a hate crime, I would ask that Mr. Cohen recuse himself from this case."

"What?" Moshe asked, his shock clearly showing on his face.

"It is very simple. If the state is going to argue that my client committed a hate crime against a Jewish person, I feel that Mr. Cohen, as a devoutly religious Jew, will be unable to be impartial with regard to my client."

"But you are also a religious Jew," Moshe shot back.

"I know, but it is my client's choice whether he wishes to retain me as counsel. He has full control. He can tell me what he wants me to argue and what he wants me to say. But he has no control over you."

Moshe was seething and Shea knew it. He had played himself into Shea's hand perfectly. By building the case based on the hate crime, Moshe had opened the door for recusal, and Shea had chosen to walk right through it.

"Are you seriously taking this motion into consideration?" Moshe asked the judge

"You can't have it both ways, Mr. Cohen. If you are going to make this case about a hate crime, then it probably wouldn't make a lot of sense to have you trying it for the prosecution. You are a good attorney and I would never accuse you of acting improperly. But I think I would actually be doing you a favor by asking you to recuse yourself. Because if the defense loses this case, you can guarantee that they will argue on appeal that you were prejudiced because of your religion."

Moshe threw Shea a look of contempt, grabbed his cell phone, and began texting, his fingers jabbing furiously at the keys. Shea pointedly gazed at his notes. He didn't feel good about what he had just done, but he knew that he had to do it. Not only was Moshe the best attorney that the DA had, Shea also hoped that because the prosecution would need to find another ADA to take Moshe's place, that would buy Shea the time that he so desperately needed.

"Your Honor," Shea began, "because of your ruling, I would understand if the prosecution would need a few more days to prepare. It might take them a while to bring a new ADA up to speed."

"I appreciate your understanding," Daniels replied. "Well, Mr. Cohen, will the state need a few extra days to prepare?"

"No, Your Honor," Moshe answered after scrutinizing the screen. "Even though Mr. Berman obviously hoped that my recusal would afford him extra time, the state will not need any additional time for preparation. We are ready to proceed immediately. Because of the nature of this case, the district attorney himself will be replacing me as lead prosecutor."

Shea's jaw dropped. He had always remembered him mother quoting the famous saying, "Be careful of what you wish for, because you might get it." Well, Shea had wanted to get Moshe off the case, but his replacement was going to be a lot tougher. District Attorney Michael Reeves had been one the most successful attorneys in all of New York before becoming the DA. Allan had told Shea some of the war stories that had taken place between him and Reeves. He had even confided to Shea that if there was any lawyer that Allan felt was his equal, it was Michael Reeves. If Allan considered Michael Reeves his equal, Shea was definitely out of his element.

"That is good to hear," Daniels stated with a satisfied smile. "So we will schedule jury selection for ten o'clock tomorrow. Have a good day, gentlemen."

Shea nodded in agreement while Moshe raced out of the room. Shea carefully packed his things and left the office.

Moshe was waiting for him.

"How could you do this?" Moshe accused him.

"I didn't do anything wrong in there," Shea defended himself. "I see how passionate you are about the case. You are way too emotional to try this case fairly. I was just doing the right thing for my client."

"Your client almost killed your rebbi! How can you just forget about that?"

"I haven't forgotten about anything, but there is nothing I can do about it. My firm assigned me the case and I am just following orders."

"Isn't that what the Nazis said?" Moshe said caustically.

"That isn't fair, Moshe. You have no idea what I am going through right now."

"You are right and that is because I would never sell out my soul and my people just to make a couple of bucks. You are pathetic, Shea, and do you know what really gets me angry?"

"What?"

"When you called me that morning, begging to know what had happened to Rabbi Felder, I really thought that you were concerned. You sure had me fooled. But now I know the truth. You are as spineless and as gutless as the rest of your defense lawyer buddies. I can't believe I ever thought that you were one of the good guys. And by the way, good luck against Michael Reeves, because you are going to need it. He is going to tear you and your client to shreds and I can't wait to see it happen."

Moshe turned on his heel and walked to the elevator, leaving Shea speechless. Shea knew that Moshe's tirade was not going to be an isolated event. Once the trial began and people saw who was at al-Jinn's side, there would be a total outrage. Shea knew that he needed to prepare himself. But right now, Shea had a bigger problem to deal with and his name was Michael Reeves.

■ ■ ■

Michael Reeves looked up from his seat and noticed someone waiting at his door. When he saw who it was, he tried to hide his surprise, but, in reality, it didn't shock him. Michael knew why he was here, and that is why he wanted him to wait. After several minutes, aware that his visitor was getting anxious, Michael motioned to the door and allowed his visitor to enter. The visitor closed the door behind him and took a seat at the desk.

"I am sorry," Michael began, "but we have a strict rule here at the district attorney's office. No suits costing more than three thousand dollars are allowed in this office."

"Well it's nice to see you to, Michael," Allan Shore replied. "And for your information, this suit cost ten thousand dollars, not three."

"Is that supposed to impress me?"

"I don't need to impress you, Michael. My hundreds of clients and my millions of dollars impress enough people just fine."

"What happened to you, Allan?"

"What do you mean?"

"I mean that when we were in school together, you wanted to change the world. You wanted to be the voice for the downtrodden who couldn't speak for themselves. You wanted to make a difference. But now look at you. You are a hired mercenary who sells his services to the highest bidder with no regard for the people that you hurt."

"Wow, that might have hurt, if it hadn't been so hypocritical."

"What are you talking about?"

"You sit behind that desk and judge me. But we both know that only a few years ago, you were also playing for the dark side. You didn't run for district attorney because you wanted to make a difference. You did it because you couldn't hack it with the big boys. I still remember going up against you in court, and frankly, you weren't that good."

Michael was silent and Allan chastised himself. He hadn't gone down to Michael's office to pick a fight. He actually needed a favor from Michael, and by the look on Michael's face, he probably wasn't going to get it.

"I am sorry about that last comment," Allan apologized. "I was out of line."

"Look Allan," Michael continued ignoring Allan's apology. "I really don't have time for chitchat. As you know, we are in the middle of big case right now, and I need to get back to work."

"Well, it's because of that case that I am here."

"Oh, I forgot," Michael said sarcastically "Your firm is defending that terrorist. Well, thanks to your junior associate, I am the one trying the case now."

"I know, he told me everything."

"Well, then you should know that unless you are coming here to plead guilty to all the charges, we have nothing to talk about."

"I didn't come here to speak about a plea."

"Then why are you here, Allan?"

"I need you to bow out of the case," Allan requested.

"What?"

"I want you to drop the case. Find some other ADA to take it over. There are probably thirty other people in this office who can try this case. You don't need to do it."

"How do you know what I need to do?"

"I know you, Michael," Allan answered. "You are a great attorney, but an even better man. Please don't let your personal vendetta against me and my firm cloud your judgment on this one."

Michael started laughing uncontrollably. Allan, not understanding what was going on, joined in the laughter.

"What are we laughing about?" Allan asked

"You," Michael replied. "You know the ADA that your guy had recused — not only is he one of my finest attorneys, but he also happens to be an Orthodox Jew. He taught me that the Jewish rabbis have a teaching. They say that a person should look at the world and say, 'for me, the world was created.' Well Allan, you really take that saying to heart, don't you?"

"I don't understand," Allan admitted.

"You are self-centered enough to believe that I am taking on this case because I have a vendetta against you and your firm? Here is a newsflash for you, Allan. Not everything I do in my life revolves around you."

"So why are you taking this case?"

"I don't have a choice. Do you know the political pressure being put on me by the members of the city council? They want your client to pay for what he did. They want to make this case a warning against any form of terrorism or bigotry. The only time they ever want to see your client's face again is when they slam his cell door shut forever."

Allan closed his eyes and sighed. He'd been fuming ever since Shea had told him that Michael was prosecuting the case. Michael and Allan's history went all the way back to when they had both been junior associates at Crane, Gardner, and Scott. They came out of Harvard together, and they were both given an opportunity to prove themselves over the course of their first year in the firm. Allan had shown himself to be the more cunning and successful lawyer, and after their first year Allan's contract was renewed and Michael's was terminated. Ever since that day, Allan had felt that Michael bore a grudge against the firm. When Shea had told Allan that Michael was taking the case, Allan thought it could only be for one reason, revenge. Now Allan understood what Michael's intentions really were.

"Is it really that serious?" Allan wondered.

"Are you kidding me? It's a media circus out there. Not only do I have the mayor breathing down my neck, but I have the governor himself wanting to be updated every fifteen minutes. I didn't ask for this case, but thanks to your boy, I have no choice but to take it."

"He made the right move by asking for a recusal," Allan defended him.

"I agree," Michael responded. "I would have done the same thing. But here is what I don't get. According to my ADA, your guy seems to be very close with the victim. So what would possess you to have him try the case?"

"I can't go into it."

"You can't or you don't want to?"

"You know how it is," Allan answered.

"I know exactly how it is," Michael responded, his eyes flashing. "You are forcing this guy to take this case, aren't you? I remember the way Jessica made us take cases that would test our resolve and compromise our ideals. But you know what is sad? I remember you telling me that when you made partner, you would never put a junior associate through what you went through. Now look at you. You are no different from Jessica and all of her cronies. So how did you do it?"

"Do what?" Allan asked.

"How did you convince this guy to defend his rabbi's attacker? Did you tell him that he would lose his job if he didn't? But if he did, he would be showing his loyalty to the firm?"

When Allan didn't respond, Michael knew he had his answer.

"I can't believe that you are actually putting this guy through this torture. You thought I would be upset about the way the firm treated me and that I would want to take revenge. I should be thanking Jessica, not hating her."

"Why?"

"Because," Michael answered, "had she not fired me, I might have ended up like you and that would have been the greatest tragedy of all."

Allan got up to leave. While he would normally have responded with a quick and witty remark, he didn't have anything to say. Though he hated to admit it, everything that Michael had said was true.

"One more thing," Michael added. "Why did you ask me to lay off the case? If he needs to win to prove his loyalty, what do you care?"

"Just drop it," Allan ordered.

"Wait one minute," Michael continued. "Is it possible that the great Allan Shore actually cares about this junior associate? Is it possible that you still have a heart?'

"He is a good guy and he has a family," Allan responded. "For your information, this wasn't my call. Jessica wanted him on the case and as you know, whatever Jessica wants Jessica gets."

"Did Jessica send you down here to convince me to get off the case?"

"No, this is all my idea. Michael, this guy Shea is a good attorney and a better person. He needs this case and frankly, though you will never hear me repeat this again, you are a very good attorney and I am afraid that he is going to lose badly against you."

"Well, you are right about that. But at this point, my hands are tied. I need to try this case and frankly, not even Jessica herself could convince me otherwise."

As he opened the door to leave, Michael called out to him. "Allan, can you do me a favor?"

"What?" Allan asked.

"If Shea Berman is really as good of a guy as you say he is, tell him that when Jessica fires him, there will be a job waiting for him right here at the district attorney's office."

"J UST MAKE SURE THAT YOU GET IT IN WRITING," JESSICA Scott ordered. "I don't trust anybody."

"When do I tell them to come in so we can prepare them for testimony?" Kyle asked.

"Right now, Merzeir is hoping for a settlement, so tell them to hold off. If Aragon Pharmaceuticals is crazy enough to go to trial, then we call them down to testify."

"Are we sure that settling would be the best move? I mean, if we have such an airtight case, wouldn't it be smarter to avoid settling at all?"

"Kyle, remind me. Who is the managing partner in the room?"

"You are," Kyle admitted sheepishly.

"And who is the junior associate in the room?"

"I am."

"Good, because from the tone in your voice I thought that you got confused for a moment. You don't offer any advice unless I ask for it. Is that understood?"

"Completely," Kyle affirmed, his voice carefully controlled.

"Good," Jessica replied. "Now get out of my office and do as you were told."

Kyle raced out of Jessica's office right past Allan, who had been waiting for their meeting to end. Allan knocked on Jessica's door. Once Jessica gave him the okay, Allan entered the office.

"Did you catch the show?" Jessica asked.

"I've seen that performance before," Allan answered.

"Performance?"

"I seem to remember you giving me that exact same speech when I was a junior associate."

"You never knew your place," Jessica laughed.

"True, but Kyle is a good lawyer and you don't want to discourage him."

"I didn't discourage him, I just bruised his ego. I needed to show him who is boss and whom he answers to."

"Well, I hope it works, because he has to be at his best for the Merzeir lawsuit."

"Not to worry," Jessica declared. "Kyle is going to be great. He is ruthless and cunning, but more importantly, he thinks that I am upset with him. That will cause him to want to excel even more because he will want to get back in my good graces. I think that was my mistake with you."

"Mistake?"

"I went too easy on you. To be fair, I was young and inexperienced. The firm was just beginning and I was short-sighted."

"What do you mean?"

"You were a great attorney and you were winning us a lot of cases and more importantly, bringing in a lot of money. So instead of guiding you, I let you do your own thing because I knew that in the end, you would get the results that you needed."

Allan had no idea where this was headed. "So why was that a bad thing?"

"Because you were reckless and defiant," Jessica answered. "You didn't listen to anybody and you did only what you wanted. The sad thing is that twenty years later, you are still that same insolent, hasty kid, maybe a few pounds heavier."

"What are you talking about?"

"I am talking about the al-Jinn case," Jessica answered curtly.

"What about it?"

"Didn't I specifically tell you not to get involved because the Merzeir lawsuit took top priority and I needed you to be fully immersed in the case?"

"I think I remember you mentioning something like that to me," Allan responded carefully.

"So you can imagine my surprise when I got a call from Michael Reeves' office. He asked me why I hadn't gone down to beg him myself. Well, since I had no idea what he was talking about, I asked him to explain."

"And he told you that I had gone down to his office, correct?" Allan interrupted.

"Yes he did, and now you can understand why I might be a little perturbed with you right now."

"For your information, I didn't beg him. I merely requested that he take himself off the case. I didn't put the firm's reputation in jeopardy."

"Are you kidding me?"

"What?"

"Are you so self-absorbed that you can't see why I would be upset at you? You think I care that you begged Michael Reeves? I couldn't care less about your sterling reputation. This may come as a shock to you, Allan Shore, but this firm is greater than any single lawyer, even you."

"So why are you upset?"

"Because you disregarded my order. I told you to stay away from the al-Jinn case and let Shea handle it himself. But as usual, you did whatever you wanted and ignored me."

"I wasn't doing it for myself. I was doing it for Shea."

"You never do anything unless you can gain something. The word *altruism* doesn't exist in your vocabulary."

"Then how do you explain my going down to Michael Reeves' office? What could I possibly gain by that?"

"It is called clearing your guilty conscience," Jessica answered.

"What are you referring to?"

"The only reason why you are trying to save Shea's job is because it is your fault that he is here in the first place."

"I have no idea what you are talking about."

"Let me refresh your memory," Jessica continued. "I specifically asked you to hire one great Harvard attorney. But as usual, you decided that you knew best. You wanted to prove to the world that all Harvard lawyers are inferior and the only lawyer that is worth anything is one that has been trained by Allan Shore. So to prove your ridiculous point, you hired a nice guy, who because of his family life and religion would stand no chance to outdo the Harvard lawyer, and had him try to outlast the Harvard lawyer. It was your own little social experiment. But now it has come to the end and your guilt is getting the better of you. So you are trying to ease your conscience and help Shea keep his job — which, between me and you, is already Kyle's."

"That isn't what you told me," Allan said, his face pale and set.

"I lied," Jessica admitted coldly.

"Yes, you lied, and not only about Shea's job. Don't you remember — or don't you want to remember — that you told me to hire two associates and have them fight it out to see which one would get the prize of keeping his job? You have a very selective memory, Jessica!"

"Don't play games with me, Allan! Whatever I may have said and whatever you remember me saying, that job is going to Kyle Ross and it's just too bad about your little Jewish friend.

"If I hadn't lied to you, you never would have gone along with the plan and Shea Berman never would have taken the case. The firm needs him to represent al-Jinn. We have to show our European friends that we aren't anti-Muslim. So I told you what you needed to hear and you did all the rest."

"You played me?" Allan asked in disgust.

"Like a fiddle," Jessica replied gleefully.

"Do you have any idea what we are putting this kid through? His whole life is going to be turned upside down because of this case. The only reason I asked him to take on this case was because I actually thought I was helping him by giving him an opportunity to prove himself. Now you are telling me that he has no chance. What makes you think that I won't go over to Shea right now and tell him what is really going on?"

Jessica cornered Allan and stuck her finger in his face. "Because you are a very smart attorney and understand what is really at stake here. Attorneys like Shea Berman come along all the time. This firm needs to be protected. We are nothing without this firm. It's the firm that attracts the client, not the lawyers. So if the firm needs a junior associate to go through a little discomfort to defend a client, then that is what the junior associate will do. And if the firm needs one of its partners to be silent while the junior associate does his job, well, we know what the partner will do, don't we?"

Allan looked at Jessica with a mixture of contempt and sadness. For the first time in years he had no answers. On the one hand, he was furious with her that he had been exploited. Allen Shore was usually the one pulling the strings, not the other way around. However, Allan knew that if he had been in her place, he would have done the same thing. In his many years in the profession Allan had learned that the only thing that mattered was the bottom line, and it didn't matter who got hurt in the process. But Allan also realized something else, and it caused him to become despondent. He had always thought of himself as courageous. He felt that he was brave because he would go to great lengths to defend his clients, no matter what obstacles stood in front of him. However, in a rare moment of clarity he now understood what true courage was. True courage was standing up for what was right, no matter the consequences. It was looking injustice in the eye and telling it to back down. As he stared at Jessica, he knew just what the right thing to do was and he knew he didn't have the courage to do it.

"Yes, we do," Allan responded quietly, hoping that Shea would be able to forgive him for what he had done.

■ ■ ■

Shea arrived early to night *seder*. Normally, he found it hard to get there on time; after getting home late from work he wanted to spend as much time as he could with Shira before venturing out to learn with his *chavrusa*, Danny Abramson. Shira and Shea would spend the time discussing each other's hectic days and sharing their individual successes and failures. But Shira still wasn't talking to him, so there was nothing to keep him at home.

Shea had come home early from work, hoping to reconcile with his wife, but to no avail. As soon as he entered the house, he was greeted by a foreign and eerie sound: silence. Shea soon discovered that his wife had put the two younger children to bed, and the eldest child, Yehuda, was sitting in his room reading. When Shea had asked Yehuda where his mother was, Yehuda responded that his mother had told him that she had a headache and needed to lie down. While his son may have thought that his mother was ailing, Shea knew the truth. In all their years of marriage, Shea had never known Shira to ever lie down because of a headache. She would never give in to the pain and would do anything to prevent herself from falling into bed. However, Shea reasoned to himself, the pain of a broken heart was too strong. Shea had thought about entering his bedroom to speak to his hurting wife, but decided against it. He gave Yehuda a kiss goodnight and drove to shul to learn.

As Shea entered the *beis medrash* and saw all the familiar faces he cringed. Even though the judge had issued a gag order, he knew that it was only a matter of time before the whole community found out who Shea Berman really was. The kind smiles that people flashed him would soon turn to angry glares and there was nothing that Shea could do about it.

Shea found his seat, opened his *gemara* and started to learn. Often, reviewing the previous day's cases made it challenging for Shea concentrate on his learning, but tonight Shea pushed everything out of his mind. The last thing he wanted to think about was Khalid al-Jinn or Michael Reeves. He only wanted to think about the *sugya* of *Eidim Zommeim*, which he and Danny were learning. He found himself truly enjoying himself, until his concentration was broken by somebody grabbing his shoulder.

"Reb Shea, how are you doing?" asked a middle-aged man with a short beard.

"Well, until you interrupted me, I was doing great, Motti"

"I am sorry," Motti apologized. "Were you learning?"

"You sound shocked," Shea remarked. "Are you trying to say that I never learn?"

"I didn't mean to insinuate anything. Of course I know that you learn, it's just that sometimes ... well ... I don't want to *chas v'shalom* ...."

"Don't worry, Motti, I'm just giving you a hard time."

Motti Holland was one of Shea's oldest friends. They had known each other since elementary school and had grown up across the street from one another.

"Look, Shea, I know that you and Danny are close, but when is the last time that you guys actually sat down to learn?"

"I think it may have been a couple of weeks ago," Shea was forced to admit.

"So why don't you join the *kollel*, already?"

Motti had started a night *kollel* in Shea's shul. He gave a *chaburah* once a week and arranged for all the participants to have *chavrusas*. Ever since it opened, Motti had been trying to convince Shea to join.

"You know the answer to that question," Shea responded. "I can't commit to anything right now. My schedule is too hectic."

"But you aren't learning with Danny either."

"It isn't all his fault. I miss just as often as he does."

"I'm not placing the blame on anybody. All I am saying is that as long as you continue to learn with Danny, neither of you is going to get any learning done."

"Here comes Danny now. Let me speak to him and we'll see."

Motti gave Danny a pleasant nod and returned to his seat.

"Hello there, counselor," Danny addressed Shea. "I think a *kiddush* might be in order."

"Why is that?"

"Because we're both at night *seder*. Not a very common occurrence."

"I know," Shea replied. "Motti was just talking to me about it. Trying to get me to join his night *kollel*. I told him that right now I can't commit to anything. My job is just too time-consuming and unpredictable."

"The hardest-working attorney in New York," Danny joked. "Any new great cases?"

Shea looked at Danny with suspicion. *Does he know what is going on in the al-Jinn case,* he wondered. It didn't seem likely, but Shea wasn't taking any chances.

"Have you heard anything about the trial of Rabbi Felder's attacker?" Shea asked.

"Nothing," Danny answered.

"Nothing? The man who lives on the Jewish blogs doesn't know anything about the trial of the century?"

"I gave up the blogs."

"What! When?"

"As soon as I heard Rabbi Felder was in the hospital. I tried to think of a way to help him, but I couldn't. Everybody was *davening* and making *kabbalos,* and I wanted to do something. I wanted to take on something that would be difficult for me but not impossible and then I thought about the blogs. I thought about all the time that I have wasted and all the *lashon hara* that I have read and I made my decision. As long as Rabbi Felder was in the hospital, I wasn't going to read a single blog or news article. I've been blog free ever since."

Shea regarded his friend with admiration. For some time Danny had been addicted to the blog sites. Whether it was Therealhock.com or Frumnewstoday.net, Danny would spend hours looking up the latest gossip. For him to give that up was no easy feat, and Shea saw his friend's love and dedication for their rebbi shining through. Thinking about the past few days, Shea felt ashamed of himself. Ever since his rebbi had been attacked, he'd spent the entire time worrying about himself — and hardly sparing a thought for his rebbi's suffering. Shea knew that he loved Rabbi Felder at least as much as Danny, but his recent actions told a different story.

"Wow," Shea said, a wistful note in his voice, "that is really impressive. I'm sure that rebbi would be really proud of you."

"It's nothing," Danny shrugged off the praise. "Everybody

reacts to tragedies in their own way. I am sure that you are doing your part to make sure that rebbi has a speedy and total recovery."

If you only knew, Shea thought.

"By the way, I did receive an email today," Danny continued. "It was from Josh Silver's office."

"The councilman? What do they want?"

"It seems that the trial will be starting soon, and they wanted to make sure that everybody knows what they are planning for the first day of the trial."

"And what are they planning?" Shea asked, trying to mask his anxiety.

"They are arranging a major rally at the courthouse, and are inviting everybody to join. Busloads from up and down the eastern seaboard will be participating."

"What are they rallying about?" Shea asked, his voice barely audible.

"The theme of the rally is 'Jewish Unity.' Silver is trying to use the attack on Rabbi Felder as an example of the extreme anti-Semitism that exists throughout the world, and even here in America. His office says they are expecting over ten thousand people to attend the rally."

Shea shook his head in dismay. If he ever had a hope of keeping his new client a secret, the rally just killed it.

"You aren't going to go, are you?" Shea asked.

"You're kidding, right? Of course I am going to go. It's going to be a madhouse. You know how Silver is. He'll be flying off the handle, screaming and yelling slogans, and I am going to enjoy watching every minute of it. But seriously, you can't forget that this is all for rebbi. I mean, can you imagine ten thousand people saying *Tehillim* together for him? It will be unbelievable! Besides, all the *rabbanim* are encouraging people to go. Aren't you going to be there?"

Shea eyed Danny. He badly wanted to tell Danny what was really going on, but how could he? Danny wouldn't understand and Shea didn't blame him.

"I wouldn't miss it for the world," Shea said, with hint of dread in his voice.

S HEA STARED AT HIS MONITOR AND TRIED TO FIGURE OUT his next move. He knew that he should have been preparing for jury selection, but he had another pressing matter on his mind. Ever since Allan had told him that Brad Jenkins, the firm's top investigator, would not be available, Shea felt lost. According to the discovery provided by the prosecution, they would call three witnesses: the forensic expert, the arresting police officer, and an eyewitness. Shea needed information on the police officer and the eyewitness, and that is where an investigator would help. But due to the Merzeir lawsuit, all of the firm's investigators were occupied. Shea had nowhere to turn.

As he struggled to find options, a solution came to mind. It was unorthodox, but desperate times called for desperate measures. Shea took his phone, located the number, and dialed.

"*Hola, amigo,*" an excited voice answered on the second ring.

"Hector, how are you?" Shea asked.

"*Muy bien.* How are you, my friend?"

"Just fine," Shea responded. "How are the wife and kids?"

"Can't complain. Hector Jr. and Hectorina both have the flu right now. So it is a little *loco* in my *casa.*"

Hector Ramirez had been one of Shea's first clients and also one of his most memorable. Hector had been running his own private investigation firm in Far Rockaway. He generally serviced high-end businesses that were suspicious of their employees' behavior. In most cases, the employers thought that their employees were stealing, and it was Hector's job to catch them in the act. Hector was good at his job and for the most part he kept out of trouble — until nine months before Hector met Shea.

It seemed that Hector's newest client, Finest Cut Steakhouse, suspected that one of their chefs, Carl Osborne, was stealing their recipes and selling them to their competitors. They were willing to pay Hector twenty thousand dollars to get the proof that they needed. Hector was not going to let an opportunity like that go to waste, and he lost no time staking out Carl's home. Through his high-tech binoculars, Hector saw Carl walk through the door after a day's work, take out a flash drive, and copy the contents onto his computer. Hector was convinced that Carl was copying recipes. But the steakhouse wanted proof, not theories, so Hector waited until Carl left the house, and then proceeded to try to acquire that proof. He opened a window on the first floor and climbed into Carl's house. In his haste, Hector had bungled when he tried to disarm the alarm system. Within minutes, he was surrounded by five police officers brandishing handcuffs.

Hector arrived at Shea's cubicle the next day, out on bail and desperately needing representation. What Hector failed to tell Shea was that this wasn't his first arrest for breaking and entering. Hector had been caught two times before and the prosecution was looking to put Hector behind bars for a long time. Shea, through some shrewd negotiating, was able to keep Hector out of jail, provided that he closed his PI firm and agreed never to practice as an investigator again. Hector was happy to oblige, telling Shea that he'd found another calling instead. Two months later, to Shea's surprise, Hector opened up his own steakhouse featuring some of the best recipes in town.

"Tell me, *muchacho*, what I can do for you?" Hector asked.

"Well, I need a favor," Shea began.

"For you, I would do anything," Hector interrupted. "I still remember what you did for me. I tried to get you to come to my restaurant, but you never do. Whattsa matter, food not good enough for you?"

"I told you Hector, I only eat kosher, and your restaurant doesn't serve kosher."

"What do you mean? I told you that I would even get a rabbi to bless the food. Anyway, what do you need me to do?"

Shea smiled. Hector meant well and Shea knew that he would be able to count on him. But Shea wanted him to know what he was in for before he agreed.

"First hear me out, before you start agreeing."

"Shoot, *amigo*."

"Have you heard about that rabbi who was attacked last week?"

"Of course. It was all over the news and it made me very upset. I may be a Christian, but my *padre* and my *madre* always taught me to respect religious men, no matter what religion they practice."

"Well, I have been asked to defend the alleged attacker."

"Ouch, *hombre*," Hector responded. "How you get saddled with that one?"

"Don't ask," Shea replied. "All you need to know is that I really have no choice and that is the only reason why I am defending this guy."

"I know you Shea. You are *un hombre muy honorable* and if you are defending this guy, you must have a good reason."

"Thank you Hector, you have no idea how much that means to me."

"*Me placer*, so what can I do for you?"

"Well, right now my firm is involved in a major lawsuit and all of its resources are being devoted to that suit. Because my case is pro bono, there are no investigators available to help me. "

"You want me to go back in the game? Don't you remember the plea deal? If I break the rules, I go to prison."

"Do you think that I would put your freedom at risk? I looked over the details of the agreement. It specifically says that you are not allowed to act as a private investigator for hire. It says nothing about your ability to volunteer as a PI."

"So you want me to get some dirt on some witnesses and you're telling me that I won't go to prison?"

"As long as you don't do anything illegal while getting the information."

"*Excellente!*" Hector exclaimed. "When do I start? Can I start now?"

"What about the business?"

"You kidding me? It doesn't take a rocket scientist to run a restaurant. Besides, my brother, Manuel, runs the daily operations. Me, I just collect the money."

"What about your kids? Aren't they sick?"

"More reason to get out of the house. They are driving me crazy."

"Great," Shea said. "I'll email you whatever I have on the witnesses. Then you do your magic."

"*No problemo. Hasta mañana.*"

"Have a great one too, Hector and thanks again."

Shea hung up and opened a file on his laptop. He studied the names of potential jurors. Normally, Shea found, jury selections were routine and went smoothly. But, as Shea was about to find out, nothing about this case was going to go smoothly.

■ ■ ■

Michael Reeves reviewed the notes on his desk. Moshe was meticulous, and without his well-kept records, Michael would have been lost. Still, Michael had some questions and he needed Moshe to answer them. He shot Moshe an email and asked him to come to his office as soon as possible. Minutes later, when Michael heard a knock at his door, he thought it was Moshe and shouted to him to enter. When he saw who the visitor was, he jumped up from his seat.

"Senator Reynolds," Michael greeted the visitor with a hand-shake. "This is an honor."

Senator Mark Reynolds was the Democratic Senator for the

State of New York. He had served in the Senate for over twenty years and headed both the Commerce Committee and Homeland Security. But, more important to Michael Reeves, he was the chairman of the New York office of the Democratic Party.

"Sit down, Mike," Senator Reynolds said with a smile. "I am not your priest or a judge; you don't need to rise for me."

Michael waved the senator to the most comfortable chair in the office. "So what brings you here?" Michael asked.

Senator Reynolds paused before answering. He looked remarkably fit for a man of his age. His silver hair was perfectly groomed and Michael couldn't see a wrinkle anywhere on his face. If there was ever a person who looked like the quintessential politician, Michael thought, it was Senator Reynolds.

"It seems that you have a pretty big case on your hands," the Senator remarked.

"Nothing that I can't handle."

"That is exactly what I think. We need confidence in our leaders. No more excuses, just results. Do you understand what I am trying to say to you?"

Michael wasn't sure where the senator was going with this, but like most politicians the senator liked to talk and Michael wasn't about to deprive him of that pleasure.

"You see, Michael, it's a crazy world out there. Chairing Homeland Security affords me access to certain information that if it were to ever see the light of day, would cause complete and total panic throughout the country. Do you know how many threats our nation receives daily from our enemies?"

"I have no idea," Michael responded meekly.

"Too many too count. Can you believe that? That means, if not for our excellent defense services, our country could be under attack every day. That is a scary thought. But let me tell you an even scarier thought. Most of the threats that we face are from those who work and live within our borders. Nowadays our enemies aren't camping in some cave out in the middle of nowhere. They are living in New York and in Los Angeles and even in Washington D.C. Do you know how that makes the American people feel?"

Michael was about to respond, but Reynolds continued speaking as if Michael weren't in the room.

"They are scared and they have a right to be. We need to show the American people that we are stronger than these cowards, and you, Mike, are the key."

At the sound of his name, Michael listened more attentively.

"Me, sir?"

"Yes, you," Reynolds responded. "And I will tell you why. I'll bet that you can't tell me what the biggest problem is for the Democratic Party today."

"The failing economy?" Michael ventured.

"No, that we can blame on the Republicans. The greatest threat to our beloved party is the former president of the United States, George W. Bush."

"Bush? You must be kidding."

"I'm absolutely serious, Mike. One thing that George Bush brought to our country, besides two wars, was a sense of invincibility. Any country that would dare to start up with us, George Bush would go all-out cowboy on them, and the American people would feel safe. John Brady is a great man and a better president than George Bush could ever be. But people aren't afraid of him. Our enemies laugh at his threats and that makes us look weak. But you have a chance to change that, Michael."

"How?"

"Right now you have a terrorist on trial. Sure, he didn't blow himself up, but he attacked an innocent American and he needs to be punished for it. Imagine what will happen if you — a proudly Democratic DA — are able to send this barbarian away for the rest of his life. People would no longer look at our party as being weak. They will see that we are the ones who are going to wrest the power away from the terrorists. That we are the ones who are instilling the sense of invincibility in America. And you are the one who is making the streets safe for our children to walk and play."

Michael was speechless, but that was the way that most people responded after a sonnet by Senator Reynolds. Did he believe every word that the senator said? No. During his years as the DA, Michael had been able to weed out the liars and he knew when somebody was telling a fish tale. But that didn't stop him from hanging on to every word the senator uttered.

"Have you ever contemplated a life in politics?" Reynolds asked.

"What do you mean?" Michael asked, confused by the unexpected turn in the conversation.

"I mean do you see yourself as a DA for the rest of your life, or do you have higher political aspirations?"

"Well, I haven't really thought about it," Michael prevaricated. In truth, ever since Michael had been voted into the DA's office, he had had his eyes set on more high-powered positions in government.

"Come on, Mike, me and you both know that isn't true. You were born to be a leader. I have had my eye on you for a long time."

"You have?"

"You aren't just a DA. You are a DA in the most dynamic city in the world. You exude power with every law that you uphold and every criminal that you put away. I see a very bright future for you. I could even see you occupying the governor's mansion one day."

"Charles Edwards is doing a fine job now."

"Charles Edwards?" Reynolds responded in disbelief. "Charles Edwards is a lame duck and everybody knows it. Besides the fact that he is older than me, all of his policies have failed miserably. He hasn't even been able to pass a new budget. The Assembly is still working with the old budget that preceded him before he got into office. Next year's election is going to bring about a change and I am here to make sure that change will keep our party in office."

"What makes you so sure that I could be the governor?"

"You are young, you are fair, and most importantly, you are great at what you do. Nothing breeds success like more success."

Michael couldn't believe what he was hearing. He had always

dreamed of this day and Reynolds was about to make his dreams a reality.

"Let me put it to you straight," Reynolds said, extending his hand. "Put away this monster and I'll make sure that you have the full support of the Democratic Party when you run for governor next year."

"I will make it happen," Michael said confidently. "You can count on me."

"I knew I could," Reynolds declared as walked to the door.

When Reynolds left the room Michael stood up and pumped his fist into the air. *Can't wait to see what Allan Shore will think of me when I am governor,* he thought. *He won't be able to throw his fancy suits and rich clients in my face anymore.*

Michael's moment of euphoria was interrupted by a knock at the door.

"You wanted to see me, boss?" Moshe Cohen asked.

Michael debated whether to tell his assistant about Reynolds' visit. Moshe was bright, but he was also still a young idealistic attorney who wouldn't understand the political angle. No, better to keep this under wraps.

"I need some help regarding page sixty of your notes. Can you clarify what you are referring to in paragraph six?"

Moshe proceeded to explain the details to Michael, but Reeves was listening with half an ear. His concentration was devoted to his conversation with Senator Reynolds and the life that would be waiting for him after he put al-Jinn away. If sticking it to Allan Shore and beating Crane, Gardner, and Scott hadn't been enough of an incentive to win, becoming the next governor surely was.

Michael Reeves wasn't going to let anything stand in his way.

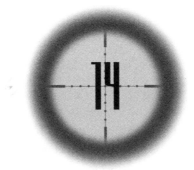

HENRI JOSEPH WALKED THE COBBLESTONE STREETS OF Neuilly-sur-Seine. As one of France's wealthiest developers, Henri was able to call this quaint and old-time suburb of Paris home. Only the wealthiest Frenchmen could afford real estate in this small suburb. For Henri and his multibillion dollar fortune, there was no better place to live.

Passing the Pavilion de Wurtenberg he saw a young couple wheeling their baby in a brand-new designer stroller. As he listened closely, he was able to hear the wife's complaints about the shortcomings of her staff of twelve, and he chuckled to himself. *They think these are problems,* Henri thought. *How about growing up without any food to eat or no heat to warm your house? How about being the laughingstock of your school because of your ragged clothing?* The people of Neuilly-sur-Seine knew nothing of that kind of life. Most of the residents had been born into wealth; their parents either had royalty in their blood or old-time money handed down from the times of Napoleon. Henri Joseph had neither. He had amassed his fortune through a series of wise business deals, and now was deemed one of the wealthiest men in France — indeed, in the world.

Although listening to those over-privileged yuppies whine about their petty problems often irritated him, Henri enjoyed the solitude and anonymity that Neuilly-sur-Siene provided. It was because of this obscurity that Henri was able to lead his double life: one as Henri Joseph, real estate developer, successful investor, and philanthropist; and one as Fareed al-Zilzal, financier of terrorism.

It hadn't always been this way. Born to a prosperous, assimilated Jewish family in Egypt, Henri had enjoyed a peaceful and pleasant childhood that came to an abrupt and fearful end with Israel's participation in the Suez Crisis. The little Jewish boy, ripped from his Arabic-speaking milieu and his luxurious existence, found himself and his family refugees from Egypt's anti-Israel violence in one of Paris' teeming slums, eating one nutritious meal a day in a kosher soup kitchen, making do with scraps and handouts the rest of the time.

In a twist that would have given great pleasure to psychologists looking for interesting cases (they wouldn't find one in Henri; as a child he'd been too poor to go for therapy; as an adult he was far too confident, and way too close-mouthed) young Henri turned his rage at his new and difficult life not onto the Muslims who had driven his family from their home after generations, but at his Jewish brethren. He had wonderful memories of his Arab school friends and the life he'd lived under Muslim rule. It was only when forced into a Jewish slum that life had turned sour. Somehow, his childish mind linked the two: misery and Jews.

As a young adult, Henri had cut himself off completely from his family and his roots. For decades he turned his considerable intellect, unyielding determination, and frightening lack of conscience to the goal of becoming a wealthy Frenchman. It was only recently, though, with his billions secure in banks in Switzerland and the Cayman Islands, and real estate and media holdings all over the globe, that he'd taken an interest in radical Islam.

It was when he had gone to the Gaza Strip aboard a flotilla that he begun to seriously believe in jihad. The flotilla had been turned back, but Henri had made his way overland via Egypt. When he saw the dire poverty of the Gazan Palestinians he remembered the gnawing pangs of hunger that he too had suffered, and he identified almost completely with the Palestinians.

Initially he only wanted to help financially, and he asked the organizer of the flotilla where he should address the first check. The organizer had told him that if he really wanted to help he needed to learn more about the cause. Interested, Henri met various Muslims who lived the life of jihad. Within a short while Henri was hooked, and he decided to adopt Islam as his religion. He changed his name to Fareed and began to research the best way to attack the Zionists who, he truly believed, were behind all the misery of the Middle East.

He searched for months, but found nothing that piqued his interest. Sure, there were opportunities to fund suicide bombers who could cause casualties and wreak havoc, but he knew the Israeli mentality too well. A few bombings wouldn't stop them. They would just go on as if nothing had happened. He wanted to do something big. He wanted to bring pain to the Israeli people, pain from which that they would never recover, and he wouldn't rest until he did so.

And then, finally, with one unexpected phone call, he found it.

As he stopped to rest on a carved bench in one of the gem-like local parks, he tried to put everything into perspective. Even though he had received a disturbing phone call from Rasheed, he was confident that the situation was being handled and that the mission would continue as planned. But if Rasheed was having reservations, there might be more issues that needed to be dealt with. He opened his cell phone but closed it immediately. Even though the couple next to him was more concerned with their domestic problems than the issues of the well-dressed, obviously wealthy Frenchman seated near them, Henri wasn't taking chances. His office was only a few blocks away and it was there that he would make the calls that would ensure that his mission would be a disastrous success.

■ ■ ■

The oppressive August sun bore down on the orange and guava orchards in Sargodha, Pakistan. The farmer, Ibrahim Yusuf, tended to his fruits like a father tends to his children. A simple man, Ibrahim was devoted to growing and harvesting his extraordinary fruits. Ibrahim was a man of intrinsic faith, and he spent his spare time, whenever he wasn't farming, reading from the Koran and praying. In a time when computers and technology ran the world, it was rare that a man would be content farming his land and living a pure and simple life. But for Ibrahim, that was all that he desired.

Walking home under the blazing sun for his afternoon rest, Ibrahim's thoughts wandered to his son. Ibrahim had tried so hard to show him the beauty of the simple life, but Jabril was mesmerized by modernity. He wanted to be educated and become wealthy like the American celebrities that he saw on the screen in the town's lone movie theater. Ibrahim had tried to teach Jabril that the lives of the Americans were empty and full of sadness, but Jabril wouldn't listen. He only wanted to be like them.

Rather than lose his son, Ibrahim had sent him to the finest school in Karachi. It was there that Jabril decided to pursue another dream: to become a teacher, rather than a Hollywood star. He told his father that he wanted to repair all the damage that was being done to youth throughout the world. He wanted to teach children to love life and not hate their enemies.

Ibrahim could not help but be proud of his son. Even when Jabril told him that he was moving to America to turn his dreams into reality, Ibrahim was sad but understanding. Jabril was a good man, and Ibrahim trusted him to make the right decisions.

As he sat at his simple wooden table, he reread Jabril's last letter. In the digital age, Ibrahim still believed in the power of the written word. Jabril had tried to convince his father to get a computer. He had told his father that with a computer Jabril would be able to send him letters much more quickly. If Ibrahim wanted to see pictures of his grandchildren, who were growing and changing every day, a computer was the way to go. But Ibrahim resisted. He wanted to preserve his way of life. Still, after intense pressure from Jabril, Ibrahim had finally caved in and bought a telephone. Ibrahim told his son that he would look forward to hearing the joyous voices of Jabril and his family. They usually spoke once a week, but this week Ibrahim had not heard from his son. He was slightly anxious, but he brushed off his concerns. Jabril was probably just busy preparing lessons to teach his students.

Ibrahim heard a voice calling his name from the road. There was a sense of urgency in the voice that sent him rushing to the door. A boy of about twelve dashed in, panting heavily. Wordlessly, he handed Ibrahim a newspaper.

Ibrahim glanced at the front page, dropped the paper to the floor, and ran to the phone. He dialed the number that he had memorized. No answer. He tried the number four more times, and understood that there would be no answer.

He looked up at the sun, which was high in the sky. There was still time to catch the daily bus to Karachi. He threw a couple of things into a bag and headed for the bus stop. He knew it was madness, to leave with no plan, no idea of what to do. But he knew that this was what he had to do.

SHEA ARRIVED IN THE COURTROOM, THIS TIME MAKING sure to be early. As it turned out, neither Michael Reeves nor Judge Daniels was there, so Shea had a few minutes to think. He remembered his first-year law professor telling him that a lawyer was only as good as his jury; if you chose the right jury, you stood a great chance of winning. With all the odds stacked against him in this case, Shea knew that picking a good jury was vital.

The jury selection process, known as *voir dire*, was a basic procedure of questioning potential jurors in order to ascertain their competence to be seated on a jury for a trial. While it was usually routine, Shea was aware that because of the intense media influence that this case was going to generate, Judge Daniels was going to do whatever he could to make sure that the members of this jury could be impartial and unbiased toward Shea's client.

There was another aspect of jury selection that Shea needed to focus on. Of course, it was important for the jury not to be biased against Shea's client, but he also needed to find jurors who would be sympathetic toward al-Khalid. While he didn't expect any juror to actually agree with what his client had allegedly done, Shea needed to find potential jurors who would listen to Shea's arguments and not judge his client before the case even began. More important, he needed to find jurors to whom he could connect. Shea had to find the juror who would smile at his jokes and be appalled at his various accusations of police mistreatment. The problem was that Shea didn't have much time with the jurors, and he needed to base his decisions solely on how the various potential jurors answered the judge's questions.

Looking at his watch, Shea saw that the proceedings were about to begin. He quickly jotted down a few questions that he wanted Judge Daniels to ask the prospective jurors, questions that would help him weed out the biased and partial jurors. If the judge chose not to ask these questions, Shea would object and if needed would use his objection as a basis for an appeal should it be necessary. There was also the matter of the ten challenges that Shea had at his disposal. Even if the jurors were able to answer the judge's questions to his satisfaction, Shea still had the right to dismiss ten potential jurors without citing a reason. This, Shea knew, was a dangerous game, for if he started to use his challenges, the prosecution could use their six challenges and remove jurors that Shea found favorable. It was like a high-stakes game of poker and Shea needed to be prepared for anything.

He was so deep in thought that he didn't realize that Michael Reeves had already arrived and was seated at the prosecution table. Shea rose from his chair to greet his counterpart.

"Mr. Reeves," Shea addressed him while extending his hand, "I have heard a lot about you from my superiors and I'm looking forward to this trial."

Michael ignored Shea's outstretched hand and addressed him coldly. "At least Allan was right about one thing. It does seem that you are a nice guy."

"When did you speak to Allan?"

"He didn't tell you?"

"Didn't tell me what?"

"It figures," Michael reasoned. "He probably didn't want to hurt your feelings."

"Why would my feelings be hurt?" Shea wondered, confused at the turn this conversation had taken.

"Look, I will put this as straight as possible. Allan came to my office and asked me to recuse myself."

"He did? He never told me about that."

"Of course he didn't. He was obviously afraid that I would embarrass you in court. He didn't want you to go into this trial knowing that he had absolutely no confidence in you. So when I told him no, he probably pretended that nothing had happened and went on, business as usual."

Shea turned away from Michael. He didn't want the DA to see his disappointment. *Why would Allan do that*, Shea wondered. *If I am supposed to use this trial as a way to prove myself, why would he ask Michael to step down?* Unless what Michael was saying were true — and that frightened Shea even more. If Allan had no confidence in him, what was the chance that the board would be impressed enough to keep him?

"Look, I am sorry, " Michael said, softening his tone, "that I had to be the one to break the news to you, but you need to know who you are fighting for when you are argue in front of that jury. You have to ask yourself the question, is this all really worth it? Because if it isn't, you might as well get out right now."

Shea mulled over Michael's words. Though he didn't think that Michael was lying about meeting with Allan, he definitely doubted Michael's motives in telling him about it. While Michael wanted Shea to believe that he was telling him all this for his own good, Shea knew that Michael was trying to get Shea to lose his focus. No matter what Allan had said or felt, Shea needed to pick a jury and he couldn't let anything affect his concentration.

Before he could frame a suitable answer to Reeves, Judge Daniels entered the courtroom. Both attorneys returned to their places.

"All rise for the Honorable Judge Daniels," the bailiff announced. "This court is now in session. Judge Andrew Daniels presiding."

"All be seated," the judge ordered. "Mr. Reeves, I am pleased that you were able to join our proceedings on such short notice."

"Although it was my desire to have an ADA try this case," Michael replied, glaring at Shea, "the defense has made that impossible. But I am happy to be able to help in any way possible. Especially if it means putting that monster in jail for the rest of his life."

Shea exclaimed, "My client has not been convicted of anything. Therefore, I take offense to the prosecutor's assumption that he is guilty. Additionally, my client is not a monster and I would appreciate if Mr. Reeves could refrain from using any derogatory terms when referring to my client."

"Mr. Berman, while you have raised fair points, I would like you to remember that the jury has not been seated and the trial has not begun. Therefore, there is no need to raise any objections. Unless you are afraid that I will be influenced by the accusations of the prosecutor, and if that is the case, then we can schedule a private meeting in my chambers."

"I am sorry," Shea apologized, realizing his mistake. "I didn't mean to imply that Your Honor would be influenced by the rantings of the prosecutor."

"I am sure that you didn't. However, I would like to remind Mr. Reeves that as soon as the jury is seated, such references will not be tolerated in my courtroom. And if they do continue, I will have no problem finding you in contempt. Is that understood?"

"Perfectly, Your Honor," Michael answered sheepishly.

Shea looked at Michael and then at the judge. While he originally thought that Daniels was going to give him a hard time, he was happy to see that Reeves wasn't beyond reproach. It seemed to Shea that the judge was going to prove difficult for both the prosecution and the defense, and that was perfectly fine. As long as the prosecution got the same tongue-lashing as the defense.

"Now that we have got that matter out of the way," the judge continued, "are we ready to pick a jury?"

"Yes," Reeves and Shea responded in unison.

"Good. Bailiff, please call down to the jury room and request that the potential jurors be brought to the courtroom."

Shea shifted his focus from the judge to the courtroom doors. In a matter of moments, forty-five people would wend their way into the courtroom and seat themselves in the gallery right behind the lawyers. Shea knew that in those precious few moments he could learn a lot about the jury, without any of them saying a word.

Allan had always told him that the key to reading a jury was first to weed out the jurors that you didn't want. Shea knew that many jurors would be excused based on their responses to the *voir dire* questions of the judge. But what about the ones whose answers weren't objectionable? For those jurors, Shea would need to observe their body language and facial expressions. If a juror looked bored and disinterested, he would normally blame the defense, because he didn't want to be on the jury and he was angry at the defendant for making him be there. If a juror was happy when he walked in that usually meant that he wanted to be part of the justice system; that was a juror that Shea wanted on the jury. If Shea would be able to poke holes in the prosecution's case, it was those jurors who would find his client innocent. A simple smile or nod from a juror could tell Shea volumes.

A few moments later, the potential jurors were seated and Shea went to work. He saw two women wearing burkas and immediately crossed them off his mental list. It wasn't that he didn't want them on his jury. Shea would have loved to have them on his side. But he knew that the prosecutor would likely use his challenges on those jurors if they survived the *voir dire* process.

Once all the potential jurors were seated, the judge addressed them.

"Good morning, ladies and gentleman. My name is Judge Andrew Daniels and I would like to thank you for being here today. The beauty of the American legal system is that when a defendant is called to trial he isn't solely judged by a cold-hearted bureaucrat like myself."

Many of the jurors smiled at the comment of the judge. However, there were some who didn't. Shea made a note of who they were.

"He is judged," the judge continued, "by his peers. People like him who get up every day and trudge though the daily grind like he does. This allows every defendant to get a fair trial and that is what makes our legal system the best in the world. I, together with the attorneys present today, thank you for your service and for taking part in our wonderful legal system."

Most of the jurors nodded, which was to be expected.

"While I would like to say that all of you would make wonderful jurors," the judge continued, "due to certain circumstances, some beyond your control, you may not be able to be a juror on this case. Therefore, we will now embark on a process called *voir dire*. This process will comprise a series of questions that I will ask to all of you. Depending on your answers we will decide whether or not you will serve on this jury. Do we all understand?"

Everyone nodded.

"Good, so let us begin." The judge proceeded to discuss the details of the case and explain the charges that were being brought. He then asked if any of the members of the jury had heard of the case before arriving in the courtroom. If they had, the judge asked them whether or not they would still be able to make an impartial judgement. A few of the jurors said no and the judge asked them to approach the bench. After seeing that their reasons made sense, the judge dismissed them and thanked them for their service. Then they left the courtroom.

This process repeated itself as the judge continued asking questions. Some of the questions were routine, dealing with whether the jurors had any previous relationship with the attorneys or the defendant. Anyone who answered in the affirmative was automatically excused.

When the judge started to ask questions based on each juror's political and judicial beliefs, Shea began to take notes.

"As a general position, do you believe that a police officer is more likely to tell the truth than a civilian witness?"

One of the jurors, an African American named Malcolm Thomas, answered first. "I don't believe anybody."

"Would you care to explain?" the judge requested.

"Sure. I believe that everybody is a liar until I know otherwise. Everybody lies, that is my credo. I don't care who is giving the testimony. It could be a police officer, doctor, even the pope himself. They all lie and I always know if someone is lying."

Shea took out a pen and noted Malcolm's name. This was a juror Shea wanted. Because Shea's whole case was based on disproving the state's case, and not on proving al-Jinn's innocence, a cynical juror like Malcolm Thomas was perfect and Shea knew that all it took was one juror to free his client.

As the judge continued, Shea hoped that Malcolm would survive the weeding-out process. The prosecution was only allowed six challenges, and Shea had a feeling he knew who Michael was going to use them on: the two women wearing burkas and four more men who openly said that they distrusted the government and felt that too many people were being sent to prison. If Malcolm was able to survive the *voir dire* process, Shea would have his one juror whom he felt might free his client.

Those hopes were dashed with the next question that the judge asked.

"Have any of you or a friend or relative of yours ever been accused of committing a serious crime?"

Again, Malcolm was the first to answer. "Sure. My brother was accused of vehicular manslaughter, about five years ago."

"What was the verdict?" Daniels inquired.

"The judge found him guilty and put him away for ten years. But he wasn't guilty."

"How did you know that?"

"Because I was in the car when the accident happened. It was me, my brother, and some white guy named Charles Spencer. Charles was the driver and he was drunk as a sailor. But you see, that isn't the way the police said it went down."

"I don't understand," Daniels interrupted. "If what you are saying is true, why wasn't Mr. Spencer behind the wheel when the police came?"

"I know that you don't understand," Malcolm said, clearly annoyed. "Charlie was driving, and he crossed over the double lines and went head-on into another car. Because of the impact, both my brother and Charlie were thrown through the windshield. It's a miracle they survived. When the cops arrived they assumed that my brother had been driving and they arrested him."

"But why couldn't you testify for your brother?"

"He didn't have any money and his court-appointed attorney thought that since I was his brother, I wouldn't be a credible witness. Oh, one thing I forgot to mention: Charles Spencer was never questioned and it just happens to be that his father is a judge."

Shea's jaw dropped when he heard the last line. There was no way that Judge Daniels was going to allow Malcolm Thomas to be a juror and Shea knew it.

"I am sorry for your experience and I hope that your brother does receive justice," Judge Daniels said, clearly keeping his emotions in check. "However, you can understand why I have to ask you to excuse yourself from the jury."

Malcolm Thomas nodded and rose from his chair to exit the room. Shea tried to hide his disappointment, but Reeves could not suppress a grin.

As the questioning continued, Shea took notes on the various jurors that he planned to dismiss or retain. While there weren't any obvious winners like Malcolm Thomas, Shea still felt that if he played his challenges correctly, he could end up with a jury that might be sympathetic to his client.

Once the judge had finished asking the questions, Shea spoke.

"I would ask the judge to please ask the panel question three on the list that I provided. I feel it is very important to see if any of the jurors had ever been to a pro-Israel rally, as it may establish them as being biased against my client."

"While I appreciate your concern, I must deny that request," Daniels responded.

"Then I would request that this denial be put on the record should an appeal be necessary."

"As I thought you would. It has been recorded if you will need it for an appeal. Mr. Reeves, are there questions that you feel should have been asked that weren't?"

"No, Your Honor. I think that you did a wonderful job and your questions will enable us to seat a fair and honest jury."

"Mr. Reeves, I always appreciate a compliment but there is no need to be so effusive."

Shea smirked at the judge's last comment. It was good to see that he wasn't going to be blinded by Reeves's flattery. However, Shea didn't have much time to enjoy that thought. The jury still had to be chosen and they were entering the final segment, the challenge phase.

Only fifteen people were needed, twelve for the actual jury and three alternates. There were thirty remaining potential jurors. The attorneys could use their challenges and dismiss whichever juror they chose. After the challenges were completed, the final jury would be seated according to the original number that the potential jurors had been assigned when they entered in the courtroom.

Shea looked at his list of the remaining jurors. There were twenty women and ten men remaining. Shea wanted as many men as possible on the jury. Though it wasn't a concrete science, his instincts were screaming to him to seat as many men as possible.

Because four of the men had expressed anti-government views, Shea felt that Michael would use four of his challenges on them. Shea also figured that Michael would use his last remaining challenges on the women wearing the burkas. That would leave Shea with eighteen women and six men. If Shea wanted to have any men on the jury, he would need to use as many challenges as possible on the women. He had observed the women during the *voir dire* process, and nearly all of them had looked sceptically at Shea at least once.

Judge Daniels usually allowed the prosecutor to use his challenges first and Shea waited his turn.

"Mr. Reeves, does the state wish to strike any jurors?"

"Yes, Your Honor. The state wishes to strike jurors five, fourteen, sixteen, nineteen, thirty-one, and thirty-two."

"Thank you, Mr. Reeves," the judge responded. He turned to the gallery and said, "If your number was called, you are excused from this jury and we thank you for your service."

Shea looked at his list and did a double-take. According to his assumptions, Reeves should have used a challenge on juror number twelve, Amir Hakaniny. From what Shea could tell, he was an Arab and would be sympathetic to al-Jinn. So why hadn't Reeves dismissed him from the jury? *It could be that he made a mistake,* Shea thought. But Michael Reeves was good and didn't make mistakes. If he was keeping Hakaniny, that meant that he assumed something about him that Shea didn't realize.

As Shea raised his voice to challenge Hakaniny, he stopped himself. What if Reeves was messing with him and he wanted Shea to waste one of his challenges on Hakaniny? Maybe Hakaniny was really an ideal juror for Shea, and Michael should have used one of his challenges on him. But maybe Michael wanted to strike other jurors and he figured that by leaving Hakaniny, Shea would assume that Hakaniny was sympathetic toward the defense and Shea would opt to strike Hakaniny. Shea's head started to spin as he thought of all the possible scenarios that could have led to Reeves keeping Hakaniny as a juror.

He realized that whatever his decision, it had to be made soon because Daniels was waiting. If there was one thing that Shea had learned, you don't keep the judge waiting.

"Mr. Berman," the judge stated, "would the defense like to strike any jurors?"

"Your Honor," Shea began, "the defense would like to strike juror number twelve."

Amir Hakaniny's eyes rose when he heard his number being called, but he showed no emotion or movement.

"Mr. Hakaniny," the judge addressed him, "the defense has chosen to use one of its challenges on you, and you are therefore excused from the jury. Thank you for your service."

"He can't do this," Hakaniny responded in a heavy Middle Eastern accent.

"Yes he can," the judge corrected him. "The defense is allowed a specified number of challenges and he can use them on whomever he wishes. He need not give a reason for his decision."

"That is not what I am referring to."

"I am not sure that I understand."

"I am saying that he," Hakaniny said, pointing at Shea, "can't defend that monster."

Shea gasped. Even Daniels was startled by Hakaniny's comment. The judge took a moment to regain his composure before replying.

"You are entitled to your opinion. However, this is not the forum in which to express your feelings."

"I am older than you and have lived through a lot more than you have, Mr. Daniels. I would ask you to respect my ability to exercise my first amendment rights."

Shea was shocked. Once a juror had been excused, he was no longer permitted to speak up. But what surprised him more was that Daniels was quiet and it seemed that he was going to allow Hakaniny to continue.

"Mr. Berman," Hakaniny continued, turning to Shea. "As you now know, my name is Amir Hakaniny. I emigrated from Iran right after the revolution, in 1981. You can't imagine the horrors that we experienced during those fearful days. Our freedoms were stripped from us and there was nothing we could do about it. There was a wealthy Jew from our community who had been executed and we were afraid that we would suffer the same fate. So we went to Qom under the pretext of peace, to seek Khomeini's assurance that we would be spared. Once we got there and we saw his true intentions, we realized that our lives would never be the same. The Ayatollah forced all of us to renounce our religion and praise Allah. He said that if we accepted Islam, we would be spared. But if we didn't, we would suffer the same fate as our friend. The next day, my family and I fled Iran to Pakistan. I would love to be able to recount the nightmare that we had experienced. How my younger two children died from the terrible hunger and cold that we had experienced on our journey. Though every step of that horrific journey is forever etched in my mind, the pain is too great to recall."

The courtroom was silent. A few of the women actually dabbed their eyes after hearing Hakaniny's painful words.

"And now, look at you, Mr. Berman. They seek to destroy us.

People like your client will never be happy unless our entire race is annihilated. When you sit there defending this evil man, I see you spitting on the graves of my children. But you are not only spitting on their graves. You are desecrating the memories of all of our brethren who died because they were Jews. How can you defend a person who seeks to destroy us? You are a traitor, Mr. Berman, and I am sorry for you. I would like to pray for your soul, but I am not sure that you have one."

Amir Hakaniny rose from his seat and exited the courtroom, but all eyes were on Shea. This had been the second time in less than a week that he had been humiliated in Judge Daniel's courtroom, and he suspected it wouldn't be the last.

As he looked again at his list Shea realized that he had been right to go with his instinct and strike Hakaniny as a juror. However, after seeing the hurt and pain in Hakaniny's eyes, that provided little consolation.

THE PORT OF KARACHI BUSTLED WITH EXCITEMENT. AS usual, traffic was at a standstill in this city of over twelve million people.

As Ibrahim Yusuf walked toward the harbor, he was overwhelmed by the noise and chaos. When Jabril had been younger, Ibrahim had taken him to visit the port during his vacation. He wasn't interested or impressed by the port's growing economic infrastructure. For Ibrahim, amassing wealth was not important. He wanted to show Jabril the history of this great city. He took him to visit the fort on Manora Island that had been built by the Talpur Mirs of Sindh right by the harbor's entrance. Ibrahim and his son had seen the Mohatta Palace Museum, built by Shivratan Chandraratan Mohatta, the successful entrepreneur, and learned all about the development of Pakistani ceramic crafts dating back thousands of years.

But Jabril was no longer a young child and Ibrahim was definitely not on vacation. He had a very clear idea of what he needed to do, and he knew he could not do it on his own.

Loitering outside the main shipyard, Ibrahim searched for his friend. While he hadn't seen him in many years, Ibrahim hoped that Anwar would not forget him in his time of need. Scanning the throngs of men in uniform, he eventually spotted his old neighbor. When he called out to him, his friend ran over to embrace him.

"Ibrahim," Anwar said in Urdu, "It has been far too long. What brings you to Karachi? How are you?"

"You look good, Anwar. It seems that Allah has been kind to you. How is your family?"

"They are doing well. Hassan is working here at the port with me while Mohamed lives in America. He has a good job and is starting a family. Life here in Karachi is a little different than it was back in Sargodha," Anwar said with a smile, "but we are enjoying it all the same."

Anwar gazed at his longtime friend, at the lines of worry that radiated from his eyes, at the tight lips. His smile faded.

"You have not answered my question, Ibrahim. You have not told me how you are feeling."

Ibrahim sighed, the worry lines growing more prominent. "I can't even explain to you the emotions that I am feeling. Here, read this and you will understand everything."

Ibrahim handed Anwar the copy of the newspaper that he had taken with him from Sargodha. Anwar scanned the front page and his genial countenance melted into a mask of shock and disbelief.

"This can't be true," Anwar said.

"I agree with you. The problem is that the newspaper says it happened."

"But surely you don't believe it."

"I have no idea what to believe. I want to believe that it isn't true, but at the same time, I cannot dismiss these words."

"So what are you going to do?" Anwar wondered

"What choice do I have? I will go to New York and see what is going on."

"New York?" Anwar asked incredulously. "You, who have never left Pakistan, who hardly has left his village, will travel to America? How do you expect to get there?"

"That is why I came to you," Ibrahim replied. "I need your

help getting on a freighter. Surely there is a ship traveling to America. Help me stow away on board and I will be able to get to America."

"Are you insane? I can't sneak you on. The Karachi Port Trust has dedicated itself to preventing stowaways. The freight companies used to complain that security at the harbor was lax and stowaways were sneaking onto the ships. The stowaways would then jump ship as it entered the waters of the United States coastline and gain entry illegally. As a result, surveillance has been tightened. I can't help you."

Ibrahim would not be deterred. "Do you remember that summer night twenty years ago in Sargodha?"

"Of course," Anwar admitted.

"Your son Mohamed had stolen oranges from Ismael bin Salam's orchard."

Anwar could visualize the scene as if it had been yesterday. His crop had failed that year and the family was starving. Young Mohamed tried to sneak into the orchard in the dark of night, but Ismael had caught him climbing the fence.

"Do you remember what they wanted to do to Mohamed?"

Anwar shivered despite the Pakistani heat. "How could I forget? Ismael grabbed him by the arm and dragged him to our house. After waking me, Ismael took out his blade. Mohamed was only six years old, but that didn't matter to him. The punishment for stealing is cutting off the hand and Ismael wanted to make sure that justice was served."

"So I am sure that you remember what I did that night," Ibrahim said quietly.

"You heard the commotion in my house and you ran over. You told Ismael that you would repay Mohamed's debt tenfold if he would let Mohamed go. Ismael released my son and we never heard about that incident again."

"I can see that you remember that story well. Please keep it in mind it as I ask you once again to help me."

"Do you know what will happen to me if I get caught? Not only will I lose my job, but I will be put in prison as well."

"There is one thing that you are forgetting," Ibrahim informed him.

"What is that?"

"If you were in my position, I would not hesitate to help you no matter what the consequences might be."

Anwar looked at him with pity. Ever since Anwar had emigrated from Ramallah, Ibrahim had been his loyal friend. It was true: Ibrahim would help him no matter the outcome. Still, matters were not quite that simple. Anwar cherished his job at the Port Trust and he didn't want to do anything to jeopardize his future. Yet, he also couldn't forget what his friend had done for him, and he knew what he needed to do.

He thought for a moment, and then spoke quietly, almost in a whisper.

"Listen to me very carefully. There is a freighter bound for New York that is leaving the harbor in three hours. I want you to return to this spot in exactly two hours. By that time I will have been able to make the necessary arrangements."

"Thank you, my friend."

"Don't thank me yet. I am not sure that I will be successful, but I know that at least I must try. Be back here in two hours. You cannot afford to be late."

"I will be here on time," Ibrahim assured him. "You need not worry about me."

Anwar nodded and turned away. Ibrahim walked in the other direction, away from the harbor. While it pained him to place his friend in such an awkward and dangerous position, he also knew how grave the stakes were. Something terribly wrong was going on and Ibrahim needed to find out what it was.

He tried to ignore the thought that kept circling in his mind: even if he succeeded in getting to America, what was he going to do when he got there?

■ ■ ■

Shea exited the elevator and strode directly to the corner office. As he passed the secretary's desk, he heard a voice call out to him.

"You can't go in there," Donna informed him. "He is in an important meeting and doesn't want to be disturbed."

"That's fine," Shea replied, his voice kept carefully under control. "Normally that would stop me. But now, I don't really care and I want some answers."

Shea threw open the door to Allan's office and saw that Allan was on the phone. With his back to the door, Allan didn't see who had entered the room.

"Donna," Allan barked, "I thought I told you that I didn't want to be disturbed."

"Donna told me that," Shea replied. "But I told her that I didn't care."

Allan turned around and looked at his protégé. When he saw the rage in Shea's eyes, he spoke to the person on the phone.

"Hey, Charlie, let me think about what you just said. I will give you a call later if I have any more information."

Allan hung up and faced Shea. He wasn't sure what Shea knew, but obviously he was upset.

"How could you?" Shea said.

"How could I what?" Allan asked, playing for time.

"Don't play dumb with me. You know exactly what you did; I just want to know why."

Allan gazed at Shea and tried to figure out what was going on in his head. Allan was a master at finding out what people knew. He earned his very considerable livelihood by being able to read people. Did Shea know about the scheme that Jessica had orchestrated? It was possible, but Allan couldn't know for sure.

"Honestly, Shea, I have no idea why you are upset. If you could tell me what is going on, I might be able to help you."

"You are really going to pretend that you didn't do anything wrong?"

"No, I probably did do something wrong. Come to think of it, there are many things that I probably did wrong. But I can't remember the specific one that you are referring to. So how about we stop playing this game and you tell me what is really on your mind."

Shea restlessly paced the floor, while Allan tried to figure out what Shea was going to say. If Shea knew about Jessica's scheme, then he would quit and there was nothing that Allan could do about it. Still, he knew that Shea would be hurt, and even Allan Shore couldn't bear to see the knowledge of his betrayal on Shea's face.

"Didn't you tell me," Shea asked, "that the only way that I could keep my job is if I won this case?"

"That is what I told you," Allan affirmed.

"So then why would Michael Reeves come over to me and tell me that you asked him to recuse himself?"

Allan breathed a sigh of relief. Shea knew nothing about Jessica's scheme. He was merely upset about what had transpired with Michael, and that was something that Allan could explain.

"Why are you so surprised?" Allan deflected him.

"If you really think that I am a good attorney, why would you ask Michael to step down?"

"Shea, you aren't getting it. This isn't a popularity contest. It is all about wins and losses. You may be a good attorney, but you aren't as good as Michael. He has many years on you and knows all the tricks. And he also has one thing going for him that you don't."

"What is that?"

"He has the pressure to succeed."

Shea was appalled. Didn't Allan remember what was at stake here? He wasn't trying this case because he wanted to. He was trying it because he had no choice.

"You don't think that I'm under pressure? Don't you remember that my job is on the line here? If that isn't pressure, I don't know what is."

"You think that Jessica and I breathing down your neck is pressure? How about having the mayor and the governor of your state calling you every five minutes for details? That is what you call pressure. If you lose this case, sure, you may be fired, but you are still young and can find another job. For him the stakes are much higher. His job isn't the only thing on the line. His career is in jeopardy too."

"So what does that matter?"

"It matters because desperate men will do desperate things. Look Shea, I don't want you to get the wrong idea here, but I need to level with you. I believe that your greatest asset can also be your greatest weakness."

"Is that supposed to make sense?"

"Hear me out for a second. Do you know why clients request you, Shea?"

"I am not sure."

"It is because you are honest and genuine. You will never steer a client wrong and your clients can feel that. When they sit down and bare their souls to you, you actually listen to them. If I was in your chair, I would probably send them packing before they open their mouths."

Shea smiled at Allan's last comment. Allan had no patience for Shea's clients. Come to think of it, Shea didn't know anybody that Allan actually had patience for.

"You are a good person, Shea, and that is a rarity in this business. However, being the good guy isn't always a good thing. Sometimes you need to have that drive. The drive that makes you want to win, no matter who gets hurt in the process. You need that killer instinct, and frankly, I don't think that you have it."

"Are you saying that I can't be mean?"

"Shea, you wouldn't know mean if it slapped you in the face."

"What are you saying? I can be ruthless. Do you remember the Levinson lawsuit? I had Mrs. Levinson on the stand and she was bawling like a baby."

"That was because she had conjunctivitis that day and she couldn't prevent her eyes from tearing. Face it, Shea, you can't be callous. I mean, do you recall our first case together, the Wilton Elementary school suit?"

Shea couldn't forget if he tried. It was his first case with Allan and Shea was sitting second chair. Wilton Elementary School in Lawrence had a contract with its teachers and the teachers wanted more money. They knew that school couldn't fire them, because then the teachers would collect a large severance package that the school could not afford. The teachers had threatened to strike. Allan had been hired by the school to reach a settlement with the teachers. However, after days of negotiations, the teachers would not settle and Allan was forced to take the case to trial. At trial, Allan had called a mother of one of the students to the stand. She had testified that the teachers were extremely committed and dedicated to the education of her son. They even, she had explained, worked extra hours in order to provide her child with the skills that he needed. While this woman had thought that she was helping the teachers, in reality she was bringing disaster upon them. The teachers had a clause in their contract that prevented them from working extra hours without the written consent of the school's board. By working longer hours, the teachers had broken the terms of their contract and now the school was able to fire them without fear of being sued. When the woman had realized that Allan had tricked her into testifying, she was heartbroken. She broke down in tears right on the stand — and Allan had orchestrated the whole thing.

"I still remember the scowl that you had on your face," Allan reminded Shea. "You were so upset with me. I actually thought that you were going to cry."

"What you did was wrong," Shea argued.

"No, it just wasn't right. I didn't break any rules and no one was hurt. Sure, the teachers wanted more money, but the school couldn't afford it. If the teachers had won, the school would have been forced to close and everybody would have lost."

"I didn't realize that," Shea admitted.

"I know you didn't. You were too caught up in a mother's sob story to realize what was really going on. But you see, Shea, that is your problem. You think with your heart and sometimes the heart is dumb."

"Even if what you are saying is true, what does this have to do with my case? Michael Reeves isn't you."

Allan winced at Shea's comment and Shea was immediately remorseful.

"I didn't mean it like that," Shea tried to explain.

"No, you definitely meant it like that, but that is fine. I know what kind of lawyer I am and I am not going to make excuses for it. But don't be fooled."

"Fooled by what?"

"You think that just because Michael works for the government that means that he is a saint and won't bend the rules in his favor. Just remember, Michael and I grew up in the same firm and got the same training. If you think for a second that he won't do whatever it takes to win this case, you are gravely mistaken."

"You don't think that I would do whatever it took to win this case?"

"If Michael calls up Rabbi Felder's wife to testify about his whereabouts that evening, could you cross examine her? Or how about his kid? Could you grill him on the stand and make him change his story? Are you really prepared to do anything?"

Shea was quiet. He could lie to Allan and tell him what he wanted to hear, but then what? Shea wasn't going to do what Allan would do and frankly, that didn't bother him. He didn't want to be ruthless and conniving. He wanted to be a moral and honest lawyer, someone who earned people's respect; more important, someone that Shea himself could live with.

"You are right," Shea agreed. "I am not like you. I won't make good people cry on the stand or bend the rules for my advantage. I was taught from a very young age that good character trumps all. So if that isn't good enough for you, then maybe I should quit right now."

"You are missing the point," Allan informed him. "I don't want you to be like me. Too many people like me aren't good for society. I want you to be the same lawyer that you have always been. You shouldn't change for anybody, especially me."

"So what am I going to do about Michael?"

"You are going to beat him," Allan said confidently. "He didn't leave the firm because he wanted to. He left this firm because he was fired. Now don't get me wrong. He is still a good lawyer and I only went to him because I knew how important this case is to you and I didn't want to take any chances. The partners won't care how well you did. They are only going to want to see if you won or lost. Having Michael oppose you, doesn't mean that you are definitely going to lose. You are just going to have to work very hard to beat him."

"Wait one second," Shea interrupted. "Michael worked for the firm?"

"Yeah, it was a long time ago. We came out of Harvard together and we were both signed up our first year out."

"Let me guess, it was you versus him and you won."

"Bingo," Allan responded proudly.

"No wonder this guy hates me," Shea said in exasperation. "He probably feels that if he can beat me it is as if he is beating you."

"Well, let him think what he wants because he could never beat me in court. But you shouldn't be worrying about that now. The only thing that matters is that you need to be at the top of your game. And I will tell you something else. I have seen you at the top of your game and when you are on, there aren't many lawyers out there who could beat you. Especially, Michael Reeves."

Shea's eyes lit up. With everything that was going wrong for him, it felt good to know that Allan had a lot of confidence in him.

"So now let's get back to business," Allan advised. "What is the game plan?"

"Well, because of the budgetary constraints that you put on me, I had to find my own investigator."

"Hold on," Allan interjected. "I never put any restrictions on you."

"Yes you did," Shea said. "You told me that because of the Merzeir case, Brad wouldn't be available."

"That's true," Allan agreed. "But that didn't mean that we wouldn't hire another investigator for you. We needed Brad for the suit, but there are plenty of private investigators that the firm uses when Brad isn't available."

"I wish you had told me that," Shea said. "I recall you telling me that there were no investigators available. So I took the initiative."

"How?"

"I asked Hector Ramirez to help me."

"I thought that he wasn't allowed to do PI work anymore."

"No," Shea corrected him, "He isn't allowed to get paid for it, but if he wants to volunteer for a job, he can do whatever he wants."

"And you got him to work for free?"

"He was the one thanking me. Turns out, the restaurant business isn't providing the excitement that Hector needs in his life."

"Are you sure that you can trust him?"

"Hector might be a little loco, but there aren't too many people that I would trust more than him. He is as thorough as they come."

"Okay, we'll accept crazy Hector," Allan said. "So how you are going to win this case?"

Shea outlined his strategy. While Allan offered a number of criticisms, overall he was pleased with Shea's approach and felt that he had a good chance.

After they finished going over some final details, Shea turned to Allan.

"Allan, I just wanted to thank you."

"Thank me for what?" Allan asked, taken aback.

"For being there for me. Right now, I have no idea who my real friends are. You know, they may be talking to me now, but who knows what will happen once the trial opens. Having you in my corner really means something to me. Because, hey, after this trial is over, you may be the only friend that I have left."

Allan nodded, trying desperately to ignore the incredible guilt he was feeling.

SPECIAL AGENT ROBERT FIELDS HASTENED THROUGH THE hallways of 26 Federal Plaza in downtown Manhattan. Because of the evening traffic, Fields was running a full ten minutes late, and the boss would not be pleased.

Fields' morning routine was pretty much the same every day. Assistant Director Stephens would give a briefing on the previous day's events; which terrorists were behind bars and what terrorist attack had been thwarted. Ever since 9/11, most of the New York office's resources had been devoted to preventing terrorist attacks in the Big Apple. Over the last couple of years there had been an increase in organized crime, and the FBI had to divert its attention to the various crime families. But ever since the death of Danny Bastetti and the disappearance of his father Eduardo, the organized crime front had been pretty quiet, and the FBI was able to return its focus to terrorist activities. For the most part, things had been rather quiet. That was why Fields was a little surprised when he received a call that the Assistant Director wanted to call an immediate meeting, even though it was ten o'clock at night.

As Fields crashed through the doors of the main conference room, he hoped that the meeting had not begun. Seeing Assistant

Director Stephens standing at the head of the conference table, he knew that his hopes had been in vain.

"Thank you, Special Agent Fields, for joining us," Stephens said sarcastically.

"I'm sorry, but the traffic from Brooklyn was impossible. Some truck got stuck in the middle of the Battery Tunnel and traffic was backed up for miles. I had to change course and take the Brooklyn Bridge, which by the way, was no picnic either."

"We are all grateful for the traffic update," Stephens interrupted. "Would you like to give us the five-day forecast as well?"

"Well, right now it is dark outside, which is the reason I am confused as to why you called us all here for a meeting."

"Had you been here ten minutes ago, Fields, you would have heard why I called you down here tonight. But since you weren't, I am going to have to repeat myself."

Fields grinned. Only a few years ago, Stephens and Fields had been at each other's throats. Fields was a maverick while Stephens went by the book. Whenever they were assigned to the same case, their styles would clash and tempers would flare. However, after working a few cases successfully together, Fields had grown to admire and respect Stephens, while Stephens had learned to tolerate Fields. Even when Fields had been offered the position of assistant director in the Washington D.C. field office, he turned it down. He was having too much fun working with Stephens.

Stephens continued the briefing. "Two weeks ago, a rabbi was assaulted in Brooklyn on the way home from his school. The perpetrator was identified as a twenty-nine-year-old Palestinian man. The police believed that it was a hate crime. Currently, the Palestinian man is being held in Rikers Island and is awaiting trial."

Fields interrupted. "And now, can you please tell us why this case, which seems to be an issue for the police, has brought me out of my comfortable house and into this office?"

"I was just about to get to that, Special Agent Fields," Stephens answered with a tinge of annoyance. "Right now, we cannot treat this incident as an isolated attack. We have to assume that other attacks or greater attacks may follow."

Fields wasn't impressed with his solemnity. "Why?"

"Because at least three militant Islamic groups have each claimed responsibility for the attack. Granted, none of these claims have been substantiated. But if these groups are claiming responsibility, we have to assume that other attacks may be on the horizon."

"Do we have any information about the suspect?" Agent James Pearson, an African-American who had recently joined the group, asked.

"We are currently working closely with the DA's office and trying to gather as much information as possible. It seems that the suspect grew up in the Jenin refugee camp. Somehow he came to America, although nobody is completely sure when."

"So if he was in the Jenin camp," Fields said, "it is safe to assume that he could have connections with Hamas, al-Aqsa Martyrs Brigade or even al-Qaida."

"Yes, anything is possible at this point. And one more thing. The summit is in less than two weeks. The Israeli Prime Minister and the Palestinian President are going to be here in New York for peace talks. If this attack is any indication about what lies ahead, we need to remain vigilant and alert."

"So where do we go from here?"

"I am still waiting to hear from the DA if he has any more information on the suspect. If we are able to find out what terrorist group he was associated with in Jenin, we will be able to focus on our potential targets. Until then, keep your eyes and ears open."

The agents nodded and rose from their seats. Stephens placed the files into his briefcase and prepared to leave. However, as he looked toward the table, he saw that Fields had stayed behind and was shaking his head.

"Scared of going home in traffic, Fields?"

Fields gave him a cool look. "I am not buying it."

"What am I selling that you aren't buying?"

"I don't believe that you called this meeting to discuss a potential attack. I know you, Leo. You don't get all hot under the collar over some nasty little attack by some nasty little Ay-rab. You have some hard evidence that something big is going down. The other agents may have bought your story, but I know you are hiding something. So you really have only two choices."

"And what would those be?"

"Either you can tell me what is really going on or I can do enough digging and find out for myself. You know what happens when I start digging. I start out mining for coal, but if I find a diamond I don't give it away. Your secrets, Leo, are my diamonds."

Stephens stared hard at Fields. While he appreciated Fields' talents and abilities, his disregard for the rules went against everything that Stephens believed in. Stephens knew that if he gave in to Fields, he would only be encouraging his rogue behavior. He also knew that Fields would stop at nothing to get to the truth, and that was something that Stephens could ill afford to have happen.

"Okay," Stephens relented. "Before I begin, obviously that which I am telling you not only is extremely and highly classified, but also officially doesn't exist. Do I make myself clear?"

"Crystal."

"You are right. There is a highly credible and dangerous threat being discussed right now. It is very real and is something that we may have to act upon."

"Stop talking like a cop show," Fields requested. "It's just you and me here. No other agents in the room. What is really going on?"

"We have received information that the life of the Israeli prime minister may be at risk."

"So what else is new? This guy gets more threats to his life than I get telemarketer phone calls."

"This threat involves his stay here in New York. As we discussed earlier, the summit is in less than two weeks. According to our intelligence reports, an attempt on his life will be made during the week that he is here in New York."

"Let's say that what you are saying is true," Fields said, pacing the room. "Why are we the only ones involved here? Why aren't we meeting with our Shin Bet liaison to discuss strategy?"

"We can't discuss this with Shin Bet," Stephens declared.

"Why not?"

But before Stephens could answer, Fields knew the reason.

"You can't discuss this with Shin Bet, because they have no idea that you know about it and they can't know that you know about it."

Stephens didn't respond, but Fields knew he had the answer. "How long have we been spying on them?" he asked.

"Remember," Stephens reminded him, "nothing that we say in this room gets out. Look, the espionage game that different countries play is older than the countries themselves. Even though Israel may be our staunchest ally, we still have conflicting views on certain issues. The decisions that the Israelis may choose to make can adversely affect the economy and safety of our country and we always need to be prepared. That being said, until recently, we only used agents to get information on the Israelis. Their computer security was the best in the world and our attempts to hack into their servers were unsuccessful. All that changed about six months ago. We commissioned a local computer security firm, Access Technologies, to develop a state-of-the-art Trojan that could infiltrate the Knesset's network. After a few months of trying, we finally achieved access, and now we have a direct link to the Knesset's main server."

Fields couldn't believe what he was hearing. He knew that the Israelis had the best computer technicians in the world. If the FBI was in fact able to infiltrate their network that meant that the technician who'd developed the Trojan must have been quite an expert.

"But how do you know that the threat is even real? Maybe Knesset was being fed a bunch of garbage."

"The threat that we are talking about originated from the Knesset."

"Are you telling me that there is somebody in the Knesset who is planning an attack on the prime minister?"

"No," Stephens answered. "We have no idea who is planning this attack. All we know is that somebody in the Knesset knows about it and he sent an email regarding it."

"Do we know who sent the email?"

"Yes. His name is Eitan Adiran and he is the head of a computer security company that services the Knesset."

"So why don't we get in contact with this guy and gently persuade him to talk."

"We already tried that and we were unsuccessful. It seems that this guy has fallen off the grid and nobody has been able to find him."

"So what is Shin Bet doing about the threat?"

"They don't know about it."

"How is it possible that they don't know about a threat to their own prime minister, but we do?"

"Whoever sent the email knew that Shin Bet was monitoring all communications. Through a proxy, he or she was able to send it without Shin Bet's knowledge. However, because he or she didn't know that we were also monitoring the system, the proxy didn't block our Trojan and we were able to read the email."

"So you are telling me that right now we have information vital to the Israeli national security that they don't know about and we can't tell them about it?"

"That is exactly what I am telling you."

Fields paused to process everything that Stephens had just told him. The FBI was in a no-win situation. If they couldn't tell their Shin Bet counterparts about the threat, then the only one who could prevent the assassination was the FBI. And if they weren't successful, the fallout could be devastating. The problem was that the intel that the FBI had on the Israeli prime minister was minimal, and the FBI needed a lot more if they wanted to thwart the attack.

"How are we going to prevent an attack on a prime minister that we know nothing about? Fields asked. "Do we even know his itinerary?"

"No," Stephens answered. "The Israelis are very confident in their security and all their plans are made in Israel. They don't keep us informed unless they have to. As long as they are using their own security forces, they won't tell us anything."

"That doesn't make any sense. Don't they know that keeping us in the loop will only ensure the safety of the prime minister?"

"You try to convince an Israeli that he is wrong," Stephens rolled his eyes. "I'd like to see how that turns out for you."

"So how do we make them keep us informed without telling them why?" Fields wondered.

"I am still working on that. But for the time being, we will just need to wait and see."

"Is that why you brought up this assault case?" Fields asked. "Do you actually believe that the two events might be connected? I mean, what possible connection could there be between the assault of an Orthodox Rabbi and the attempt on the life of the prime minister of Israel?"

"Honestly, probably nothing," Stephens conceded. "But when we have no leads, any lead, no matter how small, is valuable and worth checking into. Could it be a coincidence that only two weeks before Israeli Prime Minister Yitzchak Schechter is scheduled to arrive in New York a rabbi is brutally attacked? Yeah, it could just be a coincidence. But if there is one thing that my experience has taught me, there is no such thing as coincidences."

Fields nodded and Stephens finished placing all his files back in his briefcase. As he turned to leave, when he realized that Fields was still standing there, deep in thought.

"Look Robert," Stephens addressed him. "It's almost midnight and I need you fresh and ready for tomorrow. Go home and get some sleep. Whatever thoughts and scenarios are flowing through your brain, right now, you probably can't do anything about them. So do me a favor and get some sleep."

"Don't worry," Fields reassured. "I'll be out of here in a minute."

"Fine. And Robert, remember, not a word to anybody."

"My lips are sealed," Fields replied, laughing and making a zipper motion across his lips.

Stephens left the room, leaving Fields alone. He appreciated the solitude. He enjoyed the peace and quiet that seclusion brought. It allowed him to be free of all distractions and focus on the issue at hand. And right now, he had a pretty big issue to deal with. The

Israeli prime minister's life was in danger, and Fields was going in blind. He didn't know what the threat was and he didn't know where the attack would happen. Come to think of it, he didn't even know when the prime minister was arriving in New York. With all those questions swirling around his head, Fields needed answers. There was only one guy who could provide them and Fields needed to get in touch with him.

■ ■ ■

Traffic was surprisingly light as Shea drove home. Usually, the Garden State Parkway looked more like a parking lot during rush hour. That is why Shea normally took Route 9. Today, though, the parkway was moving just fine and Shea decided to take it all the way to Lakewood. Shea enjoyed driving on the highway when there was little traffic; it allowed him to get lost in his thoughts and hopefully emerge with some clarity. On the evening before the biggest trial of his life opened, clarity was one thing that Shea desperately needed.

Shea felt much better after his meeting with Allan. Not only had Allan given him a vote of confidence, but Shea honestly believed that Allan cared about him. As Shea turned onto the exit that led to his house, he realized how important that was.

Though he couldn't blame his wife for her behavior, it still troubled him. How could it not? During their first decade of marriage, Shea could hardly remember a disagreement that they had, let alone a fight. Even when they had a disagreement, Shea made sure that he and Shira always reconciled before they went to sleep. He had learned that from his grandmother, who had always told him to never go to sleep angry. Until recently, Bubby would have been proud of me, Shea thought. However, it had been almost a week and Shira still wasn't talking to him. He had tried everything to engage her, but she ignored him.

Part of him was angry at her. *Did she really think that I wanted to take this case? What person in their right mind would do that?* But after thinking about it more carefully, Shea understood what was really going on. Shira felt betrayed. He had lied to her and she didn't know why. Shea wanted desperately to tell her, but he couldn't bring himself to do it. The shame of what his father had done was too great for Shea to expose. Also, Shea had reasoned, his father was seen in the eyes of many as an angel. Who would believe that the great Dovid Berman would have stolen from his investors?

Now, as Shea thought about it, he realized how short-sighted he had been. Whatever embarrassment revealing his father's actions would have caused, it paled in comparison to the anguish that he felt every time he looked into his wife's eyes. Those eyes not only conveyed pain, they also expressed betrayal. If there was anybody in the world that Shea should have trusted to believe him it was Shira, and Shea had blown it.

As he pulled into his driveway, Shea saw that the light to his bedroom was off. He sighed. He wanted nothing more than to reconcile with his wife, but he simply couldn't force the issue. Her pain was real and Shea had to be patient. So as he opened the door, he was taken aback at what he saw.

■ ■ ■

Mohamed entered his modest home. After a long day of working and following Shea, the only thing he wanted was peace and quiet. However, he knew that with his current situation, peace was the last thing that would ever come to him.

He was greeted by the smell of fresh roasted lamb that his wife was preparing. Qoozi: his favorite dish. It was Mohamed's birthday, but he was in no mood for celebrating. He was tormented by the choices that he had made and he searched for a way to undo the terrible harm that he had already precipitated. He knew that his options were limited and time was not on his side.

Watching his wife setting the table for the birthday meal, he sighed. She has no idea what I have done, he thought to himself. She looks at me as if I am her hero, but I am not worthy of any respect.

When he had left his homeland three years earlier, he had promised his wife that they would have a fresh start. They would live a life of peace and acceptance, not hatred and rejection. For the first couple of years, he had been able to make good on that promise. But his former life had caught up with him and it wasn't letting go. While at the beginning he had tried to resist, its forces were too strong and he was powerless to stop them. Now, as he looked at his simple home, he realized that not only had he reneged on his promise, but he had put their lives in jeopardy.

When his wife saw him, she smiled and motioned for him to come to the table.

"Where are the boys?" he asked

"Oh, they are outside playing," his wife answered. "Would you like me to tell them that you are home?"

"No, no, let them play."

"They have been asking for you all day. They will be so excited to see that you have finally come home."

"It is really okay. You don't need to call them."

"It will only take a minute. They are only outside in the back."

"I told you no!" he yelled grabbing her hand.

His wife blanched. Although she knew that her husband had a temper, ever since they had moved to America, he had been much calmer and rarely did he ever erupt into a rage. But the look in his eyes told the whole story and she knew that something was very wrong.

Upon seeing his wife tremble, Mohamed changed his tone.

"I am sorry. I didn't mean to lash out at you like that. I have just been under a lot of pressure."

"Why? Is everything okay?"

Mohamed looked at his wife. *She would never forgive me, if she found out what I have done,* he thought.

"Let's move away," Mohamed said suddenly. "We'll go anywhere in America. It will be your choice."

"Why would we do that?" his wife said, the shock in her voice apparent. "We have a good life here. You have a well-paying job and we are trying to build a family. What is really going on?"

"I'm sorry," Mohamed relented, as reality hit him like a punch in the gut. "I am just speaking out of frustration. You need only to worry about the children. And … our child that will be born. Leave everything else to me. Whatever is bothering me, I know I can handle it."

Mohamed looked at his wife to see if she believed him. His wife was trusting, sometimes a little too much, but for now, he needed her to believe him. He knew that if she started asking too many questions, everything that was dear to them would be in danger.

"Call the boys and let us celebrate my birthday."

His wife called the boys in. The two rambunctious children ran in from the backyard. When they saw Mohamed, their eyes lit up.

"Uncle Mohamed," they shouted. "We missed you."

"I know, boys, I missed you too. Did you have a good day?"

"Sure we did. We went to the park and we had ice cream."

The younger boy's lower lip trembled a little. "Vanilla. Like Mommy likes."

"Uncle Mohamed," the older boy said, "when are Mommy and Daddy coming back?"

"I told you already. Very soon. They just needed to take a little trip but don't worry. I have spoken to your mother and she misses you very much."

"Why can't we speak to her?"

"Whenever she calls, you boys are sleeping. She knows how much you miss her and she is going to be back soon. She even told me that she is going to bring you guys a special toy because you have behaved so nicely."

Their eyes lit up and the pending tears vanished.

"So come, boys, let us have a wonderful dinner that your aunt prepared. It is my favorite dish, qoozi."

"Huh? What's that?"

"Roasted lamb with fried nuts and rice. Wonderful."

The boys rolled their eyes.

"You don't like roasted lamb?" Mohamed asked.

"Our mother always buys us pizza on Tuesday nights and

we really like pizza," the boys responded in unison, the tears returning.

Mohamed looked at his wife. With all that was going on, the last thing that he needed was to have two boys throwing tantrums. As if reading his mind, she nodded in agreement.

"If you boys want pizza, then pizza it is," Mohamed exclaimed.

The boys cheered with glee and Mohamed led them out the door.

The qoozi sat congealing in its sauce, cold, greasy, and unappreciated.

"**Y**OU LOOK SURPRISED," SHIRA SAID.

Shea's mouth hung open in shock. He had expected to find his house dark, quiet, depressing, as it had been these past few days. Instead, here was Shira seated in the dining room, presiding over the table set with the Berman's finest china and a feast usually reserved for a Shabbos or even a Yom Tov.

While Shea had no idea what was going on, he definitely was happy about it.

"I just didn't expect this," Shea responded.

"What didn't you expect?"

"Well … it's been cold takeout for the past few days. This is … well, it's a great change."

"Shea, I am sorry about the way I have been acting."

The world, which had seemed so dark, suddenly grew light and clear. "I am the one who should be sorry. I lied to you and I betrayed your trust."

"But I never should have reacted the way that I did. I should not have closed myself off. I should have worked things out. I should have trusted you. I'm sorry that I didn't."

Shea didn't know how to respond. He had many questions

for Shira, but right now he was just overjoyed to have his wife back.

"There will be time for us to discuss things later. Right now, I don't want the food to get cold."

Though she'd prepared his favorite delicacies, Shea hardly ate. He was too happy, too grateful to be hungry. And, although he suspected he should leave well enough alone, the lawyer in him was curious. Only a few hours earlier his wife had been furious with him, ignoring him completely. But now, not only was she talking to him, she had prepared a feast for them to share. Shea knew that something was up.

He managed to set his curiosity aside for awhile. Finally, he asked the question that had been bothering him all along.

"What is going on?" Shea asked.

"What are you referring to?"

"For almost a week, you haven't said a word to me. But now, all of the sudden, you are acting as if nothing happened."

"You don't seem to upset by my change in mood."

"I have never been happier in my life. Those days that you weren't talking to me were impossible to deal with. It felt as if I was torn apart."

"I am sorry," Shira said softly. "I was just hurt and angry. I had never felt so betrayed in my life. I couldn't verbalize my pain to you."

"I am not blaming you. I was the one who was wrong. I was the one who lied to you for over four months. You have nothing to be sorry for. But why the sudden change of heart?"

"Would you believe me if I told you it was because I realized that I needed to act differently?"

"No."

"Well, I guess then I better come straight out with it."

Shea looked at his wife and saw the uncertainty in her eyes. Shira was hesitant and Shea saw that. "Shira, we've had enough lies and silence. Lies are what got us into this mess. The only way out of it is the truth."

"Your father came by," Shira blurted out.

"My father?"

"Yeah, he came today."

"Why?"

"First, he told me that he was in the neighborhood and he wanted to see the house. But then, once he got here, he broke down crying."

Shea recalled the meeting that he'd had with his father months before. It was the same story. His father had come by under the pretense of seeing Shea's office. However, moments after he had arrived, his real intentions were made known.

"I am so sorry, Shea," Shira exclaimed, choking back tears.

"What are you sorry for?"

"I should have trusted you. When I found out about the money, my mind was racing and terrible thoughts were flooding it. I thought that you were paying off a gambling debt or even worse, maybe bribing a judge with the money. The only thing that I didn't think was that maybe you had a good reason for not telling me. I never gave you the benefit of the doubt."

"So he told you everything," Shea said, lowering his head.

"Yeah. He told me that the business is finished and he told me about the money that he stole. He also told me how you have been bailing him out."

"But why did he suddenly tell you now?"

"Because he never knew that I didn't know. He had no idea that you were lying to protect him. He told me that it was bad enough that his son had to bail him out. But if he was causing his son problems with *shalom bayis,* that was too much for him to bear."

"So now you know," Shea stated dejectedly.

"But why?"

"Why what?"

"Why couldn't you tell me what was really going on? Why all the secrecy and subterfuge?"

"I should have told you," Shea admitted. "You aren't the only one who should have been more trusting. When I agreed to bail my father out, I wasn't even thinking about how you would react. I only thought about one thing and that was protecting my father and my siblings. But after a while, I realized that I needed to tell you something. The house was under construction and we needed to pay for it. I knew that you were going to ask me for the money and I couldn't give it to you. Do you know how many times I just wanted to tell you the truth? The lying was killing me."

"So why didn't you?" Shira repeated.

"How could I? Look at it from my perspective. My father was perfect in the eyes of so many people. He was everybody's hero. Who would believe that he had stolen money and needed his son to bail him out?"

"I would have believed you," Shira said softly.

Shea looked at his wife and wanted to bury himself in a hole under the table.

"I know that now. I only wish I had believed it then."

Shira faced her husband. While he had definitely hurt her with his lies, she understood why he had done it. He was protecting his family. Shira would have done the same. She admired the fact that he was so committed to his family and she knew that he would do anything to protect her or the kids.

There was still one question that needed to be answered.

"So what do we do now?" Shira asked.

"Besides finishing these amazing spare ribs?"

The two of them laughed. It felt good to share a joke. But then Shira grew serious again.

"I mean, how are we going to win this case so you still have a job and your father can stay out of jail? You can't let your father sit in jail. So if the only way to keep him out is to try this case, then we are going to win this case."

Shea's eyes filled with tears.

"Shea, what's wrong?"

"Nothing is wrong and that is why I am crying. For the last week, I have had to carry this burden alone. I have been embarrassed in court and ridiculed by my opponents. I knew I needed to try the case, but with everyone against me, it was getting too hard. But now, with you behind me, I am no longer alone. I can't describe to you how that feels."

"Shea, you have my word, you will never feel alone again."

"You don't know how much that means to me."

"However, this is only on one condition."

"Name it," Shea said cautiously.

"No more lies," Shira ordered. "From this day on, we tell only the truth to each other. No matter how bad the situation looks, we will always be able to handle it together. You have to promise me that if you continue to defend this man, you will be completely honest with me. I'm not referring to the things that you can't tell me because of attorney-client privilege. I am talking about everything else. Because right now, this case isn't only going to change your life, but it is going to change my life and the kids' lives. I know that it isn't going to be easy and I need to know that I can trust you."

"You have my word."

"So be honest with me, how bad is it going to get?"

"Honestly, I don't know. So far I have been able to limit the damage. I got the judge to issue a gag order."

"What is that?"

"It means that nobody, neither me nor the prosecution, is allowed to speak to the media regarding the case."

"Why would that help us?"

"My hope is that if I don't have to give interviews to the media, then fewer people will know that I am al-Jinn's lawyer. As it is, I have been pretty successful in keeping my name out of the papers."

Shira breathed a sigh of relief. "So that's all right then. We can keep a low profile during the whole trial."

"Not quite."

"Why not?"

"Because tomorrow they are scheduling a rally for Rabbi Felder at the courthouse. They expect thousands of people to be there. If anybody who knows me sees me there, word will spread like wildfire."

"Who's to say that anybody will see you?"

"Danny is pushing me to come," Shea said.

"Why would he want you to come? Doesn't he know that you are al-Jinn's lawyer? Oh my, Shea — Danny doesn't know?"

"I couldn't tell him."

"How could you not tell him? He is your best friend and he is going to be crushed if he finds out from somebody else."

"I know, but he is going to be crushed either way. Once he finds out that I took the case, he will never understand why and he is going to hate me like everybody else."

"But Danny isn't like everybody else. He is your oldest and closest friend. You guys have been through everything together. I don't know how he will react when you tell him. But I do know how he will react if you don't."

Shea regarded his wife and chastised himself. He always thought that he had all the answers, but he now saw how shortsighted he could be. He wasn't able to see past the moment and that was why he had lied to his wife and that was why he couldn't tell Danny the truth. After finding out just how wise his wife was, Shea knew that she was right. He could only smile grimly at the sheer irony. The only reason he lied was because he was trying to protect those he loved. But in the end the lies only brought pain to those whom he was trying to protect.

"I'll call him right now," Shea responded.

"No, you won't," Shira corrected him, smiling. "We are going to continue to enjoy this meal that I prepared for you. I haven't spoken to my husband in almost a week and frankly I missed him. And don't think I haven't noticed that you've eaten very little. So do you think that you could hold off on that phone call, counselor?"

"I think I can do that for you," Shea grinned, realizing that he couldn't remember the last time that he actually felt this good.

■ ■ ■

Hector Ramirez looked at his watch and sighed. When he had agreed to help out Shea, it wasn't only because he felt that he owed Shea a favor. Hector needed a change. While the restaurant business had been lucrative and successful, Hector missed the action. He missed the chasing and the scheming that came with being a private investigator. He missed digging up information on potential opponents and having it all come out in court. But there was one thing about being a PI that Hector didn't miss and that was the stakeouts and at this moment he was in the middle of a long and boring one.

Shea had asked Hector to find out all he could about Louise Pritchard. Louise was a seventy-four-year-old grandmother who also happened to be the prosecution's sole witness. It was Louise who supposedly saw al-Jinn attack Rabbi Felder that night. Hector knew that it was going to be Shea's job to disprove Louise's testimony, but it wasn't going to be easy. Normally the defense would try to use something from the witness' past to undermine his credibility. Whether it was a preexisting bias, or some sort of addiction, the defense's job was to discredit the witness and cast doubt on their testimony. However, with Louise Pritchard, Hector was finding that to be impossible.

At the ripe old age of seventy-four Pritchard was the model witness for the prosecution. She had no known history of drinking, gambling, or any criminal activity. She paid all her bills on time and never even threw a piece of regular trash into the recycling bin. Hector couldn't even find a parking ticket in her history. With the trial coming up, Hector knew that he had to find something, or else Shea would be in trouble. So as he waited for her to leave her house, Hector hoped that Louise would lead him somewhere that could provide hope for the defense.

And boy, did she ever!

When she took her morning stroll from her apartment on Quentin Road, Louise headed toward Ocean Avenue. Not wanting to spook her, Hector followed her on foot. She stopped at the corner of Ocean and Quentin and entered an apartment building. Hector marveled at the number of tall buildings in the area. Every block seemed to have a high-rise. There were two empty adjoining lots nearby, where houses formerly stood, and signs that indicated that luxury condos were going to be built on the site. Hector couldn't understand it. Growing up in Santo Domingo, Hector's family wasn't rich, but they had a lot of land. Hector remembered playing soccer with his friends in his backyard every day after school. *What do these people have against grass*, Hector wondered. After a moment he remembered why he was there, and he followed Louise into the building. Hector noticed the sign above the door she had walked through, and it piqued his interest. He waited a minute or two, opened the door, and walked in.

He had never felt so out of place in his life.

The room was filled with senior citizens. Hector stuck out like a sore thumb. Most of the conversations were in Russian, so Hector had no idea what any of the people were talking about, but he didn't mind. His mind was focused on one thing and that was to find out why Louise Pritchard was there. As he looked around the room, he couldn't find her and that concerned him. He made his way toward the receptionist, and glanced at the papers on her desk. Yes, Louise's name was on the log. She was here somewhere. The only question was where. As he continued to look around, the receptionist turned to him.

"Can I help you?" she asked in a heavy Russian accent.

"Yes, I was looking for someone," Hector responded.

"Who may that be?"

"I was looking for Louise Pritchard. Do you know where she is?"

"Can I ask why you need to see Mrs. Pritchard?"

Hector looked into the receptionist's eyes before answering. As a private investigator, you needed to have two things, one of which Hector did not possess. You needed to be tenacious, and Hector was as persistent as anybody. But at times it was necessary to fabricate stories in order to get the information that you required and Hector was a terrible liar. It wasn't that he couldn't be convincing, it was that the stories he would tell were so outlandish, no rational thinking person would ever believe them.

"She is my grandmother," Hector lied.

"Mrs. Louise Pritchard is your grandmother," the receptionist repeated.

"Yeah, she is my mother's mother."

"So your mother is Diane?"

Hector knew that he was in trouble. He hadn't counted on the receptionist knowing Louise Pritchard's family tree.

"No," Hector countered, "Diane is my aunt."

"But Louise only has one daughter."

"That is what she tells everybody," Hector responded trying to sound sincere. "She didn't approve of my father, so she tells everybody that my mother doesn't exist."

The receptionist looked at Hector and gave him a sympathetic look. Just as he thought that she had bought his fish story, she brought him back to reality.

"How about you leave this office right now, before I call the cops," the receptionist advised. "I don't know who you are, but if you don't get out of here now, you will have to tell your story to the police officers."

"Look, lady," Hector said, backing away, "I didn't mean no harm and I am sorry for bothering you. You have a nice day, okay?"

Exiting the office, Hector realized that he needed a new plan. For some reason, Louise Pritchard was in that office and he had to find out why. Although he had his suspicions, Hector couldn't approach Shea without proof and the proof was behind closed doors. While he didn't dare go back and face that receptionist, he knew that he needed to figure out a way to get that information. As he struggled to think of another way in, something caught his attention out of the corner of his eye.

Now he knew what he had to do.

While Hector struggled at fabricating stories, he excelled at acting. Growing up, he had always wanted to be an actor and always landed the leading role in the school plays. Although he never made it to Hollywood, Hector was still able to use his acting skills when it came to investigative work. If he had to assume the role of a certain person to try to get information for his client, it was an opportunity that he relished.

So as Hector raised his eyes, he saw a way to get past the

receptionist, and that was to assume the role of the janitor. It seemed, much to Hector's delight, that the janitor had left not only his cart in the hall, but his protective overalls and cap as well. Hector figured that the janitor wouldn't mind if he borrowed them for a few minutes, and he took the uniform into the restroom. When he emerged a few minutes later, he had been transformed into Manuel the custodial engineer. Mop in hand, Hector proceeded to walk back into the office.

He pushed his cart past the receptionist and headed for the offices in the back. He found himself in another hallway with doors on each side. While he would have loved to find Louise Pritchard herself, he knew that he didn't have the time. He needed to act quickly. Suddenly he saw what he was looking for. A file with Louise Pritchard's name had been placed in a holder on one of the doors. Hector knew that he needed access to the file. The only question was how he was going to get it. An idea popped into his head and he sprang into action. He took out a sponge and a can of spray polish and started cleaning the door. As he was doing so, he knocked Louise's file onto the floor. A middle-aged woman saw what had happened and ran over.

"I sorry, I sorry," Hector cried. "I clean up, I clean up."

Giving the careless janitor a dark look, the woman left him to pick up the papers that were scattered all over the floor. As he lifted each paper, he used a small camera to take a picture of every page. Once he was satisfied that he had gotten all the information that he needed, Hector replaced the file on the door and proceeded to exit through the rear.

While Hector grinned happily and sauntered away, Manuel was busy trying to get an explanation from the receptionist on how his uniform and cart had mysteriously gone missing.

■ ■ ■

Shea wiped his mouth with his napkin. The barbecued ribs that his wife had prepared truly hit the spot. He was feeling great, and it wasn't only because of the ribs. He had his wife back in his corner and he felt that with her by his side, there was nothing he couldn't handle.

However, he knew that he had a different matter to attend to and he was dreading it. As Shira saw him contemplating his next move, she read his mind.

"You need to make that call," Shira informed him.

"I know," Shea responded. "But it doesn't make it any easier. This is going to crush him."

"Maybe he will understand."

"How can he understand? Unless they knew the truth no one could understand why I am defending al-Jinn, and telling him the real reason isn't an option."

"But he is your friend," Shira reasoned.

"And you are my wife, but that didn't stop you from being angry at me and not talking to me."

Shira turned her eyes away. Shea knew that he had made a mistake and wanted to rectify it quickly.

"I am not saying that you were wrong. If the roles had been reversed, I would have done the same thing. However, we can't deny what happened."

"But I told you that the reason why I was upset was because you lied to me, not because of what you are doing. Sure, I didn't understand how you could defend a monster like al-Jinn. But what really crushed me was your dishonesty and your deceitfulness. Had you been honest with me the entire time, things would have been different."

"I think you are right, but you don't know Danny like I do," Shea said quietly. "When he gets passionate about things, there is no stopping him. Right now he is taking this attack on Rabbi Felder and making it his cause. How is he going to react when I tell him that I am the one who he is rallying against?"

"First of all," Shira corrected him firmly, "you are not fighting against Danny. Danny is demonstrating against terror, not you. You are not your client. You may have to defend him, but you are not him! You are a good person and a great husband and father. Please, never forget who you really are."

Shea looked at his wife and lifted the receiver. He believed what she was saying, but it felt good to hear somebody else say it.

"Also," Shira continued, "I don't know Danny as well as you, but there is one thing I do know. He is a great friend and deserves your honesty. Just call him up and tell him. You have nothing to lose. But if you don't tell him and he finds out some other way, you could lose everything."

Shea nodded to his wife and dialed. While he knew that he needed to tell Danny what was really going on, he had no idea what he was going to say.

THE WAVES OF THE SEA WERE CHOPPY, BUT IBRAHIM YUSUF didn't notice. It wasn't that he was immune to sea sickness. On the contrary, every time that Ibrahim had taken Jabril either sailing or fishing, Ibrahim would invariably spend most of the time fighting off nausea. Although he suffered terribly, because Jabril loved to fish, Ibrahim had taken him whenever he wanted. He loved his son more than anything in the world, and that is why he was embarking on this perilous journey.

Although Anwar had been able to sneak him aboard the ship, Ibrahim was still in danger. Should the captain or any of the security staff on the freighter come searching for stowaways, Ibrahim would be apprehended and sent back to Karachi. But even if he was able to stay hidden for the entire journey, there was still a major obstacle that had to be dealt with. Ibrahim did not have a visa and therefore could not clear passport control when the ship docked in New York. He knew that the only chance for him to enter the United States was to jump overboard as the ship neared the harbor and swim to shore. A friend of Anwar had promised to sneak food to Ibrahim during the journey and to tell him when he should jump ship; Ibrahim prayed that when the time came he would have the courage to do so.

What bothered him even more than having to jump into total wet blackness was the fact that he still had not figured out how he was going to help Jabril. Even though the newspaper story had been clear as to what had transpired, Ibrahim couldn't believe that it was true. Jabril was a loving father who cared for everyone. He tried to change the world by spreading a message of peace and hope and not hatred and strife. He would never harm anybody. *However, maybe I don't know my son,* Ibrahim thought. He had been living in America for nearly three years. Maybe he had changed over that time. Maybe he was no longer the same Jabril Yusuf who had left Sargodha and his father's orchard.

Ibrahim shook his head. He knew Jabril and he wasn't going to allow a news article to corrupt his view of his only son. Something dreadful was going on, and Ibrahim was going to figure out what.

As he clutched the newspaper clipping in his hand, Ibrahim held tightly to another piece of paper as well. On it Anwar had written his son's Mohamed's work address. He had told Ibrahim that if he ever reached the shores of New York, he should seek out Mohamed, who would help him with his quest.

As he placed his head against a wooden crate, he struggled to fall asleep. His dreams were pervaded by heartrendering images of his beloved son calling for help, with no one there to answer.

■ ■ ■

"Hey, Danny," Shea called over the phone.

"What, Shea is that you?" Danny asked, shouting over loud background noise.

"Yeah, can you hear me?"

"Not really. I'm in the middle of a meeting for tomorrow's rally. It is really crazy over here."

"Do you have a minute to schmooze? I really need to speak with you about something."

"What did you say?" Danny asked trying to hear over the noise of the large crowd.

Before Shea could answer, he saw Hector's ID flash on his screen.

"Danny," Shea shouted, "my PI is calling in. Can you hold on for a minute?"

"Shea, I can't really hear you. Listen, I'll see you tomorrow at the rally and we can speak then."

Before Shea could stop him, Danny had hung up. Hector's number appeared again. With a shrug, Shea answered.

"Shea," Hector exclaimed, "I found it!"

"Found what?"

"The magic bullet," Hector announced, his excitement evident.

In defense attorney parlance, a magic bullet refers to a piece of evidence that could destroy the prosecution's case. Usually it was a piece of DNA evidence or a fingerprint, and since Hector had been asked only to research the witnesses, Shea was surprised.

"What are you talking about?"

"You know the witness, Louise Pritchard, I found something."

"Hector, I already told you that I am not going after her. She is a nice old lady and if I grill her on the stand the jury will think that I am a monster."

"I am not talking about any dirty laundry here," Hector responded.

"So what did you find out?"

Hector proceeded to tell Shea what he had discovered. Shea's eyes lit up.

"Are you sure about this?" Shea asked

"I saw it with my own eyes."

"But how did you find this out?"

"Shea, you have your methods and I have mine."

"You didn't do anything illegal, did you?"

"Nothing that could get me behind bars, that's for sure."

"Good," Shea responded. "Because right now, with this case, I don't have the time to defend you."

"Don't worry about me, *compadre*, you just need to figure out how you are going to bring it up in court, without the prosecution objecting to it."

Hector was right. Even though he had found the magic bullet, it would be of no use if Shea was not able to introduce it to the jury.

"Do you have the whole file?" Shea asked

"Right here on my phone."

"Send me everything that you have," Shea requested. "Let me check it out."

"No problem, Boss."

When Shea downloaded the file, his face lit up. It was a long shot, but he could see his way to getting this information before the jury without the prosecution objecting.

Yup, he had his magic bullet, and Reeves had no idea that it was coming.

■ ■ ■

Shea arrived at the Eric M. Taylor Detention Center at about five minutes to seven. He hadn't seen his client since the bail hearing. With Hector's new information, he hoped al-Jinn would realize that he had a good chance of winning his case, and that he would be more receptive this time. Although the only thing that mattered was whether or not al-Jinn went to prison, not if he liked or disliked Shea, it was still much easier to work with some-body who held you in high regard and Shea hoped that at least he would be able to gain al-Jinn's respect.

Even though visiting hours for inmates began at eight o'clock, Shea had called in a favor and asked to meet with al-Jinn at seven. He explained that the trial was due to start at ten, and Shea needed to see his client before the proceedings. The warden owed Shea a favor. Earlier that year, the warden's nephew, Scott Tolleson, was caught speeding on the Long Island Expressway at 2:30 in the morning. After he was pulled over, the officer asked him to take a breathalyzer test. Tolleson, obviously drunk, refused and attempted to flee. When he was caught, he was badly in need of representation and Shea received a call. Shea was able to negotiate a suspended license and community service, but no jail time. The warden, who was close to his nephew, remembered what Shea had done and allowed him to see al-Jinn earlier than usual.

After being thoroughly checked and searched, Shea was permitted to enter and was guided to one of the meeting rooms. Whenever Shea entered the prison, he felt sick. Though he had defended criminals in the past, he always had the same feeling while walking through the halls. When he saw those steel bars and the steel doors, it made him contemplate the ultimate depravity that a human could face. Growing up he'd been taught about the *gadlus ha'adam*, the greatness of man. His *rebbeim* had explained that man had unlimited potential to do good and to bring prosperity to himself and his surroundings. Looking at the inmates milling around aimlessly, he also saw the devastation that man could suffer, and it frightened him greatly.

Rikers Island was a jail rather than a prison. That meant that the inmates were primarily those who had been denied bail and were waiting for their day in court. Only once they had been found guilty would the inmates be moved to a state prison such as Sing Sing or Otisville. Since al-Jinn had been denied bail, he was going to spend the remainder of the trial in Rikers, but Shea hoped that his stay would be brief.

He waited while they brought al-Jinn from his cell. Shea withdrew his notes and went to work. He wanted to show al-Jinn exactly how he planned to defend him. Shea felt that absolute transparency was the only way to go when dealing with clients. If you wanted them to trust you, you needed to trust them. As he rehearsed his opening statement for the twentieth time, he heard the door open and saw his client being led in.

When Shea saw al-Jinn's face, he gasped. One of his eyes was partially closed and there were five stitches along his eyebrow. His lip was bloody and there were cuts up and down his cheek. Shea wasn't sure when it had happened, but obviously his client had been attacked while he was incarcerated.

"What happened to you?" Shea asked as al-Jinn sat down.

"Why do you care?" al-Jinn responded, his disgust evident.

"I am your lawyer and it is my job to make sure that you are protected. If somebody attacked you, then I need to know about it."

"Why? What good will it do?"

"If you need to be protected, I can arrange for you to get protection."

"How can you protect me from yourself?"

"What is that supposed to mean?"

"Do you know who attacked me?"

"No."

"It was one of your Zionist pigs," al-Jinn responded angrily.

"A Jew did that to you?"

"Not physically. I think the assailant was a large black man named Tyrone. However, I know that your people got to him."

"What are you talking about?"

"The same way your people get to everybody: with your dirty blood money. They use the money that the Zionist regime steals from my brothers and sisters in Palestine."

"You are trying to tell me that a Jew paid a thug named Tyrone to beat you up?" Shea asked incredulously.

"Why is it so hard to believe? The Israelis are constantly planning operations to wipe out Islamic freedom fighters in other countries. Why would this be any different?"

Shea couldn't believe what he was hearing, but he shouldn't have been surprised. Al-Jinn was a fundamentalist who believed the venomous hatred with which he had been indoctrinated. However, Shea had hoped that a few days in prison would have made him realize the error of his beliefs. It didn't take more than five minutes for Shea to realize that nothing had changed.

"I didn't come here to discuss philosophy. I came here to discuss strategy for your trial. So if you have any interest in knowing how I am going to keep you out of jail, I would advise you to listen closely. "

"You are such a hypocrite," al-Jinn spat out, ignoring Shea's last statement.

"What did you call me?"

"I called you a hypocrite."

"Why do you think that I am a hypocrite?" Shea asked quietly, carefully keeping his temper in check. The more he knew about al-Jinn, the better he could deal with him.

"You look at me with contempt because of the hatred and distrust that I feel toward your people. But are you really any different?"

"I would like to think so. I am not walking around spewing unfounded accusations."

"You may not be saying it, but that just makes you a coward. I know what you feel in your heart. The same hatred that I feel toward you, you feel toward me. The same distrust that I feel toward the Zionists, you feel toward the Arabs."

"That isn't true," Shea defended himself.

"Really? When you get on a bus or a plane and there are Arabs sitting across the aisle from you, tell me that you don't get nervous. Tell me that you aren't thinking that they have bombs strapped to their chest just waiting to blow themselves and everybody else up."

Shea was quiet and that just gave al-Jinn the momentum to keep going.

"You see, we are both filled with hate and suspicion. The only difference is that I am not afraid or ashamed to voice my beliefs. You may hide behind the cloak of politeness, but I know the truth. The only reason why you don't voice your hatred is not because you are refined; it is because you are a coward."

Shea looked at al-Jinn. The man was no fool; Shea couldn't deny it. Shea didn't trust Arabs and that was the simple truth. But there were two huge differences. First, his suspicion was based on reality, on the unspeakable crimes that had been committed by the Islamic terrorists throughout the years. And second: he would not raise a hand against a Muslim, except in self-defense. While al-Jinn ....

He shook himself; these thoughts were getting him nowhere.

"I am here defending you, no matter what my feelings are," Shea said, trying to bring the conversation back into his control.

"Hah," al-Jinn scoffed, "You don't think that I know why you are really here? You aren't here out of the goodness of your heart. You aren't defending me because you want to mend the scorched bridges between our people. Not only are you a coward for not voicing your true feelings, you are a coward for not standing up for what you truly believe in."

Shea took a deep breath. The man was smart, that was clear. Time to go on the offensive.

"If you hate me so much, why would you want me as an attorney? Why not ask the judge to have me recused?"

Al-Jinn's face twisted into a bitter sneer. "Because I want to make you suffer. My hatred for your people runs deep within me. Even though you probably think that I am an illiterate buffoon, you are mistaken. I am quite aware of what you will be going through because of this trial. You are going to suffer. Every moment that I am stuck in that dark cell, I will be happy because I know that my pain will pale in comparison to the torment that you will be experiencing."

Al-Jinn called for the guard to open the door and just like that, he was gone, leaving Shea speechless.

Whatever doubts that Shea had before were gone. Al-Jinn was evil, and Shea was stuck with him.

■ ■ ■

New York City councilman Josh Silver sat at his desk deep in thought. He knew that today could be the most momentous day of his career, and he didn't want to squander the opportunity. A mentor of his had once told him that in the business of politics the ones who are successful are the ones who capitalize on different situations and circumstances. Today was one of those situations and Silver knew what he needed to do.

Though he didn't personally know Rabbi Felder, many people in his district, the Forty-Fourth, knew him well and were severely shaken by the tragedy. Silver, seeing his chance, had called a massive rally. He knew a great opportunity when he saw it. It had all the buzzwords that politicians love: Jewish unity. A city trapped in fear. The battle against terrorists besieging our city.

He had fought many times with the mayor about allocating additional funds in the city's budget toward fighting terrorism. Whether it was installing security cameras on every street or providing further training to city police officers, Silver honestly felt that is was vital for his city to protect its citizens, and he was quite vocal about it. Until now, the mayor had been able to convince the other members of the council that putting the money into the city's infrastructure and schools was more important and Silver's proposals were struck down. With this attack, Silver hoped that he would be able to garner the support that he needed to push his plan through and provide the protection that his constituents deserved.

Silver wasn't naïve. He also knew that if the plan were approved, he would come out looking good. Very good. His disagreement with the mayor was public knowledge and the media knew where Silver stood. By calling this rally, Silver would be putting his agenda front and center for everybody to see. While he would never state it publicly, he hoped that with all the rallying cries for tighter security and more protection, people would realize that he had been right and the mayor had been wrong.

As Silver waited for his visitor to arrive, he knew that he couldn't do this alone. He had to avoid having the rally perceived as a cheap attempt to further his political ambitions. If he was seen as using the attack for his own self-aggrandizement, the whole plan could backfire. He wasn't a student of Rabbi Felder and officially the rally was about the rabbi and the terrible attack. Silver needed someone to speak about Rabbi Felder and give the crowd and the media a picture of the type of man whom they were all rallying around.

Last night, he had found his man and as he saw him standing in the doorway to his office, Silver smiled.

"Come in, Danny," Silver said.

M OHAMED FAROUK WAITED NERVOUSLY INSIDE THE office. The boss had said he wanted to speak with him. Not a good sign.

His hands felt cold, and his stomach was clenched as he thought about the last few weeks.

Everything had been going so well. He was making good money and had finally begun to feel that he had broken free from his earlier life. But in a frightening instant all had changed, and now Mohamed found himself in a mess with no clue as to how to get out of it.

The boss walked in. Mohamed jumped.

"You seem nervous, Mohamed," Rasheed observed.

"It is nothing. Just something I ate this morning. I think that the coffee may have been stale."

"Well, you should be nervous," Rasheed said coldly. "Today is a big day."

Mohamed tried to sound confident. "It will go well. The defendant knows what he needs to do."

"Are you sure about that?"

"Positive. He has too much riding on this for him to make a mistake."

"And what about the lawyer?"

"What about him?"

"Is he going to be a problem?"

"No," Mohamed answered. "He doesn't know anything and there is no reason to assume that he will ever find out. If we let everything play out the way we planned, the operation will go off smoothly."

"That is good to hear," Rasheed responded. "I don't want to have to remind you of what happens if this operation does not go as planned. The defendant isn't the only one who will lose everything if we fail. Is that understood?"

"Perfectly," Mohamed answered, his voice quivering.

"Good. Now get out of my office and go do your job."

Mohamed left the office and headed for his cab. His cell phone rang, breaking into his dark thoughts.

"Hello."

"Good morning, my son." Anwar Farouk's voice came over the line, thin and distant but clear.

Mohamed was surprised. Normally he phoned his father once a week, but his father rarely called him.

"How are you, my father?"

"I am doing well, my son. Mohamed, I have news. Ibrahim Yusuf is on his way to America. "

Mohamed was speechless. Ibrahim had never left Pakistan, hardly ever even left his own village.

Mohamed's face broke out in a cold sweat. He forced his voice to stay calm, though his chest tightened.

"That is interesting, Father. Why is he coming?"

"It has something to do with Jabril," Anwar responded.

"Jabril?"

"Yes. Jabril is in deep trouble. Do you know anything about this, Mohamed?"

"I haven't even seen Jabril in months."

"I gave Ibrahim your phone number and address," Anwar said.

"What?!"

"Mohamed, you must help Ibrahim. You must help Jabril. I

have not forgotten our debt, and I will not allow my son to forget it either. Ibrahim Yusuf saved your hand, and it was Jabril who ran to him and told him what was going on. If he is ever able to reach New York, you will be the first person he calls."

"Why would you send him to me?" Mohamed asked, inwardly cursing his fate. With the operation just a few days away, anything out of the ordinary could be disastrous. "I don't know what I can do to help him."

"Mohamed, your friend, your best friend, is in dire need of your help."

"But, Father."

"There are no 'but fathers' here. Ibrahim came to your aid. Now you will come to his. It is that simple."

With that Anwar Farouk hung up, leaving Mohamed to his thoughts. They were bleak indeed. The situation had just gotten much more dangerous and unstable. What his father was asking him to do wasn't easy. In fact, it was almost impossible, if Mohamed didn't want to put everything that he held dear in jeopardy. But on the other hand, even before Anwar had called him, Mohamed's conscience had been pestering him as well. It was pleading with him to do the right thing and end this nightmare.

How? Too many things were already set in motion. To change everything, without anybody getting hurt, would be impossible. And yet Mohamed also could not forget the debt that he owed and what his responsibilities were.

He needed to make a decision, and with the operation and Ibrahim's arrival only a few days away, he knew that both events were on a collision course.

He needed to decide which side he was going to be on.

■ ■ ■

Michael Reeves took one look in the mirror and smiled. *It is going to be a great day*, he thought. Not only did he have a rock-solid case, but he had picked a great jury, filled not only with intelligent people who would see through the lies and deceit that the defense would present, but who were also sympathetic individuals who were going to feel the pain that Rabbi Felder had suffered and demand justice. It also didn't hurt that the members of the jury had seen Berman humiliated by Amir Hakaniny. Michael had seen many juries through the years and there was one thing that they all had in common: they appreciated the powerful lawyer. Jurors didn't appreciate a hesitant and timid attorney standing and arguing in front of them. They wanted to see an alpha male who was strong-willed and tough and wouldn't back down to anyone. Jurors didn't like weakness and Shea Berman had displayed just that in front of everyone.

There was still another reason why Michael felt that he had the upper hand going into trial. That was because of what Michael had done just a few minutes earlier. Although he risked angering the judge, he felt it was a risk worth taking; if it worked, it could strike a major blow against the defense attorney. Only time would tell if his gamble would pay off.

As he straightened his tie once more before heading to the courthouse, Moshe Cohen raced into his office.

"Have you seen the reports?" Moshe asked. "It's traveling around the web faster than an Arizona brush fire."

"What story is that?"

"The story of Shea Berman representing Khalid al-Jinn in the attack against Rabbi Felder."

"What else does the report say?" Michael asked calmly.

"Nothing much. It only mentions that even though Shea is a religious Jew and a student of Rabbi Felder, he is still going to be defending the accused attacker, Khalid al-Jinn. Bloggers love that kind of thing."

"Well, at least they got it right for once," Michael commented.

"You don't seem surprised," Moshe said. He cast a look at his boss. "Wait one second. Did you leak the story to the press?"

"I am not admitting anything. However, between you and me, I may have called up a friend of mine who works for the New York Daily Beat and I may have told him, in total confidence, a few minor details about the case that I am about to try in court."

"But the judge issued a gag order," Moshe reminded him. "If he finds out that you leaked the information, he is going to put you in contempt."

"My friend, who may or may not have heard it from me, has been a newsman for over forty years. He isn't just some cub reporter off the street. He knows how to be discreet and he knows how to cover his tracks. Nothing that I said will ever be traced to me."

"But why do it and put yourself at risk?"

"You don't get it, do you?" Michael grinned. "Do you know what is going on right now as we speak right outside the courthouse?"

"Sure. Josh Silver is putting together some kind of rally to show support for Rabbi Felder."

"Well that, and to further his own political career. But the rally is also officially for Jewish unity."

"Yeah, I read something about that."

"So just picture this for a moment. There will be thousands of Orthodox and secular Jews rallying together against the tragedy that befell one of their own. What do you think will happen when a rally of Jewish unity confronts the lawyer who turned his back on his own people?"

Moshe nodded. Michael had played it perfectly. By feeding the media the story, everybody attending the rally would know that Shea was al-Jinn's lawyer. All of the participants' anger and frustration would be turned toward Shea. He was going to replace al-Jinn as the new face of evil. Shea was walking into a wave of hatred, and he probably didn't even know it.

"Wow," Moshe gave a low whistle.

"Yeah, the look on Berman's face as thousands of people yell and scream at him will be priceless."

"But why does it matter to you? I mean besides wanting to torture him, what other motivation is there for you?"

"Winning in court, Mark, is about psychology as much as law. More so, even. It is all about getting the upper hand. Shea Berman right now is faced with possibly the biggest case of his young career. The pressure that he is under is mind-boggling. He is probably going crazy just thinking about giving his opening statements in front of the jury. Can you imagine what the added stress of being the Jewish community's number-one villain will create? I bet you that he won't even be able to finish his opening statement. And if he fails, I will be right there to capitalize."

"Isn't that a little, I don't know, dirty?" Moshe asked his boss quietly.

"What do you mean?"

"I don't know. It just seems to me that what you are doing is something that the defense would do. We always accuse the defense of scheming and cheating, and well, this ploy of yours, seems kind of underhanded. I just thought that here at the district attorney's office we were above that kind of thing."

Michael turned to Moshe with anger in his eyes. He didn't appreciate his ADA questioning his judgment.

"You think that I am playing some sort of game? You think that I am back in high school trying to play a practical joke on somebody?"

"That isn't what I was saying," Moshe defended himself.

"This isn't a game. We are talking about justice for a man who was brutally attacked. We are talking about a community that is afraid and needs reassurance that its police and justice department will protect it."

"I know."

"Well then, you should also know that the only thing that matters here is the outcome. You think that the defense wouldn't do the exact same thing to me, if they had the chance? Allan Shore probably has given Shea forty different underhanded techniques on how to sabotage my case. And by the way, what about what *you* did?"

"What did I do?"

"Don't you play the innocent! You had al-Jinn moved from the precinct, so his lawyer wouldn't have a chance to meet with him before the bail hearing."

"But that was different."

"How?"

Moshe took a deep breath and confronted his boss. "Because I wasn't going against a direct order from the judge that could land me in prison."

Michael ignored Moshe's last statement and, experienced lawyer that he was, went on the offensive instead. "Why are you so protective of Shea? Remember, Mark, Shea was the one who got you recused. That was also playing hardball, no?"

"I haven't forgotten."

"You may think that he is a nice guy on the outside, and you know what, maybe he is. But when it comes to trial, all defense attorneys are the same. They are all devious and would sell out their own mothers to get an acquittal. You have a bright future here, but if you don't start thinking like them, they will eat you alive."

Moshe watched Michael take his papers and leave for court. While he agreed that most of the defense attorneys that he had come across were as Michael had described, with Shea he felt differently. Even though he was very angry with him after the recusal, and he had said some nasty things, Moshe had had time to reflect on what happened. Ever since he had met Shea in college, he had observed one thing: No matter the situation and no matter what was going on, Shea was the one guy you could count on to do the right thing. If anybody ever deserved the benefit of the doubt, it was Shea. Though he couldn't understand why Shea would ever take on a case like this, he felt that if Shea did, he must have had a good reason.

As he thought about what was going to happen to Shea, he took out his cell phone.

■ ■ ■

Traffic was moving surprisingly well for an early-morning rush hour on the BQE. Shea took Exit 29 and drove toward Smith Street.

The phone rang again. The caller ID flashed, and Shea's face registered surprise.

"Why are you calling me?" Shea asked coldly.

"You have a right to be angry with me," Moshe Cohen responded. "But I need you to hear me out. I still have no idea why you accepted the al-Jinn case."

"And you probably will never know."

"That might be true, but here is what I do know. You have always been a standup guy, Shea. You were always there for me in school. I mean do you remember that time when I was dating Sarah Frankel?"

"How could I forget? You thought that you were going to marry that girl."

"And if her parents hadn't felt otherwise, I may have. But do you remember what happened when she dumped me?"

"You were an absolute wreck. You were so depressed that you wouldn't even come out of your room."

"Yeah, but do you know who the only guy was who went to my professors and asked them for extensions on my papers so that I wouldn't flunk out of law school?"

"I seem to remember that was me," Shea responded.

"Yeah, it was. You were there for me then, and I should have remembered what kind of guy you are and not judged you like that."

Shea felt a surge of emotion that surprised him with its intensity.

"That means a lot to me, Moshe. It's been pretty brutal."

"I didn't just call to apologize, Shea. There's something important I have to tell you, but you didn't hear it from me. Are you on Smith Street?"

"I'm about to turn off it toward the courthouse. Why do you ask?"

"Turn off at Livingston instead."

"Why?"

"You know about the massive rally that they are having for Rabbi Felder, right?"

"Of course I know. I really wish that I could be there for him."

"Let me tell you this. You don't want to be there now."

"Why?"

"You will never hear me say this again and I will happily deny that I ever said anything. But, Michael Reeves leaked to the press that you are defending al-Jinn."

"What?" Shea asked in disbelief.

"You are going to get ambushed by the crowd. He thought that it would rattle you and the sight of ten thousand Jews calling death to your name would do the trick. So right now, Josh Silver is going to give a speech on Jewish unity and you are about to become public enemy number one."

"But what about the judge's gag order?"

"The reporter who has the story is a seasoned veteran who knows how to cover his tracks. His source will never be revealed."

Shea's mind was racing. The inevitable was finally here and Shea had no idea what to do. Though he had always known in the back of his mind that everybody would find out and he would have to deal with the fallout, he never thought it would happen before he even gave his opening statement.

"Why are you telling me this now?"

"Again, this is between you and me," Moshe said. "Something is up with Michael Reeves."

"What are you talking about?"

"Michael has always been a guy who goes by the book. He doesn't bend the rules and that is what I have always admired about him."

"So what has changed?"

"I'm not sure, but ever since he took on this case, he's become a different person. He keeps looking for ways to beat you and not how to simply prove your client is guilty. The move that he pulled, leaking your name to the press, that's the kind of move I would expect from one of you guys. Not from Michael."

"Thanks for the vote of confidence," Shea interrupted.

"Well, you do work for the dark side," Moshe said, laughing. "Anyway, once I saw the way that he was approaching the case, I realized that he wasn't playing fair and I felt that you deserved better."

"So now what?"

"What do you mean?"

"I mean, how I am going to get past the crowd without them seeing me?"

"Well, I already told you that you could go through Livingston Street." Moshe's voice took on a thoughtful note. "Now that I think about it, Shea, let's be honest, what is the point?"

"Excuse me?"

"Even if you don't show up at the rally, people are still going to know. Your name and photo are going to be plastered all over the news and the web in a matter of moments and there is nothing that you can do about it."

"So what are you saying?"

"I am telling you that if you run away and hide, you will only be proving Michael Reeves right."

"How do you figure?"

"Listen to me, whatever the reason is that you are taking on this case, do you believe in it?"

"Of course I believe in it. I wouldn't be doing this unless I did."

"So if you believe in it, show everybody that you do. If you run away from this, the public will feed on you like vultures. But if you show them that you aren't running scared, they will respect you. More importantly, you will show Michael Reeves that he can't push you around." Shea realized that Moshe was right. Whoever was going to hate him was going to hate him, whatever he did in the next few minutes. The only question was whether or not Shea was going to give Michael the satisfaction. And the more that Shea thought about it, the more he knew what his answer should be.

"You're right, Moshe. I can't let Michael dictate where I should go. I am going to that rally and I am going to stand tall and strong."

"I wouldn't have expected any less."

"Thank you so much, Moshe. I am really happy that there is no enmity between us."

"You're welcome, Shea. Hey look, I still hope that you lose this case and Rabbi Felder gets the justice that he deserves. I still believe that your client is evil and doesn't deserve to see the light of day after what he tried to do. But I hope for your sake that you walk out unscathed and are able to piece together your life after everything is done."

Shea hung up and headed to the court parking lot. There was a patrolman directing traffic and when he saw Shea's ID, he allowed him through to park. As he turned into his spot, Shea saw the massive crowd that had formed adjacent to the steps of the courthouse. He left his car and drew a deep breath. *It's now or never*, he thought, and Shea prepared himself to face the firing squad.

"**H**OW'S MY HAIR?" THE REPORTER ASKED HER cameraman.

"It looks fine," the cameraman answered. "It looks the same as it did three minutes ago when you last asked me."

"I just wanted your opinion and not your attitude. So how about you just tell me when we go on."

"We are ready now. So in five, four, three, two, one..."

"Good morning. This is Barbara Hasselman and I am reporting to you live at the corner of Schermerhorn and Smith Streets in downtown Brooklyn. Right behind me, in the Brooklyn criminal courthouse, the jury awaits what some people, at least in this neighborhood, are calling the trial of the century. Twenty-nine-year-old Khalid al-Jinn will be standing trial for the attempted murder of Rabbi Gedaliah Felder, respected rabbi and leader of the Jewish community. With opening statements just a few hours away, tension is at an all-time high.

"Right behind me you can see a mass gathering and protest, organized by council member Josh Silver. With the expected arrival of over fifteen thousand people, local law enforcement personnel have secured the area. Riot police are in full gear, hoping that their services will not be required.

"Although most of the attendees of the rally will be here to show solidarity with Rabbi Felder, there are others who are more outspoken and believe that their voices need to be heard. One such person is Eli Fishman, a business owner who lives in Brooklyn. Eli has been gracious enough to share his thoughts with us before the rally."

The camera shifted its focus from Barbara to Eli. Fishman was wearing rimless glasses and a button-down oxford shirt. His receding hairline was covered by his yarmulke, which was pushed to the front of his head.

"Eli, thank you for speaking with us," Barbara stated.

"My pleasure."

"Do you know the victim, Rabbi Felder?"

"No, I mean some of my friends do, but I don't know him personally."

"Then why are you at the rally?"

"I think that the people of the United States need to see what is really going on here."

"What are you referring to?"

"I am referring to all these Muslims who trample on our rights. Or maybe I should call them what they really are, terrorists."

"You can't seriously believe that all Muslims are terrorists."

"I wish I could say that I didn't, but look at what's going on in the world. Tell me of one act of violence that isn't perpetrated by a Muslim. Our wonderful country, the country that reaches out and helps anybody in need, is fighting two wars and both are with the Muslims. They are challenging our way of life and won't stop until we are wiped off the face of the earth. That is what this whole jihad thing is about. They don't want us here and all we do is apologize to them and make concessions. Well, I am here to say that enough is enough. No more concessions. You got a problem, you leave. Go back to Mecca or wherever else you came from because we aren't going anywhere."

"Wow," Barbara responded. "You aren't holding anything back, are you?

"Look, I don't mean to be cruel, but I call it as I see it."

"Wait, hold on a minute," the reporter told Eli while putting her hand to her ear. "I am really sorry to have to cut you off, but it seems that the rally is beginning and Councilman Silver is taking the podium. Let's hear what the councilman has to say."

The camera turned its focus from the reporter and zoomed in on Councilman Silver. He was wearing a single-breasted two-button suit with a light blue tie. On the lapel of his jacket, he wore a pin that consisted of a Jewish star with the words *One Nation One Heart*, emblazoned across it. He waited for the crowd to quiet down before he began his remarks.

"*Acheinu Beis Yisrael*," he began, "it with a heavy heart that I stand here. On the one hand, I am in awe of the thousands who came here today. You are here because you believe in Jewish unity and for that I am deeply moved. But I am struck with a feeling of sadness that a rally like this is even necessary. When will it end, I ask you, my brothers and sisters? When will we stop needing to hold these gatherings? But before I get into what I believe we can accomplish with this meeting, I ask you to listen to the words of Danny Abramson. Danny is a student of Rabbi Felder and at the end of the day, Rabbi Felder is the real reason why we are all here today. So please let us give Rabbi Felder the proper respect, and listen to the heartwarming words of his student, Danny Abramson."

Danny rose to the podium and looked over the crowd. While he was able to make out many faces, he didn't see anybody that he recognized. He hadn't thought that Yechiel or any of his brothers would attend, but he'd expected that some of his friends from high school would attend, especially Shea. As he gazed over the crowd one more time, he saw Shea coming down Smith Street with a briefcase in his hand. *Good old Shea*, Danny knew he'd come through.

"I'm not someone who normally gives speeches in front of large crowds. So when Councilman Silver asked me to address the rally, I was uncertain. The councilman told me that he wanted me to give everyone a glimpse into the man who they are rallying around. But to really know Rabbi Felder, it would take much more than a speech from me. There are so many facets to the man that I call my rebbi, one speech would fail to encapsulate all of them. I kept wondering, what could I tell you that would help you feel the anguish that I feel every moment that he lies in that hospital bed. But now as I see all of you uniting together, I know exactly what to say. Because if there was one thing that Rabbi Felder has taught me it is the importance of *Achdus*.

"He is a man who lives for his fellow Jew. He was always doing something for someone else. Either he was raising money for an orphan who had just gotten engaged, or going with a former student to a job interview to give him *chizuk*. I recall vividly that one time Rabbi Felder came late to class. A friend of mine, whose curiosity got the better of him, asked Rabbi Felder where he had been. Rabbi Felder apologized for being late but he needed to be at a local *cheder*. My friend's curiosity was not squelched and he asked Rabbi Felder why. Rabbi Felder responded that a student in the first grade had recently lost his father and he was having his *Chumash* party. Rabbi Felder explained that when this young boy would see the men attending and not see anybody there for him, he would feel sad and maybe even cry. Rabbi Felder couldn't bear the thought of a young child crying, so he went to the party to be there for this boy."

Danny waited to see the reaction of the crowd. There was total silence. Danny could have sworn that he even heard muffled crying in the stillness.

"So as we stand here today under the banner of Jewish unity, let us never forget the man who brought us here today. The sight of all of us, whether you are *chassidish, litvish,* modern Orthodox, all standing together, would make him proud. So let us *daven* together that in the *zechus* of this extraordinary gathering, he should merit a speedy recovery and a *refuah sheleimah*."

The crowd applauded as Danny left the podium. Josh Silver waited for the crowd to quiet down.

Then it was his turn to speak, and he chose to take a different tack. Very different.

"Thank you very much, Danny Abramson," the councilman

said. "Let us all give a round of applause for Danny and thank him for his strong and heartfelt words."

The crowd continued clapping and Silver joined them. After a few moments, he motioned for the crowd to quiet down and then he continued.

"We all know why we are here today. A monster is going on trial today for the brutal attack against one of our own. And if we can take what Danny has just told us to heart, it wasn't just a man who was assaulted. It was a holy person who lives his life for others. What kind of barbarian would harm such a holy individual? I'll tell you and the answer may not be popular, but it is something that I feel needs to be said. The blame for what happened to Rabbi Felder lies on our shoulders. It is our fault!"

Silver waited for the crowd to respond. He heard cries of disbelief and challenge, which was exactly what he was hoping for.

"We, in our comfortable homes, have dropped our vigilance. We have allowed our enemies to walk our streets and freely terrorize us. A mere seventy-five years ago, our parents and grandparents walked the streets of Europe with their heads held high. They thought that they had finally been accepted into society and found no reason to be afraid. Hitler, with his killing machine, changed all that. We saw true depravity and evil. And after the Nazis fell and our nation was rebuilt, we vowed that we would fight against our oppressors. So where is our anger and where is our commitment? The Reich may have fallen, but Hitler's ideology lives strong today. There is another nation that seeks our destruction and we just let them trample all over us. Why are we silent? Our silence must end, now!"

The crowd again erupted into clapping and cheering. The noise was deafening and Silver was savoring every moment.

While the cheering was its peak, Silver continued his speech.

"My dear friends, we have no reason to be afraid. We live in a wonderful country that will protect us. This isn't 1939 and we aren't living in Berlin. If we raise our voices in unison, we will not be persecuted for our rage but praised for our courage. Together, we can show our enemies that we will no longer cower in fear but we will rise up in defiance."

A seasoned speaker and politician, Josh Silver knew that while people enjoy clichés, what they really go for was the personal attack. They like black and white, good guys and bad guys; they were looking for someone to blame.

His throat growing hoarse, his eyes blazing, Silver brought out the big guns.

"There is one thing that we should be afraid of. There is something out there that threatens our existence and is more powerful than any terrorist's suicide bomb. Its power is so pervasive that it can attack our life source and destroy our very being. The theme of today's rally is Jewish unity, because without unity, we stand no chance against the enemy. We are only as strong as we are unified. If divisions are created among us, we stand no chance against them. So, as we look around and we see our brothers and sisters locked arm in arm, we can show our enemy that he will never be able to divide us. As one we are indestructible."

Silver looked out over the crowd, searching for one face. Much to his pleasure, he found his man. He was now ready to deliver the final blow.

"My friends, even while we stand here today as one proud nation in defiance of our enemies, all is not perfect. Even within this powerful alliance that we have built, there exists a weak link in our unbreakable chain. One individual who seeks to undermine all that we are trying to accomplish here today. He seeks to sell our nation to the highest bidder. This turncoat has not only turned his back on his people, he has spit in the face of the holy man he once called his rebbi. And if that were not enough, this spineless traitor has the audacity to come here today and show his face. I am referring to none other than Shea Berman, the defense attorney of that monster Khalid al-Jinn."

Silver paused, and the screen behind him zeroed in on Shea approaching the entrance of the courthouse. The crowd began to shout and scream. Danny, his face pale and set, leaped from the stage.

"But my dear brothers and sisters," Silver continued, "he is mistaken. He doesn't appreciate our nation's resolve and perseverance. There were many friends who handed over their own brethren to the Nazis in order to save themselves. But the irony was that the Nazis still burnt them in the crematorium even after they gave up their hearts."

Silver looked straight toward the courthouse and saw Shea seeking to enter the building as quickly as possible.

"Shea Berman," Silver shouted, his voice heavy with authority, "I am pleading with you to change your ways and do the right thing. Because if you don't, like the *kapos* of the past, there will be no redemption for you or for your soul."

Shea, trying desperately to disregard Silver's baiting and the screaming of the increasingly agitated crowd, saw that his entrance to the building was blocked by a reporter.

"Mr. Berman, I am Barbara Hasselman from Channel Five News. I was hoping that you could give me a comment on what just transpired."

"I am sorry ..." Shea began to say.

"Yeah, why don't you give everybody a comment, Mr. Berman," Danny said, shoving his way through the crowd, his eyes narrowed with fury.

Shea looked at his friend, ignoring the frenzied crowd surging around him. "Danny, I am so sorry. I didn't mean for you to find out this way. I tried calling you."

"Are you joking? You are telling me that this is real? You really are defending the attacker of Rabbi Felder?"

"Mr. Berman," the reporter interrupted, "can you please just give the citizens of New York a comment about the case?"

Shea stared at Danny. His friend so desperately wanted him to tell the reporter that this was all some crazy misunderstanding. Somebody leaked the wrong information and Shea was caught up right in the middle of it.

"I am sorry," Shea responded, "but due to the nature of the judge's ruling regarding this case, I am not allowed to discuss any details of the proceedings."

With that Shea walked into the courthouse, leaving behind an angry crowd and a crushed friend.

■ ■ ■

Shea sat next to al-Jinn. Al-Jinn was clad in prison garb. Shea paid little attention to him, not even giving him a nod. Because the jury was not yet seated, Shea didn't feel the need to pretend he got along with his client. Al-Jinn had made his feelings quite clear and Shea was going to respond in kind, unless the jury was in the courtroom. In that case, Shea would do everything to make the jury believe that he and al-Jinn were on the same page.

Out of the corner of his eye, Shea saw that Michael Reeves was already seated and prepared to do battle. Not wanting to give his opponent any satisfaction, Shea ignored him and focused on his upcoming statement.

Michael, however, approached him, a broad smile on his face.

"Wow, that crowd seemed pretty angry out there," Michael said.

"Really?" Shea responded, his voice nonchalant. "I barely noticed that anyone was out there. Was there some kind of rally going on?"

"You didn't see the fifteen thousand people calling death to Shea Berman? I could have been in the Bronx and still heard those cries."

"Sorry, I didn't notice. I don't know about you, but I have a client on trial and I can't bother with what people are saying. Now if you would excuse me, I have a trial to prepare for."

Michael stood for a moment, clearly disappointed, and the judge entered the courtroom.

"Please be seated," the judge ordered. "I am having the jury kept in their room, because I don't want them to hear what I am about to say."

Shea looked toward the judge with concern. Although it wasn't uncommon for the judge to address the attorneys without the jury present, this seemed to be different. Normally, the judge asked that the jury be kept in their room if various motions needed to be filed or argued. However, as far as Shea knew, Michael hadn't filed any motions; he certainly hadn't. So why wasn't the jury in the room?

"I believe myself to be a fair judge," Daniels continued. "I try to treat everyone who enters my courtroom with respect and dignity and I expect to be treated in kind. Therefore, when I issue a ruling, my expectation is that the ruling will be adhered to without exception or compromise."

Both Shea and Michael nodded in agreement. The judge then looked straight at Michael with burning eyes.

"So you can understand my surprise when my clerk received a call today from a reporter asking for a comment about Mr. al-Jinn's Jewish attorney. I was under the impression that I had issued a direct order that no party involved in this trial should give any statements to the press."

"I am sorry, Your Honor," Michael said, his voice ringing with righteous indignation. "I should have realized earlier that the defense would try to pull something like this."

Shea gasped at the man's sheer impudence. He was sorely tempted to call Michael a liar and disclose what Moshe had told him. Unfortunately, divulging what had been told to him in confidence would surely cost his friend his job.

"What are you referring to?" the judge inquired.

"Isn't it obvious? "Michael responded. "Clearly Mr. Berman is looking to frame the prosecution for something that he orchestrated himself."

"I am not sure that I understand," the judge said, fingering his jaw and never taking his eyes off Reeve's face.

"Look, the only one that stood to gain if Mr. Berman's identity was released seems to be the State. Look outside. There are thousands of Jews out there who would like nothing more than to hang Mr. Berman and feed his carcass to the wolves. Obviously, Mr. Berman figured if he leaked his own identity to the press, the judge would assume that the State had done it and would therefore call me to task."

"Those are some serious allegations, Mr. Reeves."

"Yes they are, but it isn't uncommon. It is classical misdirection and it is a tactic that I have seen used numerous times by attorneys from the firm of Crane, Gardner, and Scott."

Daniels gave him a sharp glance. "I believe you, too, were an attorney for Crane, Gardner, and Scott, Mr. Reeves."

"Well, yes, I was, but that was a very long time ago."

"Doesn't seem long enough," the judge muttered under his breath. "Mr. Berman, you seem pretty quiet over there. Do you have anything to add to our little conversation?"

Shea looked at the judge and then at Michael. The judge already appeared to doubt Michael's story and Shea, if he divulged what Moshe had told him, could issue the final blow. But this wasn't about punishing Michael Reeves. Shea needed to win to save his family, and he knew he would need Moshe's help to do that.

"Your Honor, I have nothing to respond to Mr. Reeves's accusations other than the fact that I know that I didn't leak anything to the press. I was the one who requested the gag order in the first place and no matter what Mr. Reeves says, there is nothing that I could have gained that would cause me to disobey that order. I am sorry that his opinion of me is so low that he would think that I would devise such an elaborate scheme. But frankly, I can't worry about what he thinks about me. I have a client who is facing some serious charges and right now his acquittal is my number one priority."

"Mr. Berman," the judge responded, "I am impressed with your demeanor and with your commitment to your client. Mr. Reeves, however, I am very disappointed with you. Why would you think that I would believe such an outlandish claim against Mr. Berman? Do you think that I am a fool?"

"No, Your Honor," Michael said apologetically.

"Though I will probably never be able to prove that you leaked the story, you shouldn't delude yourself and think that you pulled one over me. I have been in this business long before you were born and I know all the tricks of the trade. Consider yourself warned, Mr. Reeves. For some reason, Mr. Berman isn't calling for your head and isn't requesting that I find you in contempt. Therefore, without his pressuring and without any evidence, I am not going to throw you into jail for the evening. However, if you ever try to pull something like this again at this trial, or at any trial, I will not only find you in contempt of court, but I will also report you to the bar association and have your law license revoked. Do I make myself clear?"

"Absolutely," Michael responded, defeated.

"Good," the judge replied. "So now that we have gotten that out of the way, I am sure that both of you are ready to give your opening statements."

"Yes, we are," they replied.

"So then let's call in the jury and get this trial started."

"GOOD MORNING, LADIES AND GENTLEMEN," Michael began. "My name is Michael Reeves and I am the district attorney for the borough of Brooklyn. I would like to thank you for coming here today and I appreciate the sacrifice that all of you are making by being here with us."

Shea watched Michael with admiration. He showed no effects of what had happened in the courtroom just a few minutes earlier and he looked to be in top form.

"We are all here today because of unbridled hatred and uncontrollable rage. The defendant, Khalid al-Jinn, brutally attacked an innocent man in cold blood. He mercilessly threw him to the ground and then, with a metal rod, crushed and destroyed the bones of an elderly rabbi, breaking forty-two bones in all. Forty-two bones.

"But that wasn't enough for this barbarian. While the rabbi was writhing in pain from the horrible blows, this terrorist rammed the club into the rabbi's kidneys, puncturing them and doing massive damage. He then slammed the rod into the face of Rabbi Felder, breaking his nose. The swelling was so great that Rabbi Felder's own family was not able to recognize him when they first saw him in the hospital. One would think that would be enough.

Even for the most evil and twisted psychopaths, the pain that had been administered to Rabbi Felder surely was enough. But no, this vile creature proceeded to spit on his fallen and incapacitated victim and cry out the words, *'Allahu Akbar.'* "

Michael waited a few seconds before continuing. He knew that by recalling the words that al-Jinn had used he would play on the fears of all Americans toward radical Muslims and that is exactly what he was trying to do.

"Ladies and gentlemen of the jury, through eyewitness testimony and the actions of the client himself, you will see that there really isn't a question here. The defendant was so obstinate and brash that he left the attack weapon in clear sight of the arresting detectives, practically daring them to arrest him. Well, those detectives did their duty and now members of the jury, it is time to do yours. This isn't a question of whether or not Khalid al-Jinn is guilty; the only question is how much we should punish him. But I ask you members of the jury to remember one thing. Khalid al-Jinn showed no mercy toward his victim and I ask you to show him no mercy as well."

Michael sat down and took a drink of water. By the somber and serious look on the faces of the jurors, Shea could see that Michael had done a great job. This trial wasn't going to be easy. He rose from his seat to deliver his opening statement.

"Good morning ladies and gentlemen. My name is Shea Berman. I am a defense attorney and I am here to represent Khalid al-Jinn. I would ask you to please close your eyes and listen."

The jurors looked at each other and then looked toward the judge for guidance. Although it was unorthodox, Daniels instructed the jury to follow Shea's directions. They all closed their eyes.

"If you will listen closely, you will hear a large rally going on outside this courtroom. If you will listen even more closely, you may even hear the participants of the rally calling for my head to be served to them on a platter. This is because I am not only Jewish, but I am also a close disciple of the victim. Some people, maybe even yourselves, may question how can I defend the defendant,

Khalid al-Jinn, when he is being charged with attacking my own rabbi. The answer to that question is that under the constitution of this great country everyone deserves a proper defense no matter what the charges may be. I am sure that if you were on trial for a crime that you didn't commit, you would want the best defense possible and my client, Khalid al-Jinn, deserves no less.

"There is something else that I would like you to realize. While we are in this courtroom, we are able to ignore the noise that is going on around us. I am sure that the judge has instructed you to ignore the rallies and stories that will be associated with this case. But I am asking you to ignore a different type of noise and that is the noise of unfounded and unproven accusations. The prosecutor just presented a very heartrending story and I, as a student of Rabbi Felder, cannot sleep at night knowing what has been done to him. But just because Rabbi Felder was brutally attacked doesn't mean that my client attacked him. The prosecutor said that he will be able to prove what happened. Members of the jury, that is the key. The prosecutor can accuse all he wants, but unless he is able to prove that my client did in fact commit this terrible crime, beyond a reasonable doubt, then you, the members of the jury, must vote for acquittal. It doesn't matter if you agree or disagree with his political and religious views. You don't need to like my client, you just need to decide if the prosecution has done its job and proven that my client attacked Rabbi Felder. I am confident that by the end of this trial, you will see that the prosecution will have failed in its attempt and you will have no choice but to acquit my client of these terrible allegations."

Shea sat down and eyed the jury. Though he normally didn't think lecturing the jurors was appropriate, he felt that in this case it was important. Just the sight of al-Jinn set many of them on edge. Shea needed to remind them of their responsibility and duty in this case.

To Shea, the jurors seemed genuinely concerned and confused, which is exactly what he had hoped for. As long as he was able to continue to place doubt in the mind of the jurors, Shea could hope for an acquittal.

"Mr. Reeves," the judge addressed him. "Is the state ready to call its first witness?"

"We are, Your Honor," Michael responded. "The state calls Louise Pritchard to the stand."

An elderly woman was escorted in from the waiting room and headed toward the witness stand. Although she walked with a slight limp, Louise Pritchard held her head high as she made her way down the aisle. With her warm smile that reminded everyone of their favorite grandmother, Shea knew that Louise was the perfect opening witness.

"Good morning, Mrs. Pritchard," Michael began.

"Oh, call me Louise. My mother was Mrs. Pritchard and she has been dead for over fifty years."

"Okay, it will be Louise. How are you this morning?"

"I am doing quite well, all things considered. I mean, besides my sciatica, which has been acting up on me. I asked my doctor, you know, Dr. Rosenbaum."

"I am not sure that I have heard of him," Michael responded.

"You don't know Dr. Larry Rosenbaum? He is the best sports medicine doctor in New York. If you have a back issue, he can cure it in minutes. Now, between you and me, he is very busy. I mean, the only way that I was able to see him is because of my good friend Regina Davis. You don't know Regina, do you?"

"Mrs. Pritchard," Judge Daniels interrupted, "this is a criminal trial and you must confine your answer to the matter at hand."

"Regina and I have been friends since grade school. She taught me how to jump rope and even do double dutch. Are you married, Mr. Reeves?"

"No, I am not."

"Well then, do I have a girl for you .... Regina has a daughter. She is a stunner. Maybe a little on the heavy side, but still a wonderful girl with great personality. I think you would make a great couple."

Shea had heard enough and rose to object. Even though he found Mrs. Pritchard's ramblings and watching Michael Reeves turn color out of embarrassment to be quite humorous, it was time to put a stop to this. Shea couldn't afford to have the jury fall in love with Louise; they would hate him even more during cross examination.

"Your Honor," Shea stated, "I must object to the witness' testimony. I am sure that Mr. Reeves's personal life is of great concern to the jury. But if Your Honor could please remind the witness to limit her response to issues that are relevant to this proceeding."

"Objection sustained," the judge responded. "Mr. Reeves, please direct your witness to limit her words to events about the relevant night and acts and nothing else."

"I am sorry, Your Honor," Reeves apologized. "Louise, can you please tell me where you were on the night of September seventh of this year at 11:15 p.m.?"

"Oh, I was on my way back from the store, Made in Mecca."

"Why were you there?"

"Well, remember my friend Regina? She once told me about the best kebab in town. Now, I come from the south and we never ate kebab down in Mississippi. We had grits and vittles, but no kebabs. But Regina, she told me that I needed to try these kebabs. She told me that once I tasted it, I would never be able to go a week without eating another one. Now ...."

"Your Honor," Shea objected, "the witness' dietary preferences do not have any bearing on this case."

"Your Honor, if my witness is allowed to continue without any further interruptions by the defense, I am sure that she will be able to enlighten us all."

"The objection is overruled," the judge said. "But Mr. Reeves, my patience is running thin. So please get to the point."

"My pleasure, Your Honor. So Louise, you frequent the store, Made in Mecca, often?"

"Sure I do," Louise answered. "I go there every Monday night at exactly 11 o'clock."

"Isn't that a little late for some kebabs?"

"Mr. Reeves," Louise responded with a smile. "You have obviously never tasted these kebabs if you are going to ask me that question."

"Okay, fair enough. So every Monday night you come to the store to buy some kebabs. But isn't that a little late to be out?"

"Mr. Reeves, at my age I try to sleep as little as possible. I know that in a couple of years, I may sleeping for eternity, So I figure, why not get in as much as possible before it is too late?"

"Very wise words, Louise," Michael commented. The jury nodded in agreement with her last statement, and Shea became concerned. Michael was doing a great job of building a relationship between Louise and the jury. Shea could have found another reason to object, but he decided against it. No reason to upset the jury with repeated interruptions. Shea would just have to wait it out. He only hoped that when the time came for his cross examination, the jury would be open-minded enough to see the inconsistency in Louise's eyewitness accounts.

"And where, may I ask, is this store located?"

"On Coney Island Avenue in Brooklyn."

"Do you know the address?"

"Yes. 2253 Coney Island Avenue."

"Thank you, Louise. How do normally get to the store on Monday nights? Do you drive?"

"Oh no," Louise scolded him. "I can't stand automobiles. The good Lord gave me feet for a reason and I try to use them as much as possible. So I pretty much walk everywhere."

"So you walk from your home?"

"Objection!" Shea stated. "Counsel is leading the witness." Even though the objection had little bearing on the case, Shea had decided that raising a valid objection would break Michael's momentum and that was all he cared about.

"Sustained," the judge replied. "Mr. Reeves, please rephrase the question."

"Sure, Your Honor," Michael answered, annoyed. "Louise, is it fair to assume that you walk from your home to get to Made in Mecca?"

"Yes."

"Where do you live?"

"I live on the corner of East 12th Street and Avenue R in a small brownstone. You should just know that it hasn't been easy."

"What do you mean?"

"There isn't a day that goes by that I don't get a knock on my door from some real estate developer wanting me to sell my home. They just want to build condos on every square inch of Brooklyn. You can't see the sun anymore. But do you know what I tell them? I tell them that Louise Pritchard is not for sale. This is the home where I raised three wonderful children and I am not about to lose those memories no matter how much money they offer me."

The judge gave Louise a stern look and she realized what he was going to say. Even before the words came out of his mouth, Louise caught herself.

"I am sorry about that, Your Honor. But I am just appalled at people's lack of respect for anything other than themselves. They think that just because I am old I can be swindled into selling everything."

The judge gave her a concerned look. "While I sympathize, my courtroom is not the forum for you to retell your stories. We have a trial going on and a man's freedom is at stake. I hope you can appreciate the grave and serious nature of these proceedings. So, I am instructing you for the last time, please limit your answers and statements to information that is pertinent to this case."

"I will, Your Honor."

"You may continue, Mr. Reeves," the judge informed him.

"Very well. So as you were saying, you live on East 12th St. in Brooklyn. Therefore to get to the store you would need to go west on Coney Island Avenue. Is that correct?"

"Yes it is."

"So then, when you return home, after purchasing your kebabs, do you proceed east on Coney Island Avenue?"

"Yes I do."

"On the night in question, do you remember approximately when you started your walk home?"

"Sure I do, it was at 11:10."

"Was that earlier than normal?"

"No," Louise responded. "Achmad is usually very quick with my orders and he put everything together for me as soon as I made my choices. I paid for my food and was on my way."

"Your Honor," Michael declared, "the people introduce exhibit A." Michael proceeded to take out an enlarged photograph of the 2200 block of Coney Island Avenue. He placed it on an easel and directed Louise's attention to the image.

"Where were you when you saw the defendant attack Rabbi Felder?" Michael asked

"Objection!" Shea yelled. "The witness has not yet stated that she saw Rabbi Felder being attacked. Mr. Reeves's question assumes facts that aren't in evidence."

"Objection sustained."

"I will rephrase my question. Louise, what did you do when you left the store?"

"I was coming out of the store and I started to proceed east on Coney Island Avenue toward my home."

"Pointing to the image on display, could you show the jury exactly where you were at the time?"

Louise rose from her seat and approached the easel. There was a big red circle around the area where Rabbi Felder had been attacked. Louise took a black marker out of Michael's hand and circled a portion of the area. It was about five feet from the entranceway to Made in Mecca. She returned to her chair and awaited more questions.

"Now, had you ever met Rabbi Felder before?"

"Many times."

"When would these meetings take place?"

"Every Monday night on my way home from Made in Mecca we would cross paths. He would be on his way home and I would be on my way home."

"What was his demeanor when he would pass you?"

"He was the nicest man I had ever met. There are very few people who stop to speak to strangers on the street. Most people are always in a hurry and never have time for a friendly conversation. But that rabbi, he always had time for me. He always inquired about my health and wellbeing even when it was late and it seemed that he needed to be somewhere else."

Michael waited a moment before continuing. He wanted the jury to appreciate the virtues of the victim. Hopefully, that would make them want to punish his attacker even more.

"Can you please tell us what happened on the night of September seventh," Michael requested.

"I will try; however it is an event that I have tried my hardest to forget."

Louise closed her eyes with concentration. She wanted to make sure that she was able to retell the whole story, not leaving out any details.

"I had just walked out of the store and my mind was on the package in my hands. The steaming kebabs were so tantalizing and I couldn't wait to get home to eat them. A man, seemingly in a hurry, brushed past me and headed east on Coney Island. It was then that I looked up and saw Rabbi Felder walking toward me. He waved and smiled at me and I smiled in return. However, as he drew closer, the man who had brushed past me took a thin metal object from his pocket. I wasn't able to get a good look at what he was holding, but I was able to see perfectly what he did next. The man proceeded to use this metal object to strike Rabbi Felder across the face. Rabbi Felder grabbed onto his attacker's arm but then he fell down and the man pounced on him and continued to strike at him mercilessly. He jabbed him in the stomach and punched him on his knees. The attack only took a few seconds, but it was the most horrific and brutal thing that I had ever seen."

Louise started to shake and cry. Michael offered her a tissue, which she accepted. After she dabbed her eyes, she continued.

"I tried to find my cell phone to call the police, but I had forgotten it at home. I started screaming for help, but nobody heard. It wasn't until a few minutes later that Achmad heard me and he came out. But by that time the attacker had already fled the scene. I just wish that I could have done more for the rabbi."

"I am sure that you feel badly," Michael responded. "According to the area you circled, is it accurate to say that you were about thirty feet from the attack?"

"I guess so," Louise responded.

"Now, Louise, were you able to see the face of Rabbi Felder's attacker?"

"Yes, I was."

"But wasn't it late at night and your vision may have been unclear?"

"Mr. Reeves, what I saw that night will haunt me for the rest of my life. The horrific scene will forever be etched in my memory. I don't think I will ever be able to visit Made in Mecca again, after what happened that night."

"I understand, but Louise, that doesn't answer my question. How is the jury to believe that you were able to see the face of the attacker? Wasn't it late at night and therefore you may have made a mistake?"

"If you will look to the picture, I am sure that you will see why I was able to clearly see the attacker."

"Can you please clarify what you are referring to?"

"Certainly," Louise responded. She then asked that the easel be brought closer to her so she could demonstrate for the jury.

"The area that you circled in red is the area where Rabbi Felder was attacked. Well, that area also happens to have a large flood-light over it. I think it is because the side door to Made in Mecca is right there. That night, the light was shining brightly and clearly and I had no problem seeing the face of Rabbi Felder's attacker."

Michael paused for a moment and Shea held his breath. Shea knew what question was coming next and he knew what Louise's answer was going to be. The only question was how convincing she was going to be to the jury.

"Mrs. Pritchard, is the person that you saw attack Rabbi Felder currently in this courtroom?"

"Yes," Louise answered

"Louise, please indicate to the jury the person who attacked Rabbi Felder."

"It was him," Louise screamed, pointing her finger at Khalid al-Jinn. "He is the monster that ruthlessly attacked that defenseless man. I'll never forget his dark evil eyes staring at me after he had finished his attack. Shame on you, Mr. al-Jinn."

The courtroom was in an uproar, and the judge struggled to restore order. Louise was still yelling at al-Jinn, who looked as stoic and as heartless as ever.

"Objection!" Shea called out over the hysteria. "The witness has no right to address my client or to state her views."

"I agree with you, counselor," the judge said once the tumult had died down. "The jury will disregard the witness's statements to the defendant. Are there any more questions, Mr. Reeves?"

"No, Your Honor," Michael responded, clearly satisfied with the morning's work.

"Mr. Berman," the judge addressed him, "are you ready to cross examine the witness?"

Shea looked at his notes and went through the information that Hector had acquired. After the jury heard what Shea had to say, they should definitely doubt Louise's testimony. But Shea knew that not everything goes the way it should, especially if the jury loved Louise Pritchard so much that they would be unable to see the possibility that she could be wrong. Shea needed to disprove her testimony without attacking her, and that would not be an easy thing to do. As Shea approached the stand, he knew that he had his work cut out for him. But what else was new?

"**G**OOD MORNING, LOUISE," SHEA BEGAN.

"My friends call me Louise. *You* can call me Mrs. Pritchard."

Shea winced at the comment. Louise didn't like him very much and that wasn't a good thing. If the jury loved Louise and Louise disliked him, there could be a few very long minutes coming up.

Instead of beating around the bush, Shea decided to confront her head on.

"You don't like me very much, do you?" Shea asked.

"No, not really," Louise answered.

"Why is that?"

"Because you are defending that terrible man. What he did was unthinkable and frankly, I don't believe that he deserves a defense."

"But doesn't our Constitution guarantee everybody the right to a fair trial?"

"Well, in my book, once he attacked that rabbi, your client gave up his rights to anything. The Constitution was written for men and women, not animals. What he did to that sweet holy man wasn't human. That was pure animalistic behavior. Besides, even if he deserved a defense, he only deserves one based on the facts, not like what you are about to do."

"And what exactly am I about to do?"

"You are probably going to scheme and conjure up outlandish lies to get your client off on a technicality. All you defense attorneys are the same. I think I would trust a used car salesman before I would trust a guy like you."

"Who told you that I would try to lie my way to get an acquittal?"

"Mr. Reeves told me," Louise responded matter-of-factly.

"Objection!" Michael stated, embarrassed. "Hearsay."

"Even though I would prefer not to, I have to sustain that objection," the judge commented, glaring at Michael.

Shea looked at the judge and nodded. From what he had seen of Michael thus far, he wasn't surprised to find out that Michael had said those things to Louise. However, he did find it quite humorous that Louise had no problem telling the jury what Michael had said.

"But, Mrs. Pritchard, what if I were to tell you that I do not intend to lie or fabricate anything to achieve an acquittal for my client, I only intend to use cold hard facts. What would you say then?"

"I would say that is impossible because I know that the jury believes me, and I know what I saw. I saw your client attack Rabbi Felder. So unless you can find a way to cheat, my feeling is that your client is going to get what he deserved."

Shea saw the nods from members of the jury and he knew that he needed to act fast. It was now or never.

"But isn't this is all based on the assumption that you saw my client attack Rabbi Felder?"

"I did see your client attack Rabbi Felder."

"Are you sure about that?"

"Objection!" Michael interrupted. "Counselor's question had already been answered."

"Withdrawn," Shea responded. "But I do have a question for you, Mrs. Pritchard. Who is Leonardo Haley?"

"Objection," Michael cried out.

"On what grounds?" the judge asked.

"Relevance," Michael answered.

"If you would allow me to continue my questioning," Shea interrupted, "I am sure that the court will see the relevance."

"Your Honor," Michael countered. "The defense is embarking on a fishing expedition. The witness is not on trial and doesn't need to answer questions that aren't pertinent to this case."

"Sidebar," the judge commanded. Both lawyers approached the bench and were out of earshot of the jury and the witness.

"I am not going to have my courtroom turn into a battlefield where you two can spend the entire time fighting with each other," the judge informed them sternly. "Mr. Reeves, I am overruling your objection. However, Mr. Berman, if this in fact does turn out to be a fishing expedition, I will dismiss the witness and not allow you to finish questioning her. Is that understood?"

"Yes," both attorneys responded.

"Good. Now return to your places and let us continue this trial."

Shea felt good as he walked back to the table. He wasn't sure if Michael knew where he was going with the questions, but he saw that Michael was indeed nervous. *Good*, Shea thought, because after he was finished with his cross examination of Louise, Michael was going to have a lot of things to be nervous about.

"I will ask you the question again," Shea continued. "Who is Leonardo Haley?"

"He is my pharmacist," Louise answered.

"How often do you see him?"

"Mr. Berman, I am an old woman and many of my body parts don't work as well as they used to. I am on many different medications. Most of the time I can't keep track of all of them. But Leonardo does a great job. He makes sure that I get all my refills on time and makes sure that I am always taking the right dosage."

"So it would seem to me that you two are pretty close, correct?"

"I guess you could say that."

"So if Leonardo would tell us that you were given a certain prescription over a week ago, is he someone that we could trust?"

"Yes."

"Good. I know that you might have a hard time recalling this but can you please tell the jury why you were prescribed Naproxen on September fifth of this year?"

"Objection," Michael called out. "I don't see why the witness's medications should have any bearing on this case."

Shea knew that Michael was grasping at straws and hoping that the judge would cut him a break. However, Michael wasn't in luck.

"Overruled," the judge responded. "The witness may answer the question."

"I was prescribed Naproxen because of a surgery I had undergone," Louise responded.

"What type of surgery?"

"Well, I live alone. My daughter is always worried about me, especially when it came to my glasses. You see, I would constantly misplace my glasses. The problem is that I am extremely near-sighted and can't see anything without my glasses. So when I would lay down to rest, very often I would wake up and wouldn't be able to find my glasses. I would find myself calling my daughter, panicking that I was unable to see and I needed her help. My daughter had enough and she told me that I needed to look into Lasik surgery. She had said that if I got Lasik I would no longer need glasses and therefore I would never lose them again."

"Did you go for the surgery?"

"I did. The doctor's name is Dr. Arneslyan. His office is on Quentin Road in Brooklyn."

"Mrs. Pritchard, when did you have the Lasik surgery?"

"I got it on September fifth."

"Wasn't that just two days before the night of the attack?"

"Yes, it was."

"Your Honor, the defense would like to introduce defense exhibit B." Shea took out a sheet of paper and showed it first to the judge and then to Michael. Finally, he brought the paper to Louise.

"Mrs. Pritchard, on whose stationery is the following letter written?"

"Dr. Arneslyn's," Louise answered.

"How do you know this?"

"Because it says his name on the top of the paper and I personally recognize this letterhead from all the paperwork that I have had to sign whenever I went to his office."

"What does is say on the top of the paper?"

"It says, 'possible side effects due to Lasik surgery.'"

"Thank you," Shea responded. "Would you please read aloud side effect number three?"

"It says that within the first forty-eight hours after surgery one may experience difficulty driving at night. Glares and haloes may distort one's vision."

The members of the gallery and the jury started murmuring and that was exactly what Shea had planned.

"Now, Mrs. Pritchard," Shea continued, building his own momentum, "you had testified that you were able to see the face of my client because a floodlight was shining and had illuminated his face. Is that correct?"

"Yes," Louise answered weakly.

"But according to what you have just read to the court, isn't it possible that the direct light caused by the floodlight may have in fact compromised your ability to properly see Rabbi Felder's attacker?"

"Well, I don't know."

"According to the doctor's instructions, you may have very well seen an attack, but your sight may have also been severely distorted because of the strong light cast by the store's floodlight."

Louise sat on the witness stand looking puzzled and confused. Shea could have gone in for the kill, but he decided to choose a different approach.

"Mrs. Pritchard," Shea addressed her softly, "were you aware of the possible side effects of the surgery?"

"Not really," Louise admitted.

"Didn't the doctor give you a sheet just like the one that I gave you?"

"Of course he did."

"So then why weren't you aware of the possible side effects of the surgery?"

"I know this sounds kind of childish, but I never read those papers. Most of the time the side effects don't even occur. One of my doctors once gave me a prescription for a medication that was supposed to help my blood pressure. The paper that he gave me along with the medicine said that a possible side effect was hair loss. Now I ask you, Mr. Berman, do you see this hair on my head? This isn't a wig, son. So from that day on I stopped reading those papers. I figured that the doctors were covering themselves just in case something happened. But the chances that anything would really happen weren't very likely."

"So you are telling the court, that when you went down to the police station and picked my client out of a lineup, you genuinely thought that he was the attacker, correct?"

"Yes."

"You never thought that you could have been mistaken."

"No."

"On the contrary, you probably assumed that because of your recent surgery, your eyes were better than they had ever been and there was no way that you could have ever made a mistake."

"Exactly," Louise proclaimed.

"Louise," Shea said as he walked toward the witness stand, "nobody here is accusing you of being malicious. Everybody makes mistakes. You probably thought in your mind that my client, Khalid al-Jinn, was definitely Rabbi Felder's attacker. But now, isn't it possible that you made a mistake?"

Shea left Louise on the witness stand and didn't bother to wait for an answer. The faces of the jury told Shea everything that he needed to know. Even if Louise herself was still convinced that Khalid al-Jinn was the attacker, because of the information that Shea had provided, the jury was no longer as sure.

"Mr. Reeves, do you have questions for redirect?" the judge asked.

"Yes I do, Your Honor," Michael responded, springing up from seat. "Louise, do you see Rabbi Felder's attacker in this room?"

When Shea was in law school, a professor had told him that you never ask a question to a witness unless you are absolutely certain you know the answer. Michael, in his haste, either because he wanted to salvage his lone eyewitness, or because of the extreme pressure that he was under to win the case, committed a cardinal sin and now he was going to pay for it.

"I don't know," Louise answered sheepishly.

The gallery was in an uproar and the judge called for order. Michael's face told the whole story and Shea looked away from his opponent. Shea felt good, but he knew that things could change very quickly. And as he looked at the dark empty eyes of his client, he knew that the trial was far from over.

■ ■ ■

Shea arrived in court the next morning ready to do battle. After his masterful cross-examination of Louise Pritchard, Michael had requested a recess until the following morning to regroup and rethink strategy. Even though Shea had wanted to build on his momentum and continue his onslaught against the prosecution, Michael's request for a recess gave Shea something that he sorely needed, and that was time, precious time. So instead of objecting, Shea agreed to the recess and used the time to prepare for the state's next witness, Dr. Robert Fitzgerald, Rabbi Felder's trauma physician.

The doctor was going to testify regarding the injuries that Rabbi Felder had suffered. Michael would undoubtedly ask the doctor to go into painstaking detail about all the wounds that Rabbi Felder had suffered. There was one detail that Shea hoped the doctor would be able to clarify, but for that he was going to need to wait till his cross examination.

As he entered the courtroom geared for battle, he was greeted by an unexpected figure.

"Allan," Shea said, "what are you doing here?"

"What, I can't watch my junior associate in action?"

"You can do whatever you want. You are the managing partner

and I am the junior associate. I just was wondering why you are here. I thought that you would be working on the Merzeir lawsuit."

"The judge granted Aragon a temporary injunction and I asked Kyle to fight it. He is busy right now preparing an argument for me and I am sure that we are going to win and proceed to trial. I am so confident that I was willing to take the morning off and watch you in action."

"Wow, and if I didn't feel any pressure before ...."

"Don't worry about me," Allan reassured him. "I will be a fly on the wall."

"Sure, a fly on the wall who happens to be my boss and can fire me at any second."

"What do you have to worry about?" Allan said. "From what my sources tell me, you were fantastic yesterday. I heard that you blew up Michael's witness right before his eyes."

"I couldn't have done it without Hector's help," Shea added.

"Stop doing that."

"Doing what?"

"Stop giving credit to other people, when we both know who deserves the real credit here."

"What are you referring to?"

"Hector may have found the magic bullet, but you put it together beautifully. Another lawyer may have gotten Hector's information, and not known what to do with it. But you, you knew exactly how to use it against Michael. That was good, Shea, I mean real good."

Shea didn't know how to respond. Allan rarely praised his associates and he was laying it on thick. If Shea didn't know better, he would have thought that Allan was feeling guilty about something and was trying to placate his own conscience.

"Don't let my words go to your head," Allan advised with a smile. "You've still got a long trial ahead of you. You need to keep your focus. But make no mistake about it. If Michael thought that you were some pushover, you definitely showed him that you are a force to be reckoned with."

Shea nodded and settled in at the defense table. As his client, in his orange prison jumpsuit, was led into the courtroom, , Shea faked a smile that al-Jinn did not return.

Moments later, the judge entered the courtroom. Once the jury was seated, he asked Michael if he was ready to call his next witness, and Michael responded in the affirmative.

"The state calls Dr. Robert Fitzgerald to the stand," Michael announced.

Shea turned his head to watch the doctor approaching the stand. If he hadn't done his research, Shea would have shared the same reaction that the jury gave when they saw the doctor: surprise. Rabbi Felder's doctor looked no older than thirty and in fact he wasn't. He was only twenty-seven, with plump pink cheeks that gave him an even younger appearance, but he was already a veteran physician.

Michael didn't want the jury doubting the doctor's qualifications, so he proceeded to establish Fitzgerald's credibility.

"Dr. Fitzgerald," Michael began, "how long have you been a physician in the trauma unit at Lutheran Medical Center?"

"This is my sixth year at the hospital," Fitzgerald responded.

"Doctor, how old are you?"

"I am twenty-seven years old."

"But wouldn't that mean that you started there at the age of twenty-one?"

"Yes."

"And when did you become a physician?"

"I entered to Yale Medical School at the age of sixteen. I was able to begin my residency at Lutheran shortly after graduation and I have been there ever since."

"Doctor, can you please tell the court why you chose to be a trauma physician?"

"Objection!" Shea called out. "The doctor's reasons for his career choice have no bearing on this case."

"Overruled," the judge responded. "Dr. Fitzgerald, you may answer the question."

"Well, I became a trauma physician because I really wanted to help my patients. I understand many doctors may say that, and they probably mean it. But when you are standing over somebody who had just been in a terrible accident and the fear and shock of what has just transpired are still fresh, they are extremely vulnerable. Their families are broken and don't know where to turn. I felt that if I was able to bring stability back to those people and their families in their time of need, I could really make a difference in this world."

"Is that how you would describe the Felder family after Rabbi Felder was brought in to the hospital?"

"Actually, it was the exact opposite," the doctor corrected him.

"What do you mean?"

"When Rabbi Felder was brought in, he was in really bad shape. His wife and his youngest son, Yechiel, were at his side the whole time. But something was very different about them."

"What are you referring to?"

"With most of my patients, their families are usually an emotional wreck. They are anxious and scared. But with the Felders they were eerily calm. It seemed that they had faith that everything was going to turn out for the best. When I saw Mrs. Felder, all she did was thank me and say prayers from her prayer book. As a man of science, I can't say that I really believe in a God. But after meeting a family like the Felders, I think that my beliefs may have changed."

As opposed to his policy with Louise Pritchard, Michael believed that it was vital that the doctor stay on track. He didn't want the jury to get sidetracked and lose focus. He needed them to hear and visualize every gruesome detail the doctor would provide.

"Doctor Fitzgerald," Michael interrupted, "can you please describe the injuries suffered by Rabbi Felder."

Shea could have objected at that point due to the ambiguity of the request, but he chose not to. Actually during Dr. Fitzgerald's entire testimony, Shea did not raise one objection. Although the details made him sick to his stomach, Shea wanted the doctor to establish his credibility with the jury. Because if the jury believed and trusted Doctor Fitzgerald's assessment of Rabbi Felder's injuries, they would, hopefully, believe his assessment on how exactly Rabbi Felder received them and that was exactly what Shea, who'd spent hours going over the hospital reports, was hoping for.

Michael finished his questioning and Shea rose to cross examine the witness.

"Dr. Fitzgerald," Shea addressed him, "I would first like to express my appreciation for all you are doing for Rabbi Felder and the entire Felder family."

Dr. Fitzgerald looked at Shea, his baby face confused. He hadn't expected Shea to open with a compliment and he wasn't sure how to respond.

"It is my pleasure," the doctor said uneasily.

"But let us focus now on the task at hand," Shea continued. "Dr. Fitzgerald, you testified that Rabbi Felder received injuries to his face."

"Yes, both of his lacrimal and maxilla bones were shattered."

"Now doctor, you also testified that there were abrasions found on his knees. Can you explain what that may tell you about the attack?"

"Objection, Your Honor," Michael said loudly. "This question is beyond the expertise of the witness. The doctor is not a forensic investigator and therefore is not qualified to make statements about the nature of the attack."

"But the witness has treated many injuries and would have firsthand knowledge on how various bruises and abrasions are formed," Shea countered.

"Mr. Reeves, I must agree with the defense and overrule your objection," the judge stated. The judge motioned for the doctor to answer the question.

"It would seem that bruises and the abrasions were caused by what is known as a 'dead fall.'"

"What is a dead fall?" Shea asked.

"A dead fall is where a person will have suffered a trauma that would have caused him to fall from a standing position directly onto his knees. The force of that fall will normally cause abrasions like those that were found on the knees of Rabbi Felder."

"So according to your expert opinion, Rabbi Felder must have fallen from the standing position directly onto his knees."

"That is correct."

"Were you aware, Doctor, that the eyewitness testified that Rabbi Felder was first hit on the face with the metal rod and then fell to the ground."

"No, I was not."

"But after looking at the abrasions on Rabbi Felder's knees, would you say that the eyewitness's account of the story was accurate?"

"Mr. Berman, I cannot say whether or not the blow to Rabbi Felder's face caused him to have a dead fall. The only thing that I know is that the abrasions on Rabbi Felder's knees were due to a dead fall."

"But would it surprise you if in fact the eyewitness was correct in her assessment that Rabbi Felder did fall to the ground because of the assault to his face?"

"No, it would not surprise me at all."

"Thank you doctor," Shea remarked. "One last question, how tall is Rabbi Felder?"

"I do not recall," the doctor responded.

"It says here on his chart that you filled out that Rabbi Felder is six foot three."

"If that is what it says on the chart, then it must be accurate." Dr. Fitzgerald replied.

"Dr. Fitzgerald, do you know how tall my client is?"

"No, I do not."

"My client is five foot six."

Michael knew what question Shea was about to ask and he jumped up to object. Shea continued, relentless.

"Dr. Fitzgerald, do you believe that it is possible for my client to have attacked Rabbi Felder in the face, while being close to a foot shorter?"

"Objection!" Michael yelled. "This question is beyond the expertise of the witness."

"Dr. Fitzgerald," Shea pressed on ignoring Michael's objection. "How is it possible for my client to have been able to break another man's lacrimal and maxilla bones if he is nine full inches shorter than his victim?"

"Your Honor," Michael pleaded.

"Objection sustained," Daniels responded. "The jury is to disregard the last question posed by the defense."

Shea smiled in satisfaction. No matter what the judge said, the jury had still heard Shea's question to the doctor and his point would certainly give them something to think about.

"Question withdrawn," Shea responded. "No further questions, Your Honor."

"Mr. Reeves, do you have any questions for redirect?" the judge asked.

"No, Your Honor," Michael responded, still seething from what had just transpired.

"The witness may step down," the judge informed. "Will the state call its next witness?"

"The state calls Yechiel Felder to the stand," Michael Reeves declared.

"Objection!" Shea shouted.

S PECIAL AGENT ROBERT FIELDS TAPPED HIS KNIFE AGAINST
the table incessantly. When he was tense, he tapped, and with
everything that was going on, Fields had a lot to be tense about.

Ever since his meeting with Leo Stephens, Fields had been struggling to figure out what was going on. He knew the Americans
had credible information that the Israeli prime minister's life
was in danger, but he didn't know anything else. He knew that
Schechter was scheduled to arrive in a couple of days, but he didn't
even know his full itinerary. What made matters worse was that
Fields couldn't share his information with his Israeli counterparts,
because the only way that the Americans could have gotten the
information was by spying on the Israelis and he knew that they
wouldn't be too happy to hear that. That was why he found himself sitting alone in a restaurant waiting for his source to join him.

Looking around the restaurant, Fields realized that his source
had good but expensive taste. When the waiter brought him the
menu, Fields's mouth dropped open in amazement. Aside from
the fact that Fields couldn't pronounce the names of any of the
items, the prices were extravagant. *Fifty bucks for what!* Fields
wondered. But what really shocked him was that he was only

looking at the appetizers. When he saw what the entrees cost, he felt sick. Not too sick though: Uncle Sam was footing the bill, and an expensive meal was a small price to pay for the information that Fields needed.

When his source entered, he set the knife down on the table and focused. He was about to take his only shot at figuring out what was really going on and he didn't want to blow it.

"Rami," Fields announced as his visitor came toward the table.

"Robert," Rami Aretz responded, extending his hand. "Did you order anything while you were waiting?"

"Are you kidding me? I can't understand anything on this menu. If I tried to order something, how do I know that the waiter isn't bringing me some fish stew or something like that?"

"First of all, fish stew is called *ragoût de poisson* and I don't see it on the menu. However, you should really try their *Canard à la Rouennaise*. It is really tasty."

"What exactly is that?"

"Duck in blood sauce."

Fields made a face. "Why can't they sell normal food like hamburgers or a good steak?"

"Robert, you really need to broaden your horizons."

"That may be true, but none of my horizons are ever going to cost two hundred dollars. That is precisely what your chicken in blood sauce costs."

"First of all," Rami corrected, "it is duck and not chicken. Second, you sometimes need to pay for the finer things in life."

Fields looked at his friend as he sat across from him. At the age of fifty-one, Rami Aretz was retired and enjoying every minute of it. While he had once been the head of Shin Bet, now he enjoyed the good life. He spent his days flying first class to various countries all over the world that required his expertise. He was a security consultant and was commissioned by many governments to properly train their security officials.

"Since when did you become such a foodie?" Fields asked.

"When you visit all the countries that I have, you start to appreciate international cuisine. I spent two weeks in Paris this year.

Interpol flew me down there to give a training seminar. While I was there, I was treated to the finest restaurants in all of France. My palate has been spoiled and I can no longer appreciate simple foods."

"Well, like I told you on the phone, Uncle Sam is footing this bill, so you order whatever you want, even if it is pigeon in blood sauce."

"Thank you, Robert." Rami answered with a smile. "But before I order, I need to know why we are having this meeting."

"Besides the fact that I wanted to say hello to an old friend?"

"Robert," Rami said, as he ran his hand through his close-cropped hair, "not only do you not have time for idle chitchat and meetings, but I definitely know that Uncle Sam wouldn't be paying for this meeting if it wasn't official. So please, just come out and say it."

"You got me," Fields admitted. "We are definitely on the company clock here and I need some information from you."

"What is going on?"

"I can't tell you."

"Excuse me?"

"Look, in the past I have been completely open and honest with you and I think that is why we have had such a great relationship. But now I need you to trust me."

"Trust is a two-way street."

"Meaning?"

"Meaning that you have some information that for some reason you cannot share with me. You are asking me to trust you, but you aren't willing to trust me."

"I can't," Fields said quietly. "The way that I came to learn this information can never be shared. I may trust you, but that doesn't matter."

"But it does to me," Rami said, rising from his seat. "If you cannot be forthcoming, then we have nothing to talk about."

Fields saw his friend get up and head for the door. Now Fields had a major problem: He needed Rami's intel but couldn't disclose why without creating a foreign-relations nightmare. Fields realized that he still had one more card to play. He had hoped that he wouldn't need to use it, but desperate times called for desperate measures.

"You owe me," Fields announced to Rami's departing back.

"What are you talking about?" Rami said, swinging around.

"The fiasco with Danny Bastetti. Remember him? He put it over you just fine, got away with the schematics of the missile defense system. You were the head of the Shin Bet, and you were looking like a rookie out of basic training. If I hadn't given you a hint or two, your career would have been over. I saved you. This lifestyle that you have, Mr. Expert on intelligence and security, is all thanks to me. Had I not solved the case, you would be making copies in the Shin Bet office and running errands."

Rami walked back to the table and glared at Fields. He didn't like to remember how a gangster had almost bested him some years ago. "So what does this mean? Since you did me a favor, I become your indentured servant?"

"No," Fields replied. "All I want is a little information. Once you give it to me, we are squared. I promise you that after this conversation, I will never bring it up again."

Rami mulled over what Fields had said. In the business of espionage and security, there weren't many rules. But there was one rule that everybody followed and that was repaying a debt. Rami owed Fields and he wasn't going to deny it. But he definitely didn't want to be on the hook for the rest of his life either.

"So let us get this clear," Rami stated. "I help you on whatever you need, without asking any questions, and we are totally squared? No more of this nonsense?"

"Totally squared," Fields repeated.

"Fine," Rami relented, sitting back in his seat. "But this meal is going to cost your government some serious cash. I am going to order whatever I want."

"Fine with me."

"So what do you need to know?" Rami inquired.

"You are aware that Prime Minister Schechter is coming to New York in two days, correct?"

"Yes, I am."

"Well, what you don't know is that there is a credible threat against the prime minster that we are trying to follow up on."

"Where did you get this information?"

"Uh-uh," Fields chastised.

"Sorry, I forgot. Force of habit. Are you sure that the information is credible?"

"Trust me on this one. It is legit."

"So what do you want to know from me?"

"From what we have been able to gather, there isn't much chatter about any attack. All of our informants have come back empty-handed. Is there anything that you know that could help me?"

"I am not sure what you are referring to," Rami answered evasively.

"Let me say it straight. If somebody was going to try to take out the prime minister on American soil, is there anybody currently here that you know of who could do it?"

Rami played with his fork. Fields knew that he was thinking and didn't want to interrupt him. It looked like Rami might actually know something that could help him in this case. The real question was: was Rami going to tell Fields what he needed to know?

"If you ever attempt to verify what I am about to tell you, you won't be successful. Only a handful of people know this information, and nobody besides me will ever say a thing. Is that clear?"

"Crystal."

"Also, don't ask me why things ended up working out the way they did. I can't answer for the mistakes of the past."

"No problem."

"Robert, what do you know about the refugee camp in Jenin?"

"Not much, other than the fact that the Israeli Army has needed to enter it on various occasions."

"There is a reason why we have had to invade the camp and that is because it is a hotbed of terrorist activities. Do you know why?"

"No," Fields replied.

"The reason is simple. You have more than sixteen thousand refugees crammed into a half a kilometer of space. Poverty is rampant. Children are starving and are ravaged by disease. The blame we put solely on the Palestinians, and they put it solely on the Israelis, but the result is what really matters. Did you know that over sixty percent of the inhabitants are under the age of twenty-four?"

"I had no idea."

"So these kids, they are born into a life of starvation and sickness and there is no hope, except for one thing."

"Terrorism," Fields interrupted.

"Exactly," Rami agreed. "These terrorists brainwash these young impressionable children from the time that they are just infants. They feed them hatred and promise them salvation. There are only two official schools operating in Jenin. However, according to our intelligence, there are more than thirty terrorist schools recruiting and poisoning kids to join their jihadist army."

"So what are you doing to stop it?"

"There isn't much we can do," Rami admitted. "However, with our sources planted inside these schools, we are able to monitor the whereabouts of certain individuals we believe will do serious harm when they get older. These are either charismatic people we are afraid will recruit others, or they are very skilled in the art of military tactics and open warfare. Either way, we identify certain individuals and we keep our tabs on them."

"That seems like a great plan," Fields interrupted. "Why are you telling me this now?"

"I am telling you this now, because about three years ago, we lost track of one budding murderer."

"Lost track of him?"

"We told our informants to keep an eye on him, but one day, right before he was about to execute a major assassination attempt, he just vanished. We searched everywhere for him. He was so dangerous we alerted the local authorities throughout Israel, fearing that he would strike somewhere."

"Did you ever find him?"

"No; however, we did learn that he entered the United States shortly after he disappeared."

"Are you telling me that there has been a known dangerous terrorist living in my country who at any moment can blow himself up and many others with him?"

"He is a skilled sniper who suffers from Intermittent Explosive Disorder," Rami corrected.

"English, please."

"It means that he can have uncontrollable and explosive anger outbursts."

"But how is he different than any other crazy terrorist?"

"This guy would never blow himself up. The reason we had him on our radar was because of his ability to fire a sniper rifle. He has murdered three Israeli soldiers. He can target anything from anywhere."

"Is that supposed to make me feel any better?"

"No, just wanted you to have your facts straight."

"But how could you not tell us about this?"

"The same way that you aren't telling me how you know that the prime minister's life is in danger. I am assuming that if you are coming to me, that the Israelis don't know a thing about this. As per your request, I won't tell them. But don't go all righteous on me. We have our secrets and obviously you have yours. It is the nature of the game."

Fields didn't know what to say, because Rami was right.

"Do you have a picture of this guy?" Fields wondered

"No."

"So what do you have?"

"I have a name," Rami replied.

"Okay, let me have it."

"His name is Khalid al-Jinn," Rami replied.

■ ■ ■

"Objection? On what grounds?" Michael asked.

"On the grounds that this witness was never on the list that was submitted to me," Shea replied.

"What are you talking about?"

"The list that I have here," Shea stated, waving a paper.

The judge motioned for both attorneys to approach the bench. Shea draw near, still brandishing the piece of paper.

"I thought I warned you two about using my courtroom for a shouting match," the judge said angrily.

"You did, Your Honor, but counsel has gone too far," Shea said. "He is trying to call up a witness who was never on the witness list. Here, look for yourself."

The judge eyed the list suspiciously. After he had checked it over several times, he turned to Michael.

"It definitely seems to me that Mr. Berman has a point. I don't see the name of your witness on this list."

"Let me see that," Michael ordered, reaching to take the list from the judge. He looked it over for a second and returned it to the judge.

"Of course his name isn't on the list," Michael defended himself. "This isn't the most updated list. The updated witness list is here in my hand." Michael handed another paper to the judge, pointing to Yechiel Felder's name.

"But how does that help me?" Shea protested. "Counselor can't just concoct a new list without showing it to me before the trial."

"I gave it to the defense before the trial," Michael replied.

"I never met you or anybody from your office, besides Moshe Cohen, before the trial. When was I supposed to have received your new list?"

"I gave it to Allan Shore, Mr. Berman's colleague, when he came to my office the night before the trial," Michael declared. "I assumed that he would pass it along to you."

Shea was confused. If Allan had indeed received the list, why hadn't he given it to Shea?

There was only one way to find out. Asking Judge Daniels, who was growing increasingly irritated, for permission, Shea headed for the gallery and motioned Allan to join him outside.

"What's the holdup?" Allan asked.

"The holdup is that it seems that you received an updated

witness list from Reeves that you neglected to give me," Shea replied angrily.

"That's right, I did."

"Didn't you realize that Yechiel Felder's name was on the list?"

"Sure I did," Allan replied.

"So why didn't you tell me that they had him as a witness?"

"It just didn't seem worth the trouble. I assumed that he would not end up testifying."

"Why not?"

"Shea, Yechiel Felder will not be allowed to testify. His testimony is one hundred percent prejudicial against your client. There is nothing that he can offer as a witness other than to make the jury hate your client even more. Reeves knows that, you know that, and the judge will surely know that. It's a simple courtroom tactic. You object to him being a witness on the grounds of it being prejudicial, and the judge will have no choice but to disallow his testimony."

Shea realized that Allan was right. Because Rabbi Felder wasn't on trial, character witnesses weren't permitted. Michael was only allowed to call witnesses who could testify about the crime committed, not about the victim.

Undoubtedly, given his knowledge of the law, Allan was right. Shea should certainly object, and the objection would be sustained.

But Shea knew something that Allan didn't. Something that might help him win this case.

Something that would certainly make him hate himself even more than he already did.

"I want to hear it again," Shea said, his voice urgent.

"Hear what?"

"I want you to tell me that if I win this case, there is no way that I will be fired. I need this job and there are many people counting on me right now. I may be compelled to do something that I will regret for the rest of my life, but it will be worth it if I know that I was able to keep my job because of it. So please, Allan, tell me again, if I win, I am safe."

Allan looked at Shea. As a trained lawyer, his face stayed calm, masking the emotions surging within him: guilt, shame, sadness.

"If you win, you are safe," Allan lied.

■ ■ ■

Shira Berman walked up and down the aisles of Dovie's. Even though the store was cramped and the aisles were almost impossible to pass through, Shira loved shopping there. They had the best takeout in the city, and the staff was helpful and friendly. She always felt welcome when she walked into the store. There would be the cordial hello from Shifra the cashier, or perhaps Benny the butcher would tell her that he had saved her the last piece of rib steak.

She made one last stop at the deli counter before checking out.

"Yossi," Shira called out with a smile, "do you have my order?"

"What order?" Yossi responded coldly, not looking at her.

"What do you mean, 'what order'? The same order I put in every week."

"Oh, I must have forgotten."

"Well, can I order now?" Shira asked, as a line began to form behind her.

"You can try," Yossi answered, "but I can't say that I will be able to get to it."

"You won't be able to get to it by the end of the day?"

"No, I am not sure that I will be able to get to it by Shabbos."

"But why not?" Shira asked, puzzled. "It's only a simple order. I see that you have most of the items that I need right here in the showcase."

"Listen, lady," Yossi answered gruffly. "If you don't like the service, don't shop here. As you can see, we are really busy right now, and I don't have time to talk to you. So if you wouldn't mind, please move aside so somebody else can order."

Shira turned away. Could this be Yossi, always so pleasant, always with a joke or a piece of cooking advice? Bewildered and on the verge of tears, Shira took her groceries to the cashier to check out.

"I am sorry but I am closed," Shifra said, not looking in Shira's direction.

"But Shifra, there is someone on your line right now," Shira pointed out.

"Oh, so maybe I am closed only for you."

"What? Why would you be closed only for me?"

"Why don't you ask your husband that question? While you are at it, ask your husband where he gets the chutzpah to do what he is doing."

Shira wasn't going to take this quietly. "You have no idea what is going on," Shira said, blinking back tears. "You don't understand what my husband is going through."

Shifra's eyes flashed. "You know, when you walked into the store, I was really angry. I thought to myself, how can she have the audacity to walk around like nothing is happening? But then I decided to give you the benefit of the doubt. Maybe you didn't know what your husband is up to. But now I see that not only do you know exactly what is going on, but you are even trying to defend him. So let me tell you this. I don't care what you and your husband are going through. You both make me sick. How about you leave this store right now and never come back!"

The cashier's raised voice had attracted the attention of the other shoppers. Shira saw the faces staring at her and she ran out, leaving her full cart behind. By the time she reached her van, the hot tears were spilling down her cheeks. She had never been so humiliated in her life. Shea had told her that things weren't going to be easy, but she never dreamed that things could go this badly.

As she reached into her pocketbook to take out a tissue, she saw that a phone call was coming in. She put the phone to her ear, listened for a moment, her hot cheeks suddenly cold and pale.

"I'll be right there."

As she pulled into traffic, she called Shea. She didn't know if he was in court, and she didn't care; he had to come home. This was not something that Shira could tackle on her own.

"I AM SORRY, YOUR HONOR," SHEA STATED. "I'VE clarified the error. The defense retracts its objection. However, because I have just learned of this witness's involvement in the trial, I would ask that Your Honor allow me some leeway when I question the witness."

"I believe that is only fair," the judge responded. "Any problem, Mr. Reeves?"

Michael looked at Shea before he answered Judge Daniels. *Why hadn't Shea objected*, he wondered. Yechiel's testimony was obviously prejudicial. If Shea had the chance to keep the rabbi's son off the stand, why didn't he jump at it?

Still, Yechiel didn't have much to add to the story. Michael had only called him so he could emphasize how saintly the victim was — and what a demon the defendant had to be, to attack him so brutally.

"It shouldn't be a problem," Michael responded.

Shea nodded and Yechiel Felder walked to the stand. Shea tried to catch his eye, but Yechiel deliberately avoided eye contact.

"Mr. Felder, I would first like to express my deepest sympathies for you and your mother and the rest of your family. Your father is in all our thoughts and prayers," Michael began.

"Thank you, Mr. Reeves," Yechiel responded.

"Mr. Felder, can you recall what happened on September seventh, the way you and your family experienced it?"

"It isn't easy."

"I know. But it would clarify the events of that night."

"My mother and I were waiting for my father to return home. Normally, he came home about 11:15. By 11:30, we started to get worried."

"Why? Wasn't he only fifteen minutes late?"

"You don't know my father, Mr. Reeves. He is a man of punctuality and promptness. If he says that he will be there at 11:15, you could expect him to be there at exactly 11:15. If he is ever going to be late, even if only by a few minutes, he always calls to make sure that my mother doesn't worry."

"But that night he didn't call," Michael stated.

"Objection," Shea called out. "Mr. Reeves is leading the witness."

"I am sorry, I will rephrase. Did he call your mother that night?"

"No, he didn't."

"So what did you do?"

"Well, my mother got worried, so she tried his cell phone. After a few rings, it went to voicemail."

"Did you know what was said?"

"Objection," Shea called out. "This calls for speculation."

"Your Honor," Michael explained, "the witness was able to observe whether or not his mother's level of concern was greater due to her husband failure to answer his phone."

"I agree," the judge replied. "The witness may answer the question."

"Sure," Yechiel replied. "My father always answers my mother's calls. Since he hadn't, my mother figured that something must have happened to him and she became increasingly agitated."

"Thank you, Mr. Felder," Reeves said. "What happened next?"

"Well, my mother called Hatzalah, and asked them to canvass the area where my father normally walks home. A few minutes later, we got a call that my father had been found but was unconscious."

"Were you there when they found your father?"

"No, I was home with my mother."

"Why didn't you join the members of Hatzalah in the search?"

"Since my father had neither answered my mother's call nor returned it, I knew in my heart that something bad must have happened to him. I didn't want my mother to be alone when she received the news."

Michael stopped his questioning for a moment. He wanted the jury to appreciate the love and dedication that Yechiel felt for his mother. Once he felt that the point had resonated with the jury, he was ready to proceed.

"Yechiel, is your father well-liked?"

"Of course."

"Does he have any known enemies?"

"No, why would you think that?"

"I'm not the one who thinks that. The defense will probably try to pin the crime on a third party and I want to ascertain that it isn't possible."

"Objection," Shea called out.

"Sustained," Judge Daniels responded. "Mr. Reeves, please keep your opinions and theories to yourself."

"Yes, Your Honor. But Yechiel, getting back to the question: isn't it true that your father had no enemies?"

"Objection," Shea called out again. "Counselor is leading the witness."

"I will rephrase the question," Reeves responded, annoyed. "Do you know of any enemies that your father may have?"

"My father has the rare ability to be both loved and revered. My father will never mince words. If he sees a congregant or a student doing something wrong, he will be quick to point it out. However, it is always done out of love and is received in kind. My father is a great man and didn't deserve what happened to him."

"So you are saying that to the best of your knowledge there was no one who bore a grudge against your father and therefore the only person who would attack your father would have to be someone that he didn't know."

"I am saying that anyone who knows my father would never want to hurt him."

"Thank you, Mr. Felder. I have no more questions for this witness."

"Your witness, Mr. Berman," the judge directed.

Shea rose from his seat to face his friend. The look on Yechiel's face almost brought Shea to tears. It wasn't a look of anger. It was a look of hurt and betrayal that was saying, *Shea, how could you do this to my father?*

Not wanting to make Yechiel suffer more than he already had, Shea got straight to the point.

"Are you certain, Yechiel?" Shea asked.

"Am I certain about what?"

"Are you sure that your father had no known enemies?"

"Of course I am sure."

"Are you sure that there is no one who would want to do harm to your father?"

"Yes, I am positive that no one would ever want to hurt my father."

"You are positive?"

"Objection," Michael called out. "Counselor's question has already been answered."

"I agree," the judge said. "Mr. Berman, please move on with your next question."

"Certainly," Shea responded. "Yechiel, who is Scott Kushner?"

Yechiel stiffened. "How dare you," he said in a voice that was almost a whisper. "You know that he has nothing to do with this attack."

"How do you know that he has nothing to do with the attack?"

"I can't believe you," Yechiel said angrily, almost spitting out the words. "First you defend that madman over there and now you are trying to pin this terrible crime on an innocent man? What has happened to you, Shea?"

"I am sorry, Your Honor," Michael interrupted. "But I am genuinely confused by this line of questioning."

"As am I, counselor," the judge said. "Mr. Berman, would you kindly inform the court what you and the witness are talking about."

"The witness has testified that there is no one who would have a reason to attack his father. I intend to disprove his testimony."

A look of concern shadowed Michael's face. So that was why Shea hadn't objected to Yechiel's testimony; he wanted to introduce a third-party theory and he was going to use Yechiel to do it.

Michael knew that he needed to stop Shea before he had a chance to influence the jury.

"Sidebar, Your Honor," Michael requested. The judge motioned for the attorneys to approach.

"I have to object to this line of questioning," Michael stated.

"On what grounds?" Shea asked.

"The witness has obviously been through a horrendous trauma. His father was attacked and he hasn't left his side for the last week. Look at his eyes. They are bloodshot and red from the lack of sleep and tears that have been shed. I think we need to show the witness mercy and allow him to return to his father's bedside."

"I am sorry, Mr. Reeves," the judge said, "but if you really cared about the well-being of the witness, you wouldn't have called him to testify in the first place. I'll admit that I was a bit intrigued because Mr. Berman hadn't objected to the witness' testimony from the beginning. But since he hadn't, I am compelled to allow the testimony."

Shea smiled; he knew that it was definitely a good sign. But as Shea turned to Yechiel and saw the look in his eyes, the smile quickly faded away.

"So please," the judge requested, "let us continue the trial without any more interruptions."

Shea took a drink of water and faced Yechiel.

"Yechiel, "Shea continued, "I will ask you once again. Who is Scott Kushner?"

Yechiel looked at the judge and hoped that he wouldn't have to answer the question. However, Daniels instructed him to answer and Yechiel cleared his throat.

"Scott Kushner was the owner of Super Pita," Yechiel responded.

"What is Super Pita?" Shea asked.

"Super Pita was a restaurant located in Brooklyn."

"What happened to this restaurant?"

"It closed."

"When?"

"About four months ago."

"Why did it close?"

"People stopped coming to the restaurant and Mr. Kushner couldn't afford the rent."

"Why did people stop going to the restaurant?"

"The rabbis of the Brooklyn Rabbinical Council removed their certificate of kashrut."

"What was the basis for this?"

"Objection!" Michael called out. "The witness is not a member of the Rabbinical Council and therefore his testimony on the matter should be classified as hearsay."

"However," Shea argued "the reason became public knowledge when it was reported by the local Jewish newspapers. Therefore, it can't be classified as hearsay."

"Objection overruled," Daniels ordered.

"Scott Kushner was accused of selling non-kosher meat," Yechiel continued. "The council ordered him to turn over the invoices of the meats that he had purchased. When he refused to do so, the council removed its certification."

"What was Mr. Kushner's reaction?"

"He was obviously angry."

"At whom was his anger directed?"

"The members of the Rabbinical Council."

"Isn't it true that your father is the head of the Rabbinical Council?"

"Sure he is, but Scott Kushner was angry at everybody, not just my father. He blamed the entire council for his store closing down."

Shea went to the table and opened his handheld computer. After a few moments he approached Yechiel.

"Yechiel, do you recognize this letter," Shea asked, pointing to the document on the screen.

"Objection, Your Honor," Michael announced. "This letter was never part of discovery and it cannot be allowed as evidence."

"Your Honor," Shea replied, "this is what I meant when I was asking for leeway. Had I known that the prosecution was going to call Mr. Felder as a witness, I would have gladly turned over the letter during discovery. But, as I explained before, I did not know that he was going to be called and therefore I was unable to provide Mr. Reeves with the letter."

"Even if we are to believe that Mr. Berman didn't know about Mr. Felder's testimony," Michael countered, "that still doesn't change anything. I am unable to authenticate the letter in question. How do I know that is a legitimate letter and not some fabrication made up by the defense?"

"While I am again appalled at the accusations of Mr. Reeves," Shea responded, "I do understand his concern. That is why I am leaving the veracity of the letter in Mr. Felder's hands. If he in fact recognizes the letter, then the court and the jury will have no questions regarding its authenticity. However, if Mr. Felder denies any knowledge of the letter, then I will agree not to bring it up again and move on with my questioning."

The judge thought for a moment and turned to Michael. "I do not approve of surprises and in my book, this letter constitutes a surprise. However, I must agree with Mr. Berman. If your witness, Mr. Felder, is able to identify the letter, I see no reason to disallow it."

Shea again proffered the letter to Yechiel. Yechiel's eyes burned with anger as he addressed Shea.

"How can you?" Yechiel said, the bitterness in his voice almost palpable, after reviewing what Shea had shown him. "This letter was sent to you by my father in confidence. It was not meant to be shown to the entire world."

"Your Honor," Michael spoke, "if what Mr. Felder is saying is true, then the letter would fall under attorney-client privilege and would not be admissible in court."

"Your Honor," Shea replied, "all of my communications with Rabbi Felder are permissible. I am not his lawyer. I have never been hired by him for any legal matters. I am his student and he was reaching out to me to get my advice."

"But how do we know that Rabbi Felder didn't view your advice as privileged?" Michael countered. "It is very possible that Mr. Berman thought that he was giving his own expert advice; however, Rabbi Felder may have viewed it as communication between a lawyer and his client."

"Rabbi Felder would never have done that."

"How do you know?"

"Because he would never ask me to do a legal favor for him," Shea answered. "There were many times that I offered to be his legal counsel on various matters, but every time he declined. He would tell me that a real rebbi only gives to his students and never takes anything in return."

"While I appreciate your sentiment," the judge interrupted, "Mr. Reeves has a point. No matter what your relationship is with the victim, it is still very possible that he assumed that you were functioning as his legal counsel, and therefore all communications between you and him would be inadmissible. "

"Why don't you ask Yechiel," Shea responded, facing Yechiel. "He can speak to my relationship with his father and testify that what I am saying is true."

"Your Honor," Michael pleaded, "that would be one hundred percent speculation. The witness may be the victim's son, but he isn't the victim and cannot accurately testify to what the victim may or may not have been thinking."

The judge rubbed his jaw, obviously deep in thought, and Shea held his breath. In order for Shea to be able to establish a third-party defense, Shea needed Yechiel to testify that Rabbi Felder's life had been threatened before. Without this piece of evidence, it was going to be much more difficult.

"Mr. Berman," the judge addressed him, "while I am inclined to believe you about your relationship with Rabbi Felder, I cannot in good conscience ignore the other possibility. Even if normally

Rabbi Felder would not accept your services as an attorney, we don't know for certain that he didn't send you this document under different assumptions. I therefore have to rule the document as being inadmissible."

Michael Reeves looked jubilant and Shea crestfallen. But the judge had more to say. "I am not saying that the episode in question is inadmissible. If Mr. Felder is able to provide testimony to your alternate-party theory, than I will allow his testimony. But any references to conversations or documents between you and the victim, I will not allow."

Shea nodded and his mind began to race. Even though the judge had allowed Yechiel's testimony to continue, it was going to be a challenge for Shea to get the testimony in without Michael objecting to it. Shea closed his eyes and tried to think of a plan.

"Mr. Berman," the judge spoke a few seconds later, "are you ready to proceed with your witness?"

"Yes I am, Your Honor," Shea responded. "Yechiel, did your father ever express to you a concern that he was in danger?"

"Objection," Michael stated.

"Your Honor," Shea countered. "Even if my conversations with the victim may have been privileged, conversations with his son most certainly were not and therefore Yechiel Felder should be allowed to answer the question.

"Objection overruled," the judge responded.

"What do you mean by, 'in danger'?" Yechiel questioned, his voice still low and angry.

"Did your father ever receive threats because of his position at the Rabbinical Council?"

"Of course he received threats," Yechiel answered. "People weren't always happy with my father's rulings and they voiced their feelings rather strongly."

"Did any of them ever threaten your father with bodily harm?"

"Yes."

"To your knowledge, when was the last time that somebody threatened to physically hurt your father?"

Yechiel paused to think. "About four months ago."

"And who made those threats to your father?"

"Scott Kushner."

"No further questions," Shea stated. Because of Michael's objection, Shea was unable to have Yechiel disclose the exact details of Kushner's threats. However, Shea hoped that the fact that Scott Kushner had threatened Rabbi Felder would not be lost on the jury and would contribute to reasonable doubt.

Michael was determined not to let that happen.

"Your Honor, I have a question on redirect." Michael stated.

"Mr. Felder, in your opinion, do you believe that Mr. Kushner could have perpetrated this attack?"

"Absolutely not."

"And why is that?"

"I know Mr. Kushner and I personally spoke to him after he had made those threats against my father. To me, he seemed contrite and was genuinely sorry. I don't believe that he would ever raise a hand against my father."

Michael sat down and Shea glanced at the faces of the jury. They believed Yechiel. Even though Scott Kushner had threatened Rabbi Felder, they didn't think that he attacked him. Shea could only hope that when the jury would deliberate and go over the transcripts of the trial, they would be open to the possibility of Scott Kushner being the attacker. But for now, Michael had won that round and Shea needed to regroup. A text message lit up the screen to his phone. When he saw what it said he gasped.

"Mr. Reeves, is the state ready to call its final witness?" the judge asked.

"I am sorry Your Honor," Shea interrupted, "but I must request a recess."

"For how long?"

"Until tomorrow morning."

"Mr. Berman," the judge addressed him sternly, "I have stated that I wanted this trial to move along quickly. We already recessed early yesterday and there are still many hours left in the day to proceed."

"I understand, but an emergency has come up."

"Involving whom?"

"My son," Shea replied. "My wife just texted and told me that I am needed immediately and that something has happened to my son. I hope that the court can understand."

"Of course," the judge responded, changing his tone. "We will reconvene tomorrow morning. And Mr. Berman, I hope everything works out well with your son in the end."

"So do I, Your Honor," Shea replied, racing from the courtroom.

■ ■ ■

Robert Fields went directly to Leo Stephen's office.

"You're not going to believe this," Fields exclaimed, as he came crashing through the door.

"When normal people enter someone's office," Stephens said, rolling his eyes, "they will greet them with a formal hello, or, at the very least, just a 'hey there.' But I guess you don't fall under the category of normal so I shouldn't be surprised by your abrupt behavior."

"Come on," Fields replied with a grin, "you know me. I don't have time for all those formalities."

"What you refer to as a formality, some would call manners."

"Well, you say tomah-to and I say tomay-to."

"I have no idea what you are talking about," Stephens replied. "But anyway, you are obviously excited about something. What's on your mind?"

"You were right," Fields replied.

"About what?"

"About that assault case in Brooklyn and our assassination attempt being connected."

"How do you know?"

"I met with an anonymous source of mine."

"Who?"

"Maybe you don't know the word. A-non-y-mous. Unknown, usually by choice."

"Okay, okay. Is he legit?"

"He is better than legit."

"So what did he tell you?"

"Basically, that a couple of years back, the Israelis lost a terrorist."

"How does one lose a terrorist?"

"I am not sure. Basically, they had him under surveillance in some refugee camp in Jenin. Then one day, this terrorist disappears. The Israelis had no idea where he was. My guy told me that the guy that they lost was not only an Islamist fanatic, but also an expert marksman. He thinks that if anyone would try to pull something on American soil, this is the guy they would use."

"Okay," Stephens agreed warily. "Even if this guy could be our guy, what connection does that have with the attack on that rabbi?"

"That's the kicker. The terrorist's name is Khalid al-Jinn," Fields exclaimed.

"Al-Jinn?" Stephens asked. "Isn't that the name of the guy who is on trial for the attack?"

"Yup," Fields answered.

"Wait. So the guy that we are looking at to take out the Israeli prime minister is currently on trial for attacking some rabbi?"

"That is what it seems."

"Well, that is great," Stephens said happily.

"What do you mean?"

"Personally, I never really wanted to get involved in this mess in the first place. If the Israelis really wanted our help, then they should have shared some information with us. I mean, they aren't even telling us what the prime minister's itinerary is going to be when he gets here. Sure, they disclosed all the public appearances, but the FBI needs to know *everywhere* he plans to go. They haven't told us anything and that is their choice. However, I can make my own choices too. If they want to handle it on their own, I have no problem letting them. I have many things on my plate that can use my attention. But once we found out that there was a credible threat against the prime minister, we needed to follow up on it. Well, we did. We did our research, and according to our findings, the number-one suspect is currently behind bars or in a courtroom. Either way, he is far away from the prime minister and that is all I care about. If there is somebody else out there with an axe to grind, at least we can say, we did our due diligence and we got our man."

"So you're not doing anything else? No further follow-up? I'm not sure that's wise."

"I *am* sure, and as long as I am the field director in this office, that is the bottom line. So if you would excuse me, we have a briefing in ten minutes and I expect you to be there."

"What is the briefing on?"

"It seems that the Sanchez brothers are back to wheeling and dealing. This time their item of choice is PCP and they are looking to move it all over the East Coast. We got a bead on them but we need to move fast. You will get all the information shortly."

"Okay," Fields said as he walked out of the office.

"And Robert," Stephens stopped him.

"Yeah?"

"I really need you to let this thing go. It isn't our mess anymore. Let the Israelis handle it."

"Sure," Fields responded. But as he headed for his office, his brow was furrowed with deep thought. Something was wrong, and Fields knew it. First of all, Fields reasoned, if al-Jinn was under arrest, then why would that message have come out of the Knesset? Wouldn't they have known that the assassin was already behind bars? But more importantly, Fields couldn't figure out al-Jinn. Why would a guy who plans to assassinate the prime minister of Israel allow himself to be arrested for attacking a rabbi? Things weren't adding up and for Fields that just meant one thing: this case was far from over.

S HEA RUSHED INTO THE SCHOOL, HIS FACE PALE AND SET with worry. Shira herself didn't know much; just that she'd been called urgently to the school. Something had happened to their son.

After Shea was buzzed into the building, the secretary nodded to acknowledge his arrival and said, "Let me just tell Rabbi Hirsh that you are here; he's been waiting for you."

Shea found Shira seated in the lobby near the office. "Where is Yehudah?" he asked.

"They won't even let me see him," Shira responded.

"Why not?" Shea wondered.

"I don't know. All I know is that when they called me, I came running. I've been sitting here alone since I got here. The only person that I saw was the secretary, who told me to wait patiently till I can see Yehuda. She said that he's being kept in Rabbi Hirsh's office until you arrive, I am going crazy here."

"I know and I am sorry that I couldn't get here more quickly."

"I feel badly, you were doing your job and maybe I shouldn't have called you to come. But I didn't know where to turn."

"Are you kidding me? My place is with you and the kids. My job will never be more important than you guys."

"Speaking of the job," Shira said, glad for something to speak about that would take her mind off whatever had happened to Yehuda, "I know that you can't tell me any of the particulars, but how is the case going?"

"Surprisingly enough," Shea replied, "it is going well. It seems that the judge is starting to see all the tricks that the prosecutor has been trying to pull and he isn't letting him get away with anything."

"Great. But tell me, Shea, do you think that there is any chance?"

"Any chance that what?"

"Any chance that he didn't do it."

"Why are you asking?" Shea said.

"Well, I had terrible experience today at Dovie's."

"What happened?"

Shira told Shea what had occurred at Dovie's that morning. As she finished her story, Shira saw rage burning in Shea's eyes.

"How could they? To you, of all people."

"Shea, I was also upset," Shira interjected, "but sitting here, I have had a lot of time to think about what happened and I have tried to see it from their point of view. They don't know that you have no choice. They don't know that you are trying to save your father and your entire family. All they see is what they are shown and it isn't pretty."

"Yeah, but then they should come after me. At least Josh Silver had the guts to confront me head on."

"Josh Silver?"

"I didn't want to tell you, because I knew that you would get upset. But basically, Josh Silver made me public enemy number one."

Shea went on to recount his experiences at the rally.

"Wow," Shira exclaimed. "I guess that sort of puts my Dovie's incident into perspective."

"But it shouldn't be that way. If anybody has an issue, they should come straight to me and not take out their aggression on my innocent wife."

"Your wife can fend for herself," Shira said with a faint smile. "Wait a second, wasn't Danny at that rally?"

"Yep."

"Did you tell him?"

"I didn't get a chance to."

"Oh no," Shira groaned. "So that is why Nechama isn't returning my calls."

"I am so sorry!" Shea exclaimed. "You shouldn't have to suffer like this."

"Don't apologize. I told you that I believe in what you are doing and I support you one hundred percent. I don't care what anybody else thinks. I know why you are doing this, and I think that makes you the greatest person in the world."

Shea looked at his wife, a wave of gratitude washing over him. "I am very lucky to have a wife like you," he said quietly. "In any case, it's almost over. After tomorrow, I am going to punch such a wide hole in the state's case that a truck could drive through it. The judge is going to have no choice but to dismiss the case."

"But do you think that he did it?"

"Shira, I have told you many times that it isn't my job to think if he did it or not."

"I know, but I am your wife and I am asking you a question. The stakes are high and I get that. But I don't want a terrible person getting off on a technicality so he can hurt somebody again. So please tell me that there is a remote chance that he didn't do this."

Shea thought about what he was going to answer. Before he had taken the case, Shea, like all the rest, felt that there was no way that al-Jinn could be innocent. From his encounters with his client Shea was persuaded that al-Jinn was evil. And yet, as the case continued to develop it was becoming clearer to him that the evidence against al-Jinn was entirely circumstantial. True, everything al-Jinn said to Shea seemed to indicate that he was the attacker. His demeanor and his anger screamed to the jury that he was guilty. But things weren't adding up.

Before Shea had a chance to answer his wife's question, his son came barreling through the lobby and into his mother's arms.

■ ■ ■

Prime Minister Yitzchak Schechter looked around his office. He was about to embark on the most important journey of his political career and yet he couldn't stop thinking about the picture that was hanging over his desk. It was one of the most famous pictures in all of Israel: his father, Yehonatan Schechter, praying at the *Kosel* in his dusty, battle-worn uniform. It was taken shortly after the Yom Kippur War. For the secular Israelis, the picture symbolized the greatness of the IDF. For the *chareidim*, the picture symbolized the greatness and the power of prayer. But for Yitzchak, the picture symbolized something very different: the greatness of the man whom he was struggling to emulate; the man to whom his detractors would forever compare him.

Much to the dismay of his enemies, Yitzchak was determined not to let his father's legacy bring him down. On the contrary, Yitzchak felt motivated by the legend of his father. He wanted to make his father proud, and he hoped that the upcoming summit would be the start of a new beginning for the State of Israel and its beleaguered prime minister.

His secretary buzzed and told him that the security measures were almost in place and it would be a few minutes until they would be ready for him at Ben Gurion Airport. As he waited at his desk, deep in thought, a knock at the door disturbed him. When he saw who it was, he motioned for the visitor to approach.

"Ariel," the prime minster called out, "where is your luggage?"

"I pack very light," Ariel Moore responded. "All I need is a toothbrush and some sleeping pills, and I am good to go."

"You're lucky. My wife has been packing everything but the kitchen sink. I think we may need another plane just for her stuff."

"Your wife decided to come?"

"Of course. It's very important for our image that she comes on the trip. We're trying to show the world that we are stable and not trigger-happy. Nothing says stability like a family, don't you agree?"

Ariel looked at the prime minister and nodded. This trip was not only a momentous occasion for the State of Israel, but it could be life changing for Schechter as well. Ariel was proud of the young prime minister and had expected great things from him.

He wondered if the late Yehonatan Schechter would have been proud as well.

■ ■ ■

"Yehuda," Shea cried out, "what happened to you?"

Yehuda Berman lifted his head from his mother's embrace. He had spent the last few minutes sobbing, with his mother trying desperately to console him. Now that he could see Yehuda's face, Shea saw exactly what Yehuda was crying about. His lip was swollen and there was dried blood in the corner. The area around his eye was red and Shea figured it would turn black and blue in a couple of hours.

"They all just came after me," Yehuda answered through his sniffling and tears.

"Who came after you?" Shira asked.

"Everybody," Yehuda answered.

"Who is everybody?"

"The entire class started attacking me."

"*What?*" Shea responded, shocked.

"Well, really Shlomie Gellman started it. But then, everybody else joined in."

"What did he start?"

Yehuda was speaking with more confidence now, though he still punctuated his words with the occasional sniffle. "We went out to recess and we started choosing teams for hockey. Usually I'm one of the boys chosen first. But today, I wasn't chosen till there was no one else left. Even then, Shlomie didn't want me on his team. He started telling all the boys that he didn't even want to play, if I was on his team."

"Did you ask him why?" Shea asked, knowing the answer and dreading to hear it.

"Sure," Yehuda responded. "He told me that he didn't want to play on the same court as a *kapo's* son."

Shea's face turned white.

"Well, I asked him what a *kapo* was, and he just told me that my father was one. Soon, everybody started yelling that word and pointing at me. It made me feel terrible and I told them to stop."

"Did they?"

"No and then Shlomie got near me and pushed me to the ground."

"What did you do next?" Shira asked quietly.

"I got up and punched him in the mouth."

His quiet son Yehuda. Shea didn't know whether to be proud or horrified; a little of both. "What happened next?"

"Well, he came at me and we were both hitting each other and rolling on the ground. The next thing that I remember was my rebbi pulling me off Shlomie and me getting sent to Rabbi Israel's office."

"Where is Shlomie now?"

"He was sent back to class, but I was told that I have to wait in Rabbi Hirsh's office until my parents came. So I have been waiting and waiting for Mommy and you to come."

The secretary interrupted their conversation. "Mr. Berman, Rabbi Hirsh will see you now," she said.

Shea was surprised. It seemed to him that Yehuda's fight was a disciplinary issue. So why was he meeting with the head of the school and not the principal, Rabbi Israel? He entered the office, leaving Yehuda and Shira outside.

Rabbi Hirsh motioned for him to sit down.

"Mr. Berman," Rabbi Hirsh addressed him coldly, "thank you for coming down."

Shea looked at Rabbi Hirsh. Less than a week earlier, he had greeted Shea with a bear hug and had poured on all the accolades and compliments. Now he was cold and distant.

"It seems that your son was involved in an incident," Rabbi Hirsh continued.

"I know," Shea responded, "he told me all about it."

"Well, then you know how much we detest fighting in this school."

"I am quite aware."

"So you won't be shocked to discover that there need to be severe consequences."

"I agree. That Gellman kid should be punished for what he did to my son."

"I wasn't referring to Shlomie Gellman. I was referring to your son, Mr. Berman."

"Wait one second," Shea responded, making every effort to keep his anger in check. "My son was the victim here. That kid threw my son to the ground."

"I am aware," Rabbi Hirsh said. "However, your son did punch the boy in the face."

"But that was only after he had been thrown to the ground. Besides the entire class was ganging up against him and calling him names."

"Actually, they were calling *you* names."

"You knew what they were yelling at my son?"

"Not at first," Rabbi Hirsh responded. "But after speaking to his rebbi and to Rabbi Israel, it became quite clear what had transpired."

"So if you know what happened, what I am doing here?" Shea asked. "It's obvious that my son was the victim and not the culprit. You should be speaking with the Gellmans, not me. Besides, since when have you been handling disciplinary issues? I thought that Rabbi Israel handled all the behavior problems."

"Normally he would, except when those issues affected the integrity and future of the school."

"What issues of integrity are you referring to?"

"Do you know what those boys were calling you in front of your son?"

"Yeah, they were calling me a *kapo*."

"Why would you think that a bunch of nine-year-olds would start calling a fellow classmate's father a *kapo*?"

Shea didn't answer. He knew full well why.

"I guess I can assume, 'silence is assent,'" Rabbi Hirsh continued.

"What do you want me to say?"

"Honestly, I don't know what you could say at this point. What you have chosen to do has angered a lot of people. Children no doubt heard them discussing what a terrible thing Yehuda Berman's Tatty was doing."

"They have no idea what is really going on."

"Frankly, that probably doesn't matter to them and it definitely doesn't matter to me."

"What is that supposed to mean?"

"I have a school to run and your actions have turned it upside down. Do you know how many calls I have gotten from reporters in the last three days wanting me to comment on your involvement in the Rabbi Felder attack case?"

"How would I know?"

"How about over twenty," Rabbi Hirsh answered. "This is besides the many calls from parents wanting to pull their kids out of this yeshivah."

"Why would they want that?"

"The exposure. I have seen three television news vans parked outside the school doors every morning hoping to catch a glimpse of you or your wife. Who knows, maybe they even want to interview Yehuda. The parents in this school don't want their kids exposed to such an atmosphere."

Shea's mind was racing. While it didn't surprise him that reporters would stop at nothing to get a story, he didn't think that his son's yeshivah was much of a draw. But if they were sniffing around like Rabbi Hirsh claimed they were, that must mean they were desperate for material. With the judge's gag order in place, Shea knew why.

"Right now I think it will be for the best if your son doesn't come back to school for a while," Rabbi Hirsh said quietly.

This Shea hadn't expected. "Why?" he demanded. "He hasn't done anything wrong."

"Well, neither have the rest of the boys in this school. But every day that your son is here is detrimental to their ability to learn."

"And how am I going to explain to my son that he is no longer allowed to come to school?" Shea said, his voice shaking slightly.

"The same way that you will explain to him why his father is the most hated man in all of New Jersey," Rabbi Hirsh shot back.

Shea glared at Rabbi Hirsh. Shea was no fool; something else was going on and it wasn't pretty. Rabbi Hirsh never bowed to public pressure. When Shea and Shira had been looking for a school for Yehuda, Kol Nearim had been their first choice primarily because of Rabbi Hirsh. Throughout the years, Shea had seen firsthand many people try to challenge Rabbi Hirsh on various issues, but he never backed down and was always true to his principles. Now, all of the sudden, Rabbi Hirsh was bowing to parental pressure? Shea wasn't buying it, and as he saw something on Rabbi Hirsh's desk, he realized just why Rabbi Hirsh was acting this way.

He grabbed the paper off the desk before Rabbi Hirsh had a chance to stop him.

"So this is why you are throwing my kid under the bus," Shea accused him, thrusting the paper in Rabbi Hirsh's face.

"What is written on that paper is none of your business," Rabbi Hirsh said, flushing slightly.

"It sure is my business," Shea responded, waving the flyer inviting parents to a meeting about the yeshivah's building expansion. Now it was clear why Rabbi Hirsh was acting this way. He wasn't caving in because of protests from the parents; he was running a building campaign and he didn't want Shea ruining his plans.

"This is the reason you want my kid out of the school. You can't ask the parents for money if you have, as you put it, New Jersey's most hated man as part of your parent body."

Rabbi Hirsh was quiet.

"In all honesty, how can you rob my child of his *chinuch?*" Shea continued.

"How can I rob the other children in the school of theirs?"

"What is that supposed to mean?"

"You have seen the building. Every single time it rains, I am afraid either that we will end up with a swimming pool in the dining room or the whole roof will just cave in. Our children can't continue to learn like this. I have a donor who came to me earlier this week. He told me that he is willing to give me half the money that we need for the expansion if the parents will raise the other half. I need the parents to believe in this school and right now, having your son here with the media circus surrounding him, is not going to make parents believe in this yeshivah."

"So you are telling me that a building is more important to you than my child."

"No," Rabbi Hirsh responded diplomatically. "I care for your son like I care for all the children here at Yeshivas Kol Nearim. But sometimes my school can't facilitate the needs of every child. When that time comes, even if it will cause me great anguish and pain, it is because I care deeply for the child that I ask him to leave my school."

Shea was livid. Rabbi Hirsh could say what he wanted, but Shea knew the truth. The Bermans had become an inconvenience and Rabbi Hirsh was throwing them out like the trash. But if Rabbi Hirsh thought that Shea was going to take this sitting down, he was gravely mistaken.

SHEA AND SHIRA DROVE YEHUDA HOME IN SILENCE. IN the house Yehuda fled to his room and Shira and Shea sat at the kitchen table. Shea then told Shira all that had transpired in Rabbi Hirsh's office.

"So how did you leave it with him?" Shira asked.

"I told him that Yehuda will be in school tomorrow and that if he had a problem with it, I would bring on a nightmare that would make this mess look like child's play."

"What are you referring to?"

"I threatened him that I, with the power of my entire law firm, would sue him and the school if he didn't let Yehuda back in school."

"You threatened to sue him?" Shira asked in disbelief.

"I sure did."

"Can you even sue him?"

"That's not the point. If he is afraid of a public-relations nightmare, I can create a horror for him and the school the likes of which they have never seen. "

"But would you actually do that?"

"I don't know myself," Shea admitted. "I hope it doesn't come to that. But I needed him to know that I was serious and I wouldn't allow my son to be treated that way."

"Maybe Yehuda *shouldn't* go to school," Shira said.

"Why not?"

"Because if the other kids will be giving him a hard time, why should we put him in that situation? It isn't fair to him."

"But this isn't fair to us."

"I know," Shira responded sympathetically. "But like I told you before, we can't force them to understand and accept what you are doing. This is the reality that we are living with and we have to be able to adapt. Now while you and I are strong enough to hold our heads high while everybody throws their verbal assaults at us, we can't expect Yehuda to be able to do that. He is only a child. I think we need to protect him and not throw him to the wolves."

"But we can't just give in," Shea stated in frustration. "If we keep him home, we are showing them that they are winning."

"This isn't a war, Shea," Shira corrected him gently. "We aren't fighting our neighbors, because if we were in their position our views wouldn't be any different. They don't know the truth and because we can't tell them the truth, we are going to suffer. But we can't think of them as the enemy."

Shea regarded his wife with admiration. After everything she had been through, she was still able to look at things in this positive light. All Shea wanted was blood, to make the people that had hurt his family pay. But Shira was different, and that is why Shea respected her so much.

"You don't seem convinced," Shira pointed out.

"I can't just sit back and watch my family hurting. I feel completely helpless."

"How much longer do you think this trial will last?"

"I am not sure," Shea responded.

"Didn't you tell me that you think the trial could be over by tomorrow?"

"At least that is what I hope will happen," Shea responded.

"Okay, so if the trial is over by tomorrow, this whole craziness will pass. Hopefully over Shabbos, people will begin to forget that anything ever happened. By Monday next week, Yehuda will be able to go back to school and we can go back to living our lives."

Shea nodded, not wanting to dampen his wife's enthusiasm, but he knew the truth. Even if Shea got the mistrial he was hoping for, nobody was going to forget what Shea had done. This nightmare was here to stay and it wasn't going to end any time soon. But Shea did realize that his wife had a point. As long as the trial was going on, emotions would be high and Shea's family would be trapped in the middle. For his own safety, Yehuda couldn't go to school. However, once Shea got the dismissal, the story would be off the front pages and, hopefully, the pressure against his family would subside.

"I guess you're right," Shea admitted. "The last thing that I want to do is cause Yehuda more pain. So at least for tomorrow, we will keep him home from school."

"That is good to hear," Shira said. "By the way, your father called."

"What did he want?" Shea asked coldly.

"He said that you haven't returned his phone calls and he was starting to get worried."

"Of course I haven't returned his calls."

"Why not?"

"Because he is the reason why we are in this mess in the first place. Every time that I walk into the courthouse and I see those signs calling for my death, I can't help but think how selfish he is being."

"Who?"

"My father," Shea exclaimed angrily. "It's his fault that we are suffering right now. Yehuda should be able to go to *cheder* without being verbally attacked. You should be able to shop, without having to run out of the store in tears. But right now we are stuck and it is all his fault!"

"He really sounded sorry when he came by. I mean every time he calls, he tries to make sure that I am doing okay."

"He should be sorry! If he was really concerned with our well-being, he never should have stolen that money."

"But he was trying to help his family," Shira reasoned.

"And that is why I helped him at the beginning," Shea responded. "But now, I'm worn down carrying around his burden. Look, I pleaded with him to find another way out of his troubles and not make me take the case. But he wouldn't do it. He left me to clean up his mess. So I hope you'll understand if I can't bear to speak to him right now."

Shea saw his wife on the verge of tears. She had never seen Shea so angry.

"I am sorry I'm reacting so strongly," Shea said softly. "But with everything that has been going on, I am under a lot of stress right now."

"I know," Shira answered, "and I probably shouldn't have brought it up. Right now, you concentrate on whatever you need to do to win this case and don't worry about anything else."

"Thank you," Shea responded.

Shira went out and left Shea to his thoughts. Detective Nelson was the final witness for the state and Shea needed to be prepared for his cross examination. As Shea reviewed his notes, he actually saw a light at the end of this dark tunnel. If everything went according to plan, Shea truly felt that the judge would have to dismiss the case.

But as Shea was about to find out, nothing ever goes according to plan.

■ ■ ■

"The people call Detective Joseph Nelson to the stand," the bailiff announced.

Shea watched as the detective made his way to the witness stand. He was dressed in a suit and tie that lent him an aura of respectability and responsibility. As Nelson settled into the witness chair, Shea looked at his watch. He knew what he needed to accomplish, but he also needed to be patient. He didn't want

Nelson or Michael to realize what he had in store until it was too late for either of them to do anything about it.

"Would you please state your name for the court?" Michael requested.

"Joseph Lawrence Nelson," Detective Nelson responded.

"Detective Nelson, how long have you been on the police force?"

"I have been at the Sixty-First Precinct for the last ten years."

"Where were you before then?"

"I served in the United States Army."

"What made you leave the army?"

"My father got sick and I was needed at home to help my mother. As soon as I got back to the States, I took the police exam and entered the police academy."

"Objection!" Shea called out. "I am not sure why Detective Nelson's life story is important to this case. As we have already seen before in this trial, the state is trying to waste our time with narratives that are totally irrelevant."

"Your Honor," Michael argued, "I am only seeking to establish Detective Nelson's credibility."

"For now," Judge Stephens informed them, "I am going to overrule Mr. Berman's objection. However, Mr. Reeves, I do not want a repeat of what transpired during Mrs. Pritchard's testimony. The witness may only offer information that is pertinent to this case."

"I understand," Michael responded.

"I was taught by my parents," Detective Nelson continued, "to help people. My father would always tell me that it didn't matter how much money you made. It only mattered what kind of a difference you made in your community. I felt that by joining the police force, I could really help people and make my mark on this world."

"I know that I can speak for everybody in this room when I say thank you for your dedication and service. Have you ever received any awards or medals for your service?"

"Yes; I received a Medal of Valor and I have also received various MPDs and EPDs over my ten years of service."

"Why were you given a Medal of Valor?"

"Objection!" Shea cried out. "Is it really the court's concern why Detective Nelson received a Medal of Valor?"

Shea saw the anger flare in Nelson's eyes and that was the point. Shea knew how much Nelson had wanted to share his heroic story with the jury, but Shea wasn't going to let him.

"Objection sustained," Daniels replied. "Mr. Reeves, please move on."

Michael glared at Shea before continuing. "Detective Nelson, can you please recall the events of September seventh."

"The dispatcher sent out a general call. There had been a 10-22 on the 2200 block on Coney Island Avenue and help was needed in the area."

"What is a 10-22?"

"It means that there had been an assault."

"What happened next?"

"Well, I had been only a few blocks away, so I headed over there."

"What did you find when you arrived?"

"There were definitely a lot of bystanders milling around, but overall I felt that the situation had been contained. The paramedics were working on the victim, so I began to try to figure what had happened."

"How did you go about doing that?"

"Well, I first blocked off the area surrounding the victim. Afterward, I began searching for any eyewitnesses who would be able to tell me what had happened."

"Were you successful in your search?"

"Not at first," Detective Nelson replied. "Since there were so many people crowding around, it took some time, but at the end I was able to find somebody who could tell me exactly what had happened."

"That is when you found Louise Pritchard."

"Objection!" Shea rang out. "Counsel is leading the witness."

Michael looked annoyed. He was trying to build up the story for the jury and didn't appreciate Shea objecting on a simple technicality. But as for Shea, that is exactly what he was trying to do. He wanted to break any momentum that Michael would have, before he was able to build it.

"I will rephrase," Michael responded. "Who was the witness you found?"

"Louise Pritchard," Officer Nelson responded. "Although she had been shaken up by what she had seen, she was willing to sit with me for over an hour and recall the events exactly how she had observed them. It gave me a clear picture as to what had happened and an excellent description of the assailant."

"What happened next?"

"I started to canvass the area for clues that would assist me to identify the attacker."

"Were you successful?"

"No," Detective Nelson replied. "Because the area of the attack is heavily trafficked, collecting any relevant forensic evidence was difficult. Even immediately after the attack, with so many people walking on Coney Island Avenue, any fingerprints or DNA at the scene would have been contaminated and useless in an investigation. My only hope was that Mrs. Pritchard's description would allow us to properly identify the culprit."

"Did it?"

"In the end, we didn't even need her description."

"What do you mean?"

"A few hours into my investigation, dispatch informed me that there had been an anonymous tip received as to the whereabouts of the assailant."

"How?"

"It seemed that somebody had called the NYPD tip line and left a message."

"What was the message?"

"The message was that the attacker of Rabbi Felder could be found at 1250 Avenue T in Brooklyn."

"Was that the complete message?"

"No," Detective Nelson replied. "The person who left the message also provided the name of the attacker."

"What was the name that was given?"

"Khalid al-Jinn."

Shea had known what Nelson was going to say, so he wasn't caught off guard by the mention of his client's name. However, the rest of the people in the courtroom, including the jury, gasped, even though they have been expecting it.

"What did you do next?"

"Well, we requested a warrant for al-Jinn's arrest and were granted one by Judge Clark O'Brien. Once we had the warrant in hand, my partner and I proceeded to the address that had been left on the tip line to make our arrest."

"What happened when you arrived at Mr. al-Jinn's residence?"

"We announced ourselves and waited for Mr. al-Jinn to open the door. When he didn't, we broke in."

"Where was the defendant when you entered the residence?"

"We found him kneeling on the floor praying."

"What happened next?"

"I informed Mr. al-Jinn that he was under arrest for the attack on Rabbi Felder and that he had the right to remain silent."

"Did he say anything to you?"

"Yeah," Nelson replied smugly. "He said that all Zionists are pigs and that the rabbi got what he deserved."

"Did you find anything else in the apartment?"

"Yes, we found a metal rod."

"Did you find this as a result of a search?"

"No, we didn't have a warrant to search the premises. We were only allowed to arrest al-Jinn."

"So how were you able to find this metal rod?"

"It was in plain view. He had left it on the coffee table. It was if he was daring us to arrest him."

"Objection!" Shea stated rising from his seat. "The witness has no idea why the metal rod was left in plain sight. He is only speculating based on his own feelings toward the defendant."

This time Nelson spoke up. "I have no feelings toward your client, Mr. Berman," he declared. "I resent the fact that you would accuse me of such behavior. You lawyers make me sick."

"Excuse me?" Shea responded.

"All you lawyers are the same. You don't understand how hard it is for the police force to do its job. When we finally find a perp and arrest him for the crime, it is only a matter of time before you guys spring him loose on some bogus technicality. If it wasn't for all of you lawyers, society wouldn't find it itself in the terrible shape that it is in."

"How dare you," Shea challenged him.

"No," Nelson responded, "how dare *you*. How dare you accuse me of anything, when all I have tried to do for the last ten years is to make sure that justice is served and people feel safe when they walk the street? But you and your slimy associates put the criminals back on the street and cause chaos for every good and decent citizen in New York."

Shea remained quiet for a few moments, trying to create the impression that he was upset. In reality he was far from it. By goading Nelson into a verbal attack, Shea was setting the stage for what was to come.

Daniels looked toward Nelson with obvious disdain and Michael looked crestfallen. Shea had baited Nelson and it had worked perfectly.

"Detective Nelson," the judge addressed him, "another outburst like that and I will ask you to leave my courtroom. The jury will disregard that exchange between Mr. Berman and Detective Nelson. Furthermore, the jury will disregard Detective Nelson's statement about the defendant's desires or feelings."

Nelson was seething and Shea was glowing. According to the research that Hector had provided Shea, Nelson was known for his explosive temper. He had been to anger management counseling several times over the past ten years. Shea wanted to show the jury the extent of Nelson's anger. With Nelson's outburst, Shea was able to set the stage for his next move, which would come during cross examination.

Michael Reeves still needed information from his witness, so he waited for Nelson to calm down before he continued his questioning.

"Detective Nelson," Michael addressed him "before we were interrupted, you were telling me about the metal rod that was recovered from the residence of the defendant. Is this the metal rod that you found?"

Michael indicated a sealed evidence bag. Nelson nodded and Michael continued.

"The state enters the metal rod as exhibit D."

Michael handed the rod to the bailiff and turned to further question Nelson.

"Detective Nelson, why did you confiscate the metal rod if you didn't have a warrant to search the premises?"

"In her statement to me, Mrs. Pritchard had mentioned that the weapon that she had seen being used on the victim was a thin metal rod. So when I entered the residence and saw such an object on the table, I assumed it was the weapon that Mrs. Pritchard had described."

"Were there any fingerprints on the weapon?"

"No, it seemed that the assailant had used gloves when attacking Rabbi Felder."

"Objection!" Shea interrupted.

"Sustained," Daniels concurred.

"What happened next?"

"We took the defendant to the police station where he was searched and processed. Then we put him in a lineup and Mrs. Pritchard identified him as the person she had seen attack Rabbi Felder. I then took him to a room to interview him and attempted to get his side of the story."

"Why would you interview him after Mrs. Pritchard had already identified him? What would be the point?"

"My job is to make sure that everybody gets a chance, even those people who make terrible mistakes. Even though I had an eyewitness and a weapon, I still wanted to give Mr. al-Jinn a chance to admit to his crime."

"Why?"

"Because, sometimes, even the best of us do stupid things. If he would have admitted to what he had done, I could have used that to show the prosecution that he was a cooperating defendant and hopefully his sentence would be lighter. I personally don't feel that a jail sentence serves as a deterrent to the committing of further crime. I think we need to rehabilitate people and give them a second chance. I was hoping that Mr. al-Jinn would capitalize on that opportunity."

"And did he?"

"No, he remained defiant and obstinate. When I saw that I was unable to obtain a confession, I sent him to a holding cell to await his preliminary hearing."

"Detective Nelson, in your professional opinion, do you think that Khalid al-Jinn attacked Rabbi Gedaliah Felder?"

"I have seen many criminals in my life, but most of them, even the cold-blooded killers, have had some sort of soul. Under the depravity of their terrible actions, I have always been able to find some humanity. But not with this guy. When I looked into those dark eyes, I felt like I was looking at the devil himself. He showed no remorse for what he did, I have no doubt that he attacked that rabbi and needs to pay for his actions."

Normally Shea would have objected to that entire tirade by Nelson, but he chose not to. During cross examination he wanted the jury to remember all the negative things that Nelson had said about al-Jinn. Because Shea hoped that after he was finished with Nelson, the jury would view the detective in a totally different light.

S HEA BEGAN THE CROSS-EXAMINATION WITH AN ATTACK. "Do you really expect the jury to believe a word that you said?" Shea asked curtly.

"What are you referring to?" Nelson asked, obviously keeping his temper in check.

"I am referring to the story that you tried to sell us on how when you interviewed my client, it was only for his own good, to give him a chance to redeem himself."

"But that is the truth. I believe in giving everybody, even the most terrible criminals, a second chance."

"Is that so? What did you call my client when you were interviewing him?"

"I don't remember," Nelson answered uneasily.

"Then, as you already know, all police interviews are recorded. My investigator was able to obtain an audio copy and I heard the entire interview."

Michael saw that Nelson was becoming agitated and he rose to his feet.

"Objection!" he called out.

"On what grounds?" the judge inquired.

"The witness interviews many suspects every day and can't be expected to remember all the conversations."

"That's fine," Shea interrupted as he took a paper out of the folder on his desk. "Here is a written transcript of the interview between Detective Nelson and my client." Shea showed the paper to the judge and to Michael. When Michael saw the lines that Shea had highlighted, his mouth dropped open.

"Detective Nelson," Shea said, showing him the paper, "do you recognize the conversation in question?"

"Like I said before," Nelson responded coldly, "I interview a lot of perps and I can't remember every conversation."

"Well, let me try to refresh your memory. My client had just asked you what you wanted from him. Can you please read your response? I highlighted it for you."

Nelson looked toward Michael Reeves for help, but Michael just looked at the floor. "'Sorry to rain on your parade, Ali Baba, but I don't want anything from you.' But you don't understand."

"Please read the second highlighted line," Shea said cutting him off.

"'You see here, you little jihadist, I don't need your confession. Your case is already wrapped up.' These comments are taken totally out of context."

"You are saying that the audio recording lied?" Shea asked sarcastically.

"No, I am not saying that the audio recording lied," Nelson declared. "I am saying that the quotes don't tell the whole story."

"The only story that I can see is one where you are lying," Shea responded.

"Objection!" Michael called out.

"Withdrawn," Shea responded. "Detective Nelson, you testified that because of your compassion toward the defendants that you arrest, you try get them to admit to the crime. Why would you then refer to my client is such hateful terms if you were trying to help him?"

"Sometimes the people that I arrest don't understand how

beneficial it would be if they confess. Therefore, I need to use other methods to convince them to confess."

"So now not only are you a detective, you are a psychologist?"

"Objection!" Michael called out.

"Sustained," Daniels responded. "Mr. Berman, please refrain from sarcastic comments."

"Sorry, Your Honor," Shea said. "Detective Nelson, are you a bigot?"

"No," Nelson shot back.

"Really? Your comments to my client would indicate otherwise."

"Like I told you before, I only spoke that way hoping that your client would realize that it was in his best interests to admit to the crime that he had committed."

"You mean allegedly," Shea corrected him curtly. "Anyway, isn't it true that in the last three years you have received over ten complaints against you!"

"I am not sure," Nelson muttered.

"And isn't true that all of the complaints were filed by Muslims complaining about your behavior toward them?"

"I can't recall."

"In the last five months alone, there have been five complaints filed against you by Muslims accusing you of misconduct and malice."

"I am not sure ..."

"With all these complaints against you, how can you deny the fact that you are racist and a bigot?"

"Objection!" Michael shouted. "Counsel is badgering the witness."

"Objection sustained," Daniels replied. "Mr. Berman, watch yourself."

"I am sorry, Your Honor," Shea said. "Detective Nelson, who is Raymond Colefield?"

"You piece of trash," Nelson said angrily. "I'm done here!"

Nelson rose, intending to leave the stand, but was stopped by Judge Daniels.

"Detective Nelson, where do you think you are going?" the judge inquired.

"I am sick of this lowlife defense attorney berating me. I have had enough and frankly, I have better and more important things to do."

"I am sorry that you feel that my courtroom isn't worthy of your time, but you have been served a subpoena and you are obligated to answer all the defense's questions regarding this case."

"Then maybe you should make sure that he only asks me questions about this case and not about my deceased partner."

"Detective Nelson, be careful how you speak to me or you may find yourself in contempt. However, Mr. Berman, I would like to know what connection is there between Detective Nelson's partner and our case."

"I would gladly demonstrate the connection, if Detective Nelson answers my questions."

"Fair enough," the judge responded. "Detective Nelson, as long as I allow Mr. Berman's question, you must answer it. However, Mr. Berman, I will not permit you to waste the jury's time with frivolous questions and accusations."

"I understand," Shea responded as Nelson settled reluctantly into the witness chair. "Detective Nelson, will you please tell the court who Raymond Colefield was."

"Raymond Colefield was my partner."

"What do you mean, was?"

"I mean, that for nearly ten years he was my partner, but he isn't anymore."

"What happened?"

"He was killed."

"Was he killed in the line of duty?"

"Yes, he was."

"Would you care to share with the jury the exact circumstances that led to Officer Colefield's demise?"

"No," Nelson responded, but as he saw the glare from Judge Daniels, he changed his mind. "My partner was on his way to work, when he saw that a man needed help. He ran over to the man to help him, but the man took out a gun and shot my partner instead."

"When did you find out that he had been shot?"

"A call came in from dispatch almost immediately that Raymond had been shot. I raced to the scene and I saw him lying on the floor in a pool of blood. It was over even before I got there."

"Who informed his family of his death?"

"I did."

"Did you normally handle those responsibilities?"

"No. We have specialists who handle those types of jobs."

"So why did you break the news to Officer Colefield's family?"

"Raymond was my partner for ten years. He was like a brother to me. His kids, they were like my own nieces and nephews. The last thing that I wanted was some stoic guy in a suit breaking to them the worst news that they would ever have to hear. They needed somebody to grieve with them and that person was going to be me."

Shea saw the tears form in Detective Nelson's eyes, and he stopped. Nelson had shown a true humanity and Shea felt terrible for what he was about to do. But as he looked around the courtroom, he saw Allan in the gallery and he knew precisely what he needed to do.

"Wasn't Officer Colefield's killer a Muslim?" Shea asked

"Sure he was," Nelson answered. "But I don't see the point."

"Don't you see the pattern? First your partner is killed by a Muslim and it shatters you. Then over the next five months, five different people, all Muslims, issue complaints against you for misconduct. Obviously, you bear a grudge against Muslims — who wouldn't? They have ruined your life! So you think to yourself, what better way to get revenge than to put an innocent Muslim behind bars?"

"That isn't true."

"Your Honor," Michael declared, "counsel is making outlandish accusations without any facts."

Daniels was about to rule on Michael's latest objection, but Nelson spoke out instead.

"Your theory makes no sense," Nelson declared to Shea. "You are forgetting that we received an anonymous tip that your client was the attacker."

"Yes, you did," Shea answered. "But did you follow up on any other leads?"

"I am not sure what you mean."

"Aren't you supposed to check the validity of the tip before you follow up on it? Where was the probable cause to arrest my client?"

"Your client matched the eyewitness' description of the attacker."

"Detective Nelson, your eyewitness, Louise Pritchard, has admitted under oath that she is not sure she identified the assailant correctly when she picked Mr. al-Jinn out of the lineup. Tell me, did the anonymous tip mention anything about the alleged attacker's height or weight?"

"No," Nelson answered quietly.

"Isn't it true that the anonymous tip only gave you the name of the alleged attacker and his address?"

"Yes. But since it was only a few blocks from the scene, we felt that we had probable cause to arrest your client."

"Detective Nelson, isn't true that many people live a few blocks from the scene of the attack but my client was picked up solely because he is a Muslim?"

"You are distorting the facts," Nelson challenged him. "We interviewed an eyewitness and received an anonymous tip. Based on the description of the eyewitness coupled with the anonymous tip, we felt that we had probable cause to arrest your client. Besides, you cannot forget that we found the metal rod on his coffee table."

"You mean that you found *a* metal rod on his coffee table," Shea corrected. "Let's talk about that. Detective Nelson, you testified that there were no fingerprints on the metal rod, is that correct."

"Yes."

"What does that tell you?"

"That tells me that your client was very careful when he attacked

Rabbi Felder not to have his fingerprints all over the weapon."

"Was there any blood on the weapon?"

"No."

"In your opinion, what does that tell you?"

"That tells me that not only was your client careful not to leave fingerprints, but he wanted to make sure that there was no trace evidence at all on the weapon."

"Detective Nelson," Shea continued holding up a piece of paper, "what is luminol?"

"It is a chemical that is used by forensic investigators to detect traces of blood."

"How does it work?"

"Luminol emits a blue light when combined with an oxidizing agent, such as iron. Since there is iron in hemoglobin, if luminol comes into contact with blood, then it will emit a bluish glow."

"To the best of your knowledge, was the weapon in question sprayed with luminol to determine if in fact it had been used in this attack?"

"I am not sure," Nelson admitted.

"The defense would like to introduce exhibit C, Your Honor," Shea stated, handing the judge and Nelson a piece of paper.

"Would you kindly read for the jury the highlighted text," Shea requested.

Nelson hesitated, but after seeing the judge's glaring eyes, he proceeded to read.

"It says that, after the object was sprayed with luminol, there was no chemical reaction."

"Doesn't this mean that the metal rod admitted in evidence wasn't used in the attack?"

"Not necessarily," Nelson said defensively. "While the luminol test is good, it isn't one hundred percent foolproof. It is still completely plausible that your client washed away the evidence well enough that the luminol didn't detect the traces of blood."

Shea eyed the jury before continuing. He saw looks of doubt on their faces and that was is exactly what he aiming for.

"Let us say that you are correct and that my client did in fact remove all the trace evidence," Shea offered. "In your experience, have you found that many criminals wipe off all evidence after they have committed a crime?"

"Yes, it is very common."

"So can you explain why, if my client was so careful as to make sure that there was no trace evidence whatsoever on the weapon, he would leave the weapon out in the open for anybody to find?"

"Objection!" Michael called out. "The witness cannot know what was going on in the head of the defendant. The question calls for speculation."

"Your Honor," Shea argued, "the witness has stated that he believes that my client committed this act and that he attempted to wash away all the evidence. I feel that if he is able to make such harsh accusations, then he should have to answer my question."

"Well, Mr. Reeves," the judge stated, "I have to agree with the defense on this one. Detective Nelson has stated that he believes that the defendant did in fact use the weapon and remove the evidence. If his supposition is true, then he should be able to explain why the weapon was left out in the open."

"I have no clue why the weapon was left out," Nelson admitted. "Maybe your client isn't as smart as you think he is and he just made a boneheaded mistake like most criminals do."

"Or maybe there is a different explanation," Shea countered. "Isn't it true that Mrs. Pritchard never clearly identified the weapon that was used in the attack on Rabbi Felder?"

"Yes; however, she did describe the weapon as best as she could remember it.

"But according to her testimony, she only saw the alleged attacker take a metal rod from his pocket. Once we arrived at the scene, and saw the metal rod on the table, we concluded that that was the weapon that Mrs. Pritchard was referring to."

"But how could you come to this conclusion, if there was no trace evidence on the metal rod?"

"Well, how else could that weapon have gotten there?" Nelson questioned.

"I believe that you planted it there," Shea responded.

Nelson was fuming and Michael was on his feet. "Objection! Counsel is making accusations without any foundation."

"Isn't it true that you were so full of rage from all the anguish that Muslims had brought upon you, that you planted the club at my client's apartment?"

"Objection!"

"Sustained," Judge Daniels called out trying to cut Shea off.

"You knew that you couldn't hide it in the bedroom, because you had no right to search there. So isn't it true that you placed it on the coffee table as soon as you entered my client's residence to ensure that you get a conviction against him? That's why there was no trace evidence. Not because my client wiped off all the blood. It was because you planted it there and it had never been used in the attack!"

"Your Honor," Michael pleaded. "Counsel has gone way too far. Mr. Berman has no right to accuse the witness of planting evidence."

"I agree," the judge said sternly. "The jury will disregard whatever accusations Mr. Berman has leveled against Detective Nelson and those accusations will be stricken from the record. Mr. Berman, this is the second time that you have tried to influence the jury improperly. Don't think that I don't know what you are trying to do. I will not have you turn my court into a mockery of our fine justice system. If you embark on one of your baseless tirades again, I will find you in contempt of court."

Shea nodded solemnly and tried to hide his excitement. Even though he knew that he was treading on thin ice with the judge, because he felt that he was so close to ending the state's case, he was willing to take the risk.

There was still one more issue that Shea needed to bring up with Detective Nelson before he could totally finish off the prosecution.

"Now, Mr. Berman, do you have any more questions for the witness?" Judge Daniels asked.

"I do, Your Honor," Shea answered.

"Well then, you may proceed. But please remember that I am watching you very closely."

"Detective Nelson, do you remember the murder of Wyatt Lewis?"

"Objection!" Michael called out. "What relevance is there between the murder of Wyatt Lewis and our case?"

"If the court will allow me," Shea responded, "I would like to lay the foundation and the court will soon see the relevance."

"Your Honor, after what Mr. Berman has just done, I don't feel that we should allow him any leeway at all."

"Well, I appreciate your opinion," Daniels responded, "but I am still the presiding judge in this court. I will allow you to continue this line of questioning, but you better get to the point quickly, Mr. Berman."

"Thank you, Your Honor."

"Sure I remember the murder of Wyatt Lewis," Nelson replied. "It was my first murder investigation and we were able to catch his killer rather quickly."

"How were you able to find his killer so quickly?"

"Well," Nelson said with pride, "after the autopsy report, the coroner concluded that Wyatt Lewis had been in a very violent struggle with his killer before he was killed."

"What made the coroner reach that conclusion?"

"It seemed that Wyatt had traces of skin and blood under his fingernails. The coroner deduced that whoever had killed Wyatt probably had massive scratches on his body. Our first suspect was a coworker whom people had seen arguing with Wyatt the day before. The coworker was found to have several scratches on his neck and chest. Before we even arrested him, the coworker confessed to the crime and is now sitting behind bars."

"Had you not found any marks on the coworker, would you have thought that he had committed the crime?"

"No," Nelson said confidently. "Wyatt's fingernails had shown us that there had not only been a struggle, but that he had injured his killer as well. If we hadn't found any marks or scratches on the coworker, then there would have been no reason to assume that he had killed Wyatt."

Shea paused before continuing. He wanted the jury to believe what Nelson had just said, because Shea was going to bury him with it.

"Detective Nelson, have you had an opportunity to read Rabbi Felder's medical report?"

"No, I have not."

Shea produced the paper and brought it toward Nelson. Once he had it in his hand, Shea spoke.

"Would you please read line twelve for the jury?"

"It says that pieces of epithelial tissue mixed with blood were found under the victim's fingernails."

"Detective Nelson, do you know what epithelial tissue is?"

"Yes, it refers to skin tissue."

"So if I am to understand you correctly, Rabbi Felder's medical report states that epithelial tissue mixed with blood were found under the victim's fingernails."

"That is what it says here."

"So based on what you just testified, regarding the Wyatt Lewis murder, since dead skin mixed with traces of blood was found under the fingernails of Rabbi Felder, wouldn't you assume that his attacker should have scratches or marks on his body."

"Yes; however, not all cases are the same."

"I understand, but didn't you testify, that without the marks on the coworker's body, you wouldn't have assumed that he had committed the murder?"

"Yes," Nelson responded abruptly.

Now it was time for Shea to finish off Detective Nelson and the prosecution for good. Shea went over to his table and took out one last paper.

"Detective Nelson, do you recognize this report?" Shea asked

"Yes I do."

"Can you please identify for the court exactly what it is?"

"It is the arrest report that I filed after arresting Khalid al-Jinn."

"Can you please read line number seventeen for the court?"

As Nelson looked at the paper, his eyes widened and he

stopped. He knew why Shea wanted him to read the line and that is the last thing that he wanted to do.

"Detective Nelson," Shea repeated, "can you please read the highlighted line for the court."

Nelson didn't respond. He knew what was going to happen once he read the line, and he chastised himself. He remembered that first day when he had encountered Moshe Cohen. He had told Moshe that he had built an airtight case and if al-Jinn walked, it was going to be the prosecution's fault. But after letting himself be played like a fool by Shea, Nelson now knew exactly *whose* fault it was really going to be.

"Detective Nelson," the judge said, "please read the line for the jury."

"It says that besides a few small burn marks and scars, there were no visible marks found on the defendant."

"Wait one second," Shea said barely controlling his excitement, "are you telling the court that there were no scratches or cuts found on the defendant?"

"That is what it says here."

"But Detective Nelson, how is it possible for my client to have attacked Rabbi Felder, if there were no scratches or cuts found on my client? The medical evidence, which you had testified earlier to be conclusive, stated that the Rabbi Felder's attacker should have had scratches on his face or body."

"I don't know," Nelson responded sheepishly.

"I do know and that is because my client never attacked Rabbi Felder! No further questions, Your Honor."

Michael would have objected to Shea's last statement as being argumentative, but at this point he felt that there was no point. Shea had done a stellar job of cross examining Detective Nelson, and the only thing that Michael wanted was to have the officer leave the stand. Daniels dismissed Nelson and he walked dejectedly out of the courtroom.

"Mr. Reeves," the judge asked, "do you have any more witnesses to call?"

Michael looked at Shea and then turned away. He thought

about the meeting that he had with Senator Reynolds and how the governor's mansion had been within his grasp. But now as he looked at the smile on Shea's face, he knew where this case was headed and it wasn't going where Michael wanted.

"No, Your Honor," Michael answered quietly.

"Your Honor," Shea jumped up. "I ask that you dismiss this case without prejudice. The state has failed to prove the crimes for which the defendant was indicted."

Shea held his breath as the judge contemplated the request. Even though Daniels had admonished Shea previously for what had transpired, Shea didn't think that the judge would hold it against him. The facts were too strong for the judge to ignore; the state hadn't done its job.

"Mr. Berman," the judge responded, "In general, I would not grant a dismissal without hearing the defense present its case. I feel that if a defendant has been brought to trial, there has to be some merit to the evidence that would require him to defend himself. However, due to the state's inability to prove their arguments, I feel that the best course of action may be an immediate dismissal."

Shea's eyes widened. He knew what the judge's next words would be. He looked around the gallery and saw Allan's smile of pride at what Shea had just accomplished. He imagined Allan and Jessica's congratulatory handshakes. He could see the joy on Shira's face when he would tell her the great news that this terrible trial would be behind them. There was finally a light at the end of tunnel and it was shining brightly.

But before the judge issued his ruling, Shea saw the doors to the courtroom swing open and Moshe Cohen enter at a run. He hurried to Michael Reeves and whispered something in his ear. Michael's eyes widened and he jumped to his feet.

"Your Honor," Michael interrupted the judge as he was about to speak.

"Yes," Daniels responded, clearly impatient.

"The state has one more witness to call."

"Your Honor," Shea objected, "the state has already rested its case."

"Mr. Reeves, this is highly unusual." Daniels responded.

"I understand, Your Honor, but new evidence has come to light and this witness can testify to the veracity of the evidence."

"Who is this new witness?"

"His name is Achmad Mustafa. He is the proprietor of Made in Mecca."

"And what exactly is he testifying to?"

"To the video that I have in my hand," Michael responded, showing a disc to the judge.

"Objection!" Shea shouted, horrified.

"In my chambers, now," Daniels ordered.

THE JUDGE HASTENED INTO HIS CHAMBERS WITH MICHAEL and Shea in close pursuit. Once inside, Daniels motioned for them to close the door. Daniels then sat himself behind his desk and glared at Michael.

"Mr. Reeves, I told you at the beginning of this trial that I loathe surprises in my courtroom. In my book, a video that magically appears right before the end of your case would classify as a surprise."

"Your Honor," Michael responded, "until a few minutes ago, I had no idea that this video even existed."

"Where did the video come from?"

"My assistant, Moshe Cohen, just brought it to me."

"Where is Mr. Cohen right now?"

"He is standing outside your chambers. I can ask him to come in."

"Please do and make it quick. My patience is running low."

Shea stared at Michael's back. He couldn't believe that the judge was going to allow the video into evidence, but at the moment Shea was no longer certain of anything.

As Moshe walked through the door, Shea knew that he was about to get some answers.

"Mr. Cohen, I am hoping that you can shed some light on this mysterious video, because right now, I don't know what to make of it."

"Your Honor," Moshe responded, "I wish I could but, there isn't much to tell. At about 9 a.m., I found a man waiting in my office, holding a package. He identified himself as Achmad Mustafa. He told that me that he was the owner of Made in Mecca and that he was in possession of evidence that was vital to the Rabbi Felder attack case. When I asked him what his evidence was, he handed me the video."

"Did you have a chance to view the video?"

"Yes, I did. Once I saw what was on the disc, I immediately rushed to the courthouse."

"What is on the video?"

"It clearly shows the defendant attacking Rabbi Felder."

Shea maintained his composure with an effort. While he'd realized that the video wasn't advantageous for his client, he never thought that it would torpedo his defense completely.

"Your Honor," Shea spoke, "there is no way that this video can be allowed into evidence. It is completely prejudicial. This last-minute drama is obviously another tactic employed by the state against my client."

"What are you implying, counselor?" Daniels asked. "Are you accusing the state of burying this piece of evidence until now? Are you willing to go on record as believing that Mr. Cohen is lying, and that the state had the video the entire time, waiting till the very last minute to bring it into evidence?"

Shea stared at Moshe. Moshe had shown Shea loyalty before, and Shea wasn't about to forget that, but he needed to be sure.

"Moshe, are you telling me that you never saw this video before?" Shea asked.

"If I could swear on a *Sefer Torah*, I would. I am telling you straight, Shea. This piece of evidence was never in our possession until this morning."

Shea heard the sincerity in Moshe's voice, and he believed him. Even though he felt it wasn't beyond Michael Reeves to suppress evidence, he knew that Moshe was honest. If he said that the video had just arrived this morning, Shea was going to believe him.

"I am not challenging the video based on withholding of evidence. I believe Mr. Cohen when he says that the video just surfaced this morning. However, I feel that it is extremely prejudicial against my client to allow the video into evidence. I have built my case on the assumption that my client did not attack Rabbi Felder. I have directed my questions against the prosecution's witnesses to prove my point. The appearance of this video at this juncture undermines my entire defense and I feel that is unfair to my client."

"Your Honor," Michael retorted, "the state also knew nothing about this piece of evidence. Its appearance at this stage doesn't bode well for the prosecution either."

"Are you serious?" Shea said, appalled. "This video is exactly what you guys need. The case was going to be dismissed. You even told the jury that you had no more witnesses. This video saves you. So please don't weep crocodile tears that you aren't happy about its arrival."

"We only rested because we had no inkling that the video existed. Had we known about the video, we would have shown it right at the beginning of the trial."

"No, you wouldn't have. You have been sabotaging my case from the beginning. If you had had the video from the beginning of the trial, I am not so sure that I would ever have seen it."

"So why aren't you accusing me of burying the video?"

"Because even though I don't trust you, I trust Moshe. He has something that you know nothing about and that is integrity."

"Coming from a defense lawyer? Isn't there a saying that people in glass houses shouldn't throw stones?"

"Gentleman, enough," Daniels called out. "This childish behavior is beneath both of you. If you want to fight, take it out into the parking lot, but not in my chambers. Mr. Berman, I think that I am going to allow the video."

"I beg your pardon, Your Honor," Shea said, shocked.

"As I told you during the trial, I am a firm believer in the process of justice. If the state has been able to prove to a grand jury that your client should be put on trial, then I believe that the state should be given every opportunity to prove its case."

"But, Your Honor, the state never proved anything to the grand jury. My client waived his right before the trial."

"Be that as it may. The video is still a vital piece of evidence that I believe will shed some light on this case."

"But what about my client's rights?"

"Mr. Berman, you are not challenging this video based on withholding of evidence, correct?"

"I am not."

"So, even though it may not seem fair to you, the state has done nothing wrong in this case. Coupled with the fact that this video is essential to the prosecution's case, I feel that I must allow it to be entered into evidence."

"But Your Honor ..."

"I have made up my mind and my decision is final."

Shea couldn't believe what he was hearing. The video was completely prejudicial and no one could deny that fact. Though he knew that he might regret it, if the judge was going to sink his case, Shea wasn't going down without a fight.

"I guess I should have known all along," Shea declared.

"You should have known what?" Daniels inquired.

"When I saw you meeting with Mark Cohen that day, originally I thought nothing of it. But now, I am beginning to see things more clearly."

The judge sat up very straight behind his mahogany desk. "Be very careful with what you are about to say, Mr. Berman. While I understand that you are upset, I will not tolerate certain claims and accusations being made in my presence. Choose your words wisely, or you may find yourself spending the night in jail."

Shea closed his eyes and tried to control himself. The judge knew exactly that Shea wanted to say and Shea knew exactly what would happen if he did. And there was another angle at play that Shea couldn't ignore. With the video being allowed into evidence, the trial was far from over. Shea, no matter how angry he was, couldn't afford to alienate the judge completely. Shea needed to win and that was all that mattered.

"I am stating for the record," Shea said coldly, "that I am objecting to the admission of this video and I will cite that objection, should I need to, on appeal."

"That is your right."

"I would also like to request a private viewing for me and my investigator to make sure that this video is in fact legitimate before we proceed with the witness. I would like to be able to acquire as much information as I can before I need to question the witness."

"I don't see any reason to object to that request. Do you, Mr. Reeves?"

Michael would have loved to object, but he realized how foolish it would look. The judge was giving him a second chance, and as his mother always told him, beggars can't be choosers.

"The state does not object to Mr. Berman's request."

"Before we proceed, I will ask Your Honor to guarantee me something," Shea requested.

"What is it that you need, Mr. Berman?"

"If in fact this video turns out to be credible and it shows my client attacking Rabbi Felder, I would request that Your Honor declare a recess until Monday morning. I will need time to work up a new defense for my client, and an extra day would really help."

"Mr. Berman, I feel that we have wasted enough time already and I really don't want to prolong this trial anymore."

"I understand, Your Honor. However, the same way that you believe that the state has a right to present its case, my client has a right to a proper defense. In order for him to get his defense, I am going to need the extra time."

"Fine," Daniels relented. "If in fact, the video does show that your client did attack Rabbi Felder, I will allow the extra time."

Both Shea and Michael nodded. While for Michael things couldn't be better, Shea had to make sure that things didn't totally spiral out of control for him. Before he could worry about a new defense, Shea had to deal with the video.

"So if we are ready to proceed," the judge continued, "I will give Mr. Berman a copy of the video and allow him to view it privately. How much time do you need, Mr. Berman?"

"How long is the video?" Shea asked Moshe.

"About two minutes," Moshe responded.

"Let me call my investigator," Shea said, "and have him come to the courthouse. Once he arrives, I will have a better idea of how much time I need."

"How about this," the judge suggested. "Let's break for lunch until three. I will inform the bailiff to dismiss the jury. That should give you enough time to view the video and to allow the jury to eat lunch."

Michael and Shea agreed and followed the judge out to the courtroom. On his way, Shea took out his cell phone and dialed. It was answered immediately.

"Hector, where are you right now?" Shea asked.

"I am in Flatbush," Hector responded. "I am looking at some potential venues. I am thinking of opening a few more restaurants."

"I need you down here right now."

"Where is 'here'?"

"At the Brooklyn Criminal courthouse."

"Shea, you know that I am not allowed to be anywhere near a courtroom."

"I know. You aren't going to join me in court. I just need to show you something."

"Can't you just tell me what it is?"

"I really think you need to see it with your own eyes."

"Ok, *amigo*. If you need me, I will be there *rapido*. Just give me ten minutes and I will see you soon."

"Good. I will be waiting in conference room six. Just come to that room as soon as you get here."

Shea ended the call and headed for the conference room. On his way he saw the last person that he wanted to see at that moment.

"Shea," Allan called out, "what is going on?"

"We ran into a little bit of a problem."

"That, any idiot could see. You had Michael on the ropes and that video stunt just bought him a little time. I expected the judge to return to the courtroom and issue a dismissal. But why aren't you in the courtroom right now?"

"I requested that the judge issue a recess."

"Why?"

"Because I needed to wait till Hector got down here."

"Why would you need Hector? This case is over. You blew up the prosecution like a balloon. There is no reason why you would need Hector, unless …. You are kidding me, right?"

"I wish I was."

"But how could the judge allow the video into evidence? Didn't you challenge it?"

"Of course I challenged it, but the judge disagreed with me."

"How could he disagree with your challenge that the state buried this video? All the evidence and circumstances would support such a claim."

"But I didn't challenge it based on withholding of evidence," Shea explained. "I challenged it based on it being prejudicial."

"Why in the world would you not challenge it based on withholding of evidence? You would have had a slam-dunk objection and the judge would not have allowed the video."

"Because the ADA, Mark Cohen, told me that the video just appeared this morning."

"So what?"

"So since I believed what he told me, I opted not to challenge the video based on withholding of evidence."

"Why does it matter to your client, if you believe the prosecutor or not? My own mother could have told me that the video wasn't buried, and I still would have challenged it. You have a duty to your client, not to your conscience. Why do we never ask the client if they committed the crime or not? It's because it doesn't matter if they are innocent or guilty. We aren't their confessors, we are their lawyers. Our job is to provide them the best defense possible, even if it may go against our ideals. You failed your client!"

"You told me that you never wanted me to change," Shea returned. "You told me to always be me when I defend my clients. Well, I was being me in those chambers and I made a call that I believed in."

"I wanted you to be you when you were defending your clients, but not *instead* of defending them. You may have felt good when you trusted your friend as he looked you in the eye and told you what he believed to be the truth. But here is what I know. If that video is allowed and it shows what I know it will show, you not only lost this case, but you lost your job. I will have no answers for Jessica when she asks me how you were able to mess this one up so bad, and frankly, I don't want to answer her. Because if you were willing to sacrifice your client's future so you could sleep better at night, you have no business being a lawyer."

Allan stormed off, leaving Shea all alone. While Shea would have loved to have said something to Allan, there wasn't much to say. Allan was right, at least as far as the legal profession was concerned, and Shea knew it. With the video allowed as evidence, he knew his only option was to be able to disprove the video and show that al-Jinn hadn't committed the attack. He needed Hector's expertise to do that. So as he found his way toward conference room six, Shea hoped that his investigator had some answers, because right then Shea could use all the help he could get.

A few minutes later, Shea heard a knock at the door, followed by a familiar voice.

"I am here, boss," Hector said. "But it wasn't easy, *amigo*. I think the security guard recognized me."

"We have bigger problems right now then some guy recognizing you," Shea said.

"What is the problem? I thought the information that I dug up on Nelson was good."

"It was perfect."

"So why are we here and not in the courtroom celebrating your client's acquittal?"

"Look at the screen and you tell me."

Hector looked at the screen and Shea pressed *play.* After a few seconds, Hector turned to Shea.

"What am I looking at?"

"You are looking at a video of Rabbi Felder being attacked," Shea responded.

"Where'd you get it?"

"The prosecution got it this morning from the owner of Made in Mecca."

"Where'd did he get the video?"

"It was taken from his surveillance system."

Hector was quiet and Shea knew why. Shea waited for him to respond, but when he didn't, Shea continued talking.

"How did you miss this, Hector?" Shea said, his voice stern but controlled.

"I didn't," Hector answered hotly.

"Well, obviously you did."

"I am telling you, Shea, there wasn't any video. I checked into that store. I am not an amateur and I knew what I was doing. I went down there and asked the manager to show me the surveillance tapes. He showed me whatever he had and nothing like this ever showed up."

"Did you see the tapes from the time of the attack?"

"Sure, he showed them to me, but they were all black. According to him, it seemed that the camera was malfunctioning at that time, and he had no real footage to give me."

"And you didn't find that suspicious?"

"What?"

"The fact that at the exact moment of the attack, his cameras didn't seem to work at all."

"Shea, his surveillance system is from the nineties. The fact that it can take any videos at all to me is a miracle. That wasn't the only time the cameras malfunctioned. He showed me other times when the cameras weren't working."

"Are you telling me the truth, Hector?"

"Of course, Shea."

"You aren't just trying to make yourself look better, are you?"

"I would swear on Hectorina's eyes, if I had to. There was no video to see, let alone one that showed your client attacking Rabbi Felder."

Shea paced the room, deep in thought. He trusted Hector, but he knew that he needed more than just Hector's word.

"I need you to testify for me," Shea said.

"No can do, *compadre*. You know what happens if I go back into that courtroom."

"Why?" Shea asked. "All you will be doing is testifying as to what the owner showed you."

"Yeah, but you will have to ask me what I was doing at the restaurant. Remember, Shea, I am not supposed to be an investigator even if I was never officially hired. If the judge finds out that I was I could end up in prison."

Shea nodded. He knew what Hector was saying was true. The irony wasn't lost on Shea. Shea needed Hector's testimony, but it was Shea's deal that he had brokered with the prosecution that would prevent Hector from testifying.

As Shea reviewed what he had just seen, he knew that his options were limited. Even if what Hector was saying was true, that when he had questioned Mustafa the video wasn't there, Hector couldn't testify to that fact. So rather than focus on Hector's story, Shea knew that the only way to win this case was to find something in that video that would exonerate his client.

As he pressed *play* again, he hoped that Hector could find something. Because right now Shea's options were running thin.

■ ■ ■

The jury sat transfixed, focused on the screen in front of them. After a few seconds the image of Rabbi Felder came into view. Shea cringed as he saw his Rebbi come into view. Part of him wished that he could yell to Rabbi Felder to turn around so that this terrible nightmare would never happen. But almost instantly, a man in a dark sweatshirt appeared. He pushed off the hood that covered his face, turned toward the camera, and smiled. Then, just as Louise Pritchard had described it, he took out a metal rod and attacked Rabbi Felder viciously. After a few moments, the attacker once again turned his face to the camera. He mouthed the words *Allahu Akbar* and ran off into the night.

Less than two minutes, and all the doubt that Shea had sown, whether it was the medical improbability of al-Jinn being able to attack Rabbi Felder, or the question surrounding the weapon, was eradicated. The man smiling smugly on the video after he had mercilessly attacked Rabbi Felder was unmistakably Shea's client, Khalid al-Jinn.

Al-Jinn, for his part, was as stoic as ever. He showed absolutely no emotion as the jury and the gallery gasped at the sight of his face on the video. But Shea was mortified. There was no more reasonable doubt, and Shea didn't know where to turn.

After the video finished playing, Michael waited a moment and then proceeded to question his witness, Achmad Mustafa.

"Mr. Mustafa," Michael began, "do you recognize the video that has been shown?"

"Yes, I do," Mustafa responded in heavily accented English.

"Have you seen it before?"

"Yes, when I reviewed the footage taken by my surveillance system, I was able to see the video."

"Mr. Mustafa, is the video that has been shown in court the same video that your surveillance system took?"

"The video that we have just seen is the same video that was taken by my system."

"Mr. Mustafa, before today, had you ever seen the defendant?"

"Yes, at times he came into my store for kebabs."

"When did you last see him?"

"On the night of the attack. After Mrs. Pritchard had called out for help, I ran out of the store, but I was too late. I was only able to see him from the back."

"Objection!" Shea called out in frustration. "The witness could not have possibly identified my client, if he wasn't able to see his face."

"I agree," Daniels replied. "The objection is sustained."

Michael smiled. Shea's objection didn't really matter, because Mustafa's testimony didn't matter. The only thing that mattered was the jury seeing the video, and that Michael had already accomplished.

"I have no more questions for the witness," Michael declared.

"Mr. Berman," the judge informed him, "your witness."

Shea cleared his throat as he rose from his chair to question Mustafa. The jury's eyes were glued to him as they waited to see what great questions he would ask. Throughout the trial Shea had been able to discredit each of the state's witnesses, and clearly the jury thought that Shea would again rise to the occasion. But the truth was that Shea didn't have any more magic bullets in his arsenal. After watching the video with Hector, he had come to the realization that Khalid al-Jinn was guilty, and there was nothing that Shea could do to disprove that.

Shea knew, just as Michael did, that you don't ask a witness questions if you don't know what answers you will get. In his frustration, though, he forgot that cardinal rule.

"Mr. Mustafa," Shea asked, "when did you know about this video's existence?"

"After the rabbi was attacked. I went to check my tapes; I saw that the video was there."

"Mr. Mustafa, how long ago was Rabbi Felder attacked?"

"I am not sure. I guess about three weeks or a month ago."

"So let me get this straight. You have known about this video for over three weeks, and only now you decided to bring it to the police? Why would you wait so long before turning over this vital piece of evidence?"

Even as he asked the question, Shea realized he'd made a mistake. But it was too late.

"I was scared," Mustafa admitted.

Before Achmad had a chance to say anything more that might further damage his client, Shea spoke.

"I have no more questions for the witness."

The judge was a bit startled, but he motioned for Achmad to leave the witness stand. Not wanting to lose an opportunity,

Michael rose from his chair.

"Permission to redirect, Your Honor?"

"Permission granted," Daniels replied.

"Mr. Mustafa, what were you afraid of that prevented you from giving the video to the police?"

"Objection!" Shea called out in desperation.

"On what grounds?" Michael asked.

"Calls for speculation," Shea responded.

"Your Honor," Michael addressed, "Mr. Berman opened up this line of questioning when he asked the witness why he hadn't handed over the video. I see no reason to disallow the witness to explain the basis of his fears."

"The witness may answer the question."

"I was afraid for my life and for my family's life," Achmad replied.

"Why were you afraid?" Michael asked.

"Though it doesn't make me proud to say this, there are many people in my community who were happy when the rabbi was attacked. These people believe that if a Jew is attacked then that is a fulfillment of jihad. Like I said before, I don't agree with this belief, but many people in my community do. These people are very powerful and influential. They walked around the neighborhood warning everybody against cooperating with police. They said that Khalid al-Jinn is a hero and if anybody cooperates against him, they will suffer a terrible fate."

"So, Mr. Mustafa," Michael asked softly, "if your life is in danger, why did you agree to help the police?"

"Because I won't live in fear anymore and I will not allow these fanatics to control me. People like al-Jinn not only give good Muslims a bad name, but they incite hatred and fear among us. America has been good to my family. I have many Jewish and Christian friends and customers. I came here today to deliver a message to the defendant and to all the people like him. If you don't like this country then leave. But don't ruin it for the rest of us."

Michael looked at the faces of the jury and saw the nods and the smiles. Achmad Mustafa's testimony was brilliant, and with the video evidence in hand, a conviction of Khalid al-Jinn was a foregone conclusion.

As the judge dismissed everyone until Monday, Michael smiled. But for Shea, it was going to be a very long weekend. He needed to figure out how things had spiraled out of control so quickly, and if there was any way he could still win this case.

T O MY DEAREST SON,
We know that the Koran equates the service of Allah to one's responsibility to honor his parents. You have also heard of the conversation between Abdullah Ibn Mas'ood and the prophet, where Abdullah asked the holy prophet which deed is most beloved to Allah. The prophet in his great wisdom responded that next to praying on time, honoring one's parents is most important.

Throughout our lives together, I am sure that Allah would be proud of how you have honored me. Though it wasn't always easy, especially when your mother passed on, you have always been a wonderful and respectful son. You have always been there for me; I am hoping that I can be there for you as well.

But know this, my son. If I am unsuccessful in my quest, please understand that I bear no ill will toward you. Though I cannot understand why you chose to do certain things, I am confident that you had a reason and you allowed Allah to guide your decisions. Please be aware that I embarked on this journey because of my love for you. I have only wanted the best for you, and I am so proud of all that you have been able to accomplish.

May it be Allah's will that you never need to read this letter and I am successful in my mission. However, if it is his will and I fail, *my son, you should know that I never stopped loving you and I cherished the wonderful years that we were able to have together.*

May Allah watch over you and your family.

Your father,
Ibrahim Yusuf

Ibrahim looked at the letter that he had written to Jabril and held it close to his heart. He wasn't naïve, and he knew that the probability that he would actually reach his son was very small. That was why he had written the letter. He hoped that even if he was unsuccessful, at least Jabril would know that he tried and how much he was loved by his father.

Ibrahim folded the letter, placed it in an envelope, and waited. Anwar's friend had told him that they would be entering New York harbor shortly. Ibrahim knew what needed to be done before they reached the harbor and he waited for Anwar's friend to come for him.

As he waited for the knock on the door, Ibrahim contemplated what had transpired over the past few weeks. He thought about the photograph in the newspaper and the favor he had asked of Anwar. He hoped Anwar had not gotten in trouble because of his efforts. Ibrahim had never dreamed that he would have made it this far and he prayed that tonight wouldn't be the end of his journey. He knew that things were far from simple and Anwar's friend had warned him of the dangers that lay ahead. But he couldn't lose hope. Jabril needed him and that was all that mattered.

A few minutes later, Ibrahim heard a knock on the door. He went to open the door and saw Anwar's friend standing in the doorway.

"We need to hurry now," the man ordered.

"Why?" Ibrahim inquired. "I thought that even when we enter the harbor, we still have a few minutes before we need to leave."

"A problem has arisen."

"What?"

"It seems that somebody saw you and the captain has been asking questions about you."

"Who could have seen me? I have been very careful to leave my room only when nobody was looking."

"I don't know when he saw you. But the captain is going to search this entire vessel until he finds you."

"So what are we going to do?"

"We are going to get you off this ship immediately."

"Let me get my things and I will be ready to go."

"There is no time," the man stated. "You need to leave now."

Seeing the urgency in the man's eyes, Ibrahim relented and followed him outside. However, as he touched the letter in his pocket, he stopped.

"Why are you stopping?" the man asked gruffly.

"I need you to promise me something," Ibrahim requested.

"What?"

"You must promise me that if I do not make it to Jabril that you will get this letter to him," Ibrahim stated, handing the man the paper.

"We don't have time for this now. The captain's men will be here momentarily and you will be shipped back to Karachi. So stop worrying about a stupid letter and let me get you out of here."

"No," Ibrahim said defiantly "I will not leave until you promise me that you will do everything in your power to make sure that Jabril sees the letter."

The man eyed Ibrahim with wonder. Although Anwar had warned the man of Ibrahim's stubbornness, he couldn't believe what he was seeing. But now wasn't a time for arguing and the man realized it.

"Fine," the man relented. "I will promise to get the letter to Jabril, but I need you to leave now."

Ibrahim handed over the letter. As they entered the corridor, they could see that the way was clear and they walked briskly to the main deck. They reached a stairwell and began their ascent. The man motioned for Ibrahim to stay behind him as he opened the door slightly. Ibrahim lunged toward the door, but the man held him back.

"The captain and the security guards are on the deck right now," he said softly. "You can't go up there."

"But we can't stay here either. If they are looking for me, as you say they are, it is only a matter of moments before they head down the stairwell."

"Okay, here is what I am going to do. I will open the door and approach the captain. He knows me, so I am hoping that I can hold his attention for a few minutes. When I feel the coast is clear, I will signal to you by moving my index finger behind my back. Once you see that, it will be your sign to make a run for it. As soon as you find a spot on the deck, hoist yourself over and jump into the water."

Ibrahim nodded. The man opened the door and took a deep breath to calm his racing heart. Once he felt that he was ready, he walked directly toward the captain.

"Fareed, I was hoping to see you. How are things?" the captain asked.

"Good," Fareed answered. "Why did you want to see me?"

"It seems that a stowaway has been sighted. You know how hard we have been trying to crack down on these trespassers. The Coast Guard has threatened us with fines if we aren't able to stop these people from entering the country illegally. I am hoping we can find this stowaway before the Coast Guard boards the ship. When we do, we can turn him over to them. That will prove that we are serious about cracking down on this problem."

"That is great to hear," Fareed responded nervously. "Do you have any idea where he might be?"

"We were hoping that you might be able to help us answer that question."

Fareed's wind-burned face was not capable of growing pale, but he could feel his heart begin to beat faster. "Why me?"

"You are the head of the kitchen staff," the captain explained. "We were wondering if anyone has requested more food than usual."

Fareed breathed a quiet sigh of relief. "Now that you mention it, I do remember somebody asking for a meal to be arranged and to be delivered to room four hundred. But that room is down the corridor the other way."

As Fareed diverted the captain's attention, he moved his index finger behind his back. Ibrahim quietly opened up the door and raced across the deck. As he straddled the railing, the captain whirled around.

"Hey you, stop!"

Ibrahim froze as he saw the captain and the guards start to give chase. Realizing his window of opportunity was closing, he threw his other leg over the railing. With the captain yelling in the background, Ibrahim closed his eyes and pictured his young son playing in the orchards of Sargodha under the bright and shining sun. With a quick thrust, Ibrahim felt himself flying through the air. His son dominated his thoughts even as he headed straight into the total blackness of the nighttime tide.

■ ■ ■

Shea awoke that Shabbos morning with a splitting headache, and it wasn't because he hadn't had his morning coffee. The thought of having to go to shul and face all of his friends was less than appealing. He had managed to escape scrutiny on Friday night, as he davened in the *ezras nashim* where nobody saw him. But on Shabbos morning the women's section would be filled, and that meant Shea needed another place to *daven*.

Like most Jewish communities, PineMist had its share of politics. The first shul was established by the pioneering families that had moved to the new development. They fashioned the *davening* and the *minhagim* of the shul based on the traditions that they had grown up with. As the community grew and new families moved in, a breakoff shul was formed. Shea always *davened* in the community's original shul. More by accident than design, he rarely even socialized with people who *davened* in the new shul. On this particular Shabbos, Shea felt that was a good thing. He needed a place to *daven* where nobody would recognize him. As he walked into the new shul for the first time, Shea found a spot in the back, away from everybody, and began to *daven*. It seemed that nobody had recognized him, because Shea had been able to *daven* all morning without anybody noticing him. But just to make sure, Shea left a few minutes before *davening* was over, so that no one would have a chance to talk to him.

Walking home, he felt if he had dodged a major bullet — more like a torpedo. Part of him was amazed that he was even concerned with what people might think and say, because he knew the truth of why he had taken on the case. So why was he so bothered by others' opinions of him? But the more Shea thought about it, the more he realized that the people he was trying to avoid were his friends, and their opinion of him meant a lot. Whether it was right or wrong, that was the truth.

Shea had hoped that he would have been able to avoid confrontation and he was almost successful, but he forgot one little detail: the weekly *Kiddush*.

Most of his friends were busy professionals who didn't have time to socialize during the week. Therefore every Shabbos they would rotate hosting a *Kiddush*. Obviously, Shea had planned on missing this week's get-together. But it was taking place at Danny's house, and Danny lived right near the new shul.

As Shea made his way, he saw with increasing horror that his friends were congregating outside Danny's house and he was headed straight toward them.

Shea walked quickly past, trying to avoid eye contact. However, Motti Holland recognized him and quickly ran over.

"Shea," Motti announced, "we missed you today."

"I woke up a little late and I needed a later *minyan*," Shea answered quietly.

"Well, let's make sure that you don't make a habit of it. We need you in our shul."

"No, we don't," Danny said loudly as he walked out onto the deck that fronted his home.

"I'm sure that Danny is just kidding," Motti responded, embarrassed.

"I am definitely not kidding," Danny replied. "We don't need him in our shul and I surely don't want him on my property."

"Maybe you had a little too much Macallan, Danny. How about we go back inside," Motti said, leading Danny back toward the house.

"I didn't have too much to drink and I don't need you taking me anywhere," Danny responded, pushing Motti to the side.

"Hey," Shea intervened, "leave him alone. He was just trying to help."

"That is really rich," Danny sneered. "Where do you get off telling me or anybody what to do?"

"I wasn't telling you what to do," Shea said. "You know what, just forget it."

"You want me to forget it? Just like you want me to forget how you stabbed Rabbi Felder in the back?"

"Look, Danny, now isn't the time," Shea said, trying to keep calm.

"Why isn't now the time?" Danny asked, his voice getting even louder. "Is it because the great fraud Shea Berman told me so?"

Shea knew he shouldn't answer, but something propelled him to speak. "I am sorry for what happened. I tried to tell you, but I didn't have the chance."

"Are you kidding me? You think that this about you and me? Wow, you really are selfish. Unlike you, I know that not everything in this world is about me. You turned your back on all of us. Yechiel and Rabbi Felder were counting on you, and you just threw them to the curb. How can you live with yourself?"

Shea looked at Danny and thought about what to say. His mother had always told him to avoid all conflicts, and now was a great time to heed her advice. It also didn't help that Shea could smell the whiskey on Danny's breath. Shea started to walk away, but Danny blocked his path.

"I am really sorry that you feel this way," Shea said, trying to move away. "If you want to speak with me privately, we can arrange a time. But I don't feel comfortable speaking about this right here in front of everybody."

"Really," Danny responded, his voice surly. "You would make

time for little old me? You could squeeze me in between your meetings with Ahmadinejad and Nasralla? Those are going to be your new clients, aren't they? I heard that you are starting to advertise on al-Jazeera as the great defender of the rights of the crazy jihadists."

A crowd started to gather around Danny's house to see what the commotion was all about. Shea saw the gawking faces and realized that he needed to end the spectacle quickly.

"How about this, Danny," Shea said, struggling to remain calm. "I come over to your house later and we talk about this. But I am not going to speak with you while you are stoned off your rocker."

"You actually think that I am going to let you anywhere near my house?" Danny responded. "How about this, Shea? You take your sorry self and get off my property. While you are at it, how about you take yourself and leave this community. I don't care where you go. Just get as far away from here as possible. We don't need people like you around here."

Danny moved aside and allowed Shea to walk past. Shea nodded and hoped that would be the end of it. Though he knew it was just the beginning.

■ ■ ■

Mohamed Farouk disconsolately picked up the stale cup of coffee sitting on the table. It was going to be another long night, but that was the least of his worries. He had put in for the night shift three months earlier. Originally, he had done this for the extra pay, but now, with everything that had happened over the last few weeks, he was happy to be here at night just so he wouldn't have to look into his wife's trusting eyes and lie to her. *Soon the nightmare would end,* he tried to tell himself, and he would go back to building himself a life in America, but he knew that wasn't true. After one makes a decision like the one he'd made, there was no going back, no matter what you did.

Mohamed took his coffee and headed for his cab. His boss had called a very important meeting for later that night, and

Mohamed had no idea what Rasheed was going to say. His mind on his troubles, Mohamed tripped over a chair, spilling his coffee all over the floor. A fellow driver, Vijay, walked over and tried to help him clean up the mess.

"Man," said Vijay, "you a little clumsy tonight."

"Sorry," Mohamed replied. "Just thinking about things."

"It sure seems that way. Anything on your mind that you want to discuss, man? My momma would always say to me, 'Vijay, you got yourself a great listening ear.' She thought that I was going to become a therapist or something like that. But I wanted to move to America and get out of Jamaica. And well, the rest, as they say, is history."

The last thing that Mohamed wanted was to have his ear chewed off by Vijay. Though he knew that his friend only had good intentions, Mohamed had too much to worry about at this moment.

"Thank you for the offer," Mohamed said, trying to sound genuine, "but right now I really have a lot of things going on in my life and I am just trying to figure it all out."

"Well, just remember that if you ever need someone to talk to, I am here, okay, man."

"That's good to know."

"Just by the way, man," Vijay said, as he threw the paper towels in the garbage, "is that old guy sitting in the lobby part of your problems?"

"What old guy?" Mohamed asked suspiciously

"The old guy sitting in the lobby, freezing and wet. When I offered him a blanket to warm him, he wouldn't take it. I am not sure that he understood a word I said. He is definitely not from here, man. The only word that I understood from his mouth was your name. And man, he kept on saying it. I gave him a hot drink and told him that you would be there soon. I don't know what he wants, but he sure does want it."

Mohamed nodded like he understood and feigned an expression of confusion. However, unlike his Jamaican friend, Mohamed was very aware of what the visitor wanted.

Quickly leaving the office, Mohamed walked to the lobby and saw the man sitting on the couch. Though he hadn't seen him in several years, he looked exactly the way Mohamed remembered him. The aspect that Mohamed remembered best was the fire in his eyes, which, as Mohamed greeted him, was burning brightly.

"Ibrahim," Mohamed addressed him respectfully, "it is good to see you."

"Likewise," Ibrahim responded. "You look well, Mohamed. Your father has told me that Allah has been kind to you and you have been doing well here in America."

"Yes, we have been doing well."

"Who is 'we'? When you left Karachi, there was no 'we.'"

"I got married when I moved here."

"Wonderful news. Are there any children in your household?"

"My wife is expecting our first child at the end of the year. But Ibrahim, you are wet. Allow me to get you some warm clothes."

"I have no time for clothing. I came here for only one reason and I need to complete my mission."

"My father told me about the reason for your journey. But I am sorry to say that I don't think that I will be able to help you."

Ibrahim looked disappointed but he would not be deterred.

"Have you seen him?" Ibrahim asked.

"Seen who?"

"Have you seen Jabril?"

Mohamed avoided looking at Ibrahim. It was said that in Sargodha that Ibrahim was a human lie detector. If you weren't telling the truth, he would know in a matter of seconds. Mohamed recalled that one time Jabril had been accused of cheating on an exam. Ibrahim came down to the school and joined his son in the principal's office. When Ibrahim asked Jabril if he had cheated, Jabril told him no, and Ibrahim believed him. The principal wasn't convinced, and he still wanted to punish Jabril. Ibrahim offered to help the principal find the real culprit. Not taking no for an answer, Ibrahim marched into Jabril's classroom and questioned each boy individually. Every boy denied cheating, but Ibrahim knew who the real cheater was. He told the principal to check that boy's desk and, sure enough, inside they found a copy of all the answers. From that day on, no one ever dared to lie to Ibrahim Yusuf.

Mohamed was silent.

"Mohamed, I don't care what you have done; I just need to know how I can help Jabril. He was your best friend growing up and you know him better than anybody. I need you to help me reach him."

"What will you do then? This isn't grade school, Ibrahim. Jabril is in a lot of trouble right now."

"I cannot sit around and do nothing. *We* cannot sit around and do nothing."

I have already done too much, Mohamed thought.

"I understand your frustration, but we can't do anything," he replied. "It is out of our hands right now."

"Nothing is ever out of our hands," Ibrahim corrected him. "I have not traveled for many days, risked my own life on numerous occasions, just to be told by you or anybody that there is nothing we can do. As long as my son, your friend, is still breathing, we still have hope. Nobody can take that away from me."

Mohamed regarded Ibrahim with amazement, but then, he shouldn't have been surprised. His friend's father's resolve and commitment were legendary. If Ibrahim wanted to do something, he was going to do it no matter what obstacles lay in his path. Mohamed realized he wasn't going to convince him otherwise, and he decided to push off the issue.

"Look, it's late," Mohamed said. "How about I find you a place to sleep and we will meet in the morning. Maybe I will make some phone calls and we will see what we can do."

"I already have a place to stay," Ibrahim responded. "I am staying at the Brooklyn Hostel on Avenue U. You can call them and ask for me. The owner is a close friend of mine from Pakistan."

Again, Mohamed was amazed. Ibrahim Yusuf was a man from a different century. He barely knew how to use a cell phone, yet he was able to get from Karachi all the way to New York and settle himself in. Though he fully believed that Ibrahim's mission would end in failure, if there was anybody that could save Jabril Yusuf, it was Ibrahim.

And deep in his heart, Mohamed hoped that Ibrahim would be successful.

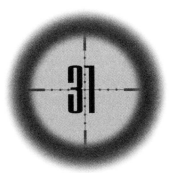

R ASHEED SALAAM LOOKED OVER THE PAPERS ON HIS desk with dismay. It wasn't as if he didn't understand them. Contrary to what he assumed most Americans thought, Rasheed wasn't an ignorant and illiterate Arab. He had graduated at the top of his class at NYU and had used the knowledge garnered from his MBA to open his own taxi company. His company, American Taxi Service, was one of the most popular car services in Brooklyn, and he had over fifty drivers in his fleet. Rasheed had been successful, but it wasn't the money that interested him. He was in America for one purpose. It had taken him many years to accomplish his goal and now he was only a few days away from success.

He threw the papers into the drawer and rose from his desk. As he paced the room, he thought about the events that had sown the seeds for what was about to come.

Rasheed hadn't always been a jihadist. His family had lived in peace and tranquility in the Carmel Mountains of Israel. His father's only wish was that his sons would go to school and be able to support their families in a respectable manner.

Everything changed in the summer of the year 2000. Because of his father's financial struggles, his family was evicted from their home, and, with no other option, they joined relatives who were living in the Jenin refugee camp. Even in the chaotic atmosphere of the camp, Rasheed went to school and remained committed to his studies, hoping to make his father proud. Life was difficult, but the family was managing. That was until April 2002, when the IDF entered Jenin and Rasheed's life was changed forever.

A man named Mahmud Tawalbe, a storeowner in Jenin, had masterminded various suicide attacks within Israel. The Israelis were committed to stopping the attacks and made plans accordingly. The inhabitants of the camp were not going to give up without a fight and chose to prepare for battle by booby-trapping numerous roads and buildings. Rasheed's father had seen the preparations and wanted to get his family out of Jenin before violence would erupt. The Israelis, for their part, encouraged the locals to evacuate by announcing their plans and offering the chance to leave. Rasheed wanted to take the Israelis up on their offer, but his mother, who had never recovered from being compelled to abandon their first home, could not bear to become homeless once again, and she refused to go. Rasheed's father pleaded with her to reconsider, but she would not. In the end, Rasheed volunteered to stay with his mother, and his father took Rasheed's other siblings out of Jenin to safety, leaving Rasheed and his mother to fend for themselves.

Rasheed had hoped that he and his mother could avoid the conflict entirely and they spent the next few days in hiding. On the third day of the conflict, Rasheed's hiding place was discovered by the IDF and they were ordered to leave the building. Again, Rasheed's mother resisted, but the soldiers were insistent. As they tried to forcibly take her from her room, Rasheed's mother reached into her pocket. An investigation later revealed that the soldier thought that she was reaching for a detonator to blow herself up. In reality, she was just trying to get a tissue to wipe the tears that were streaming down her face. Had the soldier known her true intentions, things would have ended differently, but he didn't. The soldier took aim and shot her three times in the head.

Realizing his mistake, the soldier tried to help her but it was too late. Rasheed's mother was dead, another casualty of war.

Rasheed was left to grieve alone. Something within him changed drastically in the next few hours. He was no longer the studious and peaceful son. He was now the fighter and the warrior. He got himself off the ground and vowed revenge. He would make the Israelis suffer as they had made him suffer.

During a break in the fighting, Rasheed ran to Hazem Ahmad Rayhan Qabha, who was known as "Abu Jandal," and was the leader of the resistance in the camp. Rasheed was a distant relative, and Hazem knew him well. Rasheed told Hazem that he was ready to fight against the IDF. Hazem told him that he didn't want him on the front lines. He had a different mission for Rasheed. He knew Rasheed was smart and that he would be able to use his talents to punish the Israelis in a different fashion.

Not long afterward Hazem arranged for Rasheed to study in an American university. Rasheed was told to live a life as an American and that one day he would receive a call and he would be able to get his revenge. Rasheed had gotten that call a few months earlier, and though the mission was not yet completed, he could already taste the sweetness of vengeance.

With the mission only a few days away, Rasheed needed to make sure that everything was on schedule. That was why he called this meeting, even though it was almost 3 a.m.

When his men finally entered the room, Rasheed motioned for them to close the door and be seated.

"Mohamed," Rasheed addressed him first, "Vijay tells me you had a visitor tonight."

Mohamed kept his voice even. "He was just one of my father's friends from Pakistan. He is here visiting and my father told him that I would be able to take him sightseeing. I'll do the usual with him," he forced a smile, "Statue of Liberty, Ground Zero ...."

Rasheed cut him off. "With our mission only a few days away, the last thing we want is surprises. We can't have people snooping around. Is this person going to be a problem?"

Mohamed forced himself to remain calm. With everything that

Ibrahim had already endured, the last thing he needed was to be on Rasheed Salaam's radar screen.

"Don't worry," Mohamed responded, "the old man will be no problem at all. I will make sure of it."

"You do that. Now back to business. Mohamed, how is the trial going?"

"The video was introduced and it looks like the defense is going to lose. I am sure that the lawyer will try something, but the jury seems to already be sold. You could see it on their faces."

"We need to be sure," Rasheed responded. He pointed to the two other men in the room and spoke. "Hassan, Sharif, I want you to be in the courtroom on Monday. If anything out of the ordinary happens, call me at once."

"I thought it was my job to monitor the court case," Mohamed said, startled.

"It has been your job and you have done it well. However, I need you to take care of another urgent matter."

"Which is ...?"

"With the mission only days from completion, we need to take care of all loose ends. One of them is the woman. By tomorrow, I want you to make sure she can do us no harm."

Mohamed's voice came out, strangled and thin. "You mean ...."

Rasheed answered firmly. "I mean, kill her."

Mohamed had long ago trained himself not to show emotion. He kept his voice low and even. "Why would we kill her? The deal was that as long as everything went according to plan, she would be released at the end. They have done their part. Why would you want to kill her? It's obviously not my call, but I just feel that if she did what we asked, then why are we punishing her?"

"We aren't punishing *her*. This is a war. This is our holy war against the Zionist infidels. If she needs to die, we aren't punishing her. On the contrary, we are giving her an opportunity to die for the honor of Allah. What greater reward is there?"

"But why does she need to die?"

"Because she knows too much," Rasheed answered. "She knows our voices and though we have been careful, it is possible that she has even seen our faces. We can't take any chances. She must be dealt with. If you cannot handle this yourself, I am sure that either Hassan or Sharif would welcome the opportunity to do it."

"I can do it," Mohamed said quickly, forcing himself to sound confident. "By tomorrow, she will be gone."

"That is what I wanted to hear. We are on the verge of making history, my friends. We are about to show the world the greatness of Allah and the vengeance of our jihad. Now go and take care of the tasks that I have given you."

Mohamed walked slowly out of the modest building, deep in thought. *How had everything turned so bad so quickly?* he wondered. When Rasheed had originally approached him for help, Mohamed didn't feel he had much of a choice. Refusing would have meant losing his job, and with his wife expecting a baby they needed the money. More than that; though Mohamed hadn't liked to admit it, he was afraid of Rasheed, afraid of his cruelty and of his fanaticism, and deep inside he knew saying no to him would put him and his family in danger.

At the beginning it wasn't much of a problem: he just ran errands for Rasheed, gave him information, dropped off packages. Three weeks ago everything had changed. Rasheed had told him that their mission was in a crisis and he needed Mohamed's help. At first Mohamed had offered his services, but when Rasheed had told him what he needed to do, Mohamed tried to beg off. That was when Rasheed made it clear that refusal was not an option, subtly threatening the life of both Mohamed and, even worse, his wife. Mohamed had no choice but to go along with the plan and that is how he found himself in this terrible mess.

Now, as he walked out of the building, Mohamed saw that he had no choice. No matter what terrible things he had already done, there was still time to change everything. Because he wasn't going to kill the woman. The only question was how he was going to get away with it.

■ ■ ■

Shea Berman tiptoed out the door. The kids were still asleep, but Shea needed to speak with his client before the trial resumed.

He stopped for a minute and gazed at the automobile in its carport. Though it may have been immature, Shea always took a moment to admire his vehicle, a 'ninety-eight Infiniti Q45. Shea's father had bought the car as soon as it came on the market and had treated it like a treasure. He garaged it every night and it received top-notch maintenance. He took it for a car wash once a month and made sure to get the carpets shampooed and the leather interior polished to a glistening sheen. Shea would remark that his father treated the car better than he treated his son. But it all worked out in the end, because after Shea came back from yeshivah, his father offered him the Q45. At first Shea was taken aback, but his father explained that Shea was going to need a car for social events and to get to school. Besides, Dovid Berman had reasoned, Lexus had just come out with a jeep and he was ready for a change.

Now, almost fifteen years after the car had been driven out of the showroom, Shea still loved it. Even when the firm offered him a company car, Shea declined. The powerful engine still purred like a kitten and its leather and wood trim looked brand-new. And besides, Shea joked, there weren't many 1998 Q45s on the road, so he never had a problem finding it in a crowded parking lot.

As Shea walked toward the car, he realized that something seemed off. He went to take a closer look and saw that the car was practically on the ground, all four of its tires slashed.

His first instinct was to call the police and put in a complaint, but he realized that he had a bigger issue to deal with. Court was to begin in three hours, and Shea had no way of getting there.

As he pondered his options, a car pulled up alongside him.

"What happened?" Motti Holland asked.

"I guess some guys are really angry at me," Shea responded, pointing at his exposed rims. "They slashed my tires last night."

"Are you sure they were slashed?"

"Unless I managed to drive over two curbs simultaneously in my sleep, I would say that my tires were slashed. But after what happened on Shabbos, I can't say that I am surprised."

"What do you mean?"

"Come on, Motti, you were there. You saw everybody's face when Danny was giving me that tongue lashing. They were agreeing with everything that he was saying. Danny was the only one who had the guts to say it me."

"Well, let's see what we can do about this, shall we," Motti replied, peering at the flattened tires. "Wow, whoever did this really must have hated your tires. They didn't just let the air out; they stabbed at the tires with a sharp object. You are definitely going to need new ones. Let me call my brother and see what he can do."

Ari Holland, Motti's brother, owned Tires R Us on Route 88. If anybody could help Shea quickly, it was Ari.

"Isn't it a bit early to be calling him?"

"Nah, Ari is usually up at five. He learns with Rabbi Adler before *davening* every morning."

"But why are you doing this?"

"Doing what?"

"Why are you helping me? You are also very close with Rabbi Felder. Why aren't you furious with me for defending his attacker?"

"Because of the story of Rabbi Felder and the thief. Do you remember it?"

"How could I forget? That guy walked into Rabbi Felder's house and stole everything from him."

"And do you remember what Rabbi Felder did for the thief?"

"He appeared at his sentencing and pleaded with the judge for mercy."

"Rabbi Felder taught us that we can't judge anybody, because we have no idea what is going on in their life that would make them do certain things that we may view as wrong. He felt that the guy who stole from him may have had had a reason, and later it was discovered that the thief was stealing to pay hospital bills he'd racked up when his son was dying. If a thief deserves the benefit of the doubt, why shouldn't you? I have no idea why you are defending this man. But I do know how much you love and care for Rabbi Felder. If you are doing this, I believe that you must have a good reason."

Shea smiled. Though he knew that people like Danny were only acting based on what they saw, and not the truth, it felt good to see that there were also people like Motti who could see things so differently.

"Hey, Ari," Motti spoke into his cell phone, putting it on speaker, "my friend has a '98 Infiniti Q45 and it needs four tires. Can you help him?"

"Sure," Ari answered. "I will send my guy out there right now to tow the car to the shop."

Shea motioned for Motti to give him the phone.

"Hi, Ari," Shea spoke, "this is Shea Berman."

"Hey, Shea, how have you been?"

"Honestly, not so good."

"I figured. I've seen your face all over the papers and they aren't saying anything very nice."

"I know, and I hope that it will all come to an end very soon. But can your guy just bring the tires here and change them by me?"

"Shea," Ari responded, "your car needs very specific tires, size 215/60R1694V. Not to bore you with the details, but suffice it to say, those tires are not something I keep in stock. It will take time to order them."

"How much time are we talking about?"

"At least a day, I think."

"That long?"

"Shea, your car isn't a common one and neither are its tires. If you were driving an Accord or a Buick, I could get you those tires yesterday. But if you want to drive a car that no one else drives, well, you are going to have to wait for your tires to be ordered and delivered."

Shea's mind raced. Court was scheduled for nine o'clock and he still wanted to meet with al-Jinn to discuss strategy. He considered calling the judge and explaining the situation, but since Daniels had just given Shea an extended recess, coupled with the fact that Daniels really wanted the trial to conclude, Shea knew that the judge wasn't going to be amenable if Shea asked him for yet another delay.

His wife's van was parked in the adjoining driveway, and he considered taking it into Brooklyn. But Yehuda had an appointment with an ophthalmologist in the city and Shira couldn't be left stranded without a car.

"I need to get to court," Shea pleaded with Ari.

"I am sorry, but I can't help you on that one."

"Maybe I can," Motti interjected.

"What do you mean?"

"If we hurry, you can still make the early bus that makes a stop on Coney Island Avenue. You should be able to get into Brooklyn with enough time to hail a cab to the courthouse and be there before the trial starts."

"What about my car?"

"Leave the keys in the ignition and my guy will come by and deal with it," Ari responded. "You get yourself into Brooklyn and let me worry about your car."

"Great," Shea answered, realizing that he had no choice. "Motti, are you sure you can take me to the bus?"

"Not a problem. But we better get moving."

Shea unlocked the door and placed his keys into the ignition. As he jumped into Motti's car he only hoped that he wouldn't be late for the biggest day of his professional career.

MOHAMED FAROUK COULDN'T SHAKE THE FEELING that he was being watched. Turning toward the security cameras, he knew that everything he was about to do was going to be recorded. He prayed that by the time Rasheed watched the videos, he and his wife would be long gone.

Mohamed walked down the steps toward the utility room. The other drivers rarely came to this room, isolated in the building's dark and uninviting basement. The room contained the building's electrical panel, heater, and boiler. It contained something else as well, and that was why Mohamed was here.

He opened the door, immediately shut it behind him, and went to the back wall where the electrical panel was located. He put his hand directly under the panel and felt for a lever. He pulled down the lever and the wall slid away, revealing a stairwell. Realizing the magnitude of what he was about to do, Mohamed took a deep breath and walked down the steps.

■ ■ ■

The cell was black, but the woman was wide awake. Ever since she had recognized Mohamed's voice, she'd been even more terrified. While she had originally thought that she'd been chosen at random, she now knew that wasn't the case and that frightened her greatly. Mohamed hadn't visited her since that day and she started to fear that he would never visit her again. But as she clutched the picture of her boys closely to her heart she knew that she couldn't afford to give up hope.

While her thoughts were focused on her children, she heard an opening of a door and she jumped to attention.

"Hanadi," Mohamed called, "are you there?"

"Of course I am here," the woman answered defiantly. "Where else would I be?"

Mohamed turned on his flashlight. In its bright glare Hanadi retreated toward the wall, but Mohamed was still able to see her face. The bruises that she'd sustained the night that she was taken were slowly fading, but he could see the torment in her eyes and it was alive and strong.

"Hanadi, come here," Mohamed ordered.

"How could you?" Hanadi said. "Jabril trusted you. We trusted you with everything. How could you do this to us?"

"You don't understand. You could never understand, but that doesn't matter now."

"Of course it matters now," Hanadi said, her voice rising. "Your betrayal is all that matters. "

"You need to keep your voice down," Mohamed said.

"Why should I listen to you after what you have done to us?"

"Because I was sent to kill you," he answered bluntly. "You may not trust me, but I've told you how crazy Rasheed is and you know that he wouldn't hesitate to kill you."

Hanadi's lips were quivered in fear. "If he sent you to kill me, why are you telling me this?"

"Because I don't intend to listen to him," Mohamed answered. "I know that you must think that I am a monster and no different from Rasheed. But you need to know this, I never meant for any of this to happen. I thought that nobody would get hurt and I would be able to protect my family, and yours. But I see now that I was wrong. Though I can't undo the pain that you suffered,

I intend to make sure that you never experience it again. So I beg you, come with me now."

Mohamed opened the cell door.

"You need to trust me. If we don't get out soon, Rasheed's goons will be here and they will kill us both."

Her eyes accustomed to the light, Hanadi looked into Mohamed's eyes. She could see terror there, and truth.

She followed him from the room.

Fire codes mandated more than one exit in any multistory building, and there was an almost forgotten door in a dark corner of the basement. Together, Mohamed and Hanadi hurried toward it. Mohamed rammed the rusty lock with a hammer that he'd brought with him, and with a sound of cracking wood it flew open.

They were free.

Standing in a quiet alley, Mohamed handed the woman a wad of cash. "Take this money and go to the Brooklyn Hostel."

"Why there?" Hanadi said, drawing deep breaths of fresh air. "I want to go home."

"Your husband's father is waiting there."

"Ibrahim?"

"He saw Jabril's photo in the newspaper and he traveled all the way from Sargodha to New York."

"Photo? What photo? Where is Jabril?"

"I don't have time to tell you now. All you need to worry about is getting to the Brooklyn Hostel before anybody finds out that you are missing."

"What about my sons? Rasheed told me that they would be in danger if I didn't do as he said."

"Your sons will be meeting you at the hostel. But you need to go now. Don't take a taxi; the driver might be one of Rasheed's men. There is a bus on the corner. Take it to Avenue U. The hostel is right down the block from the bus stop."

Hanadi headed toward the corner and Mohamed walked the other way. After a few seconds he heard Hanadi call out to him.

"Is Jabril going to be okay?"

Mohamed looked at her sad eyes and said the only words that

he knew to be true. "I don't know. Now you must get on that bus. Once you are with Ibrahim and the boys, you will be safe."

Mohamed got into his cab and sped off. He knew that he needed to get out of the city as quickly as possible. There wasn't much time before Rasheed would find out what really had happened to Hanadi. And once he did, he was going to demand blood. Mohamed's blood.

■ ■ ■

Al-Jinn was waiting for Shea in the conference room. Shea could still see the burning hatred in his eyes. Ever since their last encounter, Shea had done his best to avoid speaking to his client. Al-Jinn had made his wishes clear, and Shea didn't feel that there was anything to be gained by engaging him in conversation. But now that was changing

Shea's original tactics had worked beautifully, but then the video had been screened. Now Shea needed a new defense, and that defense required his client's cooperation. Shea knew that the chances of this were slim, but there were no other options left.

Shea sat across from his client and took out his notebook. Al-Jinn averted his eyes as Shea began to speak.

"How did it go with the doctor?" Shea asked.

"Why are you asking me?" al-Jinn responded coldly. "You have all the information right there in front of you."

"You are right that I do. But I wanted to know your opinion of her."

"Why should that matter?"

"Because if my own client doesn't believe in my expert witness, how will the jury?"

"The jury already believes that I am guilty, so if you are hoping that your witness will change their minds, you are wasting your time. This trial has been a sham from the beginning, but I don't really care. They are going to send me to jail no matter what that doctor says."

"You can't believe that."

"Why not? You Zionists run all the courts in this country. Even if I wasn't guilty, I would still be sent to prison."

"If you weren't guilty, you wouldn't go to prison."

"The sad thing is that you really believe that," al-Jinn said with disdain. "Here is what I know. I am an Muslim, a Jew was attacked, and I was arrested. End of story. But here is something that you can't seem to forget. I don't care. I don't care what they do to me. Allah knows the truth and he will provide me my salvation. Not some Zionist in a suit."

Shea was disheartened, but he couldn't say that he was surprised. Al-Jinn's hatred was as venomous now as it had been at the beginning of the trial. Shea had hoped that perhaps with the trial coming to an end and reality about to sink in, al-Jinn would display some humanity. But after hearing what his client had just said, he knew that this was a lost cause.

■ ■ ■

Shea looked up from the defense table while his witness was called. The previous night Shea had spent many hours on the phone with the doctor, reviewing her testimony. Michael Reeves, for his part, seemed unconcerned, clearly believing that a conviction was a foregone conclusion.

The middle-aged woman made her way to the witness stand and took a seat. Her horn-rimmed glasses provided an aura of respectability, and that is exactly what Shea was hoping for.

"Would you please state your name for the jury," Shea requested.

"Dr. Morgan Kestler," the woman responded.

"And Dr. Kestler, what is your occupation?"

"I am the head of the Department of Psychiatry at Columbia Medical Center."

"Sidebar!" Reeves called out.

The two attorneys approached the bench.

"I object to this witness' testimony," Reeves said.

"My witness hasn't said anything yet," Shea argued.

"But that is exactly the point. Dr. Kestler's views and opinions are most certainly known, and based on the Frye standard, her expert testimony should not be allowed."

"Your Honor," Shea retorted, "Dr. Kestler is a respected member of the medical community. She has authored many books and is the editor of *Psychiatric Weekly*, which is a highly respected publication."

"Nobody is debating the doctor's credentials," Reeves responded. "However, the question here is whether or not the expert's testimony will be providing scientific information that is reliable and relevant. According to Frye vs. United States, the testimony, and I quote, 'must be sufficiently established to have gained general acceptance in its particular field.'"

"I am quite aware of the Frye standard, Mr. Reeves," the judge remarked.

"Then Your Honor should have no trouble sustaining my objection to the doctor's testimony."

"Your Honor," Shea argued, "there is a precedent for the doctor's research in criminal cases. For instance, in 1976 during the Patty Hearst trial."

"Your Honor," Michael interrupted, "the jury found Ms. Hearst guilty and rejected her defense."

"But she was pardoned by President Clinton," Shea argued.

"That was only because of public opinion and outrage. As far as I can recall, we are not trying this case in the court of public opinion, but in a court of law."

"More recently," Shea continued, "during the Maryland sniper trials, the defense argued that the defendant, Lee Boyd Malvo, was brainwashed by John Allan Muhammad, and the court allowed the defense to present such an argument."

"But as in the Hearst case, the defendant was found guilty and his defense was rejected. So I am asking Your Honor to please not allow the defense to waste any of our time with unfounded and baseless theories."

"Your Honor," Shea retorted, "despite what the state would like to claim, my client has a right to a proper defense. Even if other juries have not been convinced of its efficacy, the brainwashing defense is a real defense and my witness is an expert in its effects and ramifications. So I will ask that Your Honor allow my witness to present her well-documented research to the jury."

Daniels thought for a moment and Shea held his breath. Though he knew that the chances that the jury would believe that al-Jinn had been brainwashed were slim, it was his only shot at getting his client an acquittal. If the judge sustained Reeves's objection, Shea knew that the trial was over.

"Mr. Reeves," the judge addressed the DA, "I think that you will recall that I was lenient regarding the admittance of the videotape. This was because I believe that the state should have the ability to present its case properly. If I am going to afford the prosecution the capacity to present its case, then I have no choice but to afford the same right to the defense, no matter how outlandish you believe its argument to be. I therefore overrule your objection and I will allow the witness to continue."

As a disappointed Reeves returned to his seat, Shea breathed a sigh of relief and turned to his witness.

"Dr. Kestler, you have done extensive research regarding the use of brainwashing, have you not?"

"Yes, I have."

"Would you please care to elaborate?"

"The human mind is a powerful tool. It can be used to accomplish great things. However, throughout history, we have seen that man can use his mind to commit the most horrific atrocities and not feel any remorse for doing them. While some psychiatrists would attribute the lack of remorse to a psychological condition, more commonly known as the insanity defense, my research has proven that there may be another reason that people may commit the most heinous crimes, without even understanding the gruesome nature of what they have done."

"This is because they have been brainwashed?" Shea asked.

"Objection!" Reeves called. "Counsel is leading the witness."

"I will rephrase," Shea responded. "What has your research

shown as another reason that people may commit these terrible crimes?"

"In certain situations it is because the accused perpetrator may have been brainwashed."

"What is your clinical definition of someone who is brainwashed?"

"It is where a tactic has been implemented against an individual that will subvert that person's sense of control over his or her own thinking, behavior, and actions."

"Now, wasn't there a study done after the Korean War involving soldiers who'd defected to the Communist side after supposedly being brainwashed?"

"Yes, there was."

"Isn't it true that the study found that the soldiers who had defected hadn't done so because they had been brainwashed, but because the Communists had used methods of coercion?"

"Yes," the doctor responded. "It seemed that the Communists, after torturing the soldiers through sleep deprivation and starvation, had offered the soldiers a way out of their suffering — and that was to defect."

"Were the soldiers brainwashed?"

"No."

"And how do you know this?"

"It seems that after the war most of the soldiers who had defected returned to their homes and lived their lives no differently than they had before the war had started."

"So you could say that these soldiers had control over their thinking and thought it was better to appear to defect than to suffer at the hands of their enemies."

"That would be accurate."

"So if that is not brainwashing, then, Doctor, where have you seen brainwashing overtaking a person's thinking and control?"

"In Israel," the doctor responded. "More specifically, in the city of Jenin."

"When did you observe these behaviors?"

"When I began my research, over two years ago, I was primarily intrigued by the rise of radical Islam. I, like many Americans, had seen the videos and pictures of young Muslims yelling *death to Israel and America*, and going to their own deaths willingly as suicide/homicide bombers. I wondered, as a doctor, whether I should fear these people or feel sorry for them. The real question that I struggled with was whether or not these people are responsible for the hatred that they feel and subsequently for the actions that they take."

"How did you go about researching these behaviors?" Shea inquired.

"I reached out to a friend of mine with the Red Cross and asked if he could help me. He told me that there were various groups located within Jenin that he believed engaged in brainwashing. He gave me information on one of the groups that happened to have been run by an American named Jamal. I emailed him and told him that I, as a psychiatrist, wished to observe their training techniques."

"What was his response?"

"He said that he was more than happy to allow me to observe their operation."

"Why would he have wanted to do such a thing?"

"From my understanding, he believed that my being there legitimized their plight. He wanted me, as a respected member of the American medical community, to see the terrible conditions that the people in Jenin were suffering under. He was actually convinced that he was providing these young people a life and a purpose while the Israeli oppressors sought to take everything away from them."

"What did you observe while you were there?"

"I definitely saw tactics of brainwashing being used. Jamal, along with his staff, would bring young boys and men into his home. There, he would isolate them from their families, degrade their previous lifestyles, and force them to perform repetitive tasks and drills all designed to turn these men into soldiers of jihad."

"Were they successful?"

"One man, who was about twenty-six years old with a European wife and family, divorced his wife and disowned his family after only three weeks of being at Jamal's house. I would say that Jamal and others like him are very successful in what they do."

Shea waited just a moment. The doctor was doing great, but now was the real key. Could he turn his client from assailant to victim? As he looked at the jury and saw the look of interest and, perhaps, a touch of pity in some of their eyes, Shea was convinced that he might actually stand a chance.

"Doctor Kestler," Shea continued his questioning, "did you have an opportunity to interview my client?"

"Yes, I did."

"And what did you discover during your interview?"

"It seems that your client, while he was in Jenin, also went through one of these programs that I had observed."

"Did he describe what he experienced during this stay in that program?"

"Yes, and according to what he described, it was exactly what I had seen at Jamal's house."

"And what was that?"

"That he underwent extensive programming to hate Jews and to believe that he is a soldier in a war of jihad."

"Doctor, after meeting with my client, could you say that he was brainwashed?"

"Your client is a highly educated individual who, according to my medical opinion, has been robbed of the thought processes that would allow him to discern between right and wrong when it pertains to matters involving Jews. Mr. al-Jinn has been brainwashed to hate Jews and to believe that it is his duty and mission to hurt as many of them as possible."

"Do you believe that my client should be punished for the crime that he allegedly committed?"

"Your client needs to be rehabilitated, but not punished. When committing the attack against Rabbi Felder, I believe that your client could not appreciate the heinous nature of his actions, due to the brainwashing that he had experienced while living in Jenin."

"No further questions, Your Honor," Shea said, turning toward the defense table.

"Mr. Reeves," Daniels addressed the DA, "do you have any questions for the witness?"

"Yes, Your Honor," Michael responded.

Shea watched Michael rise from his chair and waited. He knew that the doctor's research was highly controversial and it wouldn't take Michael very long to undo everything that Shea had just accomplished. However, when he heard Michael's first question to Doctor Kestler, Shea was genuinely surprised.

"Doctor Kestler," Michael began, "what was the name of the group that allegedly brainwashed Mr. al-Jinn?"

"They were known as, 'al-Adiyat,' which, translated into English means, 'the assaulters.'"

"And when did he join this group?"

"Two years ago."

"Are you positive that Mr. al-Jinn was a member of al-Adiyat two years ago?"

"I am almost positive," the doctor said. "If you would allow me to refer to my notes, I can tell you for certain."

"Please do," the prosecutor requested.

Shea looked on, perplexed, while the doctor looked through her notes. Why was Michael so interested in which group al-Jinn had joined rather than attacking her theory on brainwashing? Something was going on, but Shea had no idea what.

"It says here," the doctor said, holding a piece of paper in her hand, "that the defendant told me that he had joined the al-Adiyat group two years ago and was a member for almost three months."

"Thank you, Dr. Kestler," Michael stated. "I have no further questions for the witness."

"The witness may step down," Daniels stated.

"Your Honor," Michael called out, "the state would like to call Asraf al-Asr as a rebuttal witness."

Shea watched as a clean-shaven, dark-skinned man walked to the witness chair. Even though he didn't look imposing, Shea was absolutely frightened of this man, because he had no idea what the witness was going to say.

■ ■ ■

"Mr. al-Asr, what is your occupation?" Michael inquired.

"I work for an organization called Operation Understanding," al-Asr responded in a heavy Middle Eastern accent.

"What does this organization do?"

"We travel around the United States to different Muslim communities and try to combat the influence that radical Islam is having on the Muslim youth in this country."

"Do you find that you are having success?"

"Only time will tell. Radical Islam is rampant in many areas, because it gets the most media attention. The youth see the videos on the internet. They see the parades and they see the protests, and they want to get involved. We have to fight many battles in order to get the children's attention. But we hope that we will be successful as the years go on."

"But you weren't always fighting the influence of radical Islam, were you?" Michael asked.

"No, I wasn't."

"What were you doing before you joined Operation Understanding?"

"I was a recruiter."

"Who were you recruiting for?"

"I recruited young Muslims to join the jihad against the Israelis."

The jury gasped. Nobody could have guessed that this articulate and well-dressed man used to be a terrorist.

"Why did you stop?"

"It was one of my recruits who caused me to change. I had brought him into our group and he had asked me to promise him that I would protect him. I told him that I would and one day we went out on a protest. There was a riot and this recruit, no older than sixteen, was caught in crossfire between a Muslim jihadist and an Israeli soldier. The jihadist grabbed the boy and used him as a human shield. I ran to him as he was bleeding out, and I saw the fear and hurt in his eyes. The only thing he was able to say was, 'I trusted you.' After that, I realized that I was making a major mistake and I needed to change my lifestyle quickly."

"Mr. al-Asr, what was the name of the group that you recruited for?"

"Al-Adiyat," Al-Asr answered.

Shea glanced toward his client and saw a look of concern and worry cross his face. Al-Jinn shifted nervously in his chair and his hands stiffened. To Shea it looked as if he was trying to get away, even though he couldn't go anywhere.

"Mr. al-Asr, the defense contends that Mr. al-Jinn was a member of al-Adiyat two years ago and was brainwashed there. Do you believe that claim?"

"No, I do not."

"And why is that?"

"Because I was the recruiter for al-Adiyat during that time and I never saw the defendant until today."

The jury and the gallery again found themselves in an uproar. Daniels struggled to regain order and Shea was totally lost.

"Is it possible that Mr. al-Jinn joined al-Adiyat without you knowing it?"

"No."

"Why?"

"Since I was the only recruiter for the group, nobody entered the group without my knowledge. If Mr. al-Jinn contends that he was a member, there is only one explanation."

"And what is that?"

"That he is lying," al-Asr said, pointing his finger at al-Jinn.

Shea turned to his client for an explanation. Oddly enough, while he could readily believe that Khalid al-Jinn may have been a cold-hearted attacker, he never thought that he was a liar. In any case, why would al-Jinn lie about the group that he had joined in Jenin? There was only one person that could answer this question, and Shea was staring right at him.

"What is going on?" Shea whispered angrily into the ear of his client.

"I told you already," al-Jinn responded, "drop this now."

■ ■ ■

Rasheed Salaam glared at the phone, waiting for it to ring. When Rasheed asked Mohamed to take care of something, he was usually very quick and would report back immediately. Mohamed had taken care of the woman over twelve hours earlier, but he had not yet checked in. It was cause for concern, and that was the last thing Rasheed wanted at this moment.

As he sat by his desk, he started to review what Mohamed had said. True, the woman had done everything she had been asked, but she was still a liability and needed to be dealt with. Mohamed didn't know everything; he was aware that something big was being planned, but had no idea of the exact details. If Mohamed had known what the mission really was, he never would have questioned Rasheed's decision. He would have realized what was really at stake and that no chances could be taken. But by design, the mission was a secret, and Mohamed would need to trust Rasheed. Throughout the entire ordeal, Mohamed had never failed Rasheed, and Rasheed hoped that he wouldn't fail him now.

The ringing of the phone startled Rasheed out of his reverie, and he lifted the receiver immediately.

"Mohamed, where are you?" Rasheed barked.

"It is not Mohamed. It is me, Sharif."

"What is going on?"

"You asked me to report to you on the trial, and we may have a problem on our hands."

"What kind of problem?"

"It seems like the lawyer might be getting too close."

"Why do you think that?"

"The prosecution just brought in a witness who testified that the defendant wasn't in the al-Adiyat group two years ago."

"How did they find this witness?"

"I have no idea. Right now the lawyer seems pretty upset."

"What about the defendant?"

"He isn't talking. But I am not sure that we have a lot of time."

"Why? If the defendant is quiet, what are you worried about?"

"I am worried about the lawyer," Sharif explained. "I saw his face, and he knows that something is going on. He's a smart one, and it's only a matter of time before he figures everything out."

Rasheed narrowed his eyes. The plan seemed so perfect, but with what Sharif had just told him, he realized that it was also very close to unraveling. He needed to neutralize the lawyer and he needed to do it fast.

"I want you and Hassan to scare off the lawyer," Rasheed ordered.

"What do you mean, scare?"

"Exactly what I said. Rough him up a little if you have to, but don't kill him. If he dies, that will only focus more attention on the defendant, and that is the last thing that we want right now. Find the lawyer and give him a warning. Make sure he backs off this case. Make him understand, is that clear?"

"Perfectly," Sharif replied.

"Call me when it's done," Rasheed ordered.

Rasheed threw his phone down in disgust, scattering the papers on his desk to the floor. He had spent too much time and had gone too far to let everything unravel at the last second. His only hope was that Sharif and Hassan would be able to convince the lawyer to back off without causing any further damage.

As he bent to pick up the papers that were strewn over the floor his attention returned to Mohamed, hoping that he had succeeded in his mission and wondering why he had yet to call in.

■ ■ ■

"Would you like a drink?" the stewardess asked.

"Make it Scotch on the rocks," Mohamed replied, after a pause.

"Anything for your wife?"

Mohamed looked at his wife sleeping soundly next to him

and shook his head. The stewardess left Mohamed and promised to return shortly with his drink, which he sorely needed. Even though Islam forbade alcoholic beverages, Mohamed felt that with everything that had happened, he was entitled to some leeway. His anxiety was at an all-time high and he needed something to soothe him.

As he gazed at his wife, so calm and peaceful, he thought back to the conversation that he'd had with her a few hours earlier. When he had informed her that they were moving back to Pakistan, she was shocked and upset. If Mohamed had been doing so well, she demanded, why did they need to move? Mohamed had told her that she needed to trust him, and, like the good wife she was, she did. Looking back at everything that he had done, he realized that he didn't deserve a wife like her. He only hoped that a new life in Pakistan would provide a fresh start for him and his family.

As he settled into his seat and waited for his drink, he wondered if he should have stayed behind to help Jabril. He could have marched into a police station, admitted everything that he had done, and saved his friend. But the more he thought about it, the more he understood that doing so that might or might not have saved his friend, but he would have been putting himself and his wife in grave danger. From the beginning Mohamed had been weak, and as he sat back in seat, he realized that nothing had changed. Sure, he had released Hanadi and directed her toward Ibrahim. But when it came to helping his oldest friend, he'd run away to save himself. Mohamed knew that he was nothing more than a coward and he wasn't relishing the thought of being confronted by his father.

As Mohamed nursed the unaccustomed drink in his hand, he knew that despite everything he had done, Jabril still had one chance to survive. He only hoped for his friend's sake that his hot-shot Jewish lawyer wouldn't give up and would fight until he discovered the truth.

■ ■ ■

"Sir, we will be closing in a few minutes," the librarian informed Shea politely. "If you need to check out any materials, you can bring them to the desk."

"It's okay. I will be leaving momentarily."

Shea watched the librarian retreat to her desk and sighed. He couldn't understand how things had gone downhill so fast. He had gone from looking like a seasoned veteran on the verge of winning an unwinnable case, to a clumsy amateur unable to even get his own client's story straight. He thought that he had everything under control, but at every turn something had managed to go wrong. He would have loved to be able to analyze every aspect of the trial to find out exactly where his mistakes began, but as he looked at his watch, he knew that he had bigger issues to deal with, like how he was going to come up with a defense with no clue of how to proceed next.

To his credit, Judge Daniels had seen that Shea had been totally ambushed by the state's witness and had granted Shea a recess until morning. While normally he would have welcomed the extra time to prepare, Shea now found himself totally flummoxed. He had no idea what to do next. Though his brainwashing defense had been a longshot, at least it was a defense. But now the state had proved that al-Jinn was not only a cold-blooded attacker, but a liar as well. Shea couldn't bring himself to stand in front of the jury and try to orchestrate still another defense. He was weary and, though he'd never thought he would ever be at that point, he was ready to give up.

That is why he found himself at the small local library he used to visit as a youngster in Flatbush. It was a place that had warm memories for him, a place to hide. After all the mistakes that he had committed, he couldn't face Allan or the rest of the associates in the office. Shea had failed and there was nothing he could do about it. He knew that tomorrow could very well be his last day as an attorney for Lockhart, Gardner, and Scott and it pained him deeply. It wasn't because his pride would be hurt. He knew that whatever would happen was because Hashem wanted it, and he would have to deal with what the fallout would be. What really pained him was the thought of his wife and his family. They had endured terrible hardships during the trial, all with the hope that at the end Shea would emerge victorious and they would be able to go on living as they had before. But it seemed that their suffering had been for nothing.

He nodded farewell to the librarian, turned left from East 16th Street, and walked toward his parents' house on Avenue J. He had told Shira that he needed to work late and would sleep at his parents' house rather than return to Lakewood. With his car in the shop, he explained, it was easier for him to stay in Brooklyn. The real reason was that Shea couldn't face his wife knowing that despite all the pain she had undergone because of him, he still wasn't going to be able to keep his job.

In the fading light of day Shea turned the corner. The streets were unusually quiet; only two men were standing nearby. He assumed they were college students but as he came closer he saw they were older, and they were walking purposefully toward him. Shea was in no mood to talk to the myriads of media people who'd constantly been hounding him, and he turned back in the direction of the library. The two men picked up speed. Shea stopped for a moment to confront them; that was when he saw the blackjacks and brass knuckles.

He dashed back to the library and desperately banged tensely on the locked door. No answer. The men were almost upon him. Shea looked around. No one was passing by; there was no one to come to his aid.

He noticed a high metal fence adjoining the nearby train tracks. If he could only scale the fence, maybe he could lose them. He jumped and tried to pull himself up and over. Shea wasn't a teenager any more, and as he grabbed onto the metal and tried to hold up his body weight, his arms felt like they were on fire. With all his strength he pulled his body toward the top of the fence and he felt his legs follow suit. Soon he would reach the top, vault over, and get away.

He felt a tugging at his legs. One of his pursuers was grabbing him. Desperately, Shea tried to shake him off, but the man was too strong. Shea finally gave way and fell heavily to the hard sidewalk.

One of the men roughly picked him up. Shea turned to face his pursuers.

"I don't have any cash on me," Shea said, trying to remain calm, "so if you were looking to rob me, then I am sorry, but you guys aren't going to get much."

"We don't want your money," the taller one said.

"Then what do you want?"

Before he could answer, the other man slammed his fist into Shea's gut. Shea fell to one knee, gasping for air.

"We want you to listen very carefully to what we have to say," the tall man said quietly. The other man rammed his knee into Shea's nose. Shea struggled to remain conscious as the taste of blood entered his mouth.

"If you scream, we will kill you now," the taller man said. "Is that understood?"

Shea nodded weakly as he struggled to his feet.

"We have a message for you," the tall man continued. "Drop the case. Tell the judge that you no longer can continue. Drop this case and never think about it again. Are we clear?"

Shea again nodded his head.

"That is good," the man said. "Now, we are going to disappear, but I am watching you. If I see you make a move for your cell phone, Hassan will not hesitate to shoot you. Once we are out of your sight, you can call whoever you want. But remember, I am always watching you. And if I need to pay you another visit, you won't be getting off this lightly."

■ ■ ■

Allan Shore looked at the plaques that adorned his walls. Over the past decade, he had been awarded Attorney of the Year nine years out of ten. He gazed at the pictures of him with numerous celebrities and personalities that he had either defended or known personally. Here was a man, it seemed, who was on top of the legal world. But Allan knew the truth, and no award could convince him otherwise.

People who saw Allan Shore, with his ten-thousand-dollar suits and seven-hundred-dollar shoes, generally assumed that he came from a background of wealth and privilege. They were wrong: Allan's upbringing had been difficult and impoverished. His father was a factory worker who was never able to make ends meet. His mother struggled with depression and wasn't really there for her child. His childhood was replete with memories that he struggled to forget. But there was one incident that he remembered vividly.

Allan was fifteen, and a great student. He had the grades to prove it. It wasn't that he was so much smarter than everybody else, but he possessed a drive to excel that none of his classmates could match. His driving force was that he saw his parents' life and he was committed to make sure that he didn't end up like them.

He'd aced his biology exam and wanted to share the news with his father. But when his father came home, he told Allan something that would shape the rest of his life. His father told him that he was kicking Allan out of the house.

When Allan had asked why, his father told him that he was doing it for his own good. He explained that the world was a cruel place, not for the weak or dependent. *If you want to survive,* his father said, *you need to make it on your own.* His father gave him enough money for the first month and told Allan that he would have to fend for himself — it was either sink or swim.

While many teenagers would have used that incident as an excuse to fall into crime or drugs, Allan used it to motivate himself. He was going to make it his mission to be better than his father and failure was not going to be an option. Allan got an after-school job and used his wages to pay his room and board. Because of his exceptional grades, he was given a full scholarship to college and the rest, as they say, was history.

Allan would have loved to be able to tell himself that the reason he was so hard on Shea was because he knew what it was like to suffer. Allan hadn't forgotten what Jessica had told him, and he knew that whatever the outcome of the case, Shea still was out of a job. *So why am I making him suffer*, Allan wondered. Then he realized the answer. The man who had made it from nothing, was still no more than a nothing.

Though he knew, especially with the guilt building up inside of him, that he should call Shea and tell him the truth, Allan couldn't bring himself to do it. He believed that Jessica would not hesitate to fire him, and if the choice was between Shea and him, well, Allan Shore wasn't going to pick Shea. Still, something was compelling him to speak to Shea, give him some encouragement, even if it was false.

He picked up the phone and dialed his secretary.

"Donna," Allan called, "can you get Shea on the phone? I want to ask him how the case is doing."

"Well, you can ask him yourself because he is right here in his office."

"When did he get here?"

"About a couple of minutes ago," Donna answered. "But I gotta warn you, Allan, he doesn't look too good."

"What do you mean that he doesn't look too good?"

"His face is all swollen and he is walking a little bent over. If I had to guess, I would say that he got into some kind of a fight."

"Is he still in his cubicle?"

"Yeah. He came here and asked for you. I told him that you were busy and he told me that he would be in his cubicle to work on the case."

"I am going to see him right now," Allan declared.

■ ■ ■

Shea winced in pain as he pored over the documents in front of him. Contrary to what his attackers had intended, Shea was more focused and determined than ever. His defeatist thoughts were gone; *punched out of me*, he thought with a wry smile.

While Shea understood the risk he was taking, he also knew

what would happen if he lost the case, and he wasn't ready to give up.

His thoughts were interrupted as he heard a familiar voice call his name.

"What happened to you?" Allan asked, observing the swelling and dried blood on Shea's face.

"Whatever," Shea responded. "It's no big deal."

"No big deal? It looks like you were in a boxing match and you didn't have any gloves to fight with."

"A couple of guys came after me because of the case," Shea admitted.

"What does that mean?"

"They cornered me and attacked me. They told me that if I didn't back off the case, they would come back and finish the job."

"Did you get a good look at their faces?"

"No, it was dusk and I had other things on my mind."

"Do you remember anything about them?"

"Well, one of them referred to the other one as Hassan. That would lead me to believe that these guys were Muslims."

"Why would Muslims attack you if you are defending one of their own?"

"I have no idea. That is why I am back here."

"Did you at least go to the hospital?"

"Yeah, I stopped in for a second and when I saw the crowd in the waiting room, I got out of there as quickly as possible. I don't have the time to sit and wait while the trial is still going on."

"Why not? I am sure that Daniels will give a continuance because of the attack."

"No," Shea corrected him, "Daniels will probably have me recuse myself if he finds out what really happened. That is the same reason why I didn't go to the police. I can't lose this case, Allan."

"But after what happened today, you are already probably going to lose," Allan responded.

"Yeah, but at least the partners won't think that I am a quitter. Besides, there is another thing going on."

"What are you talking about?"

"It's like you said. Everybody knows that the trial is over. My client attacked Rabbi Felder. The judge knows it, I know it, the jury knows it. So why are they attacking me now? It makes no sense. In two days the jury is going to send al-Jinn to prison, whether I am on the case or not. So why would these guys bother to threaten me if I don't back off?"

"I have no idea," Allan admitted.

"The only thing that I can think of is that I am missing something big in my defense and it is right in front of my nose. These guys, whoever they are, don't want me continuing because they think that I am going to figure it out."

"What you are saying is ridiculous," Allan argued. "All the evidence shows that your client committed this act. Not even a miracle could save him at this point. But even if what you are saying is true, if the key to your client's freedom is out there, why would two Muslims not want you to find it?"

"I'm not sure," Shea admitted. "But that is why I am still here and not in some hospital. If there is still a way to save my job, I am going to do whatever it takes, no matter what anybody says."

If he only knew the truth, Allan said to himself. Shea was putting himself in danger, because he believed that he still stood a chance of keeping his job. As Shea grimaced in pain, Allan winced as well. If he had been upfront with Shea from the beginning, Shea never would have been attacked and his life never would have been threatened. Shea was in danger and it was all Allan's fault. But unlike in the past, Allan wasn't going to be a coward. He knew what he needed to do, and this time nothing was going to stop him.

R OBERT FIELDS COLLAPSED ONTO HIS RECLINER. AFTER A long day at work, the only thing that Fields wanted to do was fall asleep in his favorite chair. While his wife would lament that the recliner had more holes in it than a piece of Swiss cheese, for Fields it was more comfortable than anything he had ever sat in. And besides, it was his chair, or as he liked to refer to it, his throne, and that was what counted.

As he stretched out with his feet up, the day's events became a blur, which was exactly what he wanted. After a few moments his semiconscious state was interrupted by a knock on the door. He called for his wife to open it, but she was out shopping. Grumbling, he pried himself off the recliner and went to answer.

He opened the door and saw a young, tanned woman standing there. Fields eyed her peevishly.

"I don't want anything," he declared.

"Excuse me?" the woman asked in accented but proper English. She was clearly perplexed.

"Whatever it is you are selling, I have no interest. I don't care if it's knives, a way to lower my energy bill, or a timeshare in a place that I never want to visit. I am not interested and I would appreciate if you would allow me to go back to sleep."

"Pardon me, Mister Agent Fields, but I am not here to sell you anything."

Fields immediately became alert, all trace of fatigue gone. "What do you want?"

"I have no problem telling you but I feel that it would be safer for me if we spoke inside."

"Why?"

"I feel that what I am about to tell you may put me in immediate danger and I would feel much safer if I were allowed into your home."

Fields observed his visitor closely. He'd been trained in assessing a person by the nuances of body language, and this woman wasn't a likely killer looking for revenge. Still, he remained cautious.

"I don't just let strangers into my home. You are going to have to give me something before I let you in."

"Does the name Eitan Adiran ring a bell?" the woman asked.

Fields rubbed his jaw thoughtfully. The name sounded familiar but Fields couldn't place it. Suddenly it came to him. His eyes widened.

"Yes, I know that name," Fields replied. "My question for you is how do you know that name and why do you think that I would be interested in hearing about it?"

"To answer your first question, my name is Anat Adiran and Eitan was my husband."

"Was?" Fields inquired. "Last I heard he was listed as missing."

"No body has been found. I haven't heard from him in over a month. I am a realist, Agent Fields, and I am resigned to the fact that I am now a widow."

"If what you are saying is true, then I am sorry for your loss. However, why do you think that I would have known about your husband?"

"Because I know about the email that he sent right before he disappeared and I also know that the FBI read the email."

Fields was shocked and he immediately ushered Anat inside. According to Stephens, nobody in Israel knew about the Trojan that had been placed on the Knesset's server. So how did this woman know about it?

Once they were inside, Anat took the seat Fields offered her but declined a drink.

"You are surprised that I know about the email," Anat observed.

"Yes, you seem to know quite a bit. Would you mind telling me how? "

"Mr. Fields, my husband was amazing with computers. There is no way that any Trojan could be placed on a server that he was supposed to protect, without his knowledge. He knew all about it."

Fields laughed inwardly. So much for the great American technological coup. You really couldn't beat those Israelis at their own game.

"So if he knew that the Trojan was there, why didn't he do anything about it?"

"Leverage," Anat responded.

"Meaning?"

"My husband was negotiating a new contract with the Knesset. They were under the impression that with the security software that my husband had installed on their server, they would be protected and they did not need my husband's services to monitor it. Around the time that they had made this decision, my husband noticed the Trojan that the FBI had installed on the server. He decided to use it to his advantage. Of course any truly sensitive material, my husband blocked from the Trojan. However, my husband allowed the Trojan to access other information, and he documented everything. He wanted to show his bosses that his services were vital to national security."

"Risky business."

"My husband was a risk-taker, Mr. Fields."

"And how do you know all of this?"

"Not only was Eitan Adiran my husband, he was also my business partner. We built DatCom together. There was nothing that went on that I didn't know about. At least, that was true until a month ago, and that is why I believe my husband was murdered."

"What are you talking about?"

"About a month ago, I noticed some traffic on an old server of ours. I had thought that the server was obsolete, so I asked Eitan what was going on. He told me that he was just testing the server, and that there was nothing to worry about. My husband had never lied to me before, and, like a fool, I trusted him."

"What happened next?"

"When he disappeared I began to search through our files for clues. At the beginning the police didn't suspect foul play and told me that since he worked long hours, Eitan probably was just taking a vacation. But knowing my husband, I knew that wasn't the case and I searched through all of our files. When I didn't find anything, I returned to that old server and went through all the information that had been passed through. That is when I realized that my husband had gotten himself involved in something terrible."

"What?"

"Well, it seemed that he had been in contact with a man named Henri Joseph."

"The French billionaire?" Fields asked, carefully keeping his voice noncommital.

"Yes."

"He's got media interests and real estate all over the world. I couldn't imagine what Eitan would want with him. But I started to dig and found out some very startling information."

"You started to dig? How?"

"Being in the computer security business affords one contacts with others in the security profession. I contacted a friend of mine who worked for Shin Bet and asked her to tell me everything that she knew about Joseph. She told me that most of it was confidential, but suffice it to say, Joseph had his hands all over several attempted bombings throughout the Middle East. She told me that he was trying to become the modern day Osama bin Laden."

Fields kept his face expressionless. The FBI had, of course, been interested in this Henri Joseph and his less-public activities, but up until now they hadn't gotten any clear-cut evidence on him. Seems the Shin Bet was ahead of them. Again.

"And this was the guy that your husband contacted?"

"Not only did he contact him, but I am convinced that Eitan sold him something."

"Why?"

"A few days before his disappearance, I found that a large sum of money had been transferred into our savings. Originally, I thought that the transfer had come from the business, but when I saw the account number, I knew it didn't come from DatCom."

"How much money was it?" Fields asked.

"Two hundred and fifty thousand dollars," Anat answered.

"That is a quite a lot of money. What did your husband sell to this terrorist?"

Anat didn't like the tone of Fields' question. "Wait one minute. There is no evidence at all that my husband had any idea that Henri Joseph was a terrorist. According to the emails that I found, Joseph told my husband that he needed information for one of his magazines. My husband never would have sold him anything, if he knew that it was going to be used for terror."

"But what did he sell this guy? Obviously, whatever it was, it was important enough to cost a quarter of a million dollars and for your husband to get killed over it. So what was it?"

"I don't know, but here it is," Anat said, pulling out a flash drive. She put it into her laptop and then her fingers flew over the keyboard as she keyed in security information. Finally, an Excel chart appeared on the screen. "To me it is only a list of places and dates. But maybe you can figure out why Eitan was murdered for this data."

Before scanning the screen, Fields still had some serious questions for this woman.

"With all your connections in the security business, you couldn't find out what this data meant? Why didn't you take it to the Shin Bet? For that matter," he continued, trying to reenact the events that preceded Adiran's presumed murder, "why didn't your husband email the Shin Bet? Sending an email in the hopes that our Trojan will intercept it seems a bit convoluted."

"Not for Eitan. He'd been hacking into the most secure websites in the world since he was a young teen." A sweet smile suddenly lit up her care-ridden face. "He was a very unusual man, with very unusual thought processes."

"Okay, we'll accept that your husband meant for the FBI to learn that there was an assassination attempt, and that he preferred using us to the Shin Bet. Why didn't you go to your own security people?"

"Mr. Fields," Anat responded sternly, "I am not sure if you ever experienced the loss of a loved one. The pain is unbearable. Every night before I go to sleep, I hope that he will be there when I wake up and my nightmare will end. With the pain that I live with every moment of every day, the last thing that I want is the Israeli authorities turning my life upside-down and destroying my husband's reputation. No matter what his mistakes were, I know that he was a good man. If I gave them the information I've just shared with you, they would converge on my home in minutes and vilify my husband. That is not something that I can deal with right now."

"But don't you want justice for your husband?"

"Are you a religious man, Agent Fields?" Anat inquired.

"Not really."

"My family is very traditional. We kept all of the holidays and even went to synagogue on Friday nights. Though as I grew older I broke away from some of those traditions, I still believe very strongly that there is a G-d Who runs this world and He is the true administer of justice. Whether it is in this world or the next, I am confident that my husband's killers will be punished, even if I chose not to go to the authorities."

"So why come to me at all?"

"If my husband reached out to the FBI before he died, it was his dying wish that he would be able to right the terrible wrong that he had inadvertently committed. I am hoping that you can help fulfill that wish."

Fields had one more question for Anat. "So why me?"

"Why you?"

"Yeah. There's an official FBI office in Federal Plaza. Twenty-third floor. Why didn't you go to them?"

Again, she gave that sweet smile. "Because, Mr. Fields, my contacts in Shin Bet said that you're the best. That you are the most out-of-the-box agent they have in the field. And this seems to be quite an out-of-the-box problem."

Fields allowed himself a grin and then turned to the screen. It didn't take him more than a minute to figure it out. He knew exactly what this data was, and he knew why Joseph wanted it.

"Do you want to know what this is?" Fields asked.

"No," Anat replied. "There is an saying that 'ignorance is bliss.' Right now, the less I know the better it will be for me. But I am happy that you know because maybe you can help stop whatever Joseph was trying to do."

"Can I have that flash drive?"

"Yes, if you think it will help."

"It might."

Anat thanked Fields for everything and handed the drive to him. When she had gone, Fields sat back in his recliner and looked at the data. The list of dates and places that Anat couldn't decipher, Fields figured out quite easily. Eitan Adiran had sold Henri Joseph a copy of the Israeli prime minister's itinerary of his trip to America.

A quarter of a million bucks for the PM's life? Fields thought. *Not a bad bargain for a terror chief wannabee.*

Now it was up to Fields to stop an assassination. Fast.

It wouldn't be easy. There were more than forty different venues on the list. With only the itinerary to go by, Fields had no idea which location was most likely. He couldn't ask anyone from the Israeli side without exposing the way that the FBI had obtained the original information. He couldn't even ask security experts in the FBI, because Stephens had ordered him off the case.

Another problem: According to Rami Aretz, the most likely candidate to commit the attempt was a terrorist named Khalid al-Jinn and right now, al-Jinn was under lock and key in Riker's Island. Was it possible that Rami was wrong and that there was another rogue Islamic terrorist roaming the streets of New York? *Definitely*, Fields thought. But if that was the case, finding him would be one tough job. With only a week to go before the prime minister arrived, Fields didn't have the time to search.

As Fields lay back in his recliner, he knew one thing: if he didn't get his rest, nothing would get done. As he closed his eyes, Robert Fields let all the information process in his mind, and hoped that the Israeli prime minister would still be alive when he awoke.

■ ■ ■

"That is wonderful news," Jessica exclaimed on the phone as Allan entered her office. She motioned for him to have a seat and continued speaking. "I'm sure the other managing partners will be as excited as I am. We will speak early next week. Have a good one."

"You look like you're in a good mood," Allan observed. "What has you all giddy and cheerful?"

"I just got off the phone with our overseas investor," Jessica answered. "He is ecstatic at the way Shea has been trying the case. He sees that our lawyers are loyal, and he believes in our firm."

"Does that mean that Shea's job is safe?" Allan asked.

"No. I was very clear with the investor that Shea won't be staying on with us. He told me that was all right with him, as long as Shea stayed the course and finished the trial."

Allan looked dismayed, but Jessica didn't pay attention. She was too excited about the recent conversation to notice his disappointment, and she withdrew a bottle of Scotch from her cabinet to celebrate. She poured herself a glass and then offered one to Allan, which he declined.

"*You* declining a drink?" Jessica asked. "I don't think that I have ever seen you say no to a glass of good Scotch."

"I can't say that I am in the mood of celebrating," Allan responded, walking toward Jessica's desk. "And I wouldn't be so quick to celebrate, if I were you."

"What are you referring to?" Jessica asked, sipping the Scotch.

"Have you seen Shea?" Allan asked.

"No, is he even here?"

"Sure he is and he is working his tail off trying to finish this case."

"So why should I be concerned? Everything seems in order."

"If you would have seen him you would have seen that he had been attacked."

"Too bad," Jessica said uncaringly. "By whom?"

"It seems that there were two Arabs who want Shea off the case and they roughed him up pretty good."

"But Shea doesn't want to get off the case, does he?"

"No."

"Does Daniels know about the attack?"

"No, Shea doesn't want to tell him. He is afraid that Daniels will ask him to recuse himself."

"What's the problem, then? As long as Daniels doesn't find out, Shea can stay on and finish the case. So what is our concern here?"

"Are you kidding me?" Allan asked in disbelief. "One of your attorneys, the one that I am supposed to be mentoring, was brutally assaulted, and you couldn't care less."

"Of course I care," Jessica responded, "but as long as it doesn't harm the firm, what is the big deal? It isn't as if he is going to die or anything."

"Do you realize that the only reason he isn't in the hospital right now being treated is because he still feels that he has a job if he wins? How can we do this to him?"

"Who is the 'we' here? I didn't tell him anything."

"You told me to lie to him and tell him that his job is still in play."

"And if I told you to jump off a bridge, would you listen to me?"

"That isn't fair," Allan said.

"No, I will tell you what isn't fair," Jessica responded, raising her voice. "Suddenly you are feeling guilty, and you want to pin this one on me. But let's get the facts straight. You knew exactly what was going on when you told Shea about the case and you chose to lie to him."

"Only because you asked me to. You told me that it was in the best interests of the firm if Shea took the case."

"And as you can see, I was right. Because of the job that Shea has done, our investors are pleased and our European offices will be up and running. The increase in capital from those offices will triple our yearly profits. We will be rich."

"We already are rich. What we aren't is what we used to be."

"What is that supposed to mean?"

"When I originally sat down with Michael Reeves, he asked me what had happened to me. He told me that I had become everything that I swore I wouldn't."

"He is only jealous and was trying to get under your skin."

"That is what I thought also, but now I am not so sure. If I could mistreat somebody that I am supposed to mentor and guide, what kind of person am I?"

Allan glared at Jessica. Though he would never admit it, Allan had always wanted to be like her. She was a great lawyer and an amazing managing partner. She ran the firm with an iron fist and was the main reason for its tremendous success. But now, after seeing what he had done to Shea, the life she represented seemed trivial and wrong.

"Whatever happened to you, Jessica?" Allan asked. "When I came into the firm, you used to preach to me how we were going to make a difference. You would say that we were the voice for the little guy and we would be the protector of people's rights when the courts would ignore them. I remember you calling us gladiators. But now look at us. We trample on the little guys and we abuse their rights."

"Don't be so naive," Jessica scolded him. "To bring about change, you need power. In order to have power, you need money, and getting money sometimes involves doing things that may make us a little uncomfortable. I told what you needed to hear, because I wanted you to be a top-notch lawyer. And guess what. It worked. You and your methods made us a ton of money, and you may well be the best lawyer in New York. So I will not apologize for the things that I have done. This firm does a lot of good and none of that would happen without doing everything possible to ensure that success."

Allan looked at Jessica sadly. He couldn't believe that he had spent all those days and nights striving for her approval. Whatever doubts he had about what his next move was going to be, Jessica's tirade had just answered them.

"You had to do what you believe needed to be done," Allan responded. "Now, for the first time in years, I am going to do what I feel is right and also needs to be done."

"If you walk out that door and do what I think you are planning to do, we are through. Your office and your clients will go to Jennings, I can promise you that. You will never work in this firm again, and I will make sure no reputable firm will hire you. You do not want to cross me, Allan Shore."

"Goodnight, Jessica," Allan said as he walked out of her office and closed the door. He could hear her recriminations, but he tuned out what she was saying. He had never before disobeyed his boss, and as he walked toward Shea's office, he felt really good about doing it.

I BRAHIM WALKED BRISKLY TOWARD HIS INTENDED destination. The reunion with Hanadi had caught him by surprise; he had had no idea that she was even in Brooklyn. Moments after she had walked into the room at the hostel Mohamed appeared, leading two youngsters who looked excited and a little dazed. There was a burst of language, English and Urdu, with some Arabic mixed in as well. Hanadi wept, her children shouted, Mohamed, deeply ashamed, sat to the side, and Ibrahim watched the pandemonium, calmly waiting for an explanation.

It was not long in coming. After a few moments Hanadi regained her composure. In a few words she told Ibrahim what had transpired, and he, in turn, related his tale, pulling out the newspaper photo to show her. In unison they turned to Mohamed and demanded answers which he struggled to provide. When he finished, there were more discussions and more tears. And, finally, a plan.

Now Ibrahim was headed for one tall skyscraper in this city of skyscrapers. At the entrance, he took a deep breath and ventured inside. He hoped that Hanadi was right and Jabril's salvation would be found within these walls, because he realized his only son's time was running out.

■ ■ ■

"Shea," Allan poked his head into Shea's cubicle. "Do you have a moment?"

"Sure," Shea responded. "Right now, I'm just trying to figure out what is going on. Nothing makes sense to me. Why would those guys want me off the case? What are they hiding that they think I am going to uncover?"

"It doesn't matter anymore."

"What?"

"This whole case is over for you."

"What are you talking about, Allan?"

"I'm talking about the job," Allan responded. "The job that is going to Kyle, not to you."

Beneath the swelling and welts, Shea's face paled. "Why? I know that I messed up on this case, but I still can redeem myself. You have to tell Jessica to give me more time. The jury hasn't convicted my client yet."

"It doesn't matter whether they convict him or not. You aren't getting the job. To be honest, you were never getting the job."

"What!" Shea exclaimed in shock.

"You can hate me for what I am about to tell you and I wouldn't blame you, but I feel that you deserve to hear the truth. The job was never going to be yours. You never had the billables that Kyle had and that is all that mattered to Jessica."

"When was this decided?"

"Before al-Jinn was arrested."

"So why wasn't I told?"

"Because the firm needed you. We needed to show our European investors that our firm wasn't anti-Muslim and Jessica felt that you were the perfect attorney to show them. We used you, Shea. Plain and simple."

Shea couldn't believe it. While he had come to accept the reality that he was going to lose his job because of this case, he never thought that Allan would have duped him so badly. The only way that Shea had been able to deal with the insults and the abuse was because he thought that at the end he would be able to keep his job and save his family. But now it seemed that everything that he had endured was for naught.

"How could you do this to me?" Shea asked, his voice heavy with pain. "Do you have any idea of the suffering my family has gone through because of this case?"

"I am sorry, Shea," Allan said quietly.

"What is that supposed to mean?" Shea responded angrily. "Is your apology going to make my friends not hate me anymore? Will your contrition allow my wife to shop in a store without being harassed? Tell me, Allan, what exactly is your apology going to accomplish, except maybe easing what remains of your conscience?"

Shea looked at Allan and suddenly grew quiet. Through his anger and frustration Shea began to see that something else was occurring right before his eyes. In the time that he had known Allan, not once had Allan displayed any humility. For Allan, it was always about propping himself up or putting the next guy down. But now, as Allan stood before him, Shea saw a display of emotion that he never knew Allan was capable of. Allan seemed almost human, and for Shea that was a total surprise.

But it wasn't only Allan who seemed to be changing. It was Shea himself.

"I'm sorry," Shea said, after a brief, uncomfortable pause.

"Sorry? For what?"

"Allan, do you know what Rabbi Felder always said?" Shea said in a quiet, thoughtful tone, ignoring the question.

"Felder? The one who was attacked?"

"That's right. He used to tell me something that I think would apply here. He would ask: if one falls on the ground, should he punish the ground? The answer, of course, is no.

"The ground didn't cause you to fall, you happen to have fallen on the ground. That is how Rabbi Felder taught me to view life's challenges and heartaches. There is one G-d in heaven and He has a plan for all of us. And that includes me, specifically. Sometimes, for whatever the reason, part of the plan may involve my getting hurt. But if G-d didn't want me to get hurt, it never could have happened. Allan, I don't know why G-d wanted me to go through this awful trial. I had thought it was to make sure that I could keep my job. Obviously that isn't part of the plan. The one thing that I do know is that if G-d let it happen, He must have had a reason. You and Jessica were only the emissaries. Rather than focus on why you guys did this to me, I should be focusing on why G-d wanted this to happen."

Of course Allan had known about Shea's observance of Jewish tradition, but he'd always been cynical about it. *Anybody could be religious as long as things were going smoothly*, he would say; *the real test was whether or not a person would hold strong to his ideals in the face of adversity.* If Shea was able to cling to his faith and see what Jessica and Allan had done as the will of G-d, then not only was Shea's observance for real, it was something that Allan desperately wanted to be part of.

"If there is anything that I can do for you," Allan said, "please let me know. If you want me to write you a letter of recommendation or contact a rival firm to get you an appointment, whatever it is, just tell me and I will do it."

"How about you call my wife for me?" Shea asked with a wry smile.

"Anything but that!"

"If I need you I'll let you know, but right now, I need to figure out what I am going to do next."

Allan started to walk away. Before he reached the end of the hallway, he stopped. "You know, Shea, I really admire you and you really are a great lawyer. I only wish we could have parted under different circumstances."

"So do I," Shea responded solemnly. "So do I."

Allan left Shea alone with his thoughts. Although the disappointment of being used and lied to was still fresh, Shea couldn't focus on it. Right now he needed to think about reality, and it wasn't pretty. He still had to defend al-Jinn. Even if Shea didn't call any other witnesses, he would still need to deliver a closing statement, and it wasn't something that he felt any urge to tackle.

Shea put his feet up on his desk and sighed. He had tried so hard to be like them. He had wanted so badly to fit in with the rest of the big-time lawyers. On the surface Shea had justified this desire by saying that he wanted to provide for his family, and being part of the exclusive law fraternity would do just that. Deep down, though, Shea knew the real reason he wanted to succeed. He wanted to show everybody that they were wrong. He wanted people to know that even though he didn't go to Harvard and even though he couldn't work one hundred hours a week, he was a better lawyer than any of them.

Now Shea saw this life for what it really was. The people he had tried to emulate had lied to him and exploited him. He couldn't believe that he had done his utmost to be accepted by them. It was a hard lesson, but Shea was learning it very quickly.

As he warily touched his nose and felt the swelling, Shea knew what he needed to do. Without his job being in play, there was no reason to stay on as al-Jinn's attorney. While the betrayal by Shea's firm would not be grounds for recusal, Shea being attacked was a totally different story. If he informed Judge Daniels and told him what had happened, there was no way that he wouldn't grant Shea a recusal.

As he picked up the phone to dial Judge Daniel's number, he heard his name being shouted in the hallway.

"Mr. Berman," the voice cried out, "Mr. Berman, are you here?"

"Yeah, I am in my office," Shea responded.

"Okay, I am coming over there now," the voice replied.

A few seconds later, a man appeared in Shea's cubicle. Shea recognized him as Charlie Dawson, the head of building security.

"What's going on, Charlie?" Shea asked.

"I am sorry to bother you this late, but there is a matter that needs your attention."

"What is it?"

"Some old guy came by my station about fifteen minutes ago. The only word that he kept repeating was your name. When I tried to explain that the office was closed and that he would need to come back tomorrow, he became excited and started jabbering in a language that I did not understand."

"So what did you do?"

"Well, I was going to call the cops, but then the guy just broke down crying. I don't mean teary-eyed. I mean full-blown sobbing and he was just saying your name over and over ...."

After everything that Shea had gone through these last few hours, the last thing that he needed was this. He just wanted to call Daniels and get home as fast as possible. But the thought of an old man crying made Shea pause. It wouldn't be right to just leave him there, Shea realized, no matter how upset Shea was at that moment.

"Where is this guy?" Shea asked.

"He's waiting by the entrance to the building."

"Okay, let's go together and we'll see what he wants."

Shea followed Charlie and thought about the call that he was going to make. Though he wasn't a quitter by nature, since he was going to be fired anyway, he simply lacked the motivation to see the case through till the end, especially after being attacked. As he pressed the button for the ground floor, Shea made a final decision. After he helped this old man, he was going to call Daniels and end this thing once and for all.

■ ■ ■

"Here he is, Mr. Berman" Charlie announced, pointing to an elderly man sitting on a marble bench. "This is the guy that has been asking for you."

Shea approached the old man. The man jumped up and started talking rapidly in a language Shea didn't understand. When Shea heard the man say his name, he motioned for him to stop.

"English?" Shea asked. "Do you speak English?"

"*Nahi* English," the man replied. "*Mujhse* Urdu."

"Urdu? What language is Urdu?"

"I think it is spoken in Pakistan," Charlie responded.

"How do you know that?" Shea wondered.

"I've got lots of time manning the security post here at the front desk. I read all those *National Geographic* magazines. One time they had an article about a city called Sargodha."

"Sargodha," the old man repeated excitedly.

"Well, the article said that the language of the Pakistan is both Urdu and English. But it also said that there were some farmers that on principle would not learn the English language. Could be that this old man is one of those farmers."

"Okay," Shea responded, "we need to find someone who speaks Urdu. Wait, isn't there that 24-hour newsstand down the block? I could have sworn the owner is from Pakistan."

"I think you're are right. I remember when we killed bin-Laden that guy telling me that his family's home was a few miles from the compound."

"You go and get him and tell him to come over here. Meanwhile, I'll keep an eye on this old man and make sure that he doesn't go anywhere."

"Did you see that man's face?" Charlie asked. "Once he saw you, his face lit up like the New York skyline. I am telling you, as long as you are here, that man isn't going anywhere."

A few minutes later, Charlie returned with the man from the newsstand. He introduced himself as Pashto.

"Thank you for coming, Pashto," Shea said.

"Are you kidding me?" Pashto replied in heavily accented English. "Charlie here is my best customer. He buys more magazines than anybody else. I could never turn him down."

"What can I say?" Charlie grinned. "I have a lot of time on my hands."

"Can you ask this man what his name is?" Shea said, pointing at the old man.

Pashto spoke to the man and the man responded.

"He said that his name is Ibrahim Yusuf," Pashto replied.

"Ask him why he wants to speak to me."

Pashto again spoke to Ibrahim, and he became quite animated. "He says that he knows the truth about your client," Pashto replied, "and he has an unbelievable story to tell you."

Shea held his breath as he waited for Ibrahim to begin. Ibrahim's words came out rapid fire and Pashto had trouble keeping up with his translation. Even at that speed, it took several minutes until the story was finished, Shea was dumbfounded. If what Ibrahim said was true, then Shea had made a grave mistake in his defense and the truth about the attack on Rabbi Felder was still unknown. However, Shea realized that it was very possible that Ibrahim was lying and that the video told the whole story.

There was only one person who could corroborate Ibrahim's story and Shea was going to visit him in the morning. First, though, he had to speak to a few people and call in some favors.

In the meantime, the phone call to Judge Daniels would have to wait.

■ ■ ■

Shea arrived at Riker's Island at 8 a.m. the next morning. Whatever little sleep he had managed to get had been in his parents' home in Flatbush. Though he had spoken to Shira, he didn't tell her anything about being attacked. *There is no reason to worry her,* he thought. He also neglected to mention what Allan had told him. He didn't know how he was going to break the news to her and right now he needed to concentrate on his meeting with his client.

Though the story that Ibrahim had related had given Shea hope, he didn't want to get ahead of himself. The trial had proven to be a roller coaster with twists and turns at every corner. Could it be that Ibrahim had been telling the truth? Yes, Shea realized that it was a strong possibility. However, his client was the only one who could verify the story and that is why Shea found himself waiting for his client in one of the jail's meeting rooms.

While Shea waited, he recalled the first time he had met al-Jinn in this room, and all that had transpired since that day. The one thing that remained a constant had been al-Jinn's offensive demeanor and his loathing for Shea. So to say that Shea was skeptical about the veracity of Ibrahim's story would be an understatement. On the other hand, Shea had also seen the fervor and passion in Ibrahim's eyes while he told his tale. Shea had dealt with many clients throughout the years and he had a feel for when a client was lying to him. Shea was almost convinced that Ibrahim was telling the truth.

As his client entered the room, Shea knew that he was about to get some answers.

"What do you want?" al-Jinn asked angrily. "I thought that I had told you to leave me alone."

"Yes, you did," Shea responded, "but I still have a few questions."

"I told you at the trial, I am not answering any of your questions. I am resigned to go to prison for my crime and I don't need you meddling in my affairs."

"You may be resigned to go to prison, but it won't be for your crime."

"What are you talking about?" Al-Jinn asked.

"While I imagine that you have found it easy to evade my questions, I think that you may have a more difficult time explaining your actions to the person that I brought along with me."

"Who did you bring along? Another hotshot lawyer?"

"You can ask him yourself," Shea responded.

Shea walked over to the door and murmured to the guard standing on the other side. Two men entered.

Al-Jinn paled.

"This," Shea said to al-Jinn, "is Azeem Halid, an official translator of Urdu to English. The other man, I assume, you recognize."

Next followed an almost surreal scene, with the two men speaking to each other in Urdu, and Halid quietly, emotionlessly translating the words in the poignant scene as Shea and the prison guard sat, transfixed.

"Tell him the truth," Ibrahim said, his voice a plea.

"You have killed Hanadi and the boys," al-Jinn responded,

tears flowing down his cheeks. "Do you understand? They told me that if everything doesn't go exactly as they want, Hanadi and the boys will die."

"Hanadi and the boys are with me," Ibrahim reassured him. "They are safe. They have been with me since Sunday. Please just tell the lawyer the truth."

"Safe?" al-Jinn asked in disbelief, his voice rising in hope.

"They are staying at a hostel with me in Brooklyn. Hanadi told me everything. You don't have to be afraid anymore. Please let the lawyer help you. He is a good man and he will help us. But you must tell him the truth."

Al-Jinn looked at Ibrahim, speechless. For so many nights in his dark prison cell he had prayed for this moment, a moment he never thought would come. And now that it was here, it seemed unreal.

"Is this a dream? Are you really here?"

"I am here and I am never going to leave your side. But if you don't tell the lawyer the truth, I don't know what else I can do. You need to trust him."

Shea heard the entire exchange between al-Jinn and Ibrahim and he, too, was speechless. Seeing Ibrahim's deep, unabashed love for his son brought home to him his own strained relationship with his father. His father, Shea knew, felt the same love for him. And Shea? How did he feel?

But now wasn't the time to focus on his personal life. With an effort he turned his attention to Ibrahim and al-Jinn.

"I can't!" Jabril exclaimed. "Mohamed could be in danger. They took us from his house. How do I know that he will be safe if the truth comes out?"

Ibrahim regarded his son with sadness. Jabril knew nothing about Mohamed's treachery and betrayal. But he needed to know that truth, Ibrahim reasoned, no matter how much it would cause him pain.

"Mohamed was in on the whole kidnapping," Ibrahim declared.

"What? That is impossible. Mohamed is my friend and he would never do something like that to me or Hanadi."

"Mohamed was weak and he chose his own safety rather than the safety of his closest friend. His boss had threatened to harm his wife if he didn't help cover up the attack on the rabbi. Time was of the essence and he felt pressured. Rather than put her life in jeopardy, Mohamed offered Hanadi and you to help orchestrate the scheme. I wouldn't have believed it, if I hadn't heard the story from Mohamed's own mouth."

Jabril buried his head in his arms. While the pain and suffering over the past few weeks had been great, realizing that his best friend had been the cause of it all was too great to bear. Even though Shea was shocked by what he had just heard, he knew that time was running out and he couldn't proceed without getting an answer to a simple question.

"Look," Shea interrupted the father and son, "we don't have a lot of time here. I need you to answer this one question, who is Jabril Yusuf?"

Al-Jinn looked at Ibrahim and nodded.

"I am," he said.

"MY NAME IS JABRIL KAMAL YUSUF," THE PRISONER said, in perfect English. "I was born in the city of Sargodha, Pakistan on April 17, 1982. I am the proud father of two boys. Ishmael is seven and Abdul is five. I am also the devoted husband to Hanadi Yusuf. We have been married for ten wonderful years. The man who stands beside you is my father, Ibrahim. He traveled many miles to save me and make sure that you learn the truth."

Even though he had heard the story from Ibrahim, to hear it from Jabril's mouth still was a shock. Even more amazing was the change in Khalid al-Jinn — that is, Jabril Yusuf. His tone of voice, his bearing, even the expression on his face seemed to belong to a different person.

"I have so many questions," Shea said. "I hardly know where to begin. I guess the first one is, did you attack Rabbi Felder?"

"No. I have never met your rabbi and I am deeply sorry that any pain ever came to him."

"Then who is Khalid al-Jinn?"

"I don't know myself."

"But if you didn't commit this act and you have no idea who

Khalid al-Jinn is, why you did allow yourself to be arrested and pretend that you were Khalid al-Jinn?"

"I guess I should start from the beginning," Jabril replied. "I don't live in New York. My family and I live in a remote part of Wyoming called Thermopolis."

"What do you do there?"

"I am a teacher. I try to teach our youth that not all Arabs are fanatics and some of us actually want peace."

"So why were you in New York?"

"I surprised my family with a trip to the big city. My children had never been on a plane before and they were very excited. My wife had read about the amazing shopping malls and stores. We were all very excited and the trip started off wonderfully."

"Where did you stay?" Shea inquired

"My closest friend from Sargodha lives in Brooklyn. His name is Mohamed Farouk. Mohamed invited us to stay with him."

"So what changed?" Shea asked.

"I don't know exactly. All I remember was it was late at night. We had just put the kids to bed after spending the evening on Broadway. We had taken the kids to see a show and we all loved it. Anyway, there was a loud bang on the door to our room and some men in masks charged in. They threw me to the ground and grabbed Hanadi. I can still hear her screaming as I tried to fight off my abductors. After a few moments of struggling, they placed a wet cloth over my face and everything went black. The next thing that I remember, I woke up in a dark windowless room. "

"Were you alone?"

"No, there were two men holding me down and one guy, I guess he was the leader, telling them what to do."

"Did you see his face?"

"No he was always careful to cover his head. But I will never forget his voice and that icy tone. It was if he had no soul."

"What did he say to you?"

"He started telling me how lucky I was that I had been chosen for this holy mission."

"What holy mission was he referring to?"

"I don't know," Jabril responded. "I kept on telling him that I was just a simple teacher and didn't want anything to do with any holy wars."

"What did he respond when you told him that?" Shea asked.

"He said that Allah only chooses those who are worthy and if Allah chose me, then that must be my destiny."

"So what did he want from you?"

"He told me that I needed to become somebody named Khalid al-Jinn. I needed to go to his apartment and wait there for further instructions."

"Did you try to protest?"

"I couldn't. After giving me my orders, he showed me a picture of my wife gagged and bound. He told me that if I ever wanted to see her alive again, I would do exactly as I was told."

"What happened next?"

"I went with those two men to an apartment and they told me to kneel on the floor and pray. I had thought that they were going to kill me, but I then remembered what the boss had said and realized that my praying must have been part of the act. I saw them take out the metal rod and put it on the table. Then they told me what my real responsibilities were."

"To take the fall for the attack," Shea interrupted.

"They told me that the police were going to be arriving shortly and were going to arrest me for the attack on Rabbi Felder. When I had expressed my concern that I did not know what they were talking about, they told me everything. They told me exactly how and when the rabbi was assaulted. My instructions were simple; make the world believe that I was Khalid al-Jinn, the brutal attacker of Rabbi Felder. I was to allow myself to be placed under arrest and be convicted for the crime. Once I was sentenced, I was promised that my wife would be freed. However, my captors were very specific. They said if I was to veer from the plan in any way, she would be killed."

"So why have a trial at all?" Shea wondered. "Why not just walk into the police precinct and admit to the crime?"

"It had to be believable," Jabril explained. "If I was too over the top, people would start asking questions and the truth might come out. I needed to follow the script that they had outlined."

"I still don't understand," Shea said. "If the whole purpose was for you to take the fall, why not just plead guilty and go straight to prison?"

"I told you, it wouldn't have worked."

"Why not?"

"I had to make people believe that I was the real al-Jinn. People needed to see me as a maniacal monster committed to the destruction of the Western world. To do that, I needed to play my part perfectly."

"What does that have to do with not pleading guilty?"

"Have you ever wondered why every terrorist, no matter how much he hates America, never pleads guilty to any crime and always insists on going to trial?"

Jabril didn't wait for Shea to respond and continued.

"It is because they want to go on trial. They want to use the fabric of America's justice as a platform to spew their hatred and disdain for all that America stands for. They love it: using democratic institutions against democracy. If I had just pleaded guilty and gone away quietly, people might have begun to ask questions and that is something my wife's captors would not tolerate."

Shea paced the small room, trying to digest everything that Jabril had said. If his story was true, then the real attacker was still out there somewhere, and he had to be found. But the real question was: Why were Jabril's abductors so concerned about protecting Khalid al-Jinn?

He voiced the question aloud. "Do you have any idea who Khalid al-Jinn is?"

"I have been wondering that from the day that I was abducted," Jabril responded. "The only thing my captors would tell me was that he was a great hero and that Allah was going to be proud of what he was going to do."

Shea desperately wanted to believe Jabril. Partially it was because Jabril's story was so outlandish that nobody, not even the most skilled liar, could spin such a tale. Truthfully, though, the other reason was that if Jabril were telling the truth, Shea had an opportunity to redeem himself. All the people who had accused Shea of turning his back on Rabbi Felder would sing a different tune if his client's innocence could clearly be proven. But because he had a vested interest in Jabril's story being true, he also wanted to make sure that he wasn't being blinded by his own desires.

"There could also be another explanation," Shea said quietly.

"To what?" Jabril asked surprised.

"To you telling me this story right now and not telling me at the beginning."

"And what would that be?"

"That we are losing this case. Right now you could be desperate and you might be grasping at straws. You could be thinking I have no other option, so why not feed my lawyer a fish story and see if he bites?"

"Are you kidding me?" Jabril responded angrily. "The entire time I didn't care what happened to me. I gave up my right to a grand jury hearing because I wanted to get into jail as quickly as possible. After spending so much time and energy showing the jury that I wanted to go to prison, why would I suddenly decide to change my story?"

"Because maybe you realize that spending a few nights in Rikers isn't the same as spending half of your life in Otisville."

"Even if what you are saying is true, what about my father? What about his story?"

"Maybe he is your father and maybe he isn't. Even if he is your father, who says that he isn't lying to protect you? I know that I would take a bullet for my children. It wouldn't surprise me if your father lied to save you."

"You yourself said at the trial that the physical evidence doesn't make sense," Jabril reminded him. "You had that doctor up there and he said that due to my height, I was physically unable to attack the rabbi. You can't forget that!"

"And what about the video?" Shea retorted. "It shows you clearly attacking Rabbi Felder. How can you argue against that?"

"I have no idea how my face got on that video, but I will swear to you that I never assaulted that rabbi."

Jabril was obviously upset, which was exactly what Shea wanted. Shea needed his client to understand that there could be two sides to his story.

"Look," Shea said, softening his tone. "You need to understand something. Right now, even if I believe you one hundred percent, I have nothing. If you thought that I was being hard on you, that's nothing compared to what the district attorney will say if you ever get a chance to tell your story."

"What do you mean? Please, put me on the stand and let me tell my story."

"Jabril if I put you on the stand and you tell them what you just told me, the jury will laugh at you. They will see it as a desperate attempt for freedom and they won't buy it. They hate you too much, especially after seeing that video."

"What about my wife? She could testify about what happened to her."

"The state would object to her testifying on the grounds of bias and relevance. And even if your wife is able to testify to her ordeal, what bearing would it have on your case? According to what you have told me, she was never informed that you had been framed for the attack."

"I can't just keep quiet," Jabril responded.

"But I can't have you testify until I am able to find some sort of proof to corroborate your story."

"But how are you going to get the time to do that? Doesn't the judge expect us in court in a few minutes?"

"Well, that I was able to take care of," Shea responded.

"How?"

"You see the bruises on my face?"

"Yeah, did you fall or something like that?"

"No, actually I was attacked last night by two Arab men. They wanted me off the case and they hoped by attacking me that they would scare me."

"You see," Jabril said excitedly, "they must have felt that you were close to uncovering the truth. That is why they attacked you. This only proves that my story is true."

Shea had to admit it, Jabril had a point. Ever since last night, he had wondered why the two Arabs wanted him off the case. Now, with what Jabril was saying, it made perfect sense.

"I can ask the judge for a few days' recess, to allow me to recuperate. I won't get specific on how I received my injuries; I don't want him taking me off the case. Clearly, though, I need a medical leave. And if there is any proof out there that your story is true, I will have some time to uncover it."

Shea motioned to Ibrahim that it was time to go and took his laptop from the table. After a moment's hesitation he held out his hand to Jabril, who shook it firmly.

"One more thing," Jabril said. "I know that it usually doesn't matter with lawyers, but obviously in this situation it could mean everything. So please be honest with me, do *you* believe that I didn't attack Rabbi Felder?"

Shea looked into his client's eyes. Only a few weeks ago, those eyes burned with anger and fury. But now they radiated hope and pleading.

"I really want to," Shea responded, closing the door of the room.

■ ■ ■

Shea returned to the office, eager to get back to work. While less than twenty-four hours earlier Shea had been certain his case was hopeless, he now felt that there was at least a chance for acquittal, and that gave him the impetus to continue. On the way to the office he had called Hector and told him everything that Jabril had related. Hector was excited by the news and wanted a chance to make up for the video fiasco. Shea told him to meet him at the office and they would discuss strategy.

Even if Shea believed Jabril's story, there was no guarantee that anybody else would. Hector himself had been skeptical over the phone and told Shea as much. The question wasn't *if* they needed proof to back up Jabril's story, the only question was *how* they were going to get it. To figure that out, he needed Hector.

As he waited for his investigator, Shea saw that his phone was blinking, indicating that he had a voice message. He picked up the handset.

"Mr. Berman, hi, it's Lenny Williams. I know that you are a busy man and may not have time for good ol' Lenny, but I really need your help. These kids, they are eatin' Lenny out of house and home and I got no way to pay all the bills. Now I am not turnin' to you only as my lawyer. I am turnin' to you because Lenny thinks of you as a friend and I was hopin' that you could help a brother out. So please, if you have any more information on my case, give me a call. Thank you Mr. Berman."

Shea sighed. He didn't have the heart to tell Lenny that by the time his case was settled, Shea wasn't going to be employed anymore. However, Shea knew that as long as he was an attorney for Lockhart, Gardner, and Scott, he had an obligation to service all his clients. He picked up the phone and dialed Donna.

"Donna, can you do me a favor?" he asked.

"Shea, how are you feeling?" Donna asked, concerned.

"About what? About Allan and Jessica using me and then throwing me to the curb or about the bruises that are covering my face?"

"How about both of them."

"Well, I thank you for your concern and thank G-d I am doing great. But I actually had a question for you. Did the attorney for Halal Market ever send us those financials that I requested for the Lenny Williams case?"

"Sure he did," Donna responded. "He sent them over a week ago."

"Where are they?"

"I put them on your desk."

Shea replaced the receiver and shuffled some papers on his desk. After a few seconds, he got back on the phone.

"Can you please be more specific?" Shea requested.

"Well, it isn't going to hit you in the face," Donna answered. "Whoops, I'm sorry, that was a bad analogy, wasn't it?"

"It's okay," Shea responded, grinning.

"I think I put them on the right side of the desk, next to your monitor."

"Thanks, Donna, I found them," Shea said, pulling up a sheaf of papers.

"You're welcome," Donna replied. "And if it is any consolation, I am really sorry about what Allan and Jessica did. You are too good of a guy to be treated that way."

"Thanks."

He looked at the papers carefully. Shea wasn't a financial whiz by any stretch of the imagination. While some of his friends had MBA's along with their law degrees, Shea concentrated solely on the law. Numbers were never his thing and reading the figures in front of him was a bit like reading Greek. He hoped that Hector would be able to help him understand the Halal Market's financials. But before putting the papers back on his desk, something caught his eye. It seemed that the papers listed the owner of Halal Market as one Achmad Mustafa.

Mustafa, Shea realized, also happened to be the owner of Made in Mecca. That meant that Halal Market's financials might be connected to Made in Mecca's.

His interested piqued, Shea started flipping through the pages. Suddenly he stopped short. Even though Shea had trouble deciphering a spread sheet, he definitely could read a bank statement, and right in front of him were all of Made in Mecca's deposits from the last thirty days. And there it was, in bold black print: The day after the attack on Rabbi Felder, a deposit of forty thousand dollars had been transferred to Made in Mecca's account.

It was either a crazy coincidence, or Achmad Mustafa was somehow involved in this story. They key, Shea realized, was to trace where the money had come from. Maybe there was a simple explanation; perhaps the money was either a loan or an investment of some kind. Either way, Shea needed to find the source of the money.

And he knew exactly how he could find it. Trouble was, that meant making a very uncomfortable phone call.

As he debated his options, he knew what he needed to do. He buzzed Donna again. In a moment she was at his desk, a puzzled look on her face and a cell phone in her hand.

With a heavy sigh and a shrug of resignation, he keyed in a number.

"Hello," the person called out after the first ring.

"Don't hang up," Shea requested.

"Are you calling me from your cell phone?"

"No."

"So you hid behind someone else's number, so that that I would answer my phone?"

"Well, would you have answered if you knew I was calling?"

"Probably not, and that is why I am going to hang up right now."

"Danny, don't, please just hear me out."

"Why should I hear you out? There is nothing that you could say that I would want to hear."

"I know that you are angry with me."

"Really, how did you figure that one out?" Danny asked in a voice heavy with sarcasm.

"Your behavior on Shabbos sort of gave it away. Look, I am not calling to defend what I did."

"Good, because there is no defense."

"One second. I have a very good reason why I needed to defend Khalid al-Jinn. It may not be one that I can share with people, but I wouldn't have done this unless I had a real reason."

"Do you think that I am angry with you because you defended Rabbi Felder's attacker?"

"That is what you were yelling about on Shabbos."

"Well, that was because I had taken one Scotch too many and things just started flying from my mouth. I know you, Shea. I know you better than anybody, maybe even better than Shira. I know that defending that monster was probably killing you inside and if you needed to defend him, there must have been a good reason."

"So why were you so nasty to me on Shabbos?"

"Because you lied to me, Shea. I am supposed to be your best friend in the world. I always thought that our friendship was strong enough to withstand anything, even you defending out rebbi's attacker. But when I saw you at the rally ...."

"Don't you see, Danny, the whole thing was a setup. Silver planned the whole thing."

"I know that he did," Danny responded. "But still, when I saw you standing there, I was hurt. I felt betrayed but it wasn't because of what you were doing. It was because you hadn't been honest with me."

"I am so sorry, Danny. I tried to call you the night before the rally, but you weren't able to talk and I never got a chance to call you back. But I should have been more upfront with you, and I wasn't. I am really sorry."

"Well, I'm sorry that I accused you of working for al-Jazeera and for defending Ahmadinejad. But by the way, if you do ever defend him, can you ask him to shorten his last name? I mean, it is really impossible to say. You know, just ask him to change it to Achmad. Or maybe even, Jad. That would make life so much easier."

Shea smiled. It was good to have the old Danny back, bad jokes and all.

"It would be my pleasure," Shea responded. "Danny, I need a favor from you."

"What's going on?"

"It has to do with a case that I am working on, so I can't really go into the specifics."

"The whole attorney-client privilege thing?"

"Pretty much," Shea replied. "But here is what I need to know. Can you trace a bank account?"

"What type of account?"

"I am not really sure. All I know is that I have a client who is suing a local business. That business came into a lot of money one night, and I want to know where that money came from."

"It shouldn't be a problem, unless it is a Swiss account. Those things are impossible to trace. How about you give me the number and I'll see what I can dig up."

Shea gave Danny the information, and his friend promised to get back to him as soon as he had information. Shea handed the phone to Donna and returned to his thoughts. While it was great to have Danny back as a friend, the possibility that Danny might be able to get him information on the transfer was even more intriguing. Shea had a theory about the source of the money, but until Danny confirmed it, Shea wasn't going to do anything.

Amazingly, a few minutes later Shea heard his cell phone ring and saw that it was Danny on the line.

"What do you have for me?" Shea asked.

"Whatever you have gotten yourself into, you better get out as quickly as possible," Danny replied.

"I WAS ABLE TO TRACE THE ACCOUNT NUMBER THAT you gave me," Danny said.

"And what did you find?"

"Shea, are you sure that you know what you are doing?"

"Danny, I know exactly what I am doing but I really need you to tell me who that bank account belongs to."

"Have you ever heard of Lemour Holdings?"

"No. Should I have?"

"Lemour Holdings is one of the wealthiest conglomerates in all of France. They have their money in everything. They invest in real estate, in oil, in diamonds. They own newspapers and TV stations all over the planet. You name it, and they have money in it. The company is said to be worth over sixty billion dollars."

"So what does this business lesson have to do with the number that I gave you?"

"It took some time to trace how they tried to launder the money but it all went back to the main operating account of Lemour Holdings. Whoever got this money, they got it from Lemour."

"So why should I be concerned?"

"The CEO and founder of Lemour is a man named Henri Joseph."

"The name doesn't sound familiar," Shea admitted.

"Well, he is also known as Fareed al-Zilzal. Though nobody has been able to prove it, the rumor is that Interpol has been trying to arrest him for years on charges of terrorism and conspiracy. This guy is a certified religious wacko."

Shea's mind was racing. Why would Joseph, a billionaire tycoon, be concerned with a little Arab supermarket in the middle of Brooklyn? But as Shea thought about it, the connection came to him and he almost dropped the phone in excitement.

"Thank you so much, Danny," Shea exclaimed.

"You are welcome, Shea. Hey, are we on tonight?"

Shea wished he could just say yes; it seemed like forever since he and Danny had sat down to learn. "I don't know. Let me see what time I can get out of here and I'll be in touch."

Shea ended the call, poured himself a cup of steaming coffee and sank deep into thought. Jabril Yusuf contended that he had never attacked Rabbi Felder, but the store, Made in Mecca, had a video that showed otherwise, and displayed him mercilessly attacking the elderly rabbi. One day after the attack, that same store had received a large sum of money from a known Muslim sympathizer. Was it possible that Henri Joseph had ordered the attack on Rabbi Felder? *Sure*, Shea thought. *But why? What did an elderly rabbi have to do with a French billionaire? And if Joseph was behind the attack, why did he want Jabril to sit in jail?*

A cheerful voice interrupted his reverie. "Sorry it took me so long, boss," Hector apologized. "We have been trying new kind of burrito at the restaurant. It is called the 'Blazin Burrito.' I am telling you, it is *muy caliente*. There is nothing hotter and spicier than this burrito. It could melt one of those polar ice caps. I have been poppin' Alka Seltzers for the heartburn that I got from just tasting it."

"It is okay, *amigo*," Shea responded, laughing. "But right now, we need to get to the West Side, quick. Did you bring your car?"

"Of course."

Hector and Shea sped down the hallway. Shea only hoped that his plan would work and that this person would be able to help him. Because if he couldn't, Shea had no idea where else to turn.

■ ■ ■

The modest office of Access Technologies was buzzing, as usual. There was only one secretary, and she seemed to be doing forty things at once, which was why Shea and Hector found themselves just sitting in the waiting room. While Hector had wanted to go straight to the secretary and announce their arrival and purpose, Shea felt a little more reserved and waited for her to notice them. Because he would be asking her boss for a favor, the last thing that Shea wanted to come across as pushy and assertive. Even though time was a luxury that he could ill afford, Shea waited patiently until the secretary got off the phone, finished a text, and sent a batch of emails. A few agonizing minutes later, the secretary was finally free and she turned her attention to Shea and Hector.

"I am sorry about that," the secretary apologized. "You have no idea what it is like running a major company like this one all by yourself."

"You are the only secretary, Ms. ...?" Shea asked in surprise

"Marley. Lisa Marley. Yes, I run the show here. My boss doesn't really trust anybody else. Don't get me wrong, I love working for the guy, but it doesn't make the job any easier, that is for sure. But anyway, enough about me, who are you and what time is your appointment?"

"Appointment?"

"If you are sitting in the waiting room that must mean that you have an appointment. I can understand if you forgot what time, since the appointments need to be set up far in advance. So give me your name, and I will look up what time you are scheduled to meet with Mr. Carsten."

Shea looked at the secretary, trying to hide his frustration. In his haste to approach Andrew Carsten he'd forgotten one crucial thing: Andrew Carsten was one of the most difficult computer technicians to get hold of in New York City. He was in such a high demand that one needed three months' notice just to get an appointment.

In the Fatima Assad case, Shea had been able to procure Andrew's services only because Moshe Cohen, who was Andrew's close friend, had made a phone call and squeezed Shea in. But now Shea was on his own.

"I am totally sorry," Shea began, "but I don't have an appointment."

"That's okay," Lisa responded.

"It is?"

"Sure, you can make an appointment now," Lisa answered. "The earliest I can fit you in is in four months, would that work for you?"

"No, four months won't work," Shea said shortly. "Can you just tell him that I am waiting here and see if he will see me?"

"I never got your name," Lisa said.

"Shea Berman."

"Well listen, Shea. I don't mean to be rude or mean, but there is a reason that we require appointments. Mr. Carsten is extremely busy and he can't be bothered every five minutes by people who don't have appointments."

"I understand that," Shea responded, struggling to stay calm, "but this is not a normal situation. The information that I need could very well save an innocent man's life, and time is running out. So please, I understand that you have a job and normally you can't make exceptions. But I really need you to make an exception right now."

Lisa regarded Shea as he held his breath. Hector, for his part, sat in the waiting room reading a magazine, seemingly oblivious to the whole conversation. For Shea, that was just fine. Right now, he felt the only way that he was going to get in to see Andrew was if he was honest with Lisa, not with some underhanded scheme involving Hector.

"I like to follow my gut," Lisa said, "and my gut is usually right. My gut is telling me to trust you, so I am going to make that call. However, please don't prove me wrong. You seem like an honest man, and I hope that I am judging you correctly."

"You are," Shea responded.

Lisa keyed in a number. A few seconds later, Shea could hear her talking.

"Good morning, Mr. Carsten. I know how much you hate walk-ins …. Yes, I explained to him the concept of what an appointment is and how important they are. But he was very adamant about seeing you. His name is Shea Berman … are you sure? …. Okay, I'll tell him."

Shea looked at Lisa and hoped that she had the answer that he so desperately needed.

"Mr. Carsten said that he will see you now."

"Thank you so much," Shea exclaimed.

"My pleasure."

Shea and Hector walked past Lisa's desk and found Andrew's office. They knocked and a gruff voice ordered them to come in.

"Shea Berman," Andrew exclaimed, extending his hand to Shea and Hector, "the great defender of the dark side. How are you doing?"

"You have been speaking to Moshe, haven't you?"

"Of course. We learn together every Monday night."

"That's wonderful. By the way, thank you so much for helping me out on the Merzeir case. I'm telling you, what you were able to find out with that picture was amazing."

"No problem. The great thing about learning with Moshe is that it keeps me out of trouble. Anyway, he also keeps me informed of everything that is going on in his life."

"So I guess he told you about my newest case?"

"No, that I learned about from the papers. Man, you really know how to pick them, don't you?"

"Sometimes they pick me," Shea said dryly. "Andrew, this is Hector Ramirez."

Hector gave Andrew a bone-crunching handshake. "Mr. Carsten," he said, "I am real fan of your work."

"What type of work are you referring to?"

"The type that we can really use now," Shea responded.

"I'm listening."

"Right now, my client is going to be convicted for the attack on Rabbi Felder," Shea explained.

"From what I have heard that seems like a good thing. Your client is one scary guy."

"That was true."

"What do you mean, was?"

"Without being able to divulge too much information, suffice it to say, I don't think my client committed the attack. I think that he was framed."

Andrew spoke. "Don't those kinds of stories happen only in novels?"

"I used to think that," Shea agreed, "and I am the last guy in the world to believe in a conspiracy. But right now something really doesn't sit right with me and I need to find out what the truth is."

"How do you expect to do that?"

"Moshe told me that besides your amazing ability to provide computer security, you also have another talent."

"Oh, really," Andrew responded with a smile, "and what would that be?"

"He told me that you could hack into any computer system in the world. He also told me that you used to time yourself how fast you could break a firewall just for kicks."

The smile vanished. "Did Moshe also tell you that I don't do that type of work anymore?"

"No, that he didn't share with me."

"Did he happen to relate to you how my previous hacking practices almost got landed me in jail for half my life, and how I promised never to hack another computer security system again?"

"No, he didn't, and I would understand if you chose not to do what I am going to ask of you. However, please remember that we aren't talking about a game here. We are talking about a man's life. We are also talking about finding the real attacker of Rabbi Felder, who otherwise will walk about free, ready to attack again. The stakes are high and I wouldn't ask you to do this unless they were."

Andrew thought about what Shea was saying and Shea waited.

"Do you really believe that your client is innocent?" Andrew asked.

"Yes," Shea answered confidently.

"And you've got evidence to prove it?"

"That's where you come in."

"Then let's get started. I don't know what you want, but it could take a while." He buzzed the secretary. "Lisa, hold all calls."

Shea breathed a sigh of relief. "Thank you so much for doing this," he said.

"I am doing this because I trust you, Shea. If you believe that this guy is innocent, then that is good enough for me. What do you want me to do?"

"I am really not sure. I am convinced that this store, Made in Mecca, is hiding something. But I have no idea what."

"So basically, you want me to hack into this store's computer and see if I can find anything that would be useful in your search?"

"That sounds right."

"Okay, give me the address."

Shea told Andrew the address and watched Andrew go to work. He sat down to his computer and booted up a program. When Shea saw the program, he asked Andrew what it was.

"It is called, WiFind," Andrew responded. "Basically, it allows you to find any Wi-Fi signals in a certain area. If this store has a Wi-Fi connection, I will be able to find it."

Andrew put in the address of the store and pressed the search button. Immediately, several hundred Wi-Fi signals popped up on the screen. However, none of them seemed to belong to Made in Mecca.

"Bad news, Shea. If this store has internet, it doesn't seem that they have a Wi-Fi connection. If I am going to hack into their computers, I am going to have to do it manually and I don't think that either of us has the time for that now."

Shea looked crestfallen. He had hoped that Andrew would be able to provide the information that he needed, but right now that didn't seem possible. With less than 48 hours till he was due in court, Shea needed to think fast. After a moment, an idea popped into Shea's head and he turned to Andrew.

"Try this," Shea advised. "Type in the address, 850 Chambers Street and see what comes up."

Andrew put the address into the search bar and pressed enter. A moment later, a flashing light appeared over the address that Shea requested.

"We got a hit," Andrew exclaimed, his eyes glittering. "What is this place?"

"This is the Halal Market," Shea replied. "The owner of the Halal Market also owns Made in Mecca. Let's hope that their servers are connected."

"Well, if they are, I will find out in a matter of moments."

"Is their Wi-Fi connection secure?"

"Yes, but it is an easy encryption to crack. Just give me a few seconds, and it will all be done."

Shea paced around Andrew's office while Andrew went to work. A few minutes later, Andrew gave a triumphant shout. "We're in."

Shea rushed over to Andrew's desk. "What does that mean?"

"That means that I currently have access to the hard drives of both Made in Mecca and the Halal Market."

"So that means that the servers are connected?"

"I guess you got lucky on this one, Shea. But let's get down to business, what am I looking for?"

"Well, is there a file that has all of Made in Mecca's surveillance videos?"

"Let me see," Andrew said while he searched through the folders of the hard drive. A few moments later, he found the folder. He turned the screen so Shea could see it.

"Okay, what date are we looking for?"

"Check for September seventh of this year and see what you can find."

A few seconds later, Andrew found the video of that night and brought it on the screen. He then forwarded it to the time of the attack. Shea held his breath as he watched the video unfold. However, much to his dismay, Shea saw the exact video that he had seen in court.

"This can't be," Shea declared.

"What can't be?" Andrew asked

"That's the video that shows my client attacking Rabbi Felder."

"Wait one second," Andrew interrupted. "That is your client on the screen attacking Rabbi Felder?"

"Yes."

"And you saw this video before you came to me?"

"Yes, I did."

"I thought you said that you believed that your client didn't attack Rabbi Felder. How could you say that after seeing this video?"

"I found out information about my client that I am not at liberty to divulge. Suffice it to say, it was compelling enough to make me rethink my client's role in this attack."

"But how can you reconcile the fact that there is this video that proves otherwise?"

"Maybe the video is a fake," Shea offered.

"What do you mean, a fake?"

"Isn't it possible that if somebody wanted to frame my client, they could superimpose his body and make it seem that he was committing these terrible acts?"

"We aren't talking about Hollywood here," Andrew reminded him. "The probability that this video was doctored and your client was superimposed is very small."

"But humor me for a second," Shea requested. "If the video was in fact doctored, could we prove it?"

"I am not a movie editor and I wouldn't even know where to find one."

Shea struggled to control his disappointment. He had been sure that Jabril was telling the truth. But the video said otherwise and Shea didn't know how to disprove it.

"You know," Andrew said thoughtfully, "there might be something that can help you, but it won't be conclusive."

"What is it?"

"Give me a second while I check something out," Andrew requested as his fingers flew over the keyboard. "There, I think I may have something. What day did you say the attack occurred?"

"September seventh," Shea responded.

"Well, it says here that this file was modified on September twentieth."

Shea did a quick mental calculation and spoke.

"That was the day before the video showed up in court."

"It could just be a coincidence, or it could be that they reformatted the video the night before so it could be shown in court."

"But couldn't it also be because they modified the video by superimposing my client into the video?"

"It is definitely possible."

"But hardly conclusive," Shea finished off.

"I am sorry, Shea, but if you were looking for your smoking gun, this video doesn't seem like it is going to help you."

Shea wasn't willing to give up, and he pressed on. "But let's say, hypothetically, that my client was telling the truth and he wasn't the real attacker in the video. What would have happened to the original video?"

"If we are talking hypothetical here," Andrew said, with the hint of a smile, "then hypothetically, they would have deleted the original video."

"Which means my evidence is gone forever," Shea said despondently.

"Not necessarily," Andrew responded, his eyes getting that sparkle again.

"What do you mean?'

"Even when files are supposedly deleted, very often the file, or at least fragments of the file, can be found on the computer's registry. If they in fact did delete the original video, it may still be on the computer's registry."

"Can you check that for me?" Shea asked, hope rising again.

"I can," Andrew responded, "but after I do this, this search is over. I believe you that you think your client didn't attack the rabbi, but I can't continue to violate the privacy of an innocent business because of that."

"I understand and I really appreciate everything that you are doing for me."

"Okay, give me a second to run another program that we have developed called 'Recoverment.' It is able to identify any files that are still in the computer's registry and defragment them. If there is an original video, and if it was deleted, this program should be able to find it and reconstruct it. This program may take a while to do its thing. You and your investigator can wait outside in the waiting room. Whenever it finishes, I will call you guys. "

Shea and Hector thanked Andrew and left the room. Shea looked over his shoulder and saw Andrew bending over his computer, trying to work his magic. Shea felt that the chance that Andrew would be successful was remote, but he also knew that in that chance lay the only hope that he had left.

SHEA AND HECTOR FOUND THEMSELVES BACK IN THE waiting room. Once they were seated, Hector spoke.

"Man, boss, you don't look too good."

"I don't feel too good," Shea responded.

"What is wrong?"

"This whole thing is just bothering me."

"What do you mean?"

"Here I was so convinced that Jabril was innocent that I asked somebody to break the law to help me prove it. You saw his face; he didn't want to do it. But he believed in me and I told him to do it. But now, look where we are. We have no proof that Jabril's story was true and Andrew Carsten not only broke the law, but he broke a promise that he made to himself. And it was all because of me. What kind of monster am I turning into?"

"Hey, Shea, you look at me," Hector demanded, grabbing Shea by the shoulders. "Why are you doing this? Why are we here and not in a courtroom waiting for a guilty verdict?"

"Because I think that my client is innocent and I want to be able prove it," Shea responded.

"Then that is all that matters. I know you, Shea. I may not know you personally, but I know you as a lawyer who does whatever he can for his clients. That is what you did for me and that is what you're doing for this al-Jinn or Jabril or whatever his name might be. If this guy can't find the proof that we need to save your client, nobody will ever doubt your intentions. I know monsters. I deal with them all the time. You, Shea Berman, most certainly are not a monster."

"Thanks, Hector. It just seems to be all for nothing anyway."

"Hey, don't be so negative. Maybe your computer friend will be able to find something that can help us. My *madre* always said, 'Hector, *usted necesita mantener la esperanza.*'"

"What does that mean?" Shea asked.

"'You need to keep hope alive.' Don't worry, Shea. As long as you have hope, there is always a chance."

"Mr. Berman," Lisa called out from her desk. "Mr. Carsten said that he is ready for you."

They barreled down the hallway. When they entered the room they found Andrew sitting at his computer, a huge smile on his face.

"You must have *davened* real well today Shea," Andrew said. "Because Someone up there must really like you."

"What are you telling me, Andrew?" Shea said, barely daring to breathe.

"I am telling you that I was able to reconstruct a video off the hard drive. Now let's take a look."

Shea and Hector sat transfixed as Andrew brought up the file. Shea nodded to Andrew and he proceeded to press *play*. Once again, Shea saw his rebbi approach the store. The hooded figure approached Rabbi Felder, sinister, threatening. He towered over the elderly rav.

Towered over him ....

Jabril Yusuf was only five foot six.

The beating began. Shea kept his emotions under strict control, willing himself not to be distracted by the horrific scene taking place before him. Andrew, seeing the attack for the first time, looked like he was going to be sick.

Finally, it was over.

"I don't know how it helps us," Hector broke the silence.

"What do you mean?" Shea responded.

"We can't see the attacker's face. Right now, the only face that the jury can connect to the crime is the one that they saw on the first video and that was your client's."

"But this guy is huge. Almost as tall as Rabbi Felder himself. He's clearly not my client."

"You are forgetting something, *amigo*," Hector reminded him.

"What?"

"The jury will never see this video."

"Why not?"

"Because your friend obtained it illegally. He hacked into a computer and stole it from him. In my book, no judge will ever allow it to be entered into evidence."

"We can subpoena them and then obtain it legally."

"That will take too much time. The judge wants you back in court in less than two days. Anyway, how are you going to get a subpoena? Right now, we have no legal proof that the store did anything wrong that would warrant a subpoena."

Hector was right. Even with the video in his hand, Shea couldn't do anything. He had obtained it illegally and therefore it was inadmissible in court. Shea's shoulders drooped.

"If we were able to see who the guy was on the video," Hector continued, "then maybe we could track him down. But right now, all I was able to see was the back of his head and an arm. I may be a good investigator, but even Sherlock Holmes wouldn't be able to find a guy like that. Certainly not in two days."

Time, that was what they needed. Suddenly Shea straightened up. "I think I may have figured out a way," he said. "A way to buy some time. But if it's going to work, I am going to need your help, Andrew, and don't worry, you won't have to do anything illegal."

■ ■ ■

Moshe Cohen walked into the office of Access Technology.

When he'd received the phone call that Andrew wanted to learn at his office, he was happy. Michael Reeves's attention was focused on the al-Jinn case, and that meant a lighter work load for Moshe. He wasn't about to pass up an opportunity to learn with his *chavrusa*.

He waved hello to the secretary and she told him to head on into his friend's office. As he opened the door, Andrew greeted him with a smile that he happily returned. But when he saw who else was in the room, his smile quickly faded.

"What is going on here, Andrew?" Moshe barked, casting a dark look at Shea and Hector. "I thought this was about learning."

"I definitely want to learn with you, Moshe, but first, Shea has to speak to you."

"So why couldn't Shea use the phone like normal people do?" Moshe said, obviously angry.

"I needed to show you something," Shea responded.

Moshe finally deigned to address him. "So why couldn't you bring it down to my office?"

"Well, it is kind of only on Andrew's computer and anyway, I don't think bringing the file into the DA's office would have been the best idea."

Moshe eyed Shea and Andrew. Something was going on, but nobody would tell him what. Why would Andrew and Shea keep the truth from him? After a moment of thinking Moshe realized what was happening and he wasn't happy.

"You have been hacking again, haven't you?" Moshe accused him.

"It was my fault," Shea jumped to his defense. "I came to Andrew and asked him to help me."

"I thought you told me that you had stopped."

"He did," Shea interceded again, "but I asked him for a favor."

"A favor that could land him in jail."

"He only did it because I asked him to and he only agreed because you and I are friends," Shea said. "And also, because he trusted me, the same way I trusted you when you brought in that video."

"So why am I here?"

"I am about to tell you everything that has happened to me over the past 36 hours. I don't want you to say anything; I just want you to listen to me. After you have heard everything, I want to show you the file that is on Andrew's computer. If you still aren't convinced, then I will have nothing else to say. But if you believe me, then we will need to act fast."

Moshe closed his eyes and tried to think. He couldn't ignore his disgust with what had just happened. He didn't appreciate being lied to, and he definitely didn't like the fact that Andrew had broken the law and hacked into somebody's computer. However, Shea was right. Shea had trusted him, and the least Moshe could do was listen to what Shea had to say.

"I'm all ears," Moshe said.

■ ■ ■

After hearing Shea out, Moshe sat quietly, trying to take it all in. "That is one crazy story," he finally said.

"I know, and if I hadn't heard it from my client's mouth, I would never have believed a word of it. But now, I want you to watch this."

Andrew pressed *play* and the video appeared on the screen. Shea, not wanting to see the video again, walked away from the screen and allowed Moshe to view it by himself. After the video had finished, Moshe spoke to Andrew.

"Where did you find this video?"

"It was on the registry of Made in Mecca's computer. They had tried to delete the file, but I was able to reconstruct it."

"But with two videos, how do we know which one is real?"

"That is the problem," Shea responded. "If I believe my client, then I would say that the real video is the one we just saw and the fake one was presented in court. But I have no proof either way."

"So why not get an expert to refute the first video?" Moshe asked.

"I would need to find an expert and give him the proper amount of time to prove that the video is a fraud. Daniels wants me in court Wednesday morning. There is no way that I am going to be ready by then unless you help me."

"What are you talking about?"

"I need you to go Michael Reeves and have him ask for a few more days of recess."

"Why would he want to do that?"

"Because, unlike me, Michael and you don't get paid based on the number of acquittals or convictions. You get paid to administer justice and make sure that the guilty are punished and the innocent are vindicated."

"But we have no idea if your client is definitely innocent."

"But we don't know if he is guilty either," Shea retorted. "I am not asking for an acquittal. I know that I will never be able to present that video in court because of the way that I obtained it. However, I just need time to be able to prove my client's story, whether it means proving the first video was a doctored version or finding evidence to corroborate Jabril's story. With everything that I have just learned, there has to be proof out there somewhere, and I am going to find it. But I need time."

"You do realize that what you are asking me to do isn't just a simple favor."

"I know, but that is exactly why I needed you to believe in my client and his rights. Our legal system declares that all men are considered innocent before a trial and even during trial they need to be proven guilty beyond a reasonable doubt. Even if I am unable to prove that the first video was a fake, there is no way that Michael can deny that with everything that we have learned about this case, there is at least reasonable doubt here."

"So what exactly do you want?"

"I need time."

"Why don't you ask Daniels yourself?"

"He has already given me a two-day recess because of my injuries. If I request more time to disprove the prosecution, he will accuse me of stalling and will deny my request. But if Michael asks for the continuance, then Daniels won't interpret it as me stalling for time and he may agree."

"What is Michael's reason supposed to be?"

"I don't know," Shea responded. "How about the truth? Let him tell Daniels that we are examining the veracity of certain evidence."

"You don't understand, Shea," Moshe reminded. "This case is everything to Michael. There is no way that he is going to do this."

"He will, if you make him believe in my client and his plight. If I went to Michael, he would laugh me out of the room. But if you went to him, then he would have no choice but to believe. This isn't about winning and losing. It has to be about more than that. Remember, I could have objected to the video. I chose not to because I knew what was right and wrong, and I believed that you hadn't done anything illegal when you produced the video. Now I need you to do the same for me. We are talking about a man's life here. And if Michael won't do it to save my client, tell him that the real attacker is still out there and we need to find him. I don't care how you spin it, just please make sure you get me the time that I need."

Moshe eyed Shea. He knew he was putting his career on the line by going to Michael. There was a chance that Michael would question Moshe's loyalties and fire him on the spot for making such a request. However, he couldn't help but agree with Shea. The game that they played wasn't about winning and losing, it was about justice. And right now justice screamed to give Shea the time that he needed to save his client.

"Okay," Moshe agreed, "I'll do it. I can't promise that he will listen to me, but I will try my best."

"Thank you, Moshe."

"Don't thank me yet. Let's wait to see what Michael says and then you can thank me."

Moshe left the office and Shea breathed a sigh of relief and got down to work. If Michael was going to ask for the continuance, Shea needed to have an expert ready to examine the video. He made calls seeking anyone who was available to help him. He only hoped that Moshe would be successful and his search wouldn't be in vain.

MICHAEL REEVES COULDN'T HELP BUT FEEL EXCITED. He was only a few days away from winning possibly the most important case of his career. Michael envisioned the headlines after the conviction of Khalid al-Jinn. "Justice is served: Michael Reeves triumphs as Khalid al-Jinn is put behind bars."

Michael thought about the interview requests that would follow his victory. The news outlets would clamor for the firsthand story of how he, Michael Reeves, was able to protect the streets of New York.

"Oh, it was nothing," he said aloud, "I never doubted that justice would prevail and evil would be punished."

"Mr. Reeves," a voice came over the intercom.

"Yes," Michael responded, surprised and embarrassed.

"Is anyone in the office with you?"

"No."

"So who were you talking to?"

"I wasn't talking to anyone," Michael responded.

"That's odd," his secretary said. "I could have sworn I heard you talking to someone."

"You were mistaken," Michael said shortly, trying to preserve some dignity. "But is there something that you need?"

"You have a phone call on line one. Senator Reynolds. If you are busy, I can tell him to call back."

"No, put him through," Michael said hastily.

The voice on the other end was warm and confident; the perfect politician. "Hi, Mike. I just wanted to tell you that we here at the committee have been following the trial very closely."

"Really?"

"Yes, and I must admit that you had us a little nervous over there."

"What do you mean?" Michael asked, concerned.

"Well, it didn't take a Supreme Court justice to see that you were getting smoked at the beginning of the trial."

"Well, um ..."

"I mean, from what my sources told me, that Berman kid was able to take your case and slice and dice it like sautéed onions."

"He wasn't really disproving my case."

"Is it true that he got your star witness to change her story on the stand?"

"She didn't exactly change her story," Michael said, trying again to preserve some of his dignity.

"That Berman kid, it looks like he has some kind of future."

"I guess so."

"But that's okay."

"What is?"

"It is good that you were almost beaten."

"It is?"

"Sure," the Senator exclaimed. "The political world is a dog-fight. Sometimes the winner isn't the best candidate. It is the candidate who can slog it out, persevere through the struggle and come out on top."

"I am not sure what you are trying to say."

"I am telling you that you are a winner. It doesn't need to be pretty. Most guys after getting their head handed to them would have thrown in the towel and called it a day. But you, you didn't give up. You came back stronger than ever. Springing that video right at the last second was pure genius."

Even though the video wasn't Michael's doing, but Moshe's, Michael wasn't about to tell that to the Senator.

"We need winners in our party. We need people who don't give up and keep on fighting to the end. That is what you are, Michael."

Michael was glowing.

"Call me when you've got that guilty verdict, and we'll talk some more."

"Thank you, Senator," Michael responded. "I won't let you down."

Michael couldn't believe his good fortune. Though the trial had been far from smooth, it felt good to know that all Reynolds cared about was whether al-Jinn was convicted. Reeves was honest enough to admit that none of this would have happened if not for Moshe and his discovery of the video. He realized that he needed to thank his assistant, and he picked up the receiver to make the call. He set it down when he saw Moshe in the doorway of his office.

"Mark," Reeves called out. "I was just going to call you."

"You were?"

"I never thanked you for your help regarding the al-Jinn case. The video that you brought in saved us and I just wanted to tell you how much I appreciated it."

"Actually, I wanted to speak to you about that video."

"Sure, what's up?"

Moshe eyed his boss warily. Especially with everything that was riding on the case, Moshe understood that the chances that Michael would do as Shea had requested were slim to none. But Moshe wanted to see justice be served.

"I think that the video was a fake," Moshe blurted out.

"Are you nuts? Why?"

"Didn't you find it a bit strange that right before Shea was going to get a dismissal, the video magically appears?"

"Wait one second," Michael interrupted. "I wasn't the one who brought the video in. You did, remember? If you have a problem with it, why didn't you tell me this before?"

"Because before I had nothing else besides the video."

"What is that supposed to mean?"

"Even though I had my reservations about the video, I felt that there was no reason to bring them up because I had no proof that something was wrong."

"So why are you bringing these concerns up to me now?"

"I think I found my proof."

"What proof?"

"There is another video," Moshe stated bluntly.

"Another video?"

"I was shown a different surveillance video also taken by the Made in Mecca surveillance system."

"Where did you see this video?"

"I saw it at Access Technologies. My friend is the CEO and Shea Berman was there when I saw the video."

"You saw the video with the opposing counsel and I wasn't there," Michael barked angrily.

Moshe felt himself getting defensive. "My friend invited me down there under a pretext. However, once I arrived, I was informed of their true intentions."

"So why did you stay around when they made their intentions clear?"

"Because I owed Shea, and frankly, so do you."

"What is that supposed to mean?"

"Shea Berman could have objected to the video and accused me of burying evidence and Daniels never would have allowed it to be presented in court. He didn't do it because he trusted me when I told him that I hadn't buried it. Well, he asked me to trust him and I did."

Reeves voice was getting colder. "So what was on this video?"

"It was the same surveillance video, but it showed a different person attacking Rabbi Felder."

Michael Reeves possessed a strong lawyer's intuition, and an even stronger sense of self-preservation. Both were now working at full strength. "Where is this video?" he asked.

"On the computer of Access Technology," Moshe responded.

"That isn't what I am asking. Why hasn't Shea called an emergency session to determine whether or not the video is admissible in court?"

Moshe didn't answer.

"If you are here with me and I am not currently in court, I can only assume that Shea doesn't intend to produce this video in court. The question is why."

"Because of the manner in which it was obtained," Moshe reluctantly responded. He had known this wouldn't be easy, but he hadn't expected to be treated like a hostile witness.

"How exactly was it obtained?" Michael shot out.

"Shea asked my friend to hack into the computer of Made in Mecca. They found the video on the computer's registry."

Reeves' gift for effective at cross-examination was becoming more and more evident. "Are you telling me that your friend and Mr. Berman stole this video from somebody's computer?"

"Yes," Moshe admitted quietly.

"And this is the reason why you are suddenly having doubts? Because the other counsel committed a crime and stole a piece of evidence?"

"Yes."

"I cannot believe what I am hearing. Mark, do you hear yourself? They committed a crime. You abetted a crime."

Moshe tried once more. "We are talking about the truth here, and the truth is that right now there are two videos out there and we can't be sure which of one of them is legit and which one is a fake."

"You're wrong."

"Excuse me?"

"There is only one video," Michael said firmly. "This other video has never been introduced into evidence and therefore we are not required to assess it or even acknowledge it. Let alone the fact that it was obtained illegally."

"But that is only because of a technicality."

"You're a lawyer, Mark, and a good one. You know that we have rules. Our legal system guides us on how we are supposed to charge criminals and try them in a court of law. According to the rules, we have done nothing wrong and we are not required to adjust our case because of this supposed video."

"But what about the truth?"

"What about it?"

"Isn't that our job? Aren't we supposed to discover the truth and either prosecute or exonerate accordingly?"

"The truth is whatever evidence we present and whatever verdict the jury decides. That is the only truth that we need to worry about. Not some outlandish theory created by an opposing counsel."

"Even if the theory may be true?"

"That isn't my concern, and it isn't your concern. We only need to deal with what is presented to us legally in court. Not with anything else. Don't you understand why there are rules regarding the admissibility of evidence? It is precisely to protect against scenarios like this. How do you know that Shea didn't fabricate the video?"

"And how do we know that Achmad Mustafa didn't fabricate his?"

"The judge already decided that it was admissible and therefore we have no reason to assume that it was a fake."

"We aren't only talking about rules and laws here," Moshe continued heatedly, "we are talking about a man's life and what this conviction will do to his family."

"And what about another man's life?" Michael retorted. "Doesn't Rabbi Felder deserve justice? Doesn't his attacker deserve to be punished for his crime?"

"Of course he does. There is nobody in the world that wants to see justice in this case more than I do. But I want to see justice. I don't want to see an innocent man go down for a crime that he didn't commit."

"You still don't get it, do you?" Michael said. "According to the evidence that has been presented in this trial, Khalid al-Jinn is guilty. End of story. If there is any evidence that is presented in court that proves otherwise, we will deal with it at that time. But you don't expect me to question the merits of my case based on the wishes of a losing defense attorney?"

The intercom buzzed. "Mr. Reeves, Senator Reynolds is on the line again."

Reynolds! Moshe knew what that meant, and he realized just why arguing with his boss was fruitless.

"Tell him I'll be with him in one minute," Michael said to his secretary. He turned his attention back to Moshe. "Mark, I'm very busy. This conversation is at an end. Khalid al-Jinn has had a fair trial and he will get the justice he deserves. Is that understood?"

"Perfectly," Moshe responded as walked out of Michael's office, slamming the door behind him.

■ ■ ■

When Moshe returned to Access Technology, Shea and Hector were busy on their cell phones and laptops, working in an empty cubicle that Andrew had offered them. One look at Moshe's face was enough.

"I am sorry," he said, "but Michael wasn't going for it. Any luck from your end?"

"We sent both video files to Brent Charles," Shea said. "He's a film editor much respected in the industry. He said in order to check which video was falsified, he would have to break them down and examine every image for irregularities. Even if he weren't busy, it would take him at least a week to go through the two tapes. And we don't have a week."

"Not to mention the problem of getting the second video accepted as evidence," Hector added gloomily.

"So what are our options?" Moshe said, realizing, as the words left his mouth, that he was now committed to helping Shea.

"I don't know," Shea said. "I could still ask the judge to have me removed from the case and that may buy us some more time."

"Yeah, but right now, your client needs you," Hector corrected him. "You are the only one who believes that he is innocent, and you will fight for him like nobody else would. You hand him over to some public defender, and if he's lucky, he'll try to plead this one out. If you want to save your client, you need to be the one to do it."

"But right now we have nothing, and I go back to court in less than two days," Shea exclaimed.

"You don't have nothing, *amigo*," Hector said. "You still have that video."

"But what good is it if I can't present it in court?"

"Right now we have only one option," Hector said, his dark eyes dancing a little even as he tried to seem somber.

"And that is ...?"

"We need to find the real Khalid al-Jinn."

Shea rolled his eyes. "Great idea. No problem. And just how do we find him if we have can't see his face on the film?"

"People aren't just faces, boss."

Moshe broke in. "He's right, Shea. There are other ways to identify a person besides his face. We need to look at that video frame by frame. Maybe we can find something that will help us identify and find this guy."

Shea looked doubtful, but he followed Moshe and Hector to Andrew's office.

"So, what'cha got?" Andrew asked.

"I struck out with Michael Reeves," Moshe said.

"So where does that leave you?"

"With only one option," Moshe responded.

"And that is?"

"We're going to use this video to find the guy who attacked Rabbi Felder," Hector said.

"But we've looked at that video so many times, and we didn't see anything."

"But we weren't really looking," Hector said.

"What does that mean?"

"We were just looking at it to make sure that it wasn't a fake. We weren't trying to figure out who the *hombre* attacking the rabbi was."

"Well, we've got nothing to lose," Andrew shrugged. Despite his busy schedule, he was intrigued by this problem, and willing to help out. "Let me get the file and put it on the high def screen in the conference room. The image quality might let us see things we may have missed."

Andrew led the way to the conference room. Andrew hooked up his laptop to a high definition video screen mounted against the wall. Once the video was on the screen, Andrew turned off the lights and went to work. He forwarded through everything until the attacker came into view. After that, Andrew moved the video ahead frame by frame, giving everybody in the room a chance to examine the attacker. All they saw, though, was a hooded figure. As the attack was nearing its end, the assailant raised his right arm to strike the crumpled form of Rabbi Felder.

"Stop the video," Shea commanded. "Andrew, can you go back to the point where he raises his arm for the last time and freeze it? Then, can you add brightness to the picture?"

"Whatever you say, Chief."

Andrew brought the frame that Shea had requested onto the screen. He then added the necessary brightness and then turned the floor over to Shea.

"So what are we looking at?" Hector asked.

"Look at his arm and tell me what you see," Shea requested.

"I see him holding a metal rod and raising it to strike Rabbi Felder," Moshe said.

"Don't look at his hand. Look at his arm."

After a moment, all three men saw what Shea had been referring to.

"What is that?" Andrew asked.

"I have no idea," Shea responded. "It looks like some kind of a burn or something."

"Whatever it is, I have no idea how we missed that before," Moshe added.

"How does this help us?" Hector interjected. "This guy could have a burn mark the size of Texas on his arm, but we still don't know who he is."

"I am telling you that I have seen that arm before," Shea declared.

"When?"

"I don't know, and that is what I am trying to figure out."

Shea tried to shut out everything else and focus solely on the image of the scarred arm. He tried to forget the assault that he had just witnessed and all the betrayals and disappointments of the past weeks. Suddenly it came to him. In his minds' eye he could visualize the mark as vividly as the very first time he had ever seen it.

Not only did he remember where he had seen the burn mark before, he now knew exactly where he needed to go to exonerate his client.

Shea then took off out of the room like a sprinter in the forty-yard dash.

"Where are you going?" Moshe called out.

"I remembered where I saw that mark before," Shea shouted as he ran down the hallway.

"Where?"

But Shea was already out of sight.

"SO WHERE ARE WE ON THE SANCHEZ BROTHERS?"
Stephens spoke to a room filled with his agents.

"Nowhere," Glenda Tompkins, a tall slender woman who looked like a college student but in reality was one of Stephens' most reliable agents, replied. "I tried investigating their legitimate businesses and I found nothing. I thought that they would be using their sporting goods store as a front for the drugs, but it turns out that I was wrong."

"Anyone else?" Stephens asked.

When he saw that no one was replying, the Assistant Director grew frustrated.

"Come on, people," he yelled, "I have good intel that over ten million dollars' worth of drugs will be moved by the Sanchez brothers and their crew into the greater New York area within the next few days. If we don't find the source of those drugs, it will hit the streets and we will be stuck cleaning up the mess for the next few years. I want some answers now! Fields, you are awfully quiet for a change. Tell me something that will make me happy."

Fields was brought out of his stupor by the sound of his name.

With his mind clearly elsewhere, it took him a moment to gather his thoughts before responding.

"Nothing to report right now," he said, "but I may be onto something. Enrique Sanchez's brother-in-law is in from Colombia. I don't think it's because they are celebrating a family reunion. I know where he likes to hang out and I was hoping to pay him a visit later today."

"Okay," Stephens responded, "that is what I am talking about. We need to be proactive. These drugs aren't going to be delivered to our doorstep. So let's get out there and find them."

The meeting was clearly at an end, and the agents left the conference room to return to their desks. On his way out, Fields was stopped by Stephens.

"Is there something that I need to know?" Stephens asked.

"What do you mean?" Fields asked.

"I mean that you seemed to be in another planet during the meeting. "

"It's nothing. I just have some things on my mind that I am trying to figure out."

"Well, you better figure them out quickly, because right now your only concern should be those drugs. You are my top agent, Robert, and I need to know that I can count on you."

"Don't worry about me," Fields reassured him. "I'll report back to you later today if I was able to get anything from the brother-in-law."

"Perfect," Stephens responded, punching him on the arm. Once in his office, Fields sat down, put his feet up on the desk, and grinned. He hadn't been quite upfront with his boss. While it was true that Fields had to work things out, in his mind the fate of the Israeli prime minister did not count as nothing.

Ever since the meeting with Anat Adiran , Fields had spent most of his time going over the prime minister's itinerary. The fact that two days of the visit had already passed and there had yet to be an attempt on the prime minister's life provided little consolation. There was still more than a week remaining and according to the itinerary, there were plenty of opportunities for an assassin to strike. Looking over the many possible places, and with so few answers, Fields figured that only a miracle could save the Israeli prime minister.

■ ■ ■

He had spent a good few hours in Andrew Carsten's office, and it was well past 11 p.m. as Shea approached the apartment, but the lateness of the hour wasn't what was disturbing him. Shea didn't delude himself. There was a strong chance that upon hearing Shea's name, the tenant wouldn't open the door. She might even call the cops and have Shea arrested. However, Shea knew that his client's freedom might very well rest in this person's hands and that was all that mattered.

Shea rang the doorbell.

"Who is it?" a voice called from within the apartment.

"Shea Berman."

"What do you want?" the voice asked coldly.

"I know that I am probably the last person you want to speak to, but I need your help."

"Why should I help you?"

"You wouldn't be only helping me. You would be helping a man named Jabril Yusuf. A Pakistani, a Muslim. He has a wife and two children. He is innocent of the crimes that he has been accused of and right now, you are the only person who might be able to help him. Please, just listen to what I have to say. If you still don't want to help me, I will understand and I will never bother you again. But if you choose to help me, we need to act fast, because we don't have a lot of time."

Shea waited tensely, but there was no response. Well, he couldn't really blame her. With a sigh he turned toward the elevator.

A door opened.

"Mr. Berman, where are you going? I thought you had something that you wanted to discuss with me."

Shea turned around and walked to the apartment. Though Fatima Assad hadn't changed that much from the last time he had seen her, he still gasped when he saw her pale, emaciated face.

"Thank you for seeing me," Shea said.

"I am not doing this for you. I may not try to help Jabril Yusuf. I will at least listen."

Shea nodded. He knew that she bore a grudge against him, but thankfully, she was still willing to speak to him.

Shea looked around the apartment in surprise. There was almost no furniture, save for a small table and chair in the corner of the room. He did see boxes stacked to the celling.

"Are you moving?" Shea asked, trying to ease the tension.

"I am going back to Ramallah," Fatima answered. "I do not wish to die alone."

"I know it may not be worth much now, but I am really sorry."

"No, you aren't. You knew that if Merzeir won, I would have no chance of getting on that drug trial. That was my only hope and you ended it for me. So congratulations Mr. Berman, you won and now I am going to die."

"I never meant for that to happen to you," Shea responded. "I was only trying to win for my client. I played by the rules. That is all I ever did."

"But the rules were wrong," Fatima stated. "Did you know that aside from that day, I hadn't smoked for three years? And after that puff, I never smoked again. I deserved to be on that drug trial. It was never about the money. I only accused the company of discrimination because Drillings thought that it would help me get back on the drug trial. They were able to keep me off and hide behind a technicality. It isn't fair!"

"You are right," Shea admitted.

"Excuse me?"

"I agree with you. Sometimes, justice is blind. The rules that are meant to protect us sometimes end up hurting us in unimaginable ways. If it is true that you only smoked once, then the rules hurt you and I am sorry for that. But now there are rules that may hurt someone else. Someone innocent. And I need your help to prevent that."

"What are you talking about?"

"Have you heard about my latest client?"

"You mean the guy that attacked that rabbi?"

"Yes."

"Sure I have heard about it. But what does that case have to do with me?"

"There was a video that was presented in court that showed my client attacking the rabbi. However, we found another video that shows somebody else attacking Rabbi Felder. Because of a technicality I cannot show the video in court."

"And what does this have to do with me?" Fatima asked again.

"The attacker on the second video was able to hide his face. However, I was still able to see a part of his body that may allow me to identify who he is. But I first need something from you."

"What?"

"Do you have a copy of that picture?"

"Which picture?"

"The picture of you smoking with your brothers and some friends."

"Sure, I have it right here on my laptop. Why do you need it?"

"Please show it to me and I will explain everything."

Fatima slowly walked to the lone table in the room and retrieved her laptop. Oddly enough, the picture that had cost Fatima so much now served as the screensaver to her monitor.

"What are you looking for?"

"That," Shea said, pointing to a bare arm wrapped around Fatima's brother's shoulder. It was a muscular arm, scarred by a burn mark.

"The attacker on the second video had that identical mark on his arm. Can you tell me who he is?"

"I thought that your client was named Khalid al-Jinn."

"So did I."

"So then who is Jabril Yusuf?"

"That is my client's real name. Jabril was forced to take the blame for the attack, and pretend to be Khalid al-Jinn. Khalid al-Jinn is still out there and we need to find him to save Jabril Yusuf. So please, Ms. Assad, tell me where I can find this man."

Fatima was quiet and Shea waited for her to respond. With all the anger that she felt toward him, the last thing that Shea wanted to do was pressure her and have her shut down completely.

"I never met this guy," Fatima said. "I am not sure how I can help you."

"Please, Ms. Assad. Jabril Yusuf has two boys who miss and need their father. He has a wife who has experienced terrible horrors and pain because of this whole ordeal. They have gone through enough and you can end their suffering."

"How? I don't even know the man."

"If you don't know him, how did he end up in a picture with you and your brothers?"

"I am not even sure," Fatima responded. "I think he met my brothers a few years ago at a soccer match at Gaza Stadium. When he came to America, he contacted my brothers. The picture was taken the day that he arrived in America."

"Perhaps your brothers know something?"

"I don't know."

"Ms. Assad, you are our only hope."

"But I can't help you. I have been taught my entire life to never help a Jew. If my parents knew that I was considering helping you, they would disown me."

"Then don't help me. Help them. Help Jabril and his family. I have already been fired from my job and I will gain nothing if my client is freed or convicted."

"So why are you doing this? If you have nothing to gain, why would you do this?"

"I am trying to do what is right," Shea answered. "It doesn't matter what religion my client is, he is being framed for something he didn't do and that is wrong."

Fatima sat down on the lone chair, clearly drained by her illness and by the conversation.

"I will call my brother in Gaza," she finally said, "and see if he knows anything."

Fatima left Shea alone and went to call her brother. A few minutes later she returned, her pale face somber.

"I don't know if this helps you or not," she said. "My brother has no idea where Khalid lives. He told me that he hasn't been in contact with him for some time."

"Did he know anything that could help me?"

"He remembers Khalid telling him about a new job that he was starting about six months ago. It is possible that he still works there. But he doesn't know for sure."

"Where was that?"

"He worked as a gravedigger in the New Montefiore cemetery in Long Island."

"Okay," Shea responded, "at least it's a start."

Shea turned to face Fatima before he left. "I am truly sorry and I wish you a speedy recovery."

"That will not happen, Mr. Berman, but I hope you are successful in freeing your client, if he is indeed innocent."

It was close to midnight, but Shea was exultant. At least he had a starting point for his search.

He made a quick call to Shira, updating her on some of the news, and went to his parents' house for a few hours of much-needed sleep. Tomorrow, he knew, would be a long day.

■ ■ ■

"So this guy works at a Jewish cemetery," Moshe said, sitting with Shea in a Flatbush bagel shop the next morning. "You have got to appreciate the irony in that one."

"I'd love to, but I haven't had time to think about it. I've been wracking my brain trying to figure out what my next move will be."

"What do you mean, 'my next move'?"

"Don't get me wrong, Moshe," Shea tried to explain. "I really appreciate everything that you've done for me. But I can't ask you to see this through to the end. If Michael finds out what you're doing, your job will be in jeopardy. I can't afford to have you on the unemployment line with me." He managed a laugh. "There's no way that I want to compete with you for a job."

"You don't get it," Moshe protested. "It's not about my job. It's about finding whoever attacked Rabbi Felder and putting him behind bars for a very long time. For me, that's the only thing that matters right now."

Shea made a gesture of surrender; in truth, he was relieved to have Moshe aboard. "So what's our next move?" he asked.

"Find al-Jinn. Get evidence against him. Have him arrested."

"Nice agenda, but how are we going to do that? We can't exactly go after him ourselves. After what he did to Rabbi Felder, I don't think that he would hesitate to kill both of us if we confronted him." Shea rubbed his bruises ruefully. "I'm not made for combat, Moshe. And neither are you."

"Well, going to the police isn't an option either," Moshe stated.

"Why not? Don't tell me it is because of the way that I treated Nelson on the stand. It wasn't personal; I was just doing my job."

"Nothing to do with that. I heard from one of the other ADA's this morning that after I went to Michael, he specifically told Lieutenant Simpson that nothing should be done on the al-Jinn case without Michael's approval. I guess I spooked him really badly, and he wants to make sure that he doesn't lose this case. That means that no leads will be looked into and no suspects will be arrested without Michael's knowledge."

"Michael can do that?"

"When you are the District Attorney, with the kind of contacts and clout that Michael has, you can do whatever you want."

"So what do we do now?" Shea wondered. "You can't tell me that we have absolutely no way of apprehending this guy."

Moshe sipped his latte thoughtfully. "The police won't help, but maybe …."

"Yes?"

"What about the FBI?"

Shea laughed bitterly. "Moshe, you're an attorney. You know you can't just walk into the FBI offices and ask them to pretty please take care of a police matter. There are some pretty heavy questions of jurisdiction to be answered here, especially since we have no real evidence. They'd laugh us out of there."

"I wasn't talking about an official approach. I happen to know an agent in the FBI's New York office. Remember how Andrew told you that he had sworn off hacking into computer systems? Long story, I'll tell you one day, but bottom line is he'd gotten himself into some pretty deep trouble, and even the FBI got involved. I was helping out Andrew, and we met an agent who really impressed us."

Shea put down a generous tip and stood up. "So what are we waiting for?"

"A GENT FIELDS," THE SECRETARY CHIMED.
"Yes."

"Somebody is here to see you."

Fields looked at his desk. He had the prime minister's itinerary on one side and a list of all known relatives of Enrique Sanchez on the other. To say that he was busy would be an understatement. Unless this guy was coming to tell Fields that he had just won the lottery, he was going to have to tell him to come back later.

"Please tell him that I am really busy right now and I don't have time for visitors."

"He says his name is Mark Cohen. He says that you know him from somewhere."

Fields sighed. He did remember this Cohen; a promising, up-and-coming attorney whose hacker friend had gotten himself into hot water and had almost been cooked. Nice fellow.

"Tell Mark that I say hello and I would love to speak to him, but right now, I really don't have the time."

"I told them that, but they were insistent."

"They? Who is 'they'?"

"Mark Cohen and Shea Berman. Mr. Berman says he is the

lawyer for someone named Khalid al-Jinn and he has something to tell you about the case."

Fields froze. With around a week left to the prime minister's visit, was it possible that Shea Berman had found a way to get al-Jinn acquitted? If he did, then al-Jinn would have plenty of time to carry out his assassination attempt. But why would Berman come and tell this to the FBI?

There was only one way to find out.

"Send them in," Fields requested.

Within minutes, Shea and Moshe were in Fields' cluttered office. "Mark," Fields announced, "it's good to see you again."

"Same here, Mr. Fields. This is my friend, Shea Berman."

Enough polite amenities; Fields was in a rush. "So Mr. Berman, you're defending Khalid al-Jinn, are you? Got some information for me?"

Shea, too, had no time to waste, and he appreciated Fields' direct manner. "I have been defending Mr. al-Jinn ever since he was arrested for attacking Rabbi Gedaliah Felder. However, we have just learned that the person that I have been defending isn't really Khalid al-Jinn."

An old pro, Fields kept his face expressionless, though this certainly wasn't what he'd expected Shea to say.

"How do you know this?"

Once again Shea retold the story he'd heard from Jabril and Ibrahim.

Fields let out a low whistle. "And you believe your client?"

"Throughout the trial there were many issues with the evidence. The video introduced by the prosecution seemed definitive, but my reservations were confirmed when I discovered another video, the one I believe is the true video, that showed Rabbi Felder being attacked, but not by my client."

Shea gave Fields a very abridged version of how they'd found the surveillance video, carefully omitting any mention of Andrew Carsten.

"That's some story. So why are you coming to me and not taking the video to the DA?"

"We tried to," Moshe answered briefly, "but he wasn't listening. He has his evidence, he's got his verdict sewn up neatly. That's enough for him."

"And why come to me?" Fields asked again.

"My client needs justice, Agent Fields," Shea responded. "He is a loving father who has had his life shattered into a million pieces. He doesn't deserve to suffer when the real culprit is walking the streets as a free man."

Fields nodded, carefully concealing all reaction. It seemed that Shea and Moshe knew nothing about the plot against the prime minister, and Fields intended to keep it that way. If what Shea was saying was true, the real al-Jinn had been out there the whole time and was waiting for the opportunity to strike. Shea's mention of Lemour Holdings' involvement only increased Fields' anxiety; Henri Joseph was big-time, and the stakes must be enormous for him to go to such trouble to shield al-Jinn. It was clear: Khalid al-Jinn was going to kill the Israeli prime minister, unless Fields could find him first.

"Mr. Berman, how can you expect to find one man in a city of over eight million people? And that's assuming he's here in New York."

"I know where he is right now," Shea responded. "I have information that he is working at the New Montefiore cemetery in Long Island. I would have confronted him myself, but after what he did to Rabbi Felder I don't believe I would come out alive."

"What did you just say?"

"I said I think Khalid al-Jinn will kill me if I try to confront him by myself."

"I heard that already. Where did you say he is employed?

"He works at a cemetery in Long Island called the New Montefiore Cemetery."

Fields glanced surreptitiously at the itinerary on his desk. "How do you know this?" he shot out.

"I found out from somebody who knows him."

Again, Fields looked at the itinerary. He forced himself to look calm. "Gentlemen, your information interests me," he told them, dismissing the two with a handshake. "I'll see what I can do."

Minutes later Fields was in his car, gunning the engine and praying he'd be in time.

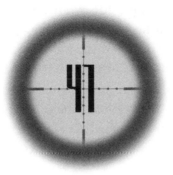

K HALID AL-JINN ROSE FROM HIS CROUCH AND PEERED
out the window. Though the accommodations that he had
arranged were less than ideal, they provided the perfect cover for
the mission he was about to complete. The dogs brought by the
Israeli agents to search the area weren't able to pick up his scent
as he'd been hidden behind bags of manure that were stored in
the equipment shed. A weaker man might have cringed at the
thought of spending a full night inhaling the stench of manure.
But Khalid al-Jinn wasn't weak, and for this mission he would
endure anything. Khalid had been ready for this day ever since
Rasheed's first visit.

As he adjusted the scope on his rifle, Khalid thought about
everything that had transpired over the last month. Rasheed had
been furious when Khalid had told him about the attack on the
rabbi, accusing Khalid of sabotaging the mission. Khalid had
argued that it was Rasheed's fault. By forcing him to take medication to contain his anger, Khalid could no longer control his rage
without the help of his pills. At Rasheed's orders he'd skipped the
meds, and an attack of some kind had been inevitable.

Rasheed had ordered Khalid to go to Rasheed's apartment and

wait until he received further instructions. It wasn't until the following morning that Khalid found out what Rasheed had pulled off, and he was quite impressed.

Khalid felt no remorse for what he'd done to the rabbi. His only regret was that he hadn't been able to wait and admire his handiwork while he watched the rabbi bleed out on the pavement. Khalid didn't even know if the rabbi had survived the attack. Rasheed had forbidden him from reading any of the papers or checking the news. He wanted Khalid completely focused on the mission. The tactic had worked, and as he eyed his target through his scope, Khalid was one hundred percent focused.

■ ■ ■

Prime Minister Yitzchak Schechter approached the headstone with great trepidation. Only a few stones adorned the stone, which didn't surprise Yitzchak. His mother wasn't well-known and Yitzchak was her only family.

For most Israelis, the name Hadassah Leibowitz meant nothing. When she had met Yehonatan Schechter, he had not yet become the Great War Hero and had not entered the world of Israeli politics. Yehonatan and Hadassah were barely out of their teens. Both of them had been studying at Bar-Ilan University and that is where they met. He was studying political science and she engineering. Their courtship was brief and only a few months after their initial encounter, they were married. Life was blissful for the new couple, and in their first year of marriage, Yitzchak was born.

Everything changed after the Yom Kippur War.

■ ■ ■

Yehonatan returned from battle not only a hero, but also a changed man. The horrors that he had witnessed on the battlefield gave him a new purpose and mission in life. He wanted to make sure that State of Israel, the country that he had so valiantly defended during the war, would endure forever. Yehonatan decided to dedicate all his time and effort to his new cause. In this new life, Yehonatan realized, that there was no room for a wife or a family. Not long afterward, the couple divorced. Yehonatan gave full custody to Hadassah and she and her young son moved back to the United States where she had been born.

This arrangement worked out nicely for everybody. Yehonatan was able to concentrate on his dream of building the State of Israel, and Hadassah was able to live peacefully with her parents in her childhood home. Yitzchak rarely saw his father, and his maternal grandfather was his father figure for the first eight years of Yitzchak's life. When he had just turned nine, his mother suddenly collapsed. It was later discovered that she had suffered an aneurism. Just like that, Yitzchak was an orphan. Hadassah's parents, devastated over the loss of their only daughter and facing some serious health issues themselves, requested that Yitzchak be reunited with his father in Israel. Yehonatan, recognizing his responsibility, agreed and immediately after the funeral he took his only son back to Israel.

As Yitzchak bent down to place a stone on the tombstone, he stopped. He wondered what his mother would have thought of him if she could see him now. His mother had been the quintessential pacifist. She always preached to him the importance of peace and he knew that she hated war more than anything in the world. Though many had blamed the divorce on Yehonatan, what they hadn't realized was that the war also affected Hadassah. While she had understood why her husband had joined the army and fought in the Yom Kippur War, once he had returned from battle, and she knew that her husband had done his share of killing people, Hadassah could no longer look Yehonatan in the eyes without seeing a murderer.

For Yitzchak, this trip, his first in many years, was about fulfilling the visions of both of his parents. For the legacy of his father, Yitzchak sought to protect Israel's right to exist. But for the legacy of his mother, he hoped that he could do it through peaceful methods.

■ ■ ■

Fields slammed the door of his car and jumped out. He ran toward the main gate of the cemetery. Immediately a tall, burly man approached him.

"Excuse me," a man said in accented English. "You are not allowed to be here. This is a restricted area."

"I am FBI Special Agent Robert Fields," Fields responded, flashing his FBI badge. "I have reason to suspect that the prime minister's life is in danger and I'm here to help neutralize the threat."

"I don't know of any threat, but I do know that you are not allowed to be here. So I will ask you to please leave the area."

"Are you listening to a word that I am saying?" Fields asked incredulously. "Your boss's life is in danger. So kindly move aside and let me save him."

Another tall, sun-bronzed man appeared. "What's the commotion?" He glanced at the FBI ID and held his hand out to Fields. "Gavi Shachar. I am in charge of the prime minister's security. Tell me what the concern is."

"Have you ever heard the name Khalid al-Jinn?"

Shachar gave him a serious look. "I have."

"I have reason to believe that he is here right now and he plans to kill the prime minister."

"Impossible," Gavi responded.

"Why?"

"The entire cemetery has been closed off since early this morning. We were here with our dogs before the PM arrived and we searched the entire premises. It's clean. Since then, nobody has entered the cemetery."

Fields gasped in frustration. He had been convinced that Khalid would make his attempt at the cemetery. It was the only scenario that made perfect sense. But if the Israelis had properly searched the area, was it possible that Khalid wasn't even there?

"One second," he said, as he saw a man wearing overalls walking outside near the gate. "You, over there, come here please."

A large man with a bushy beard and a baseball cap perched on his head approached Fields and Gavi.

"I am FBI Special Agent Robert Fields and this is Gavi Shachar from the Shin Bet in Israel. Can I ask what you are doing here?"

"Wow," the big man responded in a decidedly southern accent. "I never met me a real FBI agent before. I don't want no trouble."

"Why are you hanging around the cemetery?" Gavi asked.

"I'm Big Earl. I am a gravedigger and I work in this here cemetery. My supervisor told me to come to work late today on account that there was some big shot visiting the cemetery and it would be closed off to the public. I am just waiting till we reopen."

"You are a gravedigger here?" Fields asked.

"I know it isn't a big-time job like you got. But it is honest work and I do it with pride."

"I wasn't trying to be cynical," Fields responded. "I just wanted to know if you know another gravedigger who works in this cemetery. His name is Khalid al-Jinn."

"Khalid al-who?"

"Khalid al-Jinn," Fields repeated. "He is an Arab and about six foot three. He is in his late twenties."

"Oh, you mean Khali," Earl responded.

"Khali?" Fields and Gavi repeated in unison.

"Yeah, Khali. He has been working here for a short while. Round about six months. Never knew what his full name was. He just told us that it was Khali and it was short for something that we probably wouldn't be able to pronounce."

"When is the last time that you saw Khali?"

"That was last night."

"What time?"

"Well, it was at about 8 p.m. We was all leaving to go home, like we normally do."

"Did Khali leave with you?"

"Well, no. I mean, I live here on Long Island, Inwood if you want to know, but Khali lives in Brooklyn. Can you believe that he drives here every day?"

"I don't mean if he went home with you," Fields said. "I only wanted to know if you are certain that you saw him leave the cemetery."

"Sure. We all left together like we normally do. Then Khali ...

y'know, now that you mention it, I'm not sure if he left last night," Earl said slowly.

"What do you mean?"

"Well, me and the guys was gettin' ready to head home. Normally, Khali comes with us to the parking lot, and then we go on our separate ways. But last night, Khali told me that he needed to head back inside to get something from the equipment shed."

"Did he say what he was getting?" Fields asked.

"Nope."

"But did you see him leave after that?" Gavi asked.

"I was sayin' before. Me and the guys usually carpool and the guys were leaving so I didn't have a chance to stick around and see if Khali made it out. But I can't imagine that he wouldn't have left. Why would he want to stay in the cemetery all night?"

You don't want to know, Fields thought.

"Where is this equipment shed?" he asked

"It is right between First Avenue North and Second Avenue North."

Gavi's composure was shattered. "That's only thirty yards from where the prime minister's mother is buried," he burst out.

"Get the PM out of there!" Fields directed. "Once the prime minister is secured, we can go after al-Jinn."

Gavi began shouting in Hebrew over his radio. Fields took off running, hoping they had time to prevent the impending disaster.

■ ■ ■

Khalid al-Jinn rolled up his prayer rug and put it to the side. Finally, it was time. No more listening to Big Earl's stupid stories and laughing at his corny jokes. The thought of spending one more moment digging with those losers was too much to bear. On numerous occasions over the past few months, Khalid had wanted to quit. The fact that he, once a celebrated and notorious soldier fighting for his people, was now digging graves for Jews alongside these infidel Christian enemies of Islam was an insult to his legacy. Rasheed had told him that he needed to be patient and that all of his suffering and frustration would be worth it in the end. As he fingered the trigger and felt the rush of excitement and elation, he knew that Rasheed had been right.

■ ■ ■

"I miss you, Ema, and I hope that you are watching over me," Yitzchak Schechter murmured under his breath, bending over to pick up a stone to place on the grave. "I hope you will be proud of what I intend to accomplish."

As he straightened his body, he felt the weight of one of his security detail come crashing down on him.

"Sir, stay down," the agent ordered.

"What is going on?" Schechter demanded.

"Just stay down sir," the agent replied. He spoke into his headset. "I have the Prime Minster secured. Where is the suspect?"

■ ■ ■

As he shifted the rifle on his shoulder and drew the target into his sights, his finger steady on the trigger, al-Jinn saw a figure jump onto the prime minister. Hastily he debated his options. He could fire on the agent and hope that one of the bullets would penetrate to the person beneath him. Khalid realized that while he might wound the prime minister, there was almost no way to be sure of actually killing him. And if Khalid did indeed fire, the security forces would easily trace the bullet's trajectory and he would be caught in seconds. It was one thing to die for Allah, but to be caught and not accomplish one's mission, that was something that al-Jinn would not let happen.

Al-Jinn pulled his weapon away from the window and began to plan his escape.

■ ■ ■

Fields raced toward the shed where Khalid was supposedly located, keeping in radio contact with Gavi Shachar.

"Do you have a location?" Fields asked Gavi.

"Affirmative. My men report a rifle poking through the window in the shed."

"Can your man see the suspect?"

"Negative. The window seems to be caked with mud. We are going to need to approach the shed, break down the door, and take him down."

"You will not take him down," Fields ordered. "For all we know, this guy wasn't working alone and we need to find who else is involved in this plot. We are going to arrest him. This area is under United States jurisdiction, and I am now in charge."

Shachar was unimpressed. "If I feel that he represents danger to the prime minister, it is my duty to protect him. The prime minister's safety is my number-one concern."

"Is the prime minister secured?"

"Yes."

"So then let me do my job," Fields snapped. He grabbed a megaphone from one of the security men and spoke into it.

"Khalid al-Jinn, this is the FBI. You are surrounded. Come out with your hands up."

A L-JINN HEARD HIS NAME, BUT HE DID NOT RESPOND. Though the disappointment of his mission's failure was still fresh and throbbing, Khalid knew he needed to focus on his next objective, and that was his survival. He moved toward the back wall of the shed, inching his way to freedom.

"Khalid al-Jinn," Fields repeated. "This is the FBI. You have nowhere to run. Your only option is to turn yourself in."

"Agent Fields," Gavi chimed in.

"Go."

"My team is ready to advance on the shed and I am going to give them the green light."

"I want the suspect taken alive. He has nowhere to run. If you go in there, there will be a firefight."

"Fine," Gavi relented. "We will give him a few more minutes and see if he comes out. If he doesn't, I will have my man use tear gas. That will flush him out for sure."

"From what I know about the suspect, the less provocation, the better for everybody. So let's see if he comes out on his own. The last thing that we need is a gun battle where the odds are some-one will get hurt."

"I completely agree with you," Gavi replied. "However, I will not allow this guy to slip through our fingers again. If we've got him, I won't lose him."

"Gavi," Fields responded, "al-Jinn is boxed in. We have the lone entrance covered. There is no way that he is getting out."

■ ■ ■

Al-Jinn positioned himself behind the bags of fertilizer and searched blindly for the spot. He couldn't risk rising from his position and exposing himself to the agents surrounding the shed. He smiled grimly as he located what he was looking for. Rasheed had told him that in every great plan, there had to be an even greater plan of escape. Though originally Khalid didn't want to accept that failure was a possibility, he was happy that he hadn't given in to his ego. Because now, even though the agents had foiled his plan, he was going to live to attack again.

Still in a crouch, Khalid faced the rear of the shed. With both hands, he carefully and quietly removed the two loose pieces of wood from the wall that separated the shed from the cemetery grounds. He pulled the planks into the shed and admired his handiwork. Though the hole was narrow, for a man as wiry and thin as Khalid the size was perfect. He crawled through the small opening, which led him under the pickup truck that he had parked next to the shed. Now all Khalid needed to do was wait for the agents to storm the shed and provide the diversion that he needed to complete his escape.

■ ■ ■

"This guy isn't coming out, Agent Fields," Gavi informed him a few minutes later. "I am sending my men in."

Fields didn't choose to argue. He had offered al-Jinn a chance to surrender, which the terrorist declined. Though Fields wanted more than anything to be able to question the suspect, he knew that the longer they waited the more they were putting others' lives in danger.

"Throw in the tear gas and let us see what happens," Fields offered.

"Ten-Four," Gavi responded and gave the order. An Israeli agent ran toward the shed and flung a tear gas canister through the window. The shed quickly filled with the acrid smell, and Fields watched for al-Jinn to come racing out.

The gas dissipated. There was no sign of al-Jinn.

"Did you see the suspect leave the shed?" Gavi inquired.

"Negative," Fields responded. "Nobody left that shed. Are we even sure that he is in there?"

"There is only one way to find out." Gavi ordered his men to approach the shed.

■ ■ ■

Khalid slid on his stomach under the truck to the driver's side. Then he grabbed onto the door handle. He opened it slowly and waited. When he heard the agents converging on the shed, he realized that it was now or never. He pulled the door open, turned onto his back and slid out from under the truck. In one fluid motion he pulled himself into the driver's seat, still in a crouch so he wouldn't be seen, grabbed his keys, and placed them into the ignition. But before putting the truck into drive, Khalid removed a small detonator from his pocket and exposed the switch.

The agents, their faces covered with gas masks, walked cautiously into the shed.

■ ■ ■

In the short time that Khalid al-Jinn had been at the al-Adiyat camp, he had learned the fine art of bomb making and he was excited to finally be able to show off his talents. The five packs of C-4 explosives that he had hidden in the bags of fertilizer were wirelessly connected to the detonator that he held in his hand. Khalid marveled at the simplicity of his creation and the sheer awesomeness of its power of destruction. He only wished he could have seen his victims' faces as the bomb went off . But he needed to escape, and his window of opportunity was closing fast.

As always, Khalid said a short prayer that he succeed and then pressed the button. He immediately threw the truck into drive and sped toward the gate. The time-release mechanism gave him the distance he needed. Within seconds the shed exploded into a bright orange fireball.

■ ■ ■

The impact of the blast threw Fields to the ground as the heat seared through his body. When he was finally able to rise, he swiftly surveyed the damage. The shed was completely destroyed; the bodies of the fallen agents were strewn everywhere. Gavi and those agents who hadn't been in the shed rushed to the aid of the wounded. As soon as Fields got his bearings, he shifted his focus. He was going to take down Khalid al-Jinn.

He saw the pickup barreling down the narrow cemetery streets and raced after it, his gun in hand. He aimed for the tires as he tried to cripple the fleeing vehicle. No use: he couldn't outrun a vehicle, even an old pickup truck like the one al-Jinn was driving. Fields swerved and ran to his own car, but by the time he reached his government-issue cruiser, al-Jinn had already exited the cemetery on his way toward the Southern State Parkway. Fields knew he needed to catch him before he got onto the Parkway and more people got hurt.

■ ■ ■

Al-Jinn had a considerable head start. As he gunned the engine in pursuit, Fields keyed in the State Police emergency number.

"This is Special Agent Robert Fields, FBI ID 22734," he yelled into his speakerphone. "There's been a multi-victim bombing in Montefiore cemetery in Long Island."

"What is your current status, Fields?" the dispatcher asked.

"I'm fine, but there are casualties. We need a bus, a medevac, and a coroner. Send the bomb squad also."

"Where are you now, Agent Fields?"

"I am currently pursuing the suspect on the Southern State Parkway eastbound."

"Do you have a license plate for the vehicle?"

"Yes, alpha, beta, alpha, four six nine five."

"Approximately where are you?"

"I just passed Exit 37."

"Can you see the suspect?"

"He is right in front of me."

"Are you requesting backup?"

"No," Fields answered emphatically. "The suspect is armed and dangerous and I don't want to put anybody else in danger. Right now I'll keep following him and see where he heads."

"Agent Fields," the dispatcher responded, "we have five state troopers in the area. They can be there in about three minutes."

"Keep them on ice until we see what this guy is going to do. Tell them to shut down the highway from Exit 37 on. If this thing goes ugly, I don't want any innocent people getting hurt."

"Will do. Keep in touch and I will give the state troopers your cell number so they can be in contact with you."

Fields ended the call and eyed the truck in front of him.

■ ■ ■

Al-Jinn looked through rear view mirror again and saw the agent's cruiser on his tail. The cruiser's sirens were blaring, but al-Jinn saw no other police cars in the area. He breathed a sigh of relief, took one more look at the agent trailing him, and pulled a lever.

■ ■ ■

Fields had been taught that when pursuing a suspect one should maintain a safe distance just in case the suspect made a sudden move. As Fields watched the bed of the truck open and its contents fly onto on to the roadway, he was glad that he had listened to his instructors. Fields had enough time to slam on his brakes and guided his vehicle to the shoulder to avoid the debris that al-Jinn had emptied onto the roadway. However, the skid took him off the highway, leaving al-Jinn free to zoom ahead. Trying desperately to get his car back on the road, Fields watched his quarry drive off Exit 39 and take Route 231 toward Deer Park. While he had no idea why al-Jinn had chosen to exit there, he knew that his suspect was slowly getting away.

■ ■ ■

As the distance between him and his pursuer expanded, al-Jinn smiled grimly. This FBI agent was a formidable opponent, and Khalid al-Jinn liked a challenge.

He'd almost reached the spot he was looking for and he was pleased since he wasn't sure how much longer the old pickup could last. While he had hoped that the agent would have blown a tire on the debris, at least his tactic had bought him time.

Khalid veered off the road and exited the truck. He knew that eventually the agent would find his vehicle, and that was exactly what he wanted.

■ ■ ■

Fields drove down the road and keeping a lookout for al-Jinn. Though he'd lost a couple of minutes in the chase, knowing the condition of the pickup Fields realized that al-Jinn could not have gotten far. But where was he? The last thing Fields wanted was al-Jinn loose among innocent civilians in this rural town. Then he saw it: a pickup truck that looked exactly like al-Jinn's abandoned at a crazy angle on the road. The plates were identical.

Fields warily jumped from his car, his gun in hand. On the muddy ground he could see the fresh imprint of boots heading into the forest in front of him. Al-Jinn was in there somewhere, and if Fields didn't know any better, it seemed that he was waiting for him. Rather than go in blind, Fields took out his phone and made a call.

■ ■ ■

Al-Jinn gripped his rifle and listened for his prey. This was the same spot that he'd visited as a hunter one month earlier. For al-Jinn, this spot represented his rebirth. For the past few years, he had lived a lie. Those drugs had robbed him of his soul, of what he was destined to be. They had made him into a mindless robot. That all changed a month ago, when with precision and skill he stalked that deer and with sheer cruelty and anger he killed it. He could still smell the animal's fear, and it gave him life. It brought him out of his stupor and made him remember again who he was. Now he was free. He was free to fight his war and take his revenge.

As he waited for the FBI agent to approach, Khalid smiled. Death was imminent and he was ecstatic.

■ ■ ■

"This is Stephens."

"Leo, it's me," Fields responded.

"Robert? Where are you? I just heard the reports. They say that the prime minister is fine, but some agents were killed in a blast? And they said you were there. What is going on?"

"I can't go into it now. If you want a full report, I'll give it to you when I get back. But I need something from you."

"Why can't we go through this now?" Leo asked stubbornly.

"I am standing right near the suspect's truck. He seems to have escaped into the forest and if I had to bet, he's waiting there for me to chase him."

"Robert, don't you dare go in there without backup."

"They'll never get here in time."

"What about the local police force?"

"Leo, this guy is a trained killer. We are talking Navy Seal type. I am not having some country bumpkin get killed because I sent him into the forest with a madman."

"So what are you going to do?"

"The longer I wait, the better chance he has to escape. I am going in there to get him."

"But I thought that you said he is waiting for you."

"That is what I think, but I can't be sure. If he is fleeing on foot, then I need to chase him down."

"Alone?"

"What other choice do I have?"

"I am your superior officer and I will not allow you to go on a suicide mission."

"Honestly Leo, this won't be the first order of yours that I ignore and hopefully it won't be the last. This guy is pure evil and someone needs to stop him."

Stephens was silent on the phone and Fields felt the uneasiness. Even though they quarreled often, Leo and Robert respected each other, and Stephens did not want Robert to be harmed.

"Look," Fields said hoping to calm his fears. "I am going in with a vest. And if he's waiting for me, I'll find a big rock to hide behind."

"Until when?"

"Until you send me some air support."

"Where are you exactly?"

"I'm not sure, but GPS my phone and you should have my location."

A few seconds later, Stephens spoke. "I got you on the screen and I gave the order for the air support. They can't get there for fifteen minutes."

"Okay," Fields responded. "I am going in and I'll do my best to stay alive for fifteen minutes. If anything changes, I'll call you."

Fields ended the call and slipped on his bulletproof vest. He checked that his gun was fully loaded and took an extra magazine just in case. He examined the footprints. Somewhere out there, behind one of those large trees, al-Jinn would be waiting to fire on Fields.

Before he headed into the forest, Fields said a silent prayer. Though he never thought of himself as religious, he believed the maxim that there are no atheists in a foxhole, and Fields needed all the help he could get. Then he cocked his gun and started down the path.

■ ■ ■

Al-Jinn pointed the rifle toward the path. He had heard the slamming of a car door only minutes earlier and he knew that the agent was very close. His exhilaration was building and al-Jinn struggled to maintain focus. As he saw his prey come into his line of sight al-Jinn took a deep breath. He knew that he was ready for this moment.

He pulled the trigger.

The bullet passed a few inches to the right of Fields, causing him to drop to the ground and fire his own weapon wildly. He hadn't expected al-Jinn to fire that soon and he struggled to find cover. He saw a huge old oak tree not too far off and he realized that it was his only chance to survive. He fired again toward where he thought the shots were coming from as he made his move toward the tree.

As he dove behind the trunk, he heard a mocking, high-pitched voice call out to him.

"I am disappointed in you, Agent Fields," Khalid cried in heavily accented English. "I thought you were going to be more of a challenge. Where is that bravado that you were showing at the cemetery? Didn't you dare me to come out because I had nowhere to go? Well, look where we are, Agent Fields. The hunter becomes the hunted."

Fields remained silent. The last thing that he wanted to do was start a conversation with al-Jinn and expose his location. After a few moments of silence, Fields felt another bullet whiz by, this time landing only a few feet away.

"Answer me!" Khalid cried. "You think that I cannot see where you are? I see you perfectly, behind that oak tree. And if you think that your vest will protect you, you are very much mistaken. I have armor-piercing bullets in my rifle."

A few more shots rang out from al-Jinn's rifle and the tree protecting Fields began to splinter.

"How much longer do you think that tree can protect you, Agent Fields? Answer me now, or I will end your pathetic existence."

Fields glanced at his watch. If Stephens' estimate was correct, he still had five minutes until his air support arrived. If he wanted to live, Fields needed to stall al-Jinn.

"You are a hypocrite," Fields cried out.

"Hypocrite?"

"You talk to me about courage but you are a coward. You hide behind your sniper rifle and try to pick me off like some animal. If you were a real man, you would show yourself and we could end this like real men."

"You call yourself a real man?" Khalid yelled. "You and the rest of your Zionist infidels are the lowest form of life on Allah's wonderful earth ...."

"Allah, or whatever you pray to, would never condone inflicting pain and violence on innocent people."

"You think that those agents and the soldiers I have killed are innocent? Do you know the crimes that they have committed against my people? My family starved in Jenin when my father couldn't find work because of the checkpoints around the city. When my younger brother was dying of fever, we couldn't afford medicine because of our situation. His blood is on their hands and I will avenge it."

■ ■ ■

"You can't keep this up forever. You are going to be caught or you are going to die. Is this really worth it?"

"You American fool!" Khalid raged. "You think that I am afraid of dying! I relish the opportunity to die for the sake of Allah, and now you will get the same opportunity."

Khalid looked through the lens and got Fields in his sights. The oak tree had not really protected the agent. Al-Jinn had seen him, but he'd enjoyed toying with the agent, as he enjoyed toying with each of his prey. He wanted him to feel the shock of the first bullet. Al-Jinn wasn't going to kill him quickly. He was going to turn the agent's body into a sieve and enjoy every moment of it.

But he'd had enough. It was time to finish the game. As he fingered the trigger his eyes were suddenly blinded by a harsh light, and he heard the explosive sound of an automatic weapon.

"Khalid al-Jinn," a voice blared from the chopper above. "This is the FBI and that was a warning shot. Turn yourself in, or we will be forced to fire on you."

■ ■ ■

As Fields prepared for the thud of a bullet entering his body, he suddenly heard the rotors of the FBI chopper, and he knew that he was safe. A moment later, he felt his phone vibrate.

"Robert," the voice said.

"Leo, where are you?"

"I am in the chopper."

"I thought you never go out into the field."

"When my best agent is in trouble, I am not going to leave it to someone else to save him."

"Thanks, Leo."

"Look, we'll spend time crying on each other's shoulder later. But I have got this guy in my crosshairs. What do you want me to do with him?"

Fields thought about what had happened at the cemetery. He visualized the bodies of those fallen agents and the screams and cries of the wounded. This was for them.

"Blow him away," Fields said.

THE DRIVE TOWARD HAZEN STREET PASSED IN SILENCE, but that was just fine. It wasn't a nervous or an awkward silence. The passengers in the vehicle were quietly savoring the moment. With everything that had transpired over the past month, the possibility of this morning's meeting seemed like a fantasy out of a storybook. As they drove over the Rikers Island Bridge, they realized their wishes had come true and their elation was great.

Shea, in the driver's seat of the minivan, couldn't have been happier. The nightmare that had taken over and almost ruined his life was coming to an end. His client's release was being processed that very moment and, ironically, it seemed that he owed a great deal of thanks to Michael Reeves.

According to the information that Shea had been able to piece together, FBI Agent Fields had tracked down the real al-Jinn at the New Montefiore Cemetery while he was attempting to assassinate the prime minister of Israel. Fields ultimately followed al-Jinn to a wooded area, where an armed agent in a helicopter shot and killed him.

When Shea had heard that the real al-Jinn had been killed

Shea was crestfallen. The only way to prove that his client was innocent was if Khalid al-Jinn would admit to the attack on Rabbi Felder. With al-Jinn dead, it had seemed that Jabril Yusuf would be convicted for a crime that he didn't commit.

And then, unbelievably, Michael Reeves stepped in. Once Michael learned of the attempted assassination and discovered the identity of the would-be assassin, he had Achmad Mustafa arrested for obstruction of justice. In the interrogation room, Mustafa broke down crying. He admitted that he had received a payoff from a wealthy European man who'd offered him forty thousand dollars to erase the original surveillance video and submit the doctored video in its place. Even though he knew that the new video would incriminate an innocent man, the money was too tempting to turn down. With Mustafa's confession in his hand, coupled with the discovery of a blood-soaked hooded sweatshirt that had been found in al-Jinn's Brooklyn apartment, Michael agreed to drop the charges against Jabril Yusuf.

While Shea would have loved to attribute Michael's change of heart to his thirst for the truth and belief in justice, Shea suspected another motive. The real Khalid al-Jinn was at present the most notirous villain in America and Michael wanted to be associated with his downfall in any way possible.

As they entered the parking lot, Shea saw his client waiting in the doorway. This time, he wasn't wearing an orange jumpsuit. In his button-down shirt, corduroy slacks, and blazer, he no longer looked like Khalid al-Jinn the terrorist, but like Jabril Yusuf, the teacher.

Jabril hastened to his family and embraced them, while Shea watched. The tears flowed down Hanadi's face as she saw her husband lift their sons and toss them into the air.

Jabril then approached his father, who had never lost faith in his son. Jabril collapsed into his father's arms, sobbing uncontrollably. Shea felt his own eyes grow moist as he again thought about his relationship with his own father and how he had treated him. Shea knew that his father, whatever mistakes he had made, loved him no less than Ibrahim loved Jabril. Shea knew what he needed to do, and he was going to make sure that he did it before the end of the day.

Feeling a bit like an outsider, Shea decided to go back to the van and wait for the emotional reunion to conclude. As he turned away, he heard his name being called.

"Mr. Berman," Jabril called out.

"Yes?"

"Where are you going?"

"I figured that you wanted some time alone with your family."

"Mr. Berman, after what you did for me, you are my family. We are forever indebted to you for your kindness and dedication."

"I didn't do anything," Shea responded, embarrassed.

"You believed in me," Jabril countered. "After everything that I said to you and after all the pain and torment that you suffered because of me, you still fought for my release. You are a good man, Shea Berman. Mr. Berman, I have a confession to make."

"What is it?"

"Growing up in Sargodha, my father preached to us to love all mankind. He said that we need to respect everyone, even if we don't agree with them. But there were those who spread hatred throughout my town and those lies entered my home. I left Sargodha because I didn't want to end up like so many of my friends. I dedicated myself to teaching, hoping that I would be able to erase all the negativity that I had been exposed to. But abhorrence is like a fungus and no matter how hard I tried, I could not rid myself of the negative feelings that I felt for the Jews. That was until I met you. Once I saw the way that you personified truth and kindness, I was able to feel in my heart how wonderful the Jewish people are. Thank you, Shea, for giving me that gift."

Shea stretched his hand toward Jabril. Jabril ignored Shea's hand and grabbed Shea in a powerful hug.

Shea smiled. All the time that he had been defending Jabril, Shira's question haunted him. What kind of man was Shea fighting for? How many more people would be harmed if his client was released? But seeing who Jabril truly was, Shea felt wonderful:

not only did Rabbi Felder get the justice that he deserved, but Shea was able to save a good man in the process.

■ ■ ■

Robert Fields again found himself nestled in his favorite chair, trying to rest. This time his wife was out with her friends doing Zumba. Robert had no idea what Zumba was and frankly he had no interest in finding out. As long as his wife was happy doing it and it got her out of the house, that made Robert happy as well. It wasn't that he didn't enjoy his wife's company, but after the previous day's events, Robert craved peace and quiet.

The reporters were calling him a hero and that was the last thing that Robert wanted. He stayed away from the front pages because he felt that the more publicity there was, the more that could compromise his job. That is why he felt very good about what he had told the director of the FBI.

When Fields had returned to the office, the director was there waiting for him. He wanted to congratulate him for a job well-done, but Fields wanted no part of it. Besides his abhorrence for praise, Fields felt terrible for what had happened to those Israeli agents at the cemetery. Though nobody would ever blame him for their deaths, Fields wished he had realized that the shed could be a trap. Perhaps those men would still be alive.

Speaking with the director, Fields gave all the credit to the man who knew what to do with it, and that was Stephens. Stephens, for his part, went along with the charade and took credit for the entire operation. For Fields it was a perfect solution. Stephens got the accolades that he so badly wanted and Fields avoided the publicity that he so greatly detested.

So as Fields cranked the old chair into a reclining position, he stopped and listened. He heard nothing, and to Fields, that was music to his ears.

■ ■ ■

"Where are you going with those boxes?" Donna asked, as she saw Shea walk past her desk. "You aren't clearing out your office, are you?"

"I am just speeding up the inevitable. I figured that now that my client is freed, it might as well be better to go out on top."

"But you can't just leave!"

"Obviously, that choice isn't mine. Jessica and Allan made that decision a while ago."

"But the decision isn't supposed to be official till next week."

"Yeah," Shea agreed, "but I think I would rather go out on my own terms and try to salvage the small bit of pride that I may still have left."

"Wow," Donna said. "Like I told you before, it was really nice meeting you, Shea, and I am sure that you will land on your feet. And when you do, you will have major success."

"Thanks."

Shea headed for his cubicle. Most of the associates were in court, so the row was pretty quiet, which was exactly what Shea had wanted. After everything that he had been through, tearful goodbyes weren't something that he wanted to experience. He just wanted to take his things and get out. He was going to email Allan explaining his decision, and he would wait to receive his official dismissal letter in the mail. Though it may have been a little cold and distant, after what Allan and Jessica had done to him, Shea did not feel any ties or allegiance to Allan or the firm.

His desk was pretty clear, so there wasn't much to put in the box. Shea had tried to keep his family life separate from work and that is why he never put pictures of his wife or kids anywhere in his cubicle. There was one thing that he did take with him and that was the thank-you letter from Dennis Merzeir.

Shea found it hard to believe that he had received that letter only one month earlier. With everything that had happened, those days seemed like centuries ago. But the letter gave Shea hope that those heady days of success were still within his grasp and hopefully would return soon.

As Shea deposited the last remnants of his life at Gardner,

Crane, and Scott, into his box, he heard his name being called.

"Shea, is it?" a man inquired from the doorway of Shea's cubicle.

"Yes, that is my name," Shea responded.

"What kind of name is that?"

Shea regarded his visitor. He looked to be in his mid-sixties and his silver hair was groomed perfectly. There were almost no wrinkles on his well-tanned face. If Shea could have envisioned what Allan would look like in fifteen years, it would be exactly like his visitor.

"It happens to be a nickname," Shea responded.

"For what?"

"There was a famous Jewish leader named Joshua. In Hebrew, it is pronounced, Yehoshua. Shea is short for Yehoshua."

"Thank you for that etymological lesson," the man laughed. "You are probably wondering why I was so concerned about your name and who I am."

"You could say that," Shea agreed.

"Well, to be honest, I really don't have an interest in your name, but as you can obviously see, I am not very good at making small talk. To answer your second question, my name is Peter Crane."

Shea immediately set the box he was holding on the desk. Peter Crane was the original founding partner of the firm. Shea had never met him. *What was he doing here,* Shea wondered.

As if he were reading Shea's mind, Peter continued.

"By the look on your face, I guess you have heard of me and you want to know what I am doing at your cubicle."

"I would say that."

"Well, I first wanted to congratulate you."

"On what?"

"Your client, this Mr. Yusuf, it seemed that you were able to get him out of prison."

"I had a lot of help."

"There you go again, Mr. Berman."

"What do you mean?"

"Just because I spend most of my time in the Chicago office, doesn't mean that I don't do my research on my associates. According to your file, you are a great lawyer, but also a very humble man. You are speaking to the head of your firm, and after I compliment you, the first thing that you do is give other people the credit. I am very impressed with you, Mr. Berman."

"Thank you, Mr. Crane."

"And by the looks of that box in your hand, I would deduce that you are clearing out your desk."

"Yes, it seems that I will be terminated by the end of the week. I figured that I might as well get a head start on looking for new employment."

"Now Shea, I won't promise anything, but what would happen if I told you that I could get you your old job back?"

Shea stopped. He had come to accept that he was going to lose his job and Peter's words came as a complete surprise. However, he wasn't about to forget everything that he had experienced.

"Mr. Crane, if you have done your research, I am sure you know how I have been mistreated."

"I am aware of my colleagues' deception and I am sincerely sorry for what has happened. I am also extremely impressed with your devotion to your client, and that even after you had been informed that your job was lost, you still fought on his behalf. That is very commendable, Shea. That is the type of lawyer that we need in this firm."

"I appreciate your kind words. However, I am sure you can understand why after what I have experienced, I will have to decline your offer."

"I do understand," Peter Lockhart responded, "and I am sorry that things couldn't have worked out differently."

"So am I," Shea replied.

"But can you do me one favor?"

"What do you need?"

"I am here to take care of some important business. There is a meeting of the partners and I have decided to announce something at the meeting. I would very much appreciate if you were there when I made my announcement."

"Why do you want me there?" Shea wondered.

"I understand why you do not want to return to the firm. However, I am very serious when I tell you that I am appalled by what was done to you. Though my announcement will not take away the pain and anguish that you suffered because of your superiors' deception, I am sure that you will take solace in the knowledge that no bad deed goes unpunished."

Shea looked at his watch. He still had a couple of hours before he needed to be at his next destination. Driven by curiosity, he followed Peter Crane to the main boardroom.

When they entered, the partners were sitting around a large table with Jessica at its head. Shea found himself a corner and tried to blend into the woodwork. Peter Crane, however, went directly to the head of the table.

When Jessica noticed him she didn't seem very pleased.

"Peter," Jessica addressed him coldly, "what are you doing here?"

"It still does say my name on the letterhead of this firm, doesn't it? If I want to come to my office in New York, I most certainly have a right to do so."

"I didn't mean it in that way," Jessica responded, embarrassed. "I just wanted to know why you are here. You spend most of the time in Chicago and I wasn't notified of your plans. Had I known that you were coming, I would have postponed the partners' meeting until you had arrived."

"I came to speak to the partners about our European expansion."

"We have already been over this months ago," Jessica interrupted. "We put the expansion to a vote and you lost. I won and we decided to go ahead with an office in Paris. So please, no more sour grapes, Peter. It is unbecoming for a man of your stature."

"Oh, don't worry," Peter responded with a smile. "There are no sour grapes. I intend to give full credit for our expansion to you, Jessica, and all of your efforts."

"What are you talking about?" Jessica asked suspiciously.

"Everyone in this room knows that you are trying to use the firm's European expansion as leverage to wrest this firm from me."

"I would never do such a thing," Jessica responded with a fabricated look of shock.

"Jessica, remember who you are talking to. We all know how much you love power and how much you hate me."

"Fine," Jessica responded. "I'll admit it. I do want your seat at the head of this firm. I believe that I am more qualified to lead this firm in the digital age of social media. Our European expansion is only a small example of what I can do if I am given managing partner status."

"I am happy that you brought that up," Peter replied. "I have information that I believe the partners would find very interesting regarding our new European office."

"And what would that be?"

"As head of the European expansion, it was your job to seek investors for the project, was it not?" Peter asked.

"Yes, and I found a wonderful and respected investor who agreed to provide all the capital that we would need to open our European branch."

"You are referring to Lemour Holdings, are you not?"

"Yes."

"Well, have you informed the partners that as of this moment, the head of Lemour Holdings, Henri Joseph, has been indicted on charges of conspiracy to assassinate the Israeli prime minister?"

Jessica looked horrified and Peter loved it.

"And did you happen to tell the partners that because he has been indicted, all of his assets have been frozen? Not only that, but because he has invested in this firm, we are now going to be part of an ongoing investigation in which all of our books may be subject to a subpoena. Did you happen to share this bit of information with your fellow partners?"

"I had no idea," Jessica defended herself, looking at the other partners for help. "Henri was always courteous and pleasant when we spoke. I had no clue that he was a terrorist. Are you sure?"

"It will be all over the papers and internet by tonight. The bloggers will have a field day on this one. You have exposed the firm to shame and put its existence in jeopardy. If you are basing your ability to lead this firm on the success of our new European venture, I can confidently say that you aren't qualified to lead anything."

Jessica looked around the room for support from the other partners, but nobody would look her in the eye. She was on her own.

"Fine," Jessica said to Peter, "you win. We will find a way to work together. With whatever negative publicity that may arise from the investigation, we will need to work together to combat it."

"I am sorry, but you are mistaken again," Peter informed her.

"What?"

"You don't just get a pass on this one. You gambled away all your chips with this expansion and now you are going to have to pay the piper."

"What are you talking about?"

"You have shown gross negligence by bringing in an investor and not properly vetting him. I believe that your egregious errors are cause for dismissal from the firm."

"You can't fire me," Jessica stated angrily.

"You are right; however, a joint vote by the partners can have you removed from the firm."

"You need a unanimous vote from all the partners and you don't have the votes."

"Let us see about that," Peter said. He turned to the rest of the seated partners. "I am calling for a vote right now regarding the immediate dismissal of Jessica Scott from this firm. Not only has she exposed us to grave and serious accusations, but her overall conduct with other partners and associates has been replete with lies and deception. I move to have Jessica removed from this firm immediately. All in favor raise your right hand."

Jessica watched as almost every hand around the table went up. However, one hand had yet to be raised and she hoped that person would save her job.

"Allan," Peter addressed him, "it is up to you. I can't tell you how to vote, but I am sure that you know better than anyone about Jessica's deceptions. The choice is yours. Are you voting for Jessica's dismissal or not?"

Allan looked toward Jessica and saw her pleading eyes. Though he always loved positions of power, he realized that Jessica's career was in his hands, and the thought frightened him.

Jessica was his boss and he owed a debt of loyalty to her. But then, out of the corner of his eye, he saw Shea sitting in a corner. What about the loyalty that he owed Shea, loyalty that he had ignored? He remembered telling Shea how sorry he was for what had happened. Now he had the opportunity to show Shea that he really was sorry.

Allan locked eyes with Jessica and then averted his gaze and raised his hand. The boardroom erupted in pandemonium. Jessica grabbed her agenda and laptop and rushed from the boardroom in fury.

Shea, for his part, was mesmerized by the whole episode and he almost didn't realize that his phone was ringing. When he saw who it was his eyes lit up and he raced from the room to answer it.

■ ■ ■

"Thank you so much, Tzvi," Dovid Berman said on the phone. "I won't let you down."

Dovid Berman hung up, a broad smile on his face. He hadn't felt this good in a while and he wanted to share his news with Shea. He took out his cell phone to call him, but stopped when he saw his son waiting at the door to his office.

"Shea," Dovid exclaimed, "I was just going to call and give you some great news."

"Well, I also have great news to tell you. You know what, I'd rather just show you."

Shea withdrew a large manila envelope from his attaché case and placed it on Dovid Berman's desk. Dovid opened the envelope and his eyes widened in surprise.

"Where did you get all this money?" Dovid asked, pouring the contents of the envelope onto his desk.

"In that envelope, you will find the entire forty thousand dollars. You can put the money back into the account and your investors need never know anything about it."

"But where did you get the money? Shira told me that you were being fired from your job."

"Well, actually I was kind of offered my job back this morning."

"That's great to hear."

"But I turned it down."

"You turned it down? Why?"

"It's a long story. I'll tell you about it one of these days."

"So where did you get the money?"

"I got it from a client of mine."

"Shea, I can't have you borrowing money because of me. Especially that now you no longer have a job. Take the money and give it back to whomever you borrowed it from. I just got off the phone with a friend of mine who runs a *gemach*. I told him that I needed the money and he didn't even ask any questions. He trusted me to pay it back and I will."

"You don't need to borrow from a *gemach*. You can take the money that I just gave you."

"But how are you going to pay back the money, if you don't have a job?" Dovid Berman objected.

"I do have a job," Shea informed him.

"I'm confused. Didn't you just tell me that you were fired? How did you get a job so quickly?"

"My firm is going through some major issues right now. One of their biggest clients, Merzeir Pharmaceuticals, got wind of the impending problems and called me to make sure that everything was okay. When I informed Dennis Merzeir that I was leaving the firm, he asked me to be his sole legal counsel. I explained that I didn't even have a place to work, and he said he would take care of everything. He told me that he would give me space in his office to build and expand my own firm."

"That is amazing."

"But it gets better," Shea continued. "He gave me a retainer of two hundred thousand dollars for starters. Right now, he is in the midst of a major lawsuit and he wants me to take over. With that money, I am able to give forty thousand dollars to you."

"I can't take the money," Dovid responded strongly. "I need to answer for my mistakes. I was wrong for taking that money and it wasn't only because I put my family in danger. I was wrong because I broke the law and went against the Torah. I stole money and I can't have my son cover for my mistakes any longer."

"I am not giving you this money as a gift," Shea corrected. "You are going to pay me back every single dime."

"How"

"Because you are going to work for it."

"Excuse me?"

"Merzeir told me that I had to find a contractor to convert his storage space into office space for me. When I informed him that you ran a contracting company, he asked if you were any good. I gave him several of your references and he said that if they check out, he would use you for the renovations to his more than thirty offices."

Dovid Berman leaped from his chair and embraced his son. Tears rolled down the cheeks of both father and son, but this time they weren't tears of fear and apprehension. These were tears of joy and happiness. They were tears that declared that no matter how dark and despondent things had been, the future ahead of them was full of brightness and potential.

■ ■ ■

Shea walked through the halls of the hospital toward his rebbi's room. Though he had been informed that his rebbi was still unconscious, Shea hadn't had the opportunity to visit him since the beginning of the trial and he wanted to see him. The policeman who had been manning the door a month earlier was nowhere to be seen. With Khalid al-Jinn out of the picture, there was no longer cause for concern or fear. Shea opened the door to the room and approached his rebbi.

Still hooked up to the various machines, Rabbi Felder's large frame looked frail and diminished. Shea saw that the swelling had receded and it seemed that he was regaining color in his face. His rebbi was starting to resemble himself again; however, Shea knew that the struggle was far from over.

Shea took a chair, sat next to his rebbi's bed and gently took his hand. It felt cold and Shea began to rub it softly.

"I don't know if rebbi can hear me," Shea began, "but I have so much to say. I hope rebbi would have been proud of me. I was able to find rebbi's attacker and save an innocent man in the process. I was even able to have a part in the saving of the life of the Israeli prime minister. I wish you could have seen it. I think you will be happy to know that my wife found out about what I was doing for my father and in the end, she was really supportive of me. I was also able to get the entire sum of money for my father and I am going to be working for myself for now on. Things really did work out like you said they always would. *Refuah before the makah*, right? But I can't do this alone. I need your guidance, rebbi. I am excited about the prospects of the future but I need your help in guiding me. Please Rebbi, for all of us, you need to get better. You need to be there for your children and your students."

Shea continued to stroke his rebbi's hand as he *davened* that he should get better. After some time, Shea looked at his watch and realized he had to go. Shira was expecting him home early for supper. Now that he was his own boss, he could afford the time off, and he told his wife that he would be taking her and the kids out for pizza. He placed his rebbi's hand on the bed and prepared to depart.

And at that moment Shea realized that everything was going to be okay. Because as Shea began to leave his rebbi's side, Rabbi Felder's seemingly-lifeless hand grabbed onto his, begging him not to leave.

■ ■ ■

From across the street Rasheed Salaam watched the FBI agents streaming into his building. He had known that after the real

Khalid al-Jinn had been uncovered that it would only be a matter of time before he too would be discovered, and the mission would have failed. That is why he had a contingency plan and that is why he was able to view the procession of the FBI agents without any fear of being caught.

Rasheed realized that the agents would seize all of his computers and question all of his employees to find out more information about him, but he had been careful and he made sure that there was nothing on his computers that could be linked to him. As for his employees, none of them knew anything personal about him and therefore none of them would be able to provide any useful information to the FBI. Even if they were to run his fingerprints through the system, they would come up empty, as Rasheed had been able to avoid being processed ever since he illegally entered the United States.

As he watched the agents remove boxes laden with various files, Rasheed's mind began to race. Though his plot had been foiled, Rasheed realized that the war was far from over.

Let the Israelis be happy, Rasheed said to himself. *They may have dodged the bullet, but next time, they will not be able to escape me.*

Acknowledgments

Mimi Zakon: Your tireless dedication on this project was remarkable, even though at times you felt like a "first-year law student." I appreciated your praise, but valued your critiques. You transformed a good story into a great novel.

Judi Dick: Your attention to detail is remarkable. Thank you for the countless hours that you spent "nitpicking" through my novel and ensuring that it was the best it could be.

Felice Eisner: Your proficiency and thoroughness are evident on every single page.

Eli Kroen: Your creativity and ability to distill a book into a single image is on full display in your attractive cover design.

Estie Dicker: You typeset the book with skill and proficiency.

Adina Gewirtz: You were my first editor and you encouraged me to continue writing no matter what obstacles lay ahead. I can only say that had it not been for the many hours that you spent reading and reviewing my previous manuscripts, I never would have persevered to write this novel.

Akiva Gross Esq.: Your expertise on all legal matters was invaluable. You answered all my questions, (and there were many) succinctly and clearly. I could not have completed this project without you.

Jessica: It seems like it has been forever since "Moshe the Yid." But you were the first one to encourage me to write, and I hate to think of what would have happened had we not written that script together. All I can say is *thank you.*

To my parents: Thank you again for your endless support for me and my family and for taking pride in all of my accomplishments. A special thank you to Ema: *Diste Hector el poder de hablar. Te quiero.*

To my in-laws: Thank you for always being there for us.

Yaakov, Tzippy, and Dovie: Thank you for allowing me to bury myself in my office and write while you waited patiently for me to finish. I love you guys so much!

Rochel: Words cannot accurately describe how much you have helped me through the years, especially on this project. You listened to every word that I wrote and provided poignant insight that helped shape the story. Everything that I am, is yours. Thank you!